'Both timely and timeless, a sophisticated work of fiction that addresses the anxieties of the present moment as well as the most profound questions of history, art, love and loss. A magnificent novel.'

Emily Bitto author of *The Strays* **and** *Wild Abandon*

'It takes a phenomenal control of craft, and a keenly honed intelligence, to do what Cunningham has done with this novel: to interrogate politics and art and culture, to take on love and sex and suffering and loyalty, while all the while ensuring that the reader remains buoyant and captivated by narratives that leap across space and time . . . I loved this book. I *absolutely* loved it.'

Christos Tsiolkas, author of *The Slap* **and** *7½*

'*This Devastating Fever* is thrillingly audacious fiction. Sophie Cunningham's entwined subjects are profound—Leonard Woolf and colonialism, the crises of the present day, the challenges of creative work—and she writes commandingly and inventively about them all. The result is an extraordinary novel.'

Michelle de Kretser, author of *Questions of Travel* **and** *Scary Monsters*

'A book of big ideas that reads as a page turner. I was thrilled to keep returning to the page.'

Kate Mildenhall, author of *Skylarking* **and** *The Mother Fault*

THIS DEVASTATING FEVER

SOPHIE CUNNINGHAM

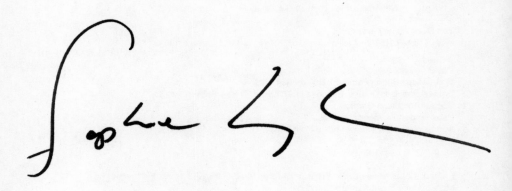

ultimo
press

Published in 2022 by Ultimo Press,
an imprint of Hardie Grant Publishing

Ultimo Press   Ultimo Press (London)
Gadigal Country   5th & 6th Floors
7, 45 Jones Street   52–54 Southwark Street
Ultimo, NSW 2007   London SE1 1UN
ultimopress.com.au

A catalogue record for this
book is available from the
National Library of Australia

This Devastating Fever
ISBN 978 1 76115 093 7 (paperback) | 978 1 76115 152 1 (paperback)

Cover design Akiko Chan
Text design Simon Paterson, Bookhouse, Sydney
Typesetting Bookhouse, Sydney | 11.8/17.6 pt ITC New Baskerville Std
Copyeditor Elena Gomez
Proofreader Rebecca Hamilton
Author photo Courtesy of Alana Holmberg

10 9 8 7 6 5 4 3 2 1

Printed in Australia by Griffin Press, an Accredited ISO AS/NZS 14001 Environmental
Management System printer.

The paper this book is printed on is certified against the
Forest Stewardship Council® Standards. Griffin Press holds chain of
custody certification SGSHK-COC-005088. FSC® promotes
environmentally responsible, socially beneficial and economically
viable management of the world's forests.

Ultimo Press acknowledges the Traditional Owners of the country on which we work,
the Gadigal people of the Eora nation and the Wurundjeri people of the Kulin nation,
and recognises their continuing connection to the land, waters and culture.
We pay our respects to their Elders past and present.

I very rarely think either of my past or my future, but the moment that one contemplates writing an autobiography . . . one is forced to regard oneself as an entity carried along for a brief period in the stream of time, emerging at a particular moment from darkness and nothingness and shortly to disappear at a particular moment into nothingness and darkness.

LEONARD WOOLF, 1960

Apart from Knox, and later Leonard Woolf in his novel, A Village in the Jungle, *very few foreigners knew where they were.*

MICHAEL ONDAATJE, 1982

What a life he has led, and how he has led it!

EM FORSTER, 1970

I
FICTION AND NON-FICTION

1936

When Leonard stood up he was taller than expected. After more than twenty years of marriage you would have thought Virginia would have the measure of her husband, but she did not. Leonard leaned towards her. Virginia held his face in hers and admired its deep lines. She found it rather marvellous that the two of them seemed to have grown tighter like this. Not just in spirit but appearance.

'We must prepare for Vanessa's,' she said.

'Your headache?'

'Of no account. She misses Julian. Besides, there are to be dress-ups.'

Leonard looked hangdog. He didn't mind how ridiculous they would seem once in costume; he had dressed up as all manner of creatures over the years: Prince Albert, March Hares, Mad Hatters. It was his wife's health that concerned him.

'We are going to the party,' Virginia continued, 'and I have worked out exactly what we are to wear.'

Leonard raised an eyebrow.

'I've had Louie set aside some boxes. That is all it will take.'

He waited.

'Bookshelves!' Virginia clapped her hands together. 'Each of us a bookshelf. One labelled Fiction, the other Non-fiction.'

'Which of us will be which?'

'Seriously, Leo. Do you even have to ask?'

2020

Alice Fox had not expected to spend the twenty-first century writing about Leonard Woolf. When she'd stood on Morell Bridge watching fireworks explode from the top of Melbourne's taller buildings at midnight on the first day of the year 2000 she'd had only two thoughts. One was: the fireworks are better in Sydney. The other was: is Y2K going to be a thing?

Y2K was not a thing. But, as it turned out, there were other things. Environmental collapse. Hen's collapse. The return of fascism. Wars. Plague.

In the early days of writing her novel, Alice's agent, Sarah, would occasionally take her to lunch and ask what was taking so long. Alice had explained once, twice, many times that she had hoped to write a novel about September 11, and been inspired by Leonard's response to the assassination of Archduke Franz Ferdinand.

> *Then the shot was fired in Sarajevo which destroyed the civilization and the way of life which I had known in the first 34 years of my life.*
>
> LEONARD WOOLF, 1964

4

Alice had experienced a similar foreboding on September 11 as she watched the towers come down. Her pursuit of echoes, of resonance, had gone on from there.

'Interesting,' Sarah had responded, once, twice, many times. 'But not, in and of itself, a novel.'

Alice would return to first principles: at the beginning of their relationship she and her not-yet wife, Edith, drove to Seymour to buy their second Burmese kitten. The first had been lonely, so they'd returned to purchase the only sibling from the litter that hadn't sold. Apparently his square, oversized head and crackly meow made him less appealing, though his square head was, as far as Alice and Edith were concerned, exactly what made him magnificent. They named him Wilson. Wilson, and his sister, Iris, became quite the distraction.

Once she had two cats, Alice would try to identify the correct position to put their baskets on her desk, next to the photo of her baby self being held aloft by her father, sometime in 1964. Black and white. Her little embroidered dress. Bloomers. She was gazing into her father's eyes. He was gazing into hers. They were both laughing at the joy of being there, together, loving each other, making the world anew.

It was hard to fit all this—computer, sentimental items, books, cats—onto her desk. Perhaps she needed a bigger one. She might have to get into the car and drive to Ikea, which would mean getting caught behind a tram. She might buy a Linnmon/Oddvald combination then realise she needed another Billy for her books. These would have to be put together.

Sarah—who was, like Alice, a white Australian woman, well north of middle age by 2020, and, as a consequence, used to non-sequiturs—would try to rein in these meanderings.

'Are you telling me you can't finish your novel because you have cats?'

'That is one reason, yes.'

'I'm going to send you a book to read,' Sarah said. 'It's by Geoff Dyer and is about how he tried to write about DH Lawrence but couldn't.'

> *All over the world people are taking notes as a way of postponing,*
> *putting off and standing in for.*
>
> GEOFF DYER, 1997

Over the course of two decades and many awkward exchanges, the lunches became less regular, though the excuses Alice came up with continued apace: climate change anxiety. The need to make an income. Dengue fever. The writing of books that were not the novel. Caring for Hen.

Caring for Hen had led to a crisis regarding the nature of narrative itself and when Sarah asked why, Alice tried to explain that dementia was a form of discontinuous narrative. Tried to explain how she'd felt simultaneously fascinated and devastated as she watched new forms of logic assert themselves in her friend's brain: words detached, language floated apart, yet some relationship, some tension, some bond, continued to organise the sounds the woman Alice loved into Hen-shaped molecules of meaning.

Another pressing issue, not particular to Alice alone, was that it stopped being possible to make a living writing novels. This meant, that sometime in the twenteens, Alice started teaching people How to Write a Novel™. She enjoyed the work but wished she was able to model How to Write a Novel™ for her students by ACTUALLY WRITING A NOVEL. But, as she explained to them, her novel was a shapeshifter, a series of mirages. Drafts took shape. Shimmered. Disappeared.

Alice took to sending plaintive emails to Sarah, in an attempt to reignite her interest. For example, did Sarah understand that in Sri Lanka, Leonard Woolf was a rock star, albeit a rock star of the colonial era? Did she understand that Leonard's famous wife was of no account there? Sarah responded equitably. Said she was concerned that while Alice was writing about a man who may (or, to be honest, may not) have been the equivalent of rock star in Sri Lanka back in the day, he was certainly not one anywhere else. Alice countered that his series of autobiographies had been bestsellers in the 1960s. Sarah, who had been an adult in the sixties, was very aware of just how long ago, and irrelevant, the sixties would seem to most of the book-buying public. However: she was also keen to support clients based in Melbourne. A hundred days of lockdown (and counting) had sent everyone in Melbourne mad. One of the reasons Sarah was a good agent was that she coped better than most with proliferating technologies—Zoom, Google Meet, Microsoft Teams, Slack, FaceTime—all of which allowed people to see a face that was ageing exponentially, as the pandemic, work stress and drinking far too much alone at home took its toll.

Alice, though younger, was coping less well. She was also keen to take advantage of her agent's sympathy. They organised to meet over Zoom.

It was early in the morning. Alice, who was holding a coffee, appeared to be standing on the Marin County side of the Golden Gate Bridge, with her back to San Francisco Bay and the city skyline. Sarah appeared to hover in space with a decrepit Jack Russell terrier on her lap, somewhere over North America. After an ice-breaking chat about the fact they needed to better customise their backgrounds, they got down to business.

Alice had prepared a list of titles for Sarah so that she could present the draft that would be finished any day now to a range of publishers. She read the list out loud. '1. *The Precipice.* 2. *Once in a Hundred Years.* 3. *This Devastating Fever.* 4. *Waiting for Leonard.* I want to go with three. It's a phrase Leonard used about himself to describe lust and the problems of repression. It strikes me as even better now because of the whole COVID thing.'

Sarah was underwhelmed.

'Do any of them describe what's in the jar?' Sarah asked, what's in the jar being one of her favourite phrases. This annoyed Alice, particularly as she was certain the phrase was 'in the tin'. Sarah, for her part, was remembering a lunch thirteen years earlier when she'd been so mean to her client that Alice had stopped writing for several years. Sarah prided herself on being a straight shooter but it's possible she crossed a line sometimes. Sarah's problem was this: what was in Alice's jar seemed to change constantly and twenty years of conversations like this one had earned Sarah 15 per cent of sweet fuck all. Liking a client only got you so far. Was she a saint? She was not. Did she have to be? She did not. If you think authors are always broke, imagine earning 15 per cent of what they earn. (Sarah did not say these words out loud. In fact, she seemed unaware that she often thought these words so loudly that she might as well have spoken them. But she tried. Oh, how she tried.)

Alice didn't pick up on the tension emanating from Sarah. This might have been a Zoom thing, but was also a phone thing. She'd failed to put on Do Not Disturb, and now the daily barrage regarding Hen was vibrating through her body. Five missed calls, and one message. The days of Hen being able to send messages herself had gone.

Please call Ageing Disgracefully soonest regarding Hen Aetós

Alice was distracted. Sarah was asking another question. 'Where are we at on the fiction or non-fiction front?'

'It's both.'

'And where do you propose that booksellers put it?'

'In the window? On the New Release table?'

'Which table?'

'Fiction!' Alice said decisively. 'It's fiction.'

Say it and it be true.

There were versions of the novel in which Alice, inspired by The Avalanches album *Since I Left You*, and Dadaism, tried to write the novel as a series of samples, or cut ups. She then tried for straight historical but almost died of boredom. Literary styles moved in, and out, of fashion: Realist, magical realist, grunge, metafiction, autofiction, historical, rhetorical, satirical, postcolonial, feminist, fantasy, sci-fi.

Software evolved: Microsoft, Pages, Scrivener, Aeon.

Prime ministers, presidents, they came, they went: Howard, Rudd x 2, Gillard, Abbott, Turnbull, Morrison; Bush, Obama, Trump, Blair, Brown, Cameron, May, Johnson.

Hardware evolved: MacBook, MacAir, iPad, iPhone.

The United Kingdom joined the European Union. The United Kingdom left the European Union.

Pets were born, were loved, lived, died.

Drafts unfurled over years, over decades, Alice let a thousand flowers bloom, wore out the soil, and, to continue the metaphor, added fertiliser.

Over the years Alice received a range of advice from Sarah and other readers. That advice could be summarised as 'more focus needed'. It was suggested she cut the footnotes and overly complicated timelines. She was advised to lose her favourite fictional character, [Redacted]. It had been painful to lose [Redacted] and by extension [Redacted]'s lover, her father and her grandmother. Alice had become attached to all of them. But no.

In.

the

(digital) bin.

One oft-recurring suggestion was that Alice cut loose Ghost Virginia, the concern being that she was a poorly executed ghost, and not central to a novel about Leonard Woolf. Sarah had gone so far as to suggest *no Virginia at all*. Alice had some sympathy for the suggestion that she remove Virginia from her novel—Virginia was one of the most written about women of the twentieth century, and she tended to take things over. However, Virginia refused to be edited out so there was not much Alice could do about that.

Other advice:

More Leonard! (This was a good idea in theory, however, Leonard lived a long life. Eighty-nine years of Leonard might be more than anyone wanted or needed.)

More Ceylon! (Alice liked this idea.)

Less Ceylon! (No. She wasn't going to kill that darling.)

More of the Bloomsbury Set in general!

Less of the Bloomsbury Set in general! (White. Entitled. Middle-to-upper-class. Irrelevant.) Alice agreed with all of this except the irrelevant bit, but then of course she would not think they were irrelevant because she too was white and middle class. She liked to think she wasn't entitled but clearly was too close to the situation to judge. She loved all of the Bloomsbury Set, and that included the obscure ones. (Desmond and Molly MacCarthy.*) The queer ones, which was all of them—except, perhaps, Leonard—and the boring ones. (Including but not limited to Virginia's brother Adrian Stephen[†] and his wife Karin Costelloe[‡].) In fact, the problem was that even the boring ones were not boring to Alice.

In short, if a *Trivial Pursuit* game was developed asking questions about the lives of these people, Alice would have trounced everyone she played, every time she played them. Unfortunately for Alice, writing a novel was not the same as playing a game of *Trivial Pursuit*. It was much harder to win at writing a novel.

The most various range of opinions among her readers related to whether Alice, who was, in one iteration of the manuscript, called 'The Author', should and could exist. Sarah thought that she could

---

* Sir Charles Otto Desmond MacCarthy was born in 1877. He was a little-regarded writer and a highly-regarded literary critic. Has also been described as a literary flop: a man who failed to live up to his promise. Lady Mary MacCarthy, known as Molly, was a British writer and married to Desmond MacCarthy. In later life she suffered from severe hearing loss.

† Adrian Stephen, like most members of the Bloomsbury Set, was bisexual and had a relationship with Duncan Grant before Grant entered a long-term relationship with Adrian's sister, Vanessa. Adrian and his wife were among the first people in Britain to engage with the theories of Sigmund Freud, then practise as Freudian psychoanalysts. Alice diligently read Adrian's papers on the psychoanalytic meaning of impotence, made assumptions, but then failed to effectively weave these details into the narrative at hand.

‡ Karin Stephen (née Costelloe) was a psychoanalyst and psychologist. She first rose to prominence/notoriety in 1913 when she was part of a group who started a legal action to compel the Law Society to admit women to its preliminary examinations. The action failed. She wrote several books, including *Psychoanalysis & Medicine: A study of the wish to fall ill,* which Alice read, was fascinated by and found pertinent, but failed to effectively weave into the narrative at hand. Karin became deaf in later life and committed suicide in 1953. Virginia hated her. Leonard published her.

(should) stay but that the protagonist should have a life that aligned with the actual author's life. The novel could, perhaps, explore:

- Alice's bisexuality
- Alice's marriage
- Alice's work as a publisher
- Alice's childlessness
- Alice's parentless-ness
- Alice's relationships with paternalistic father figures, romantic and otherwise
- Instances in Alice's life that, according to the mores of her day, were not considered sexual abuse or assault, but, in hindsight, were a form of sexual abuse or assault.

This kind of personal revelation was Not. Going. To. Happen.

'I think an exploration of the writing process would provide the kind of conventional narrative arc readers seem to require,' Alice would offer, brightly, from time to time. 'Alongside the collapse of civilisation.'

Zoom time was almost over. Sarah decided to make one last push on this question of narrative momentum and asked Alice to consider writing about one bond that she and Leonard shared: the role of carer. 'You once described to me the weight of that feeling,' Sarah said, 'of waking every day feeling convinced that both your own fate and the fate of the person you are caring for are conjoined. That you might be able to, if you try hard enough, save them.'

'I said that?' Alice asked, regretting, as usual, her propensity for oversharing. 'Hen's not such a big deal. Just a neighbour who doesn't have anyone else.'

There was more to it than that and everyone knew it. Hen Aetós had moved in next door to the Fox family in the early seventies. She was a knockout: the short but lean body of a marathon runner (which she had been as a young woman) teamed with bright red hair that was obviously dyed but looked so good it didn't matter. She had divorced young, married even younger. Hen and Alice's parents became quite the threesome until, a few years later, Alice's mother had died (cancer), and her father had drowned (in self-pity, alcohol), leaving a note for his three children on the kitchen table: *Heading north. The house is paid off. $400 a month should cover costs. Hen's agreed to keep an eye on you.*

That note had been followed by weekly postcards full of declarations of love, guilt and shame, sent from a range of tropical locations. The money was useful. The postcards were not. Most useful of all were the meals Hen made for them every night for the next five years until first Diana, then Alice, and finally the youngest of them, Doug, left home. As Hen put it, in a letter she sent to Alice who had been smoking hash somewhere in the Himalayas: *My last falcon has fledged!*

'Getting Parkinson's, with dementia, at only forty-eight years of age is a big deal,' Sarah said. 'How old were you when Hen was diagnosed? Thirty-six? And wasn't she messy from day one?'

'Messy is beside the point. Let me share this,' Alice said, keen to change the topic. 'Here's an outline I've written.' Then the screen went blank and silence fell over the meeting. Technology had defeated Alice and she'd somehow disabled Screen Share. She rallied, and launched into an enthusiastic pitch in which she tried to convey the fact that, as with the *I Ching*, as with the Tarot, one can find, in the writings of Leonard Woolf, in the writings of his wife, Virginia, commentary on events of the present day.

'Perky as fuck,' Sarah said. 'But save it for the publishers.'

'Think of it,' Alice pushed on, 'as *How Proust Can Change Your Life* but with Leonard Woolf and nihilism.'

'Jesus, I hated that book,' Sarah said, her background flickering and blurring ominously as her internet began to fail. 'Apologies. This happens every morning at nine when school starts up. I'll freeze any . . .'

'. . . moment,' Alice finished for her, looking down at her lap to the empty space where (sometimes) Iris and (sometimes) Wilson once sat. She hadn't mentioned those recent deaths to Sarah, who had been uninterested in living cats let alone dead ones. Furthermore, in Alice's experience, people thought her love for her cats was somewhat deranged. They were old, right? What was the problem? Only three people—Edith, Hen and Leonard—understood the intensity of her feelings for the animals she lived with. Her phone vibrated again. This time it was Edith, who, as if reading her mind, had sent a message from the next room.

A pandemic kitten. It's time.

II
COMET

1910

Up here, two miles above the sea and the populous plains, it was almost silent. The to-and-fro of the workers on tea plantations couldn't be heard. There was nothing but the occasional echo of chanting, which drifted up from the temples below. It was cool, cold even, compared to the coast, which was not so far away. Down there, the heat was so intense it was like a living thing: the constant buzz of cicadas; lowing cattle; sun beating down onto salt pans. Some days Leonard fancied he could hear water being sucked up from the earth by the hot air, waterholes shrinking into a muddy ooze, the low moan of the animals gathered around. The jungle that pressed up against the edges of the compound in which he lived never ceased its murmuring: the call of birds; the clack-clack-clack of a leopard's teeth, the hysterical chattering of the monkeys in the moments before they misjudged the distances between branches and fell into the leopard's jaws.

At this altitude though, just the whip of wind and clip of hooves. The wind, ever present, sang its way through the air, twisting the rhododendrons into a magnificent old age. Though gnarled they stood tall and in raging bloom: white, pink, red, yellow. Nothing like the neat, safe bushes to be found in an English garden. On this morning the fog was so thick he could see neither the rhododendron beside him nor the path ahead. It was as if he was riding across an English moor on a grey winter's afternoon instead of this, galloping towards World's End on the morning of a day that would be fine.

A herd of deer skittered away before them, clearing the path. The strong and well-bred Arab knew the way as well as his master and moved fast, sure-footed, despite the rocks on the track, until suddenly there they were, faced with a swirling wall of cloud so thick that neither horse nor man could see what they both knew was there: a precipice, half a mile straight down to the plains. It will be any minute now, Leonard said, to himself, to his horse. His hands trembled, perhaps with impatience, and the horse pawed at the ground. Suddenly the mist twirled and danced about them, dissipating in puff after great puff, leaving them high on a cliff, Ceylon spread out below them. Leonard imagined, for a brief second, the joy of flight, before returning to this fact: he needed his fellow animal to get himself down. So, this day as on others, they took the dizzying descent together. Plunged from the heights of World's End to the sea.

2004

Alice left her hotel room in Brighton early in the morning, her shoulders hunched together by way of protection as the wind barrelled across the English Channel, up the narrow lane, and slammed into her. Bam. She was wearing the wrong clothes, having not packed the right ones. Summery cotton flapped around her legs and arms: she looked a ridiculous bird, confused by the weather, flying in the wrong direction.

This is good, Alice thought as she staggered to the bus stop. She could practically see the scene she was going to write—Leonard pushing through the rain and the wind on the Downs as he contemplated his courtship with Virginia. The seeming impossibility of drawing her close to him.

She got off the bus half an hour later, went to the reading room in the library at the University of Sussex, and introduced herself to the librarian; a nice woman, new at the job, and not overly familiar with the Leonard Woolf archives. Left Alice on her own with several hundred boxes, or, to think of it another way, 60,000 documents, mainly letters, for company. Some dozen or so boxes, pre-ordered, were piled up on the table. The man had developed extensive filing systems, kept track of everything.

EVERYTHING included quantities of salt produced in Hambantota in 1910, Virginia's menstrual cycle in 1914, and whether Mahler had been played, using their new gramophone, on any given night over, say, that final winter of 1941.

Alice, feeling, and possibly looking, like a hoarder trapped inside her own house, opened a box titled 'Pets'. There, her romantic attempts to explore the profundity of Leonard's relationship with animals was stonewalled by a box of notes on the genetic lines of Siamese cats, cocker spaniels and thoughts on gene combination. She moved on to a box of index cards which had been notated every day for some years to indicate the music Leonard and Virginia listened to every night after they'd played bowls. The day drew on: bills, lists, endless letters to editors, which she supposed were literary history but which were also more than she could take.

Alice kept going after she left the library that first day, spent her evening on the internet and came across an account by a schoolboy who'd been evacuated to Rodmell during WWII. The little boy had been playing in Church Lane when he heard that Virginia Woolf had drowned. He hadn't liked her very much because she was 'a bit odd' but he'd always liked Mr Woolf who sometimes brought apples to school for them to eat, and one Christmas had taken all the village children to a pantomime and then tea in Brighton.

Alice found this story about Leonard and the apples and the pantomime cheering. She could work with this. A man who grew apples, who ate them, who gave them away to children in the hungry times of war. However, evenings spent on the internet were not going to help Alice trawl through hundreds of boxes and thousands of documents, some of which were significant, many of which were not.

Help arrived in the form of a dinner in Lewes. Alistair, a friend of Leonard's, asked Alice to join him, his wife, Vivienne, and a retired Special Collections curator from the University of Sussex called Heather. None of them had met Virginia, but they had known Trekkie, Leonard's partner after Virginia's death. They agreed with the rumours that Trekkie was far easier to get along with than Virginia. Alice tried to find out more about Leonard's sex life (did he have one?) and Alistair told her that Leonard had told him he'd had an affair with his cook in Ceylon.

Alice was learning something very important. Leonard and Virginia were not myths but people. People who lived both ordinary and extraordinary lives. They were made of flesh and blood. They were annoying. They grew apples. They picked them as the bombs fell. They ate them. They gave them away to children.

When Alice described her project, Heather reeled off a list of the boxes that would be relevant to her, by number. Alice wanted to fling herself at and kiss the woman but she was quite elderly so Alice desisted. Librarians were to the writer, she felt, as superheroes to the imperilled citizens of Gotham City. Thanks to Heather, when Alice's three weeks were done she would have written down many quotes, transcribed many pages, photographed dozens of others for later analysis. Her notebooks would be full, her computer, her memory cards.

The day after this auspicious dinner, Alice returned to the library and opened a box that contained a TJ & J Smiths small scribbling diary, Almanak No. 6. 1911. The diary was interleaved with blotting paper and cost Leonard one shilling. Alice put on her white cotton gloves and begin to flick through its pages and there they were! Lashings of Sinhalese cypher. Colonialism right there, curled inside those snail shells, slivers of alphabet moulded to private, perhaps even sinister use.

Very occasionally in times of crisis, when I want to make the record unintelligible to anyone but myself, I make my entries in cypher mainly composed of a mixture of Sinhalese and Tamil letters.

LEONARD WOOLF, 1964

Leonard was trying to hide the fact he was falling in love with Virginia. The subterfuge escalated. He used code when he analysed the act of sodomy with Duncan Grant* but soon began to use it when

---

* Duncan Grant was born in 1885 and became a British painter and designer of textiles, pottery, theatre sets and costumes. His lovers included his cousin, the writer Lytton Strachey and the economist John Maynard Keynes. He enjoyed a forty-year domestic and creative relationship with Vanessa Bell, and was the father of her youngest child, Angelica. His murals in Berwick church have been described as 'a desire to create a happy, uplifting space in which the imagination is awakened and set free to rise above the darkness and horror of war.'

he visited doctors to ask about Virginia's condition. He used code to describe the details of Virginia's illness, and the drugs he gave her.

Alongside the diaries were translations of the code done by Olivier Bell. There were further translations, jotted in pencil when Leonard had gone back to the diaries after fifty years and tried to decipher them—or perhaps to remember them—himself. There is one word that is never translated. That word, as far as Alice could judge from the context, was 'violent'.

One night, to try and break the obsessiveness of the rhythms she was developing, Alice went to a movie at the Odeon. The film was called *The Day After Tomorrow* and it riffed on a scenario known as Abrupt Climate Change. The melting Arctic forced too much fresh water into the North Atlantic and triggered a flip of the Atlantic Meridional Overturning Circulation Currents (or something). Hero-scientists frantically drilled for ice cores. Their work was interrupted when an 'ice sheet the size of Rhode Island' broke away. (How big was Rhode Island? Alice had no idea.) Soon enough there were speeches being made about global warming and 'the cost of doing nothing' versus the cost of doing something. Dennis Quaid, who played a paleoclimatologist, made eloquent pleas to the vice president—Alice thought of him as Fake Dick Cheney—regarding the fate of children, of grandchildren. He chased Fake Dick Cheney down a hallway yelling, 'Mr Vice President, if we don't act now, it's going to be too late'. Dennis Quaid's pretend son, Jake Gyllenhaal, looked moody and flew to some giant quiz meet-up in New York. The next day he and his friends visited the American Natural History Museum and looked at a mammoth that was snap-frozen 10,000 years ago; the day after that they were trapped in the New York Public Library as a storm surge engulfed lower Manhattan. Ships floated down Fifth Avenue. The temperature began to drop rapidly and within a couple of days Jake and his friends were burning books so they didn't become snap-frozen, *like mammoths*. 'As far as I'm concerned, the written word is mankind's greatest achievement,' said the librarian, as he clutched the Gutenberg Bible to his bosom. Further south, hundreds of thousands of Americans waded across the Rio Grande trying to break into Mexico. Dennis Quaid shuffled past the Statue of Liberty in his snowshoes, musing that humankind survived the last ice age and would therefore survive this one. 'It all depends if we're capable of learning from our mistakes,' he told his friend, a friend who, inexplicably, had walked from Philadelphia to New York, through the biggest storm in 10,000 years, just to be with Dennis Quaid.

Over the weekends, when the library was closed, Alice began to walk the South Downs. Spring lambs sproinged. Dandelions danced on the breeze. She walked past a circle of charismatic trees sitting high on a hill and consulted her guidebook. She was, apparently, standing by Chanctonbury Ring, a prehistoric hill fort built in 700 BC. The trees were replacements of birches first planted in the mid-1700s. Those trees had blown down in the Great Storm of 1987.

The South Downs billowed before and to either side of her. The slopes were steeper than expected, the light harder and brighter. Grass sap green, dashes of red poppies, sunny buttercups, white and yellow daisies gave way to fields of rapeseed flowering all around her. Brilliant yellow, throb of heat. Alice walked across the face of the sun. She listened out for the pulse of crickets, the shrill of cicadas, other invertebrate sounds. But things were quiet, quieter than it seemed they should be.

Fewer insects.

Fewer birds.

That night, sitting in a pub with a pint of stout (disgusting stuff, she had no idea why she'd ordered it), she turned to the random gentleman who had joined her—possibly to pick her up, but happy to make do with vigorous conversation—and asked him about the insects. The nameless man explained to her that the New Forest cicada—clear wings, gold stripes—was possibly extinct, but as the nymphs spent around eight years underground there was still hope: it was only four years since they'd last been seen. As for crickets, they were precipitously declining.

This gave Alice pause. Visiting Sussex was not going to acquaint her with Leonard and Virginia's Sussex. No, it was not. She was going to have to exercise her fictional chops and use her imagination if she planned to write about what Sussex looked and sounded like a century ago.

Alice's walk continued. Took her to Monk's House. Leonard's garden. Virginia's studio. She walked out the back gate and across a field to the deep and rapidly flowing River Ouse. She stared at the water a while and tried to imagine what it would be like to jump, and why one would jump, but became distracted by the white swans that paddled up and down. To her eye they lacked the majesty of the black swans of Australia, the drama of red beaks tapering to white.

Alice walked past the frescoes in Berwick church, which Duncan Grant had painted with Vanessa and Quentin Bell during WWII. The paintings were dilapidated, their tones darkened by age, but no less the moving for it. She visited Charleston, whereupon she admired the bed Maynard Keynes slept in whenever he stayed with Vanessa and Clive Bell. It was only three-quarters as long as modern beds, and had a sloping headboard that allowed him to sleep semi-reclined. Something to do with the damp and British lungs according to the guide that led a large group through the series of small rooms.*

On the last day of Alice's walk she finally moved into a landscape that had not changed for centuries. Emerald green set atop dazzling pure white, chalk cliffs plunging down to pebbled beaches. Violet stars—tiny daisies, perhaps—growing, so it seemed, out of the chalk itself. Vermillion. White. An undulating series of chalk cliffs billowed along the coast all the way to Eastbourne. She walked up the flanks of the first Sister, then looked across the English Channel. The sense that nothing had changed, the beauty, the height, made her feel vertiginous. This, this, was why she walked.

Once Alice's dizziness subsided she looked down at the rocky beach. There was a pile of clothes lying there on the pebbles. The day was warm, hot even, but the ocean, Alice knew, would be close to freezing. She made her way down to the water, stepping around an old bicycle that had been thrown carelessly to one side of the path.

The pile of clothes consisted of an old pair of cords, leather shoes and a plain cotton shirt. A second pile of clothes lay next to the first,

---

* Baron John Maynard Keynes was born in 1883. He became one of the most influential economists of the twentieth century and his writings paved the way for what is now known as Keynesian economics. He was an advisor to the Treaty of Versailles, and crucial to rethinking economic problems during the Great Depression. Alice hoped that renewed interest in Keynes' work would allow her to work details such as Keynes three-quarter-length bed into her narrative in an organic fashion. But no: Keynes, despite being one of the most significant economists of the twentieth century, despite being an intimate friend of both Leonard and Virginia, and despite Alice reading a 1000-page biography about his extraordinarily interesting life, will barely receive a mention in the pages that follow.

a detail she hadn't been able to make out from up high. This pile was stranger. It looked like a uniform of some sort from a vintage costume hire place.

Alice considered the channel. It didn't seem as clear as it had from her former vantage. Rain, or perhaps a sea mist, was rolling in from France. (She loved the idea of that. Of weather crossing the channel.) In the mist she could see two men. It was hard to make out any details but they were breaststroking towards each other, calling out as they swam.

'It's war!' one man shouted, his voice carrying across the water, across the century.

The second man stopped swimming; seemed to be treading water.

'Are you sure?' he called, before answering his own question. 'Of course it is. Expected. Has been since Sarajevo.'

'But still, a shock.'

'Will you sign up?' Leonard asked the man, for there was no doubt it was him. Which meant the other man out there, Alice understood, was the local policeman. Leonard, she knew, had ridden his bike from Asheham to Seaford to bathe the day war was declared because it was unseasonably hot. He would, Alice also knew, despite the heat, walk between Asheham and Lewes—no small distance—several times over the next few days to get more news about this war with the Germans.

'I will, though the force also needs me. You, sir. Are you ready to fight?'

The conversation carried clearly, through time and over distance. Alice's legs gave way. She sat down for a moment. Closed her eyes. Began to shiver. When she opened her eyes she seemed to be in an old warehouse in London. Dozens of men were standing around, Leonard among them. He, like her, was covered in goosebumps.

Alice had the sense she was standing beside Leonard, who had been forced to strip and stand in a room full of other naked men and left standing in the cold for more than an hour—though if that was the case he didn't seem to notice her among the room full of short men, fat men, flat-footed men, men in thick glasses, limping men and Leonard, trembling like a greyhound, ribcage jutting, arms held over his chest, jogging on the spot to keep warm. He looked down at his skinny legs and knobbly knees—no one got enough food these days—then found himself afflicted with an attack of modesty and he cupped his genitals in a gesture both protective and ashamed.

His cock. What a useless thing that was proving to be. (Was she in his head now? Was this a case of over identification with the subject?) Virginia's birthday last he'd snuck into her bed at dawn with her small present. They'd embraced and kissed and held on to each other, tightly, with great emotion. Castaways on a stormy sea. Would it be enough? Could they keep each other safe?

British schooling was a form of military training, which meant that most of the men were stoic in the face of these attempts to humiliate them. By the time Leonard was finally called in though, some had fainted. Exhaustion, he supposed.

'On what grounds are you claiming exemption?' one of the doctors asked—Leonard couldn't tell which one for they all looked the same.

'My tremor,' Leonard said. Holding out a hand, which twitched, as if on demand, quite uncontrollably.

The doctor looked at Leonard's hand and then his penis. 'A Jew. I see.'

There were other conversations Leonard would have preferred to have with the doctors. He'd been surveying the working poor of North England. Had developed an interest in socialism. His 'International Study of the Legal Profession' was underway. He'd travelled regularly to industrial Lancashire to lecture on Sanctions and Disarmament. He'd edited a collection of articles called *The Framework of a Lasting Peace.* He spent several hours a day spoon-feeding his wife porridge. It was this latter point that led to his current situation: the need to stay out of a war he longed to fight.

'Letter?' another doctor asked.

'In my coat pocket in the changing room,' Leonard admitted and was then sent scurrying, like one of the men he'd once lorded over in Hambantota, to retrieve it.

Lytton had not been humiliated in this fashion. He'd been afforded all the dignities of his class. Sat in a courtroom talking in serious tones about pacifism and haemorrhoids, digestive problems and asthma. His lungs were diseased, his ailments of operatic proportions. He had received an exemption on medical grounds rather than on matters of conscience and had suggested that to Leonard as a way forward.

Five minutes later Leonard was back before his interrogators holding out a sheet paper.

I hereby certify that I have this day seen and examined Mr. L.S. Woolf. He first consulted me in March, 1914, when I found that he was suffering from marked nerve exhaustion symptoms. He had a general tremor which I regarded as a permanent one, which was most marked in the hands and arms; sleep was defective and he had severe headaches. He has improved to a certain extent, but the tremor, as I expected, persists, and headaches easily come on with fatigue. Owing to his highly nervous state I have no hesitation in saying that I regard him as quite unfit for military service, and that if he attempts it, he will almost certainly break down within a short time. I may further add that his wife has had several severe mental breakdowns during the last sixteen years, and I have been consulted about her on many occasions since 1913. Her husband, Mr. L.S. Woolf, has personally nursed her through these attacks, and she is still in a highly unstable condition and if his care is removed, I am of opinion that the effect will be highly detrimental to her and may bring about a severe mental breakdown. I may add that it is only in cases where I know the personal element to be of vital importance that I am willing to express such an opinion to a tribunal.

DR. MAURICE CRAIG, 10 MAY 1916

By the time they finished reading, Leonard was so racked with tremors that one of the doctors wondered out loud if he was putting it on, but others could see that he was not. They waved their dismissal. Exempt.

Alice woke, curled up on pebbles. Had she been dreaming? It was one thing to have a vivid imagination but this felt like another thing entirely. Freezing water licked at her feet. There were no swimmers, the clothes had gone, the weather broken and the mist she'd seen transformed into the storm that was now upon her. She got up, leaned into the wind and kept walking. She had a way to go yet before she reached her destination.

1904

Leonard Woolf strained against the taffrail of P&O *Syria* as the ship snaked slowly down the Thames; he peered into the thick and dirty fog, hoping for a last glimpse of his mother, his sister, his friends, of England. In the end he could only imagine that his family were waving (they were), that Lytton was crying (he was), and that England would miss him (unlikely).

Leonard's bags were stowed in his cabin. In them, if you cared to look, were several green silk cravats, a miniature edition of

Shakespeare, four volumes of Milton and ninety volumes of Voltaire. His most important cargo, his fox terrier, Charles, was on a second ship, one that allowed animals. As they sailed, Leonard liked to imagine Charles, on all four of his seafarer's legs, sniffing the salt air and yapping in a wild excitement. He hoped that one day they might be able to engage in a conversation so he could ask Charles how he had, in fact, passed his days.

It had always been assumed, by Leonard, by his mother, Marie, that he'd do well. Study barely seemed necessary for a man of his intellect—that had been Leonard's thinking—but as a consequence he'd done poorly in his exams. What was unfortunate if a man came from money was catastrophic if a man did not. A job was necessary. He considered becoming a teacher, but Jews were not— everyone said so—cut out for that kind of thing. He sat the civil service exams instead and passed those, in a lacklustre fashion, the result of which was that instead of being sent to the jewel in England's crown, India, he was dispatched to the semi-precious stone that was Ceylon. Leonard Woolf, a third-rate citizen, a third-rate student, sent to do time in a third-rate colony. When Leonard had wondered out loud what might be expected of him once he arrived, Lytton had exhorted: 'Administrate!' Though in truth Lytton didn't really know what administration was, despite the fact that several generations of his family had plied that trade in India and most of his family had been born there.

After several weeks apart Leonard and Charles were reunited. They enjoyed a brief holiday in Colombo before being dispatched to the Northern Province: Leonard, Charles, the cravats, the Voltaire, travelled 149 miles, first by train, then atop a pile of mail bags on a bullock cart. Several days on the rattling cart was almost the end of Leonard, an end that threatened just as he was beginning: a straight road, trees on either side, the dazzle of sunlight and flit of brightly coloured birds. Over those few days Charles would be lost, then found, and Leonard's old life would be shaken from him so forcefully that when he finally arrived in Jaffna he was unable to walk; helpless as a newborn, he was manoeuvred upright and then supported as he took his first steps. It was the middle of the day. Mad dogs. Englishmen. All that. He stood under a broad blue sky. Sunlight bounced off the grand white buildings that stood along the wide main street. The people who held on to Leonard as he recovered his land legs were, it seemed to him, a startling shade of brown. Other than sky and skin, everything was bleached of colour.

Office Assistant Thomas Southorn approached with a formal smile. Leonard, a socially awkward man at best, attempted a polite greeting. The men were to room together. Indeed, some decades hence, Southorn would marry Leonard's sister, Bella. These intertwined fates did not, however, mean the men liked each other. Quite the opposite. Loathed would be a more accurate word. It was immediate. Visceral.

Various superintendents of police joined them. Leonard was escorted around the town. His cravats and Voltaire were commented on. His awkwardness was not, and besides, Charles saved the day, a glorious distraction, by leaping a wall, yelping loudly, then returning, with a large, dead, tabby cat in his mouth. The tour continued to the ramparts of the fort, whereupon Charles pounced upon a large snake and shook it wildly until it was a dead. Leonard was not unaware that this was a useful turn of events. Could see his companions thinking: this strange man, with his books and his excellent dog, is clearly a man to be reckoned with.

And so Leonard became one of a cadre of white men and women some thirty people strong. He moved into Southorn's house, which sat among and under the clawed and draping roots of an immense Banyan tree. He consolidated his social position by playing a good game of tennis and a strong hand of bridge. And, in his role as a cadet attached to the Government Agent (GA) John Perry, he ensured his professional future by making it clear that he was a man of determination. A man who could check accounts, issue licenses, attend to correspondence, files. A man who could manage a pearl fishery and, once he did manage it, was capable of working both himself and the people who worked under him, until they were close to death.

A year later. The Palk Strait. A man could watch the sun rise and set here, so wide was the vista, so flat the northern part of the land. The beach was covered with rotting oysters. Lean men, wearing nothing but lungis, picked their way around them to get to the water. Leonard followed these men, waving a staff in front of him, like a scythe, to clear the way.

The putrescent oysters were incongruous when the sea was so clear, the beach in the distance so white. And the stench! If it was a liquid it would have been thick as tar, if a temperature it would be boiling, if a sound it would be a siren. You could fancy that this coastline was a long room in an enormous house, the flies a dark shimmering rug. It was the flies: they covered everything. It seemed impossible that so many tiny living things could make such a solid mass. Underneath them lay shells so sharp they sliced through flesh. In England the animals within were a delicacy, a briny succulence that slid down the throat suggesting oceans and bigger worlds. But here it was what irritated the oyster that was prized. Some pearls were misshapen; some were white, some black, some pink. Some were perfect translucent spheres—or would be discovered to be so when the oysters had decomposed and the slime washed away. Some pearls would be returned to the loin-clothed divers: they curved out and away from the boats, a rope tied to their ankles, and plunged down to ocean floors. It was only the peg on their nose that kept the sea from their lungs and stopped them haemorrhaging.

Leonard did not know what it was to almost drown every day, lungs full to bursting, tight pain in the chest transformed to red sheen behind the eyes. But working here might kill him; there was no doubt about that. As he thwacked his stick—to the left, to the right—the gesture became more of a flailing. A tall diver, some six feet tall, almost knocked him over as he ran towards the shore, then held a hand to his heart and bowed slightly, in apology. Leonard nodded his head. 'No harm done,' he said, though his words sounded insubstantial. He couldn't be heard over the insect hum. The rug was pulled from under his feet; he crumpled into the surging mass of men, of flies, of rotting flesh. Divers held him aloft. They carried him to his tent. The voices in his head spilled out of him, the chatter of a family and a lifetime. He was a Jew, nothing but a Jew. His temper uncontrollable. His father died he left them poor his mother's talk won't ever stop and oh there is a girl he is disgusted she is disgusting her dark lips opened and inside her a pale pink glistening.

Leonard had never been safer than he was among these strong men. They didn't understand a word he said. Some part of him would remember this. Language was a mask; you could hide behind it. A man put a wet cloth to Leonard's brow, a bullock and tray were hitched, and with a shudder he was slowly carted inland, to a doctor. It was ten days before he became conscious, but during that subterranean time—he dreamt he was trapped in a dream in which he struggled to wake up—the smell of rotting things never left him: it was in his nostrils, his hair. It filled his throat, the cells of all his organs. And as the smell never left him, nor did the memory of his first flash of a silver white pearl among the festering grey.

Over the years and decades that followed Leonard would never quite erase this knowledge: there was beauty to be found everywhere. In gunmetal skies of war-torn London, in the ravings of his wife. When she looked at him during her days of madness, it was with a rage so pure it seemed to him a kind of evil. All jungles are evil. Oh, to be hated as she hated him. Oh, to be loved as she loved him. She would not take him into her body, she would not give into what was rotten about her. One day she would write a letter to him:

> *I don't think any two people could have been happier than we have been.*
> VIRGINIA WOOLF TO LEONARD WOOLF, 1941

The pearl. That is the pearl she will give him.

2004

Alice read Stephen Trombley on the train from Sussex to London. He wasn't encouraging. Virginia Woolf was elusive and, being dead, now unable to provide updated commentary on her life, but at the same time she had lived . . . *the most fully documented literary life of the twentieth century* which meant, of course that many of the intimate details of Leonard Woolf's life had also been trawled. Yet she was sure that this would not present a problem, didn't doubt she would find a way to produce fresh and relevant fiction where many before her had failed.

Alice had organised to stay at the Goodenough Club in Mecklenburgh Square, Bloomsbury—it was only later that she realised that the name of the club could be seen as some kind of curse:

was she good enough?—and had chosen it so she could be close to the last London home that Leonard and Virginia had shared. Also because it had an excellent breakfast buffet. On her first morning, after breakfast sausages, eggs, tomatoes and mushrooms, she headed around the corner to get the vibe of the place, however the house Leonard and Virginia once lived in was no longer there. The entire row had been taken out on the night of 11 September 1940. The vibe was, therefore, that the blitz had been extremely thorough.

Alice then caught the tube to Harley Street because she wanted to see the rooms of Dr George Savage, the famed author of *Insanity and Allied Neuroses* (1884), and one of Virginia's doctors.

She didn't find them.

Undeterred, Alice returned to her room and wrote a scene in which Virginia visited the doctor in 1911, utilising her own impressions of Harley Street in 2004. An hour later she read what she had written and deleted it. Tried again. Deleted that as well. Gave up and wrote two long letters back home, one to Hen and one to a librarian called Edith she had recently chatted to when sitting under the dome in the reading room at the State Library. Alice and Edith had talked for so long that the Year 12 students sharing the space complained to another librarian, and Edith had been moved to a section of the library where she wouldn't distract or be distracted by members of the public. Alice was uncertain as to how the letter would be received as she had no idea whether Edith, or indeed she, was interested in women in *that way*, nor whether she would welcome hearing from someone who had put her job at risk. The letter writing proved to be an enjoyable distraction but a distraction nonetheless.

The next morning, given that going gonzo was getting her nowhere, and she was now at the pointy end of her trip, Alice went to the rare manuscripts room of the British Library where she planned to bunker down for her final days. The archives dated back centuries, the room she sat in no more than ten years. Blond wood furniture. Spotless white ceiling. Virginia Stephen's early travel diaries. The notebooks [Paper; ff. vii/140. 188 x 140mm. Binding of green cloth] were small. Virginia's handwriting was hard to decipher but it seemed that she'd gone to Greece with Thoby and Vanessa, spent drachmas on a cloak, silk, scissors, Turkish delight, cabs and lanterns. Alice, delighted, diligently transcribed:

> *To lead (of) places is food, but best of all it is to dream hard of x in a flip-pant(?)afternoon in Athens for the ~~light of the~~ street cut in clear colours and washed in bright air—has a something something levity you think of strange/ strong Yorkshire moors(?)cool smells blowing off the heath, something, a light or two in the hollow. Or you think of a great London Square, where the lamps just lit, and all the windows stand closed(?)for the virtuous evening. The central heat(?)was lodged in Greece; as we drew near the whole of this little bridge from ~~country to country~~ crumpled up and disappeared. I write bad English I know, but I mean(?)state merely that we reached Patra at 6.30am on this day morning, & some day I will find the date. You get a little mad/vague(?)with much travelling, & after a day spent in looking at soaring hills & x valley from the steamer the mind will throb x little faster for the name of Greece. That indeed must sink in legitimately, as it surely does by its own authentic fire . . . found Thoby . . .*

AUTHOR'S TRANSCRIPTION, 2004

It was all rather hard to make out, though some phrases, like 'for the virtuous evening', leapt out at her, minnows into her net. Towards the end of her allotted time Alice moved to the diaries of 1908 but they were different somehow. Flat. Sad. When she asked the reference librarian—one of those hot young librarians that London seemed to be full of—why that might be, the hot-young-librarian looked at Alice as if the answer were obvious.

'Thoby,' she said, 'changed everything.' She then pointed Alice in the direction of various reference books. As Alice walked away, the hot-young-librarian raised her voice quite loudly given where she worked. 'Don't forget to read the footnotes!' Librarians change everything, Alice thought to herself. Without librarians, hot or not, this novel wouldn't amount to anything.

Alice read the footnotes. And in one of those footnotes she learnt that Leonard had been a guest at the Stephen's house for a farewell dinner just before he left for Ceylon. It was there that he met Virginia for a second time. She met him for the first time in Thoby's rooms at Trinity in 1903.

What Alice learned from the reference books was that the story of Virginia Woolf was a tale of many brothers.

Thoby, also known as the Goth, was born in 1880 and everyone had the highest of hopes for him. Those hopes were dashed. He was dead by the end of 1906, of typhoid, caught when travelling in Greece with Virginia.

Death stalked the family, yet the weakling, Adrian, survived. He was a slow developer, nervous, 'stunted'. Being the youngest he was his mother's favourite but she died when he was eleven, leaving him to the not-so-tender mercies of his sisters. Virginia found him depressing, exasperating, silent, lethargic and maudlin. Worst of all he was sentimental. Virginia threw pats of butter at him. He threw them at her. They hated each other; perhaps they loved each other but Adrian always knew that the wrong brother had died of typhoid in November 1906. After some years of trying, Adrian gave up on impressing his sisters and married Karin Costelloe, became one of Britain's first Freudian analysts and made a family of his own.

Then there were the half-brothers, Gerald and George Duckworth*, the sons Julia Stephen† had by her first husband—a Mr Duckworth, Alice assumed. Julia also had another daughter, Stella‡, whom Vanessa and Virginia had adored, and who had died as a young woman.

Who would want to be a woman in Victorian England? Alice wondered, as she speed-read a series of textbooks that laid out this gruesome, but not unusual family history. Then she put her head on the desk—a habit picked up in the Monash University stacks in the 1980s—and fell asleep. A young Virginia, possibly a teenager, shy, luminous, infiltrated her dreams: appearing to be nodding in furious agreement as if to say: who *would* want to be a woman in Victorian England? Really? WHO?

---

* Sir George Herbert Duckworth was born in 1886, educated at Eton, then studied at Trinity College, Cambridge. He went on to work as a public servant. After they were married, Vanessa and Virginia accused George and his brother—their half-brother—Gerald of sexually abusing them. The Duckworth brothers consistently denied all such allegations.

† Julia Prinsep Stephen, formerly Julia Duckworth, was born in Calcutta to an Anglo-Indian family. As a younger woman she was famed for her beauty and her aunt, the photographer Julia Margaret Cameron, took dozens of portraits of her. She was also a philanthropist. Her husband Herbert Duckworth died at the age of 37 of a ruptured abscess. The abscess ruptured as he reached to pluck a fig from a tree, to give his wife. They had three children. George Duckworth, Stella Duckworth, Gerald Duckworth. Julia then married the biographer Leslie Stephen and had four more children: Virginia, Adrian, Thoby and Vanessa. Julia died in 1895 at her home following an episode of rheumatic fever at the age of 49.

‡ Stella Duckworth, daughter of Julia Prinsep and half-sister of Virginia Woolf. After the premature death of her mother she took over the parenting of Virginia, Vanessa, Thoby and Adrian. She then married Jack Hills, returned ill from her honeymoon and was said to be pregnant but also diagnosed with 'peritonitis', though no operation was performed for some months. She died in 1897 at the age of twenty-nine.

Alice pulled herself out of her dream state and went back to work. The body count rose. Julia Stephen got the flu, which weakened her heart, and died in her forties. The patriarch, Leslie*, died also. He'd previously been married to a Thackery, who died after a series of miscarriages and gave birth to a daughter who was institutionalised and never spoken of. (Who indeed, Alice, or was it Virginia, thought to herself. *Who indeed.*)

George Duckworth became head of the family, but to his surprise, his half-sisters did not want to be fondled while doing Greek lessons. They did not want to be fondled in their bedrooms nor in their beds, they did not want to dress up in formal regalia to hang off their half-brother's arm, and they did not want to be fondled under dining-room tables.

Thoby and Adrian moved to Gordon Square, Bloomsbury, and asked their sisters to join them, which they gratefully did, whereupon George sold the family home in Kensington. The entire situation was an embarrassment to him: a group of young people living in a house together in a shabby part of London. Thoby invited friends from Cambridge over for a Thursday evening discussion group. And so Bloomsbury was born, though, soon enough, its founder died.

You must be prepared for something terrible.

LYTTON STRACHEY TO LEONARD WOOLF, 21 NOVEMBER 1906

Virginia, heartbroken but undeterred, wrote letters to a friend in which Thoby recovered his health. She turned him into fiction for an entire month.

---

* Sir Leslie Stephen was born in 1832 and died in 1904. He was an author, critic, historian, biographer, and mountaineer, and, as the father of Virginia, Thoby, Vanessa and Adrian, could also be described as the father of Bloomsbury. Not that he would have approved of it.

Thoby is going on splendidly. He is very cross with his nurses, because they won't give him mutton chops and beer; he asks why he can't go for a ride with Bell, and look for wild geese.

VIRGINIA STEPHEN TO VIOLET DICKINSON, 25 NOVEMBER 1906

Lytton, for his part, kept Thoby alive by asking Virginia to marry him.

Yes, she said.

Then, the following day, thank goodness: No. Lytton turned to matchmaking. He wrote to Leonard Woolf and asked him to consider taking Virginia for himself.

Clive Bell kept Thoby alive by asking Thoby's other sister, Vanessa, to marry him. She said yes, didn't change her mind, got married.

Once Virginia finally acknowledged her brother's death, she took over the literary salons and distributed his books. For Leonard Woolf—a man her dead brother knew from his years at Cambridge, a man that Thoby loved, a man who loved her dead brother, a man she barely knew—she set aside a volume of Milton.

1909

Bella and Leonard Woolf walked along the waterfront of the Galle Fort on their way to the hotel where they planned to lunch. Bella*

---

* Bella Sidney Woolf was one of Leonard's older sisters. An English writer, she was married first to Robert Heath Lock, then to the colonial administrator Tom Southorn, who was a Colonial Secretary of Hong Kong, and then Governor of the Gambia. Both her first and second husbands were colleagues of Leonard's during his time in Ceylon.

held her hat close to her head. Leonard staggered as a gust of wind hit him. The sea writhed. Rain sheeted across the water. It was, Bella thought, as if a hand had reached down from the heavens and was sweeping the turbulent water towards land. Shafts of sunlight shot between clouds that rose, high as mountains. As day turned to night the roiling sky seemed a ceiling as vivid as the Sistine Chapel.

'The atmosphere is positively biblical,' Bella said. 'Look!' She pointed to the column of water that joined sea to sky, before twisting off on its own course.

'There are two monsoons,' Leonard yelled, over the gathering storm. He had in fact explained this to his sister ten times over since her arrival in Ceylon. 'One is barely through the buffeting you get in the north-east then this second one is upon you. Those in the dry zone do not have to endure such uncertainty.'

'There is nothing uncertain about it, Leo. It happens every year, twice a year. It is to be expected. You will have to learn not to be so surprised about something so predictable.'

Sister and brother walked swiftly now. Moved so carelessly their hands briefly brushed and, within a flash, Leonard was a small boy, taking Bella's hand and running down the street in Lexham Gardens, two children growing up in genteel poverty after the death of their eminent barrister father.

The illusion was brief. Returned to adulthood they made their way up the stairs of the hotel, walked across chequerboard tiles and towards their usual table. The fans above them moved rapidly as wind gusted. Staff swirled around them, left, then right. Canvas rolls were loosened and anchored to the top of balustrade. None of this activity stopped the inevitable: the curtain figs alongside the hotel curved and shuddered for a moment, before the rain exploded, coming in sideways to spray the diners as if with a hundred small bullets.

Leonard's loneliness had been more acute since Charles had died some years ago. He continued to live with dogs and a menagerie of snakes, deer, monkeys and even a leopard, but Charles had been one of his greatest companions, hard to replace, so he was grateful to the only one of his many sisters who had been so moved by his description of solitude, psychic and otherwise, that she'd arranged to join him in Ceylon. It mattered not that her motivation included self-interest. Bella was over thirty years old and her options limited. She had began the work of finding a husband on the boat over, where she spent many hours in conversation with a young botanist called Robert Lock*, known to those who loved him as Bertie. Bella found Bertie quite marvellous. So marvellous, in fact, that she found herself keen to know more about his work on developing a robust strain of rubber plant and the new field of science known as 'genetics'. Talk of rubber led to a desire to explore central Ceylon together. Such a step, however, required Leonard as a chaperone, and Leonard, at first, resisted his duties on the grounds that he had already seen the sites that Bella hoped to visit.

'Is it Bertie you object to?'

'On the contrary. I consider him a friend.'

---

* Robert Heath Lock was a botanist and friend of Leonard Woolf's. By thirty years of age he'd published a significant work in the new field of genetics: 'Recent Progress in the Study of Variation, Heredity, and Evolution'. In 1902 he became Scientific Assistant to the Director of the Royal Botanic Gardens at Peradeniya and in 1905 he became the Curator of the Cambridge University Herbarium. He returned to Peradeniya in 1908 as Assistant Director, then Acting Director of their botanic gardens. He married Bella Woolf in 1910, and they returned to England together in 1912. He died in 1915.

'Then what?'

'Touring is just another form of imperialism,' Leonard said.

Clever young men. They would be the end of Bella. 'That's a bit rich coming from you, Leo.'

Leonard ploughed on. 'My point is not just that we are imperialists, but that, as builders of empire, we love to swoon over its remnants. The local people don't care about ruined palaces and failing tanks and the rulers that would have once forced them into slavery. We all share a meal with Harry Bell and gush over the fact he discovered these cities, but their "discovery" has been no surprise whatsoever to any fellow worshipping at the Temple of the Tooth, bringing tea to my office, or any woman selling her goods by the side of the road. Men like Bell, by the way, would use the daughters and wives of the planters around here as servants of his own personal pleasure.'

Bella was well used to the hypocrisies of both sex and class. 'Mr Bell is not alone in that particular indulgence,' she said. 'And I think the fellows making your tea and the women selling their goods by the side of the road are rather pleased about the tanks around here. It's so terribly dry for much of the year. I also think these people you love have a case to answer if they let such significant and beautiful historical sites fall back into the jungle.'

Leonard was no longer listening to Bella so much as pursuing his own irritation. 'The English love to discover a place that was getting on perfectly well without it.'

'Now you're just talking rot, Leo. You could hardly say that the people around here were doing perfectly well. Many of them were starving.'

'Still are.'

'You spend fourteen hours a day holding court, and sorting out whether this situation is equitable, or that. The people rely on you. You are proud of that fact. I know you are.'

This was true. Leonard had made terrific inroads since he'd arrived. His edict that all letters were to be answered within a single day—as opposed to up to a year after receipt—had been transformative. Thus flattered, Leonard paused for a moment or two, then agreed. 'I'll come.'

Bella managed to borrow one of the few gasoline cars that existed in the colony. A man was sent ahead, by horse, to prepare the rest house for their arrival. Bertie sat behind the driver's wheel. As well as Bertie there was Rachel, one of the daughters of the planter on a local tea plantation whom Bella had invited in the hope of encouraging a family connection. What Bella didn't know, in part because Leonard had shown some discretion on the matter, was that he thought Rachel rather lovely but as he did not wish to marry her, had already decided to leave things well alone.

The vehicle moved at a snail's pace. It took them several hours to drive the fifty-five miles to Sigiriya, giving Leonard plenty of time to become even more self-conscious and awkward about interactions with Rachel. Worse, the drama of the landscape they were driving through was denied them till they were close upon the rock, at which point it loomed up out of the jungle, as if out of nowhere.

Finally the group clambered out of their car and up an iron stairway. It had only been put in some ten years ago but was already weathered; rusted and somewhat perilous. Rachel and Bella pulled up their skirts and tucked them into the modest bloomers they wore underneath, which meant they looked, for all the world, like young gentlemen in pants.

Leonard was irritated. Bertie's enormous moustache hid his expression but his eyes suggested amusement.

'Ladies wear them to ride bicycles,' Bella said, responding to their alarm.

Rachel, perhaps concerned that Leonard might think the less of her said, 'Bella lent me a pair of hers. They are rather wonderful, aren't they?'

'Soon my sister will be telling you that women should have the vote,' Leonard said.

Rachel said nothing. Composed her face as neutrally as possible, an expression she'd been trained to maintain since the day she was born.

Bella suggested they stop at one of the lower galleries to appreciate the frescoes, though her research had in no way prepared her for the magnificence of the place. Images adorned the walls of chambers in the rock as they did the stone walls of a chapel. They were the equal of frescoes they had all seen in Europe but also suggestive of a passion that was more than spiritual. It was not just the colours—reds, ochres, yellows and oranges—indeed Leonard was hard pressed to identify what the problem was. The atmosphere felt pagan rather than Christian. Perhaps that was it. Princesses and their attendants carried offerings of fruits and flowers. A simple act, but also a suggestive one. The uncovered breasts—and there were many of them—were large and full as if inviting a man to reach out and touch them, all the more spectacular for being viewed in candlelight.

'Well,' Leonard breathed out slowly. 'I must admit that the trip has been worth it for these images alone.'

Rachel, dark-haired, slight, stood by his side and Leonard felt, as he always did in her presence, a yearning. These irrational longings were a frustration to him. They made his tremor more acute.

'Such extraordinary art in such unexpected places.' Bella was behind them, perhaps sensing she'd put both Rachel and Leonard in a spot. These paintings were rather encouraging. Bertie had, sensibly enough, already gone back outside. 'It was said that the entire western side of the rock was once covered in such works. Let us keep going, before the heat of the day envelops us.'

'What did Sigiriya look like when it was first built?' Bertie asked as he clambered from platform to platform, though he was compelled to stop for a moment, as a troupe of monkeys swung past him, and to duck as one threw a piece of its own dung in his direction. The heat was close and the wind was rising.

Bella adored questions like this. Indeed she had travelled to Ceylon with HCP Bell's volume on the archaeological history of Ceylon, so she was in a position to answer them. Bella, like Leonard, was intelligent, and like Leonard was always keen to share her learning.

'King Kasyapa built it 500 years after the birth of Christ. He'd killed his father, and the paranoia that ensued such an unnatural act made him fear for his life. This walled city was once tier upon tier of roofs. In the centre there was a tower that was in turn capped by a citadel, which rose sheer from the edge of the precipice and could only be reached by the gallery, which zig-zagged to the summit. It was one of the grandest buildings the world has ever seen. The king lived here for eighteen years, before descending with an army to fight his brother on the plains. When it became clear he was losing the battle he committed suicide.'

'All this work for eighteen years habitation?' Bertie asked.

Bella did not have time to respond. 'Look out!' she called to Leonard, who'd almost walked straight into a large sheet of honey-comb. The low hum of wild bees was all around.

'Look out for hornets, and wasps!' Bella commanded. 'There is danger everywhere! Bell and his men were constantly under attack.'

The following day the party dozed in the rattling dark until the sun rose over their next destination: Polonnaruwa. They were headed for a rest house set on a small peninsula that protruded into Polonnaruwa's tank. The water was a muddy brown, shot through with flashes of the pink, purple and white water lilies that idled on the surface. The breeze blew mosquitoes away, rather than towards them, which meant they could drink their cups of tea on the chairs and tables by the water and take in the scene. A lazy flock of ibis lifted themselves out of the trees, then floated through the air to land beside them. There was jungle all round: a tumble of green vines, a jumble of sounds. Monkeys chattered as they swung from tree to tree, wild boar snorted and birds called to each other. Plant and animal life had swarmed all over the ruins of this city for several centuries, only recently being beaten back. Leonard found himself strangely moved by the vista. He felt the landscape was speaking to him: *our city fell, all cities fall.*

'It is sobering, is it not, to realise that civilisations can disappear in not much more than the blink of an eye?' he announced.

'Why do they call them tanks?' Bella asked, not much interested in questions of extinction. 'They are as large as lakes.'

'But constructed by men, nonetheless,' Leonard said. 'Therefore known as tanks. They are the pride of Ceylon, you know. I never knew how many conversations it was possible to have about irrigation before I moved here. The entire civilisation was built on the engineering of water.'

'Is this the tank that a chieftain deliberately spiked with malaria in an effort to destroy the people?' Bella asked.

It was Bertie who replied, 'I believe that malaria was endemic here by the twelfth century. I had not heard it was used as a weapon.'

'It's more impressive than I had imagined possible,' Bella said. 'Practically Roman.'

'You should consider writing some kind of guide,' Leonard suggested. 'While you are here. Bell's archaeological work has made quite an impression on the travelling Englishman. They arrive in greater numbers every year.'

'And you detest them for it.'

'Detest is a strong word,' Leonard protested, though it was, in fact, the correct one.

The party broke up. Rachel needed to rest. Bertie wanted to pursue his interest in the semi-circular carved doorsteps known as moonstones. That left Leonard and Bella to step out together.

As the day grew hotter the ruins pulsed with white heat, light, waves of sound. Leonard noted that Bella seemed somehow to be at the centre of this: moving through monoliths and rubble wearing a hat draped with netting to protect herself from sun and mosquitoes. Sweat ran down her face, darkened patches of her dress, a dress that was slimmer than the ones she wore in England. More pleasing. Bella had, he realised, been released not just by the death of Queen Victoria but by having left England and its relentless snobberies behind.

The siblings rounded a stupa. They walked through a profusion of tropical growth to find four of the finest statues of the Buddha that Bella and Leonard—indeed the entire world—had ever seen. The Ananda statue stood some twenty-five feet tall. Two others were seated. A fourth, reclining, was almost fifty feet long. Buddha's peaceful features were depicted more delicately here than on most renaissance statuary. Gal Vihara. Buddha entering nirvana-after-death. A state of grace.

2006

In an attempt to understand why Alice felt so—well, she supposed the word was 'haunted'—by Leonard she enrolled in a PhD program in Creative Writing. She continued to read Leonard's letters from the time that he was a colonial administrator. She read his first novel. She read all personal and official diaries written during his time in Ceylon. Much of what she read struck her as vivid and insightful—alongside the moments of cringe that accompanied any reading of a writer from the olden days. She read books on postcolonialism. She read essays written by Sri Lankan academics, in which Leonard Woolf's contributions to Ceylonese society were alternately critiqued and praised. One of the things that Alice was trying to understand was why Leonard found his voice once he left England. Was it the power? Was it being released from the grip of Victorian England? Both? Was colonialism a form of vampirism? Was she a vampire too? Other people's stories. Always so interesting. Always more interesting than her own.

To this end Alice decided to visit Sri Lanka. Her guides would be *The Village in the Jungle*, *How to See Ceylon* and, if she willed it so, maybe even Leonard himself. She would go by the path until she came to a boutique where they sold balls of rice and sugar. Go on to another boutique where they sold kanji. She would see flamboyant trees in full blossom, and at those trees she would choose to follow the path that followed the direction of the hand with which she ate rice.

How to See Ceylon
by Bella Woolf, 1914
HINTS TO TRAVELLERS

1. On motoring tours it is well to be provided with a supply of quinine and aspirin tabloids, chlorodyne, citronella oil, mosquitol (for keeping off mosquitoes), brandy. Essence of Cinnamon is excellent for colds.

2. Insist on boiled milk at hotels, rest-houses. A supply of tinned milk should be taken in the car.

3. Avoid Shell-fish at hotels.

4. Do not sleep under a fan, unless a blanket is wrapped round your body. Dangerous chills are caught from fans.

5. A raincoat is indispensable in the country. A Burberry is the most satisfactory.

6. Avoid sitting in draughts during the North-East Monsoon, as the 'land wind' is responsible for many chills.

7. Never touch water except in a private bungalow where it is guaranteed filtered and even then the servants are not always reliable. A 'kurumba' (young coconut) can always be obtained for a few cents, and the milk is most refreshing.

8. A topee should always be worn until 4 to 4.30pm even on dull days.

9. Any indisposition should be regarded as more serious than at home and a doctor consulted if it does not yield at once to ordinary treatment.

10. Some visitors prefer to engage a travelling servant, who can look after the luggage and meet the motor at various points. Messrs Thomas Cook & Sons have a number of these servants on their books. Many of them have been round India several times and have given great satisfaction. Messrs. Cook & Sons take no risk when recommending these men, but the servants know that if they treat the visitor badly, they will be given no further employment by the Firm. This has usually enough effect to keep all in order.

On her first night in Colombo, Alice attended a lecture at the Wildlife and Nature Protection Society. She wanted to have a sense of what modern Sri Lanka was like, to better compare it to colonial Ceylon. The news wasn't good.

'One in every six species of indigenous inland vertebrates in Sri Lanka was facing a high risk of extinction. One hundred and twenty-two species were Critically Endangered. Of the thirty-four species of amphibians confirmed as extinct worldwide, nineteen were from Sri Lanka. One in every two species of freshwater fish, reptiles and mammals and one in every five species of birds on the island were facing the risk of becoming extinct in the wild.'

Pesticides were unregulated. Bees were on the way out.

Alice watched the carousel of slides spin round and round: shrews, bats, the Sri Lankan purple-faced langur, the red slender loris, leopards, elephants, the rusty-spotted cat, the fishing cat, sloth bears, civets, wild buffalo, hog deer, pygmy mouse deer, giant flying squirrels, whales, crocodiles, sea turtles, horn lizards, geckos and snakes. She left before the talk ended—it was too much, too much—and walked down Galle Road looking for the kottu roti joint that people suggested she try but it seemed to have gone. Everything was changing. The Sri Lanka Leonard had lived in a hundred years ago was gone. She was writing about a place that no longer existed.

Perhaps it never had.

The next day Alice headed to Galle. Once there she sat on the tiled verandah of one of the oldest and most expensive hotels in the old fort town. She drank gin and tonics from 3 pm, and at some point over the afternoon Leonard joined her. He wore a pith helmet, was tall, dark and handsome in a somewhat two-dimensional way, and a fox terrier sat at his feet. At first he seemed shy, and sipped quietly on his G&T, without uttering a word. But then the fans picked up speed and shuddered as gusts of wind rose up. The curtain figs that ran alongside the hotel curled like a breaking wave into the side of the verandah as the rain set in. The staff ran to let canvas rolls loose and anchor them to the top of balustrade.

'There are two monsoons,' Imaginary Leonard, suddenly animated, said. 'They hit you quite unexpectedly from every side. Once you're in the dry zone you will not have to endure such uncertainty.'

Alice wasn't quite sure what to say. Finally: 'Weren't you cremated?'

'Yes,' Imaginary Leonard said. 'But I can hardly come to you as an urn, or a flurry of ashes.'

'I suppose not,' Alice said, then ordered another drink.

'Are you going to Jaffna?' Leonard enquired. 'People hated me there. I was accused of horsewhipping a man of some standing and was shocked that it was believed that I would deliberately hit a Tamil. I would not. And at that moment I began to understand that I was an imperialist and that we, the imperialists, were not welcome.'

Alice let Leonard's early play for sympathy go uncommented upon. Word was he'd taken up his role as a colonial administrator with great enthusiasm. The regrets were to come later. Leonard continued.

'English education does tend to make one feel that one ought to be able to do anything . . . I went up to Jaffna as a cadet. I hadn't the vaguest notion about Ceylon or anything to do with it. But about three weeks after I go there the GA went on circuit and the office assistant had to go away to Colombo. And I was left in charge of a province . . . I had to make up my mind what to do three weeks after I got to Ceylon, for a whole province.'*

---

* Leonard Woolf actually made these comments during an interview with Michael Roberts in 1965.

Alice was certain she'd read an interview with a far older Leonard where he said exactly that. No matter, she answered his question, spoke words out loud, as if he really was sitting right beside her. 'I planned to go to Jaffna but it's not safe. More than 5000 people have been killed since the assassination of the foreign minister a year ago.'

Leonard looked confused. 'I thought the civil war was over. I do find it hard to keep track. The longer I've been dead, the more details elude me.'

'Virginia was not nice about your Ceylonese friends, was she?'

'She was not,' Leonard said. 'Few English people were. I was particularly unhappy with her reception of the lawyer EW Perera, the lion of Kotte, an educated man of high standing. I had asked him to tea at Hogarth House, as I was supporting his political work. The British government was wrong to suppress the demonstrations which had taken place in Ceylon. Perera was a noble, proud and educated man, and he gave Virginia a souvenir from Ceylon as was the custom. An envelope of lace. She described him as a mahogany wretch and his gift as a bribe.'

'How did you put up with her?' Alice asked. 'Treating him, and by extension you, so badly.'

'I had no expectation of being respected or understood. And in that way we found some peace which, in turn, led to some mutual respect and understanding. Perhaps a more relevant question is what caused the riots? As far as I could ascertain, economic questions had led to embittered feelings between the Buddhist Sinhalese and the Moslem Moormen. The English felt the need to clamp down on this with extreme violence. It would not be an exaggeration to say that the 1915 riots made an anti-imperialist of me.'

'Some would say too late,' Alice said.

'What other people say is of no account to me,' Leonard said, before being whisked away by a powerful gust of wind.

The next day, a hungover Alice was driven slowly west by a driver and guide called Mohammed. The roads were still in a state of disrepair though the tsunami had been eighteen months ago. Sections of coastline where the reefs were intact had not fared too badly. The damage was far worse on parts of the coast where dynamite fishing had destroyed the coral. Hambantota itself had almost disappeared under the sea, swallowing the colonial history Alice was so determined to get to the bottom of. More than 4000 people died there; 2500 of the bodies were found in the lagoon near the town.

Leonard's bungalow had unaccountably survived: survived the end of Ceylon, the civil war, and the tsunami. It was now listed as an archaeological site, and on it stood the Gallows Tree, the only one still standing in Sri Lanka. Seven convicts had been hanged during Leonard's time and he had watched them being executed from the upper floor of his residence. Alice found that fact hard to square with the genuine concern that Imaginary Leonard had expressed for the plight of the Ceylonese over his G&T.

Alice decided to focus on more appealing aspects of his nature. His love of flamingos for example. Flocks of thousands were once not unusual but now the population was perilously low. You might see half a dozen, if you were lucky. Nonetheless, for the entire time she was there, Alice rose every dawn in the hope of seeing a stream of flamingos in single file along the coastline, before turning sharply at the headland in a flash of pink. For three mornings in a row, she looked up into the wingless air.

Alice's next stop was Yala National Park, land that had once fallen under Leonard's jurisdiction but was now the domain of wildlife and the tourism industry. After ignoring Bella Woolf's advice and eating shellfish from the hotel buffet, she became ill and had to postpone her leopard safari. This was frustrating, as the whiteboard in the foyer of the lodge had promised several leopards. (It was unrealistic of Alice to believe the whiteboard. The leopards had been hunted by poachers, lost their habitat, and there were only about a thousand of them left in the wild.)

The following day Alice sat in a jeep for some hours and peered into the scrub. She saw neither a leopard nor a sloth bear. She did, however, see a family of jackals trot across the salt pans at dawn and a dozen peacocks. She smelt wild boar, saw buffaloes, saw deer and antlered stags. A mongoose was disembowelled by a sea eagle, and snakes lifted their bodies, straight as sticks, into the air. She saw a baby elephant being breastfed and a very pregnant female using her trunk to strip leaves off a tree. Crocodiles lay around in the heat opening and closing their mouth to cool themselves down. She saw flamingos (finally!), painted storks, egrets, Indian darters and tiny, shiny green bee-eaters.

When Mohammed parked in the shade by a tank during the heat of the day, Alice saw a sunbird—metallic purple feathers turning to green-blue—zipping from one tall and bright flower to another. Suddenly it pivoted in such a manner as to display the deep red of its breast.

Vulnerable, fearless. Perfect.

And then it was gone.

When they headed back to their lodge, Mohammed drove Alice past the ruins of the area's original hotel, which had been taken out by the tsunami. Dozens had drowned there, travellers and staff alike.

Mohammed got out of the jeep, walked towards the rubble, took off his cap and held it out with both hands as if it were an offering. He stood like that for some minutes before returning to the jeep.

'Did friends of yours work here?' Alice asked.

'Of course.'

'Why did so many more people die here than at the other lodge?'

'The sand dunes were removed to provide a better view. For the government officials. For the tourists.'

'Was there any warning?'

'The birds acted strangely and sang strange songs. The elephants heard it through their feet, and headed inland. Many animals followed them. It is humans who do not know how to protect themselves.'

'I'm sorry,' Alice said.

Mohammed put his cap on, then his sunglasses, and got back in the jeep. 'We go back to the lodge now.' It wasn't a question.

Mohammed drove. Imaginary Leonard took up residence in the passenger seat up next to him. Alice noticed that Leonard was filling out. He was more three-dimensional. More convincing. He turned to Alice. 'Let me tell you more about the animals in this place.'

Alice smiled encouragingly.

'This sanctuary lies in the driest part of Ceylon. It is April now, but no rain falls between the end of May and the middle of September. In June all the small tanks are dry. Then comes a terrible time for the animals. The deer wander around the waterholes for days, sniffing at the mud. They die from thirst and exhaustion. That is when the leopards and jackals catch them, and carry off the fawns. Only the elephants are able to remember from year to year where water might be found, and when the drought begins, they make off for the jungles bordering the two rivers. Never underestimate an elephant. That is what I wanted to say to you.'

Alice implied, through vigorous nodding, that she would never underestimate an elephant.

'There were four particularly well-known elephants in this area,' Imaginary Leonard continued. 'One and two: a tusker and cow. We always found them together. They were dull, by the standards of elephants. Obviously of the middle classes. Number four was a rogue. He would chase people, sometimes charge as if going to commit an act of violence, and then he would come to a sudden stop and wander off. In this manner he entertained himself. These three—elephants one, two and four would sometimes charge each other as well—with some violence. Again, I believe this was for entertainment. The final elephant of the herd of which I speak was a very lovely lady. She would stand to one side when this was going on, and chew quietly.'

Having said what he came to say, Imaginary Leonard began to dissolve into motes of sunlight. Before disappearing altogether he suggested to Alice that she visit the Bundala Tank that evening. 'Ask your man to take you.'

Alice leaned towards the front of the jeep. 'Mohammed, before the sun sets, could we visit the Bundala Tank?'

The sun had almost set when they arrived. The breeze had come up but was still warm. Alice stood by the tank—which to her Australian eyes looked like a dam—and Imaginary Leonard joined her once more. He looked older than he had only a few hours ago. His hair was white. He peered at her in a way that suggested his eyesight was bad. There was a certain frailty about him. He seemed confused, as if he wasn't quite sure what he was doing there.

'Where are the flamingos?' Imaginary Leonard asked. 'There always used to be so many of them.'

Alice asked Mohammed where the flamingos were, and he, some-what shockingly, pulled out a pistol and fired a shot into the air so that the birds startled and lifted out of the water, off the banks.

'I'm sorry there are so few,' Mohammed said. 'I'm told that once there would have been many more.'

But all Alice saw was abundance.

'At first only a dozen lift up into the air.' Imaginary Leonard reached his long-fingered hands towards the sky as if he were magicking the birds out of thin air. 'Then suddenly there are hundreds. Look!' He was beaming, looking towards the heavens. 'Look!'

Alice looked up to sky that was thick with the flurry of wings. Pink, black, white. Leonard staggered under the weight of the glory of it all, the place that made him, before evaporating, like a mirage, into the heat of the plain.

After Yala, Mohammed kept driving west, towards Arugam Bay, where Alice hoped to take a few days holiday.

'Four hundred and twenty people died in the village we are visiting,' Mohammed told Alice, as he drove. 'It was very badly hit.' But when Alice suggested they should turn back, that perhaps it would be disrespectful to continue, he said, 'Go there and spend a lot of money. Go there even though it is a sad place to be. That is the kind of respect we need in Sri Lanka, right now. You will see. The surfers have returned. You will see them everywhere.'

Four hundred plus deaths seemed surprisingly few given the devastation that greeted them on arrival. As they crossed the newly built bridge, the road fell away; it became bits of asphalt surrounded by potholes. The buildings that lined what had once been the main thoroughfare were reduced to their foundations: a few columns here, a brightly painted wall there. Mohammed gestured at a pile of rubble to his left—'That's your hotel'—and pulled up in front of a single whitewashed building surrounded by piles of bricks and dirt.

It had been another long day of driving. The sun was setting over the lagoon. Alice could see a yoga class underway: lots of white people attempting headstands, their legs flapping in the air as they tried to hold their pose. Beyond them lay the beach where covered women walked, a few steps behind their husbands. Two young tourists walked up from the beach wearing nothing but string bikinis. In the few minutes Alice sat there taking it all in, the sky darkened from blue to purple to black.

'I will leave you here,' Mohammed said finally. 'I will come back in three days. My family is from this area. I will stay with them.' Then he pulled Alice's suitcase from the back of the van and walked towards a patch of sand and a desk that was, she supposed, the reception area. The young man who greeted her explained: the hotel had only recently reopened; the well water was still contaminated and limited fresh water was being provided by the army; electricity was provided by a generator; their restaurant was still considered to be one of the best in Sri Lanka.

After a walk on the beach, Alice sat down in the hotel restaurant and ordered a beer. A man walked a tiny monkey on a lead and it grabbed a passing cat by the tail, then climbed onto its back for a ride. Pretty grey tabby kittens dotted the laps of the restaurant patrons and lounged on bags of rice. They were from an earlier litter of a very pregnant tabby who lay exhausted, on the floor near the bar. Alice asked the waiter—his name was Andrew—how the cat survived and he told Alice that she'd been found up a tree.

'And you?' Alice asked.

'I climbed a tree. Like the cat. Old people, children, they're not so good at climbing palm trees.' Alice looked around her at the coconut palms that had not so much as a foothold.

'Did you lose family?' Alice asked.

Andrew glared at her. 'I suppose you are writing a book?'

'I . . .'

'Everyone is very interested in what has happened to us here. Tourists come. Tourists go. I would rather not talk about the deaths and the loss.' He offered Alice the menu. 'Would you like to hear about our specials?'

Alice shook her head. She'd planned to ask if the fish curry used fresh fish but it didn't seem the time so she ordered it and all the added extras. As she waited for the meal to arrive she read a series of statements scrawled on a whiteboard that was stuck above the improvised bar. The faintest of these read: *This event is not the end! Remember: it's a new beginning and a great chance for us all. Posted 20 hrs, December 26 2004.* A second sign promised that a satellite system was now in place that would give two or three hours warning of another tsunami. A third said that any tips will go to the homeless and a fourth warned women not to walk alone because of the danger of rape.

After she'd eaten her (spectacularly good) curry, the hotel's owner approached Alice and asked if she could join her. 'Of course,' Alice said, embarrassed. It was clear that the owner was attempting to make amends for her staff, though Alice knew that it was she who should apologise.

'My name is Sofia,' the owner said. 'Let me buy you a drink.' Sofia was Danish but she'd lived in Arugam Bay a long time. She told Alice what had happened that day. She seemed to feel a need to tell her story. Perhaps she would tell it until it seemed real.

'You could hardly believe you were under ten fathoms of water . . . it was like a dream,' Sofia said, waving her hands wildly in the air as re-enactment. 'I was under for so long I thought I would drown, but suddenly I was breathing air again. I could see the sky.' She was found, injured, on the roof of what was left of her hotel; the body of her husband was found three days later and three kilometres away, on the other side of the lagoon. 'A friend,' Sofia continued, 'was dragged by the wave, slammed into a wall and his clothes torn off. His wife and daughter were washed into the local library but got out a window before the water reached the ceiling. Another friend had been heading home from the markets when the wave made land. He dropped his shopping and leapt onto his motorbike, but it was already too far under water to start, so he grabbed hold of the closest palm tree and began to climb. When he made it home, he found his entire family drowned. He helped survivors to higher ground before the next round of waves hit.'

Alice said nothing. Why was she here? She felt nothing but shame.

'What I want most,' Sofia said, patting Alice's hand, 'is to return to my garden.' She pointed at the well-lit bare sand out the front of the restaurant. 'That used to be full of flowers, palm trees, palmyras. Every day, we used to cut fresh flowers there. Just there.'

Alice told Sofia about Australia, about her cats, about her parents and Hen. Around the time the chairs were being put on the tables, Sofia gave Alice a hug and the two women clung to each other for some time. 'Closing time,' Sofia said. 'I don't like it so much these days. But I can't bring myself to leave this place.'

As Alice walked back to her cabin she looked up at the sky and saw Mars, high and dark red in the night sky. Once inside she lay on her bed and under a fan, ignoring Bella's advice once again. She listened to men chat as they poured concrete and thatched roofs until well after midnight. The surf crashed onto the beach. How loud it must have sounded that Boxing Day, as it pulled back and then surged in, swallowing the coast.

1910

Leonard always woke before dawn. Not just because his days were long, though they were—it hardly seemed possible that a man could work as hard as he did without dropping dead of disease, or a stopped heart, before he turned thirty—but because there was a gentleness in the minutes between sleeping and wakefulness, one which made everything else seem possible. When he first arrived in Hambantota Leonard had not imagined he could sleep through the crash and thud of the waves as they broke just a few feet below his verandah. But he slept well on his first night, and all the nights thereafter. Then, at around four every morning, the roar of the surf intruded on his dreams; slowly at first, then louder and louder, until there was no doubt about it, he was awake. There were other sounds too. The crow of the cocks, the chatter of waking birds and monkeys. But these were faint notes, sound waves rippling under actual waves.

When he finally opened his eyes, Leonard saw, first of all, the gauze of the mosquito net that he had become tangled in. Past that there were squares cut into the side of the bungalow that framed the leaves of the trees outside, which in turn filtered the view of the sea beyond. If it was still dark he might be lucky enough to glimpse stars or the moon setting over the ocean: slivers of silver-white against a velvet-black disc. Often he chose to keep his eyes closed for an extra minute, or two or three, and imagine that the waves below rose up and engulfed him. It was not a terrible thought, this fantasy he had of the sea swallowing the coast and him being drowned. Afterwards, there would be nothing. He believed that with all his heart. The learning of this fact, his shedding of God, had brought him much tumult, and entailed its own kind of tossing and dumping in a wild ocean, but now the idea soothed him and the thud of the surf reassured him that death was near. He could choose it any time. Once he had done that, imagined his end, he could begin his day. After sound, then sight, it was smell that came to him. This day the first thing he smelt was smoke. It caught in his chest.

'Damn it.' His voice was raised loud enough that the mongrel's ears pricked up, and his pet monkey, Henry* woke with a start and a screech.

Leonard pulled the net aside and swung out of bed. Why did the villagers insist on burning jungle plots, their chena, so close to where he lived? He tried, of course, to be reasonable. In fact, had been severely reprimanded for his support of the local people when he'd written to his managers, noting that if the burning of plots was not allowed, people would starve to death and villages would cease to exist.

But despite his relative lenience, Leonard did enforce the order. He wanted plots to be measured out and the headman's initials carved into a tree on each corner of the piece of land. It made little difference. Even those rules were ignored. As far as the villagers were concerned the stakes were too high to care about recrimination. Drought reduced them and the land around them to a husk. The amount of rice the chena provided them with would be barely enough to feed a family for a year and then all would be barren. This pattern would repeat, ad infinitum, until death.

---

* Henry was named after Sir Henry Edward McCallum, the Governor of British Ceylon from 1907 until 1913.

Leonard pulled on his trousers and stepped onto the verandah. Charles's successor, Voltaire, followed close at his heels. The two of them stood together and sniffed at the air. Leonard looked down at the creature, whom he loved, despite his nondescript beige coat and unkempt appearance. Voltaire's nose twitched then he bared his teeth at the ash that rained around them.

The ayah came around the corner of the balcony with some tea. Leonard sipped on the milky sweetness, a ritual timed to coincide with the morning flights of flamingos along the coast. There were usually three dozen of them, west to east, turning just above his head, in a sudden flash of pink. Every morning, at the same time, that gift was given to him.

Voltaire leapt the several feet off the balcony and trotted down the beach. Leonard would have followed him but Henry was rattling her cage and needed to be let off her chain.

'Shhh.' Leonard stepped back into the bungalow and released Henry, who immediately leapt onto his head as if she were some extraordinary furry hat. She rested her feet upon his ears and began to pick at his hair. Despite the absurdity of this, Leonard turned his mind to the business of the day, business which was various in form and detail. Since he'd come to Ceylon, Leonard had been an administrator, policeman, customs authority, judge, veterinarian, agronomist and examining magistrate. Now, at the age of twenty-seven, he was in charge of 1000 square miles and 100,000 souls, and his responsibilities extended to revenue collection and expenditure, municipal and local government, the sale and development of Crown land, the supervision of prisons, schools, salt works, hospitals, irrigation works, pilgrimages and festivals.

Today Leonard planned to show the villagers what could be achieved with the use of a good plough. He'd asked them all to be on the beach by nine that morning, despite the fact this would take them from their fields during the cooler time of the day. It will be worth it, he assured them, in his hesitant Sinhalese. He spoke it badly but there was some grudging admiration for his efforts. Few Englishmen bothered.

It was, of course, close to midday before the crowd gathered, and while Leonard grumbled to himself that these people had no idea of time, the truth was they'd had no intention of coming at the specified time but had been too polite to say so.

Leonard felt nervous as he walked down to the beach. It was as if he was stepping onto a stage. Certainly he was wearing clothes suitable for a performance: white pants and jacket with a boater on his head to protect him from the sun. As if struck by stage fright he felt his tremor come upon him and tried to tame his left hand by holding it to his chest with his right. After a few moments he let go and repeated the process, left holding down right. Leonard feared this trembling made him seem a coward. Weak. Worse, he suspected it made a bully of him, his temper escalating in accord with his tremor.

The black bull that Leonard's men brought to him where he stood waiting on the beach was not inclined to behave. Leonard spent half an hour trying to shackle the cumbersome creature to the plough, but it kept shaking its hump and throwing Leonard's concentration. This happened four times over. If the bull didn't misbehave, Leonard's tremor did. The villagers, listless in the heat, watched this performance with something approaching boredom. Who was this crazy man who made them farm salt and stand in the midday sun, who behaved as if he were a king? Leonard heard the snickering, and kept his back turned on the crowd so as to hide the flush in his cheeks. He fixed his gaze firmly on the metal, and, if he lifted his eyes, the ocean beyond.

Finally it was done. Leonard stood back and took the bull by the ring in his nose. He encouraged it to walk along the beach with loud clicks and hard tugs. He needed the line to be straight enough that the villagers could see the striations grooved in the sand.

'You see?' he yelled. 'You throw the seed in here,' he gestured towards the furrow. 'It goes in deep. The soil protects it and keeps the seed safe.'

Leonard bent down and mimed sprinkling seed into the sand then covering it up. This seemed to go well enough so he began to 'water' the imaginary seeds. At this point the bull took off, moving as fast as it could towards the scrub that lined the beach, the plough rattling alarmingly behind it. Leonard chased the beast, cursing himself under his breath. He should have practised this. If only he hadn't come in so late last night, exhausted after his two-week tour of the district. When Leonard finally stopped the animal he allowed himself to look at his audience. He expected to see silent laughter in their eyes, or rows of men politely staring at their feet, but no, it was worse than that. Most of them had simply wandered off. Leonard tried, but failed, not to see himself as they must: an absurdly dressed parangi, who oversaw absurd laws and stood in the heat of the midday sun. A heat that even a bull had the sense to get out of.

I am not wanted here, Leonard admitted to himself. Possibly not even needed.

His afternoon was barely an improvement. Leonard was to talk with the local Chief Headman, or Muhandiram, one Mr Nallaperuma*. Try

---

* Leonard Woolf worked with several Muhandiram in his time in Ceylon. While Woolf did meet men with the name Mr Nallaperuma, the name is not an unusual one and this Mr Nallaperuma is an entirely fictional character.

to explain to him the devastation of the soil caused by the burning of the chena. They met in his house, over tea. This was Leonard's way of extending respect to the headman, a man he admired. Mr Nallaperuma spoke several languages and, unlike Leonard, had the charisma of a born leader.

Regular bouts of illness had rendered Leonard thin as a sapling. Mr Nallaperuma was no taller than Leonard but powerful looking: older, a ball of knotted muscle. After tea had been served, Leonard began. 'I have been reading the work of Sir Albert Howard and I really feel that the East Indian approach to soil cultivation, the use of manure and so forth, is much more conducive to agriculture than this chena business. Howard writes of the connection between healthy soil and healthy populations, livestock and crop. And in these places where the soil is healthier the cattle do not get rinderpest.'

'We have been growing our crops in this fashion for thousands of years, sir.'

Leonard smiled, sympathetic to the curtness of the 'sir', which he appreciated even though he didn't feel like a sir. In England he barely was one. He couldn't really understand how he had got to where he was. Arrogance, Leonard supposed, bleakly, not sure if it were a trait to be regretted or celebrated. As for Mr Nallaperuma, Leonard sometimes wondered if he should call *him* sir. Certainly he never addressed him casually, or used Mr Nallaperuma's first name.

'You cannot slash and burn this land for a thousand years to come. Tradition is no longer respected. Soil is not left fallow long enough. It grows weaker and weaker.'

Mr Nallaperuma would not give in. 'I am fairly certain that is not why your government tries to break our tradition. Is not the Governor's concern that the land we used to cultivate in this fashion is now considered English land? By what law does land that was ours now become yours? Because you say so? Please explain this to me, sir.'

Leonard too had reservations on this matter but could not be seen to show them. 'The law is the Cultivation of Wastelands Ordinance. It allows you to buy land for private use. Surely you can see the advantage in that.'

'And do you know any Ceylonese gentlemen, sir, that have bought land in this way?' Mr Nallaperuma flicked his hand in the air, in a dismissive gesture, and shook his head. 'My question to you is this. Can a law that drives men from their homes in their very own land be considered a fair law? Can the law force families from their home and force them to starve?'

Was it fair? No. Yet Leonard persisted. 'The last king of Kandy was a bloodthirsty tyrant who forfeited the support of his own people. The chiefs invited the British to rid them of Sri Vikrama. Once the king was captured the laws were changed. The chiefs were duly consulted.'

'Englishmen are very skilled at setting the rulers of the lands they administrate against each other. It is the working man who suffers.'

Leonard looked Mr Nallaperuma in the eye. 'I do not know if I think it is a fair law. But I sincerely believe that this slashing and burning is a bad thing for the land. No matter who owns it.' He felt calmer now, on firmer ground. 'I think we must care for the soil and we are not doing so. I fear there will soon be no jungle left.'

'You do not even like the jungle, sir. Yet you very much like eating mun, kurrakan, maize, green gram, beans, chilies, and melons. How would you have us grow them? In waste? For is that not what you are suggesting with your talks of these Indian methods? Human waste!'

Leonard had had enough. 'Cattle dung is preferable, but then it is needed for fires. These are difficult questions. We are done, Mr Nallaperuma. I have work to do.'

Leonard did not, in fact, have pressing work that evening. His friend Engelbrecht had asked him to join him on a hunt, but Leonard had wondered if his time would be better spent by looking in on the Sinhalese woman who'd recently borne Engelbrecht's child. Leonard had ordered his friend to pay maintenance, though Mr Nallaperuma had informed Leonard that the Boer had refused to do so unless the woman continued to act as his mistress. As she refused to provide sexual services it seemed she and Engelbrecht were at an impasse. These were complicated matters but something about the woman's handsome, intelligent features had drawn Leonard in. He planned to drop by personally, enquire after the child and leave her with some money to tide her over.

Leonard's visit took longer than planned. Voltaire gave up waiting for him and trotted back home to flop on the verandah. The stallion was left to stand for some hours, unwatered, tail switching. If the stallion understood exactly why he was left in such uncomfortable circumstances for so much time he did not convey his irritation. After Leonard strode out of the house with a look that was a curious mixture of shame and over excitement the stallion tossed his mane in salutation and waited for Leonard to mount him. Leonard's ayah had also been left waiting many hours, as it was her job to serve him dinner no matter what time he arrived home. It was past midnight when he got home and Leonard found her, head in her arms on the dining-room table.

Leonard started when he saw her. 'You're still up?' He sounded angry.

She nodded, half asleep.

'I've eaten,' Leonard said. 'Go to bed. We both have to be up in four hours.'

As it turned out Leonard did not rise from his bed in four hours but stayed for four days. The source of his fever was unclear. It was impossible to describe how devastating these attacks were. Embarrassing that they always struck the times Leonard took advantage of his position, whenever he'd given in to the urges of his degraded, his disgusting, his physical needs. A silent war was fought within his blood, his bones, in the throb behind his brow.

Leonard tried to use these times of crisis to catch up on his personal correspondence, though he had been finding, for some years now, that correspondence from home was increasingly foreign to him. Lytton, Saxon, Forster, his sister, all described to him a world where relations were changing: human, class, imperial. They took little care to hide their various perversions, this, despite the spectre of Oscar Wilde's fate. More disconcerting than homosexuality, as far as Leonard was concerned, was this notion that men could be friends with women. Leonard barely saw a woman for months on end—if by 'woman' one meant a white woman, which is exactly what Leonard meant.

Queen Victoria had been dead some nine years but, like an old tree, she still stood, knotted, burled, bent over, at the centre of the empire. King Edward VII would die of a heart attack before his boughs could cast any shade, but the young Edwardians ploughed ahead, socialising, scandalising, and meanwhile Leonard's friends, and their sisters, were painting! Writing! Conversing! Drinking!

One particular sister of a friend, Virginia, became an endless source of fascination. In fact, both Thoby Stephen's sisters seemed to be figuring in letters sent by his various correspondents with increasing frequency. When Leonard had dined with the family the night before his departure to Ceylon, Virginia and Vanessa had struck him as nervous and wild: finely bred mares you might think you could ride only to find yourself in danger of being bucked. Their beauty struck him with the force of a blow, and the sisters came to represent all he would lose once he stepped on the boat: in their long white dresses, with their hats and parasols, it was impossible, he agreed with Lytton, not to fall in love with them.

Various of these correspondents tried to explain to Leonard both the hilarity and outrage caused by Virginia, her brother Adrian and others, when they blackened their faces, wore turbans and robes and claimed to be Abyssinian royalty. They headed to Paddington Station then, via a luncheon car on the train, continued to visit the Channel Fleet at Weymouth. A telegram had been sent ahead to the Admiral, demanding they be given a tour of the *Dreadnought*, the Royal Navy's newest battleship. They were welcomed with a guard of honour and, as the navy did not have an Abyssinian flag to hand, were compelled to raise Zanzibar's flag instead. The royal party spoke a combination of Swahili, Latin and Greek while inspecting the fleet. They asked for prayer mats and made other various ceremonial gestures. During the visit, the 'royals' repeatedly showed amazement or appreciation by exclaiming 'Bunga, bunga!' Despite the absurdity of all this, the battleship's commander, an actual cousin of Virginia and Adrian's, failed to recognise either of them.

The prank was intended as a critique, a political action. Well, that was one version of events. Another was that one of the hoaxers had friends on a rival battleship who had asked him to pull the *Dreadnought*'s leg, as it were. Whatever the intention, they made the navy a laughing stock.

Leonard failed to understand the point of any version of the story. What was so amusing about humiliating naval officers? Or dressing up as African royalty? Then there was the matter of Duncan being kidnapped after the hoax, driven out to a field in pyjamas and dressing gown, and ceremonially caned on the buttocks. Everyone seemed to think this hilarious. The entire carry on made England seem very far away, and Leonard was grateful he had his own patch of sand to plough.

But there was one letter, a letter from Lytton, that Leonard held close to his heart.

> *You must marry Virginia. She's sitting waiting for you,*
> *is there any objection?*
>
> LYTTON STRACHEY TO LEONARD WOOLF, 21 AUGUST 1909

2006

At the end of her time in Sri Lanka, Alice spent two days at Peradeniya University's main library, for that was where the original 264-page manuscript of *The Village in the Jungle* lived, inside a tattered envelope, inside a steel safe. To get the manuscript she had to sign the visitor's book, which gave her a chance to see who had last taken the manuscript out. Victoria Glendinning had, apparently. She was a British biographer, who was working on a biography of Leonard Woolf that was shortly to be published. That gave Alice quite the adrenalin rush.

Well, she thought to herself. I had better get a move on.

The manuscript had been given to the library in 1974 by Trekkie Parsons, Leonard's companion and then executor of his estate. Its various sections were held together with paperclips. The room Alice was given to work in had dark timber tables, heavy chairs and louvred windows open to the tropical weather. The humidity seemed to have led to rusting paperclips and therefore marks on the manuscript. Alice was concerned about this, which led, at the end of her first day at the library, to a conversation between her and the librarian about humidity and its perils.

On her second day, Alice wrote extensive notes regarding the handwritten edits and changes scrawled over this particular draft of the manuscript. Quite a few sections had been edited out of the printed book. These included detailed descriptions of a young woman's pain when she lost her virginity, and the mocking the village subjected her to thereafter.

> *Last night the leopard howled: how pleasant to share his bed: lift your cloth,*
> *Dingihami & show us his scratches on your thighs: surely this time you will*
> *bear him a cub.*
>
> LEONARD WOOLF, 1913

The next morning, when Alice returned to her desk in the room in the library, she noticed that her notes on *The Village in the Jungle* had been typed up on a series of index cards (who used typewriters anymore? Who used index cards?) and laid out neatly and chronologically on her desk. Imaginary Leonard was sitting there, waiting for her, in quite a smart pair of pants and a jacket. This was, clearly, Leonard the publisher. The editor.

'Good morning,' he said. 'I wanted to visit you in this glorious library. I was here—though not on this very spot—in 1960 when this superb university was being built. They gave me an honorary degree, you know. I also visited because I have become quite invested in this project of yours, and hoped to contribute to your research.'

Alice wondered how she would manage to maintain the requisite amount of objectivity now that Leonard was becoming so involved in the process, but hoped that the fact he was imaginary might help her maintain appropriate boundaries.

'Thank you,' she said.

'In terms of *The Village in the Jungle*, I thought you would find it useful to know that Edward Arnold did not give me an advance on royalties, but I received 10 per cent on the first thousand sold and 15 per cent thereafter. By 1929 I had sold 2149 copies. Perhaps one of the most extraordinary aspects of my achievement is that I've never been out of print in Ceylon—apologies, Sri Lanka—nor in England. I believe you also have had two novels published? I'm to be your third? What was your first novel about?'

'Sex,' said Alice.

'Ah, an excellent subject for a novel. I wrote quite a lot about it in both my novels, though Arnold insisted on incising some contentious sections. This was frustrating as I had wanted Victorian readers to understand that humans are animals. Sexual animals. I'm sure you'd agree. Your second novel, was that also about sex?'

'Buddhism. It tanked.'

'Another thing we have in common,' Leonard said. 'An interest in Buddhism and a failed second novel. I do understand why you've become so attracted to me.'

Attracted? Was that the word? Regardless, it seemed to Alice that now was the time to ask Leonard how he felt about sex, though he had, in fact, written enough on the subject already.

> *How dense the barbaric darkness was in which the Victorian middle-class boy and youth was left to drift sexually is shown by the fact that no relation or teacher, indeed no adult, ever mentioned the subject to me. No information or advice on this devastating fever in one's blood and brain*

was ever given to me. Love and lust, like the functions of the bowels and
bladder, were subjects which could not be discussed or even mentioned. The
effect of this was, I believe, wholly bad, leading to an unhealthy obsession
and a buttoning up of mind and emotion.

LEONARD WOOLF, 1960

'You had lovers when you were young. But with Virginia, with Trekkie, you never . . . Did you . . . mind?'

'I am not prepared to discuss what I did, or did not do, with either of my loves. But as for sexual relations, well yes, I would have preferred more of them. Would have certainly preferred to spend my final hours on earth fucking, instead of marking up the proofs of my latest book.'

'Right,' said Alice. The time did not feel right to suggest that, for a man who claimed to enjoy fucking, he spent more than fifty years of his life with women he did not, in fact, fuck, which suggested some ambivalence on the subject of fucking. She wanted to raise a more concerning issue. The exchange of letters between Strachey and Woolf about a rape case Leonard had adjudicated in Ceylon. A task he had undertaken with great enthusiasm and total ignorance, describing the event as 'astonishing' and 'sordid' and the woman as a 'hag' who'd asked for it.

She looked at Leonard, who returned her gaze quizzically. 'Is there something else you wish to discuss?'

Alice lost her nerve, shook her head.

'Good then. Now to my correspondence and reviews,' Leonard said. 'You have worked with British publishers and agents I believe?'

'Back in the day,' Alice said, remembering, in fact, a very particular day in which she'd been trying to negotiate a sale of an Australian novel but been told by an English publisher that they couldn't possibly make the numbers work 'without the colonies'.

'And how did you find us?' Leonard asked.

'It's a longer conversation than we have time for today, perhaps,' Alice said, diplomatically. After all, she'd undertaken the task of restoring Leonard Woolf to a level of complexity that history had denied him. That was going to be hard to do if she didn't make an effort to be polite.

'Yes, you're right,' Leonard said. 'First, to my publisher, Edward Arnold.'

> We . . . should be very glad to publish it, if you could see your way to 'bowoleriging' it slightly here and there, in small details which would not interfere with the general effect.
>
> EDWARD ARNOLD TO LEONARD WOOLF, 11 NOVEMBER 1912

'What's bowoleriging mean?' Alice asked.

'Bowoleriging?' Leonard leaned down, picked up the handwritten original and looked at it closely. 'The handwriting is quite difficult, I agree. I'm afraid I can't remember what the word may have been, but the intent is obviously that I should cut sections people found objectionable.'

> I do not advise a sub-title, which always seems to me to detract a little from the force of the title. The jungle conveys the idea of either India or Ceylon and the British reader won't need to distinguish!
>
> EDWARD ARNOLD TO LEONARD WOOLF, 5 DECEMBER 1912

> I do not think you will find any difficulty in making slight omissions or changes, and I hope you will agree with me that it is just as well to respect the conventions of many readers, even if one does not agree with them.
>
> EDWARD ARNOLD TO LEONARD WOOLF, 22 NOVEMBER 1912

I was very sorry to hear what trouble you have recently had with Mrs. Woolf's health but I hope it has not compelled you to relinquish writing altogether.

EDWARD ARNOLD TO LEONARD WOOLF, 7 JANUARY 1914

Alice read the letters carefully. Possibly too carefully, and soon Imaginary Leonard was tapping his fingers on Alice's desk. 'Please hurry, my dear. It is demanding to remain an apparition for such an extended time. I must go soon. Now to the reviews.'

'Must I read them all?' Alice asked. 'While you are sitting there?'

'Well perhaps just the one,' Leonard leaned down and emitted a gust of stale air from his mouth which pushed three of the cards towards Alice. This was a new development, one Alice did not approve of. She tried not to recoil.*

It requires no small skill to write a story wholly about natives, in whatever part of the world they may be, without introducing civilised man as an occasional relief; but Mr. L. S. Woolf in 'The Village in the Jungle' (Arnold, 5 s net) has accomplished this feat with conspicuous success. Except for the English representatives of law and order, who are nameless, there are no Europeans in this tragedy of struggle against the forces of nature in their most relentless aspects and economic pressure in the Ceylonese jungle.

OVERLAND MAIL, 22 MARCH 1913

---

* 'Some ghost hunters and paranormals propose that poltergeists are actually the emotions of troubled individuals—built up during times of stress. This theory, known as Spontaneous Recurring Psychokinesis, suggests that this built-up stress then unconsciously projects outwards in the form of mental energy, which effects the physical environment and produces the phenomena attributed to poltergeists. But there is little evidence to support this notion.'—'Eight things you need to know about poltergeists—just in time for Halloween', Neil Dagnall and Ken Drinkwater, *The Conversation*, 26 October 2017.

'And what are these?' Alice asked.

Leonard picked up several cards. 'A letter asking permission to bring out a Ceylonese edition of *The Village in the Jungle* in both English and Sinhalese. A letter—1956—confirming that the novel is to be serialised in the *Ceylon Observer* for a sum of one pound per thousand words. And this is my favourite.' Leonard pointed to a card on the desk.

> *It is no exaggeration to say that* 'The Village in the Jungle' *is one of the finest pieces of social analysis which British Ceylon produced.*
>
> T.J. BARRON, 1977

'You've read articles that have been written about you since you died?'

'It's harder to focus these days,' Imaginary Leonard said modestly. 'My eyes are failing. But I do my best to keep up.'

1910

Halley's Comet skated close to the planet, brilliant and bright: hanging low in the sky for an entire two months, its tail so tangible you could imagine grabbing on to it. On one particularly spectacular evening, Leonard walked to the cliff with Mr Nallaperuma to enjoy the view. The comet's head had sunk towards the horizon, its tail blazed up and over their heads. They looked out at the ocean and the comet and the stars reflected in the velvety, black sea. It really was something, this ball of rock and gas. It burned with such brilliance that it could be seen in the daylight hours. Some said that in all the comet's apparitions it had never before been so visible and would not be again for untold centuries to come.

The dome of the northern hemisphere hung heavy over him, and when Leonard tipped back his head he imagined it smothering him. A damp, thick blanket sprinkled with stars. The air in Ceylon seemed heavier than in England. Leonard was unsure whether that was just a feeling or a fact, a fact that could be scientifically proved. Something to do with humidity and the weight of water.

Leonard wondered whether the silence that had fallen between him and Mr Nallaperuma was an involuntary human response in the face of being awestruck. Leonard liked to think not. Since he'd abandoned God, awe seemed to Leonard a deeply irrational emotion. It made him uncomfortable. Certainly there were more pressing reasons for silence. The rains had come too early for the harvest; the terrible case of the dead girl. The child had caught pneumonia but her parents thought it measles. She was soon so weak that she could barely crawl around the compound. She didn't want food but craved cold water to bathe in. Finally the child had crawled away to a find a channel of water and there she died.

The jungle behind the two men inched closer. Some nights its rustlings, grunts and calls were so loud Leonard expected the trees to step out towards him as if he stood before Great Birnam Wood. (Though Lytton had always said that if Leonard was to be a character out of Shakespeare he was more likely to be Othello. Something to do with the colour of people he lorded over. Something, too, to do with the quality of the extensive stories he spun to Lytton during their correspondence, which was extensive. Voluminous.)

Leonard turned to Mr Nallaperuma. 'Don't you think it absurd the way the comets race around the sun at impossible speed through illimitable empty space?'

'No,' Mr Nallaperuma replied. 'Not at all.'

'When I first arrived here,' Leonard said, 'I sailed alone, in an open boat from Jaffna to Marichchukaddi. For a time I was becalmed. Abandoned by the breeze to lie entirely alone in a small boat on a large ocean. I lay on a mattress. The sun beat down upon me. Later I slept under an immense canopy of stars. Not unlike these stars.'

'I believe that my life and character, everyone's life and character, is determined by the placement of these planets and stars,' Mr Nallaperuma said.

'I do not know that I believe that,' Leonard said, 'but I lost track of time. I was at its centre. Absolutely and totally still. And I wasn't, for a single second, afraid to be such an inconsequential creature in such a large universe.'

'This is a very important experience to have had,' Mr Nallaperuma acknowledged. 'So perhaps explain to me why you do not believe in the predictive power of the stars. Given that you have felt their power.'

Leonard understood that both he and Mr Nallaperuma were thinking about the fate of small girls, who fell ill and crawled through the dust towards puddles of water in which they drowned. Mr Nallaperuma continued, 'Did you know that when a girl child is born her horoscope is done? And that horoscope can predict the hour and day she will begin to menstruate?'

'You don't actually believe that.' Leonard tried, and failed, to hide a certain contempt.

'It is accurate. One hundred per cent,' Mr Nallaperuma said, mildly. He was used to being patronised. 'You think this superstition but your English colleagues in Colombo believe that the earth is soon to slip through the comet's tail. We are all to meet our deaths in clouds of cyanide.'

'Yes,' Leonard acknowledged. 'A French astronomer has claimed that the gas in the comet's tail is poisonous, will snuff out all life on the planet. There is panic because people cannot get their hands on comet pills. Apparently this pill protects you from the gases.'

'But you don't believe it?'

'I do not. Though there is something in the opinion that Germany will invade us at some point—England, that is. I assume the cause, though, to be politics, not a comet.'

'The death of Edward VII? The floods in Paris? The comet is also blamed for this, is it not?'

The floods in Paris had seeped upwards, surprising people in their beds. Well, that was how Lytton had described it in his latest letter. Leonard found it hard to imagine—either the flood, or that city. After six years away, Europe seemed like a mirage.

'The comet has been held responsible for many things over the centuries.' Leonard was turning this conversation into a clumsy lecture. 'The fall of Jerusalem; the entombment of Pompei; William the Conqueror prevailing over England; the Black Plague; and even, an American friend tells me, the fall of the Alamo.'

'What is the Alamo?'

'Some contested territory in the Mexican–American war,' Leonard said tentatively. He'd never really got a handle on America, nor understood what the point of it was.

As they'd been speaking the two men had begun to wind their way down the clifftop path to the beach. Mr Nallaperuma changed the subject. He had more pressing things he wanted to talk about. Despite being a very frustrating person, Mr Woolf was always available to have an argument about important matters and had been known to be critical of English administrators. He had even been asked by those more senior than him to restrain the supercilious tone of his reports, to more carefully choose his words, and to generally avoid being so jarring.

'My question is this, sir. The salt is a mineral that occurs naturally from our own sea water, on our own coast. By what right does this now belong to the English?' The tide was low and the white sand glowed as the moon rose, lighting their way.

While Leonard knew that the criticisms Mr Nallaperuma made were a form of sedition, he could not bring himself to stop their conversations. Mr Nallaperuma's logic was often irrefutable. Nonetheless, Leonard argued back.

'What you say may be true. But if salt is to be mined, does it not make sense that it be done efficiently? If not collected promptly, it only takes a night of heavy rain to destroy it.'

Leonard had had a nightmare on this matter just the night before. It rained through the night, and the sound of the rain had stolen into his dreams, transporting him into a flamingo's view of the coast. He could only watch as water fell from blue skies onto a crystalline white that shimmered before melting away into the mud. He woke, at his usual time, with a hammering heart.

'Of course, sir. But you pay the men so little per ton for its removal.'

Ah, so that's what this particular conversation was about. The tale of Leonard's long walk with the salt contractor Abdul Rahman was getting around. Leonard's version of the story was this: contractors had formed a cabal and were refusing to drop their prices. When negotiations regarding the cost per ton stalled, Leonard asked the man to accompany him for a short walk. Then Leonard walked, and he walked, despite the heat, despite Abdul Rahman's size and age, until, in a state of exhaustion, Rahman agreed to sell Leonard the salt at 1.80 Rs a ton. Leonard felt a curious mixture of shame and pride in having broken the man.

'But you must concede that the difference between the weight of the salt record, and the actual weight of the salt has led to a black market. No matter who owns the salt, that kind of dishonesty must be stamped out.'

'Honesty is a noble thing,' Mr Nallaperuma smiled. 'But it seems to me that honesty is of much greater interest to the English when it is financially advantageous for it to be so.'

Leonard couldn't be seen to agree so remained silent. He was, he realised—was always realising, he wished he could stop—a tiny human imposing absurd laws on a thankless people on a small planet in a godless universe. He found himself haunted by the horse he'd once beaten—her body was flecked with blood and foam, she'd almost died—another victim of his attempts to discipline the unruly. The horse had survived but refused to acknowledge Leonard again, registering him from a distance each time he approached before turning her elegant head to one side and moving slowly to the other side of the field. The disdain in her gesture was one of the reasons Leonard no longer underestimated the intelligence of animals. He understood that that horse would never take him into her confidence again: an entire world had been lost to him. If he was not careful, humans would also refuse him. Perhaps he should discuss this with Mr Nallaperuma?

Perhaps not.

The air had cooled. Darkness fallen. There were flashes of sparkling green as the waves broke along the shore and it was obvious to both men that some kind of living creature was responsible for the tiny lights that dusted the beach, leading Mr Nallaperuma to observe that all the mysteries of the world were not yet discovered by men of science.

Soon after that conversation, the earth slipped through the comet's tail. There were strange bands of light in the sky, but the world did not end. It would not be long before the locals would present the government with a list of the ills that had befallen them as result of Halley's Comet. A Jew had been appointed to lord over them. He was too strict. The taxes were too high. The cattle had begun to die.

2007

Alice finished the first draft of *This Devastating Fever* soon after her return to Australia. The novel ended in WWI as the worst of the battles that raged within one of the more complicated marriages of the twentieth century drew to a close. She created a narrative arc that embraced the fact that, to quote the Dada Manifesto (as she did, as she would):

> *A thousand-year-old culture disintegrates. There are no columns and no supports, no foundations anymore—they have all been blown up . . . The meaning of the world has disappeared.*
>
> HUGO BALL, 1916

Alice wrote 60,000 words in a matter of weeks—she was on a high, barely slept, was catching a wave. Flow! She had flow!—and sent them to Sarah.

Sarah sat on the manuscript for three months, during which time Alice became increasingly anxious. Sarah finally called and asked, somewhat formally, if they could meet for lunch.

'Of course,' Alice said, agreeing to meet at Tiamo the next day, rather than doing what she was desperate to do, which was ask Sarah over the phone what she thought of the manuscript.

When Alice arrived, Sarah was already there, glass of red in hand at 11.55 am.

'I'm having the bolognese,' Sarah offered. Alice ordered the carbonara, said no to wine.

'Order one,' Sarah said. 'Really.'

Sarah was a beautiful woman of an indeterminate age. Short. Slightly fragile. Fine featured with a severe black bob she'd been wearing for so long that no one remembered what colour her hair had originally been, though it was clear that it was white under the black dye these days. Her physical fragility meant that Alice forgot her agent could be, when required, vicious.

'Firstly, we need to discuss your use of contemporary Australian references in a novel about a British icon. I really don't think English publishers are going to enjoy those.'

'I'm assuming that British publishers won't care for much that an Australian novelist has to say about Leonard or Virginia Woolf full stop,' Alice replied, nervous, feisty.

'And what's with the footnotes? Promise me. No more.'

Alice opened her mouth but Sarah held up a hand.

'Do not mention *Infinite Jest* to me. And do *not* tell me you are following academic protocols. I don't give a flying fuck. This is not a discussion. It's an intervention.'

Alice pushed her carbonara aside. She took Sarah's advice and ordered a glass of wine, then stared into the middle distance willing herself not to cry in public.

'And I need you to explain to me why there is not more sex in this novel. Your first novel was wall-to-wall fucking. You brought a great deal of enthusiasm to the genre. Frankly, the sex life of the Bloomsbury group is possibly the most interesting thing about them.'

'Sex is not always sexy,' Alice replied, all feist gone. She wasn't quite sure what else to say, given that Sarah was clearly several glasses in and not listening.

'Sex sold your first book,' Sarah said. 'Also, it can very definitely be sexy. My job is to sell your book. Unless you don't want me to sell your book?'

The conversation continued in that vein. Desultory and aggressive by turns. Alice was pissed by the time lunch was done, went home, made an annotated Sex List and emailed it to Sarah in an act of self-destructive passive aggression.

SEX LIST or Who fucked Who

- Clive Bell: married Vanessa Bell, fathered two children with her, and took responsibility for a third, Angelica. Open marriage. Heterosexual.
- Julian Bell: son of Clive and Vanessa. Bisexual. Lost his virginity to the spy Anthony Blunt. Got in trouble while living in China for having an affair with a married woman.
- Vanessa Bell: married Clive Bell, had many affairs, including one with Roger Fry. Settled into a long-term, passionate but largely platonic relationship with Duncan Grant. Vanessa, like her sister, Virginia, was sexually abused by her two half-brothers, George and Gerald Duckworth.
- Dora Carrington: a generation younger than the rest of Bloomsbury. Bisexual. Had a (platonic?) long-term relationship with Lytton Strachey. Married (and was sexually involved with) Strachey's lover Ralph Partridge. Gender presentation these days would be considered non-binary.
- EM Forster: homosexual. Oppressively close relationship with his mother, who he cared for until she died at the age of ninety. This meant he was a late starter, sexually speaking. He tended to have sex with men of a different generation, race and class. Spent his final years in a threesome with a policeman called

Bob and his wife, May. Forster's sexuality didn't come out until after he died and his posthumous novel, *Maurice*, was published. In a terrible act of betrayal Bob denied their physical involvement after Forster's death.

- Roger Fry: married to Helen Coombe, who suffered from serious mental illness. Fry was loyal but had affairs. Fell desperately in love with Vanessa Bell. Also had an affair with Lady Ottoline Morrell.

- Angelica Garnett, née Bell: believed she was the daughter of Clive and Vanessa Bell. Was unaware that the older man she married, Bunny Garnett, was the long-term lover of her biological father, Duncan Grant, until after her marriage.

- David (Bunny) Garnett: bisexual. As an older man, he married the daughter of his long-time lover Duncan Grant, Angelica.

- Duncan Grant: Lytton Strachey's cousin. Very beautiful. Fucked absolutely everybody.

- John Maynard Keynes: bisexual tending to homosexual. Had an affair with Duncan Grant. Like Leonard, Maynard was a keeper of lists and these lists included detailed records of all sexual encounters. These began with his fellow Etonians, at seventeen years of age. They stopped when he fell in love with a younger woman, the Russian ballet dancer, Lydia Lopokova. They married in 1925 and took Wittgenstein on their honeymoon.

- Henry Lamb: heterosexual. Australian. Had a love affair with Lady Ottoline Morrell. Lust object of homosexuals.

- DH Lawrence: briefly courted by Bloomsbury but was repelled by the number of homosexuals in the group—so he said— and broke contact. Used the word 'cunt' a lot. Heterosexual, APPARENTLY. Married to Frieda.

- Lydia Lopokova: heterosexual. Had many lovers before becoming happily married to Maynard Keynes.
- Desmond MacCarthy: heterosexual. Married to Molly, had affairs.
- Mary (Molly) MacCarthy: heterosexual. Married to Desmond, had affairs, including one with Clive Bell.
- Lady Ottoline Morrell: bisexual tending to hetero. Lived in an open marriage with politician Phillip Morrell, was a patron of Bloomsbury, had affairs with Henry Lamb, Dora Carrington (maybe), Roger Fry and Bertrand Russell.
- Harold Nicolson: bisexual tending to homosexual. Long, devoted, open marriage to Vita Sackville-West. Had two sons, Benedict and Nigel.
- Vita Sackville-West: bisexual tending to homosexual. Open marriage to Harold Nicolson. Cross-dresser. Enjoyed seducing women away from their marriages then returning to the safety of hers. Her most famous relationship before Virginia was with Violet Trefusis, whose mother, Alice Keppel, was the mistress of Edward VII. Vita and Violet shared fifteen years of 'mutual psychosexual obsession'. At one point her husband Harold flew a plane to Paris to wrest (kidnap?) his cross-dressing wife away from her lover.
- Adrian Stephen: bisexual. Lovers included Duncan Grant. He caught tertiary syphilis from a prostitute and illness haunted him, much as it did his sister. He married Karin Costelloe in 1914.
- Lytton Strachey: homosexual. Constantly fell in love with straight men including Thoby Stephen and Henry Lamb. Had a love affair with his cousin, Duncan Grant. Lived with Dora Carrington for fifteen years and in a threesome (of sorts) with

Dora and her husband, Ralph Partridge, for some years. In his final years was involved in an S&M relationship with Roger Senhouse, the publisher at Secker & Warburg.

- Leonard Woolf: heterosexual. Visited prostitutes in the years before his marriage to Virginia Woolf. Many rumours of affairs in Ceylon, as well as some, less substantiated, rumours of affairs in England. In his final years he was involved with Marjorie (Trekkie) Parsons, who was married to Ian Parsons, a publisher at Chatto & Windus. Available evidence suggests that neither of his long-term relationships with women were conventionally consummated but were certainly erotic and romantic relationships.

- Virginia Woolf née Stephen: bisexual tending to homosexual. Erotic attachments included Violet Dickinson, her sister's husband Clive Bell, Leonard Woolf, Vita Sackville-West and Ethel Smyth. Was sexually abused by her two half-brothers, George and Gerald Duckworth.

Sarah's response was curt: *It would be more grammatically correct to ask who fucked whom.*

After that soul-destroying episode, a group of Alice's friends, several of whom were writers, met her at her local pub, patted her on the back and told her it could've been worse. (It couldn't have been.) They regaled her with stories of entire manuscripts chucked in the bin.

In one case a friend had embraced the drama of the failure, printing the manuscript out, then setting it alight. Everyone laughed uproariously and Alice bought them a round of drinks, remembering too late that drinks were expensive these days and her novel was not only just not making her money, it was actually costing her money. There seemed to be no suggestion it would make her money in the near future. In any future.

1910

When the rinderpest hit, it had the force of a cyclone, and Leonard learned just how quickly things could unravel. Jurisprudence rendered him powerless. All he could do was watch people go about their work between his district and the next, then wait until bulls dragging carts full of salt to Hambantota staggered into the local herd.

And that was that.

Leonard issued orders that cattle be tethered. He personally shot the cattle of villagers who disobeyed him. He even shot two bullocks owned by a man he thought of as a friend, while that man pleaded with him and lay prostrate across the bullocks' bodies. By the time that scene was over, half the village was gathered around him, and Leonard thought for a moment that he was going to be stoned. It was Mr Nallaperuma who finally saved Leonard and pulled him away from the crowd.

'Come,' he said, leading Leonard to the local tank. 'I have something to show you.'

Despite all that had happened, Leonard was unprepared for the scene before them. Dead bullocks lay everywhere, many of them on the water's edge, infecting the water supply. Further along the tank lay several sambar deer. One hapless bullock, its face half-eaten by maggots, blundered past. Leonard got out his gun, took aim and fired. A large beast, it seemed to take several minutes to register the blow and finally die.

'This is what hell looks like. Or would look like. If I believed in it.'

Mr Nallaperuma explained that when a bullock was struck ill it ran wildly. The dying animal could cover long distances in its final days.

'Why?' Leonard asked.

'So as to die where it was born.'

'But surely not all these bullocks were born here? This is an example of evolution at work. Of cunning. A virus evolving so as to ensure maximum chance of survival.'

'I am not a believer in evolution.' Mr Nallaperuma's smile was strained. He did not think now was the time for conversation. Was deeply concerned by the terrible losses the village was sustaining. 'But I think we can agree that these bullocks will soon be dead.'

As they stood by the waterhole surrounded by dead animals, the red of a mongoose's eye flashed in the corner of Leonard's vision before darting into the belly of a pig. The men moved close to inspect the carcass. Pigs can't catch rinderpest. To judge by the mauling, a leopard had killed it, then feasted before leaving the scraps for the other pigs.

'Sir,' Mr Nallaperuma said, 'this leopard is killing the few animals we have left.'

The two men slowly dragged the heavy carcasses of several bullocks to a spot away from the waterhole. It was exhausting work and Leonard feared Mr Nallaperuma would have a heart attack, but he clearly couldn't have moved the bodies alone. After a good hour's work they had a pile of bullocks arranged in the hope that they might seem a tempting meal. This was Mr Nallaperuma's plan, though Leonard argued with him all the while.

'Do you really think a leopard would eat such diseased creatures?'

'This plan is better than no plan,' was the terse response.

Mr Nallaperuma and Leonard hid a few yards away in a rough hide they'd made out of branches.

They waited.

And waited.

Leonard had learned to tolerate the heat, and the thirst, but it was wearing nonetheless.

The sun set. The moon rose. Full and bright.

Another hour passed.

Suddenly a second, and then a third mongoose dashed across Leonard's line of vision, swiftly followed by a larger shadow. Leonard blinked and pulled his shotgun closer. In the time it took him to close then open his eyes, the cat had moved, silently, to face him. So much for the hide.

The leopard's eyes were gold. It stared at him directly. Leonard thought that he had never, in his entire life, beheld a creature more beautiful. He met the frank gaze, imagined that they were having some kind of communication, that the leopard was enquiring, 'Do you really plan to shoot me?' Leonard's reply was to put his gun to one side.

Mr Nallaperuma was frantically tapping Leonard on the thigh as if to say 'Shoot! Shoot now!' but it was clear to Leonard that he would not, and anyway, he could not, for the leopard disappeared as silently and suddenly as it had arrived.

Mr Nallaperuma hauled himself out of the dust and began to walk back to the village, too angry to even throw Leonard a backwards glance. Leonard, on the other hand, felt happier than he had in months. As he scrambled to his feet, he witnessed a sight even more extraordinary than the last.

A jackal stood entirely alone. The creature flung itself into the air and did a somersault. Landing, it twisted to the left, then the right, in a series of deliberate and intricate steps, totally absorbed in its task. It was, Leonard, realised, dancing in the moonlight. He'd seen something similar among March hares in Sussex. Suddenly, it struck him that all animals danced like this when they thought they were truly alone. When they felt joy. Or when they were gripped by desire for a mate.

Over the coming weeks, despite the spread of the disease and the endless smell of burning bullock flesh as the bodies were torched, Leonard found himself thinking of the dancing jackal more and more. Thoughts would follow, thereafter, of Virginia. In his final year of isolation, the idea of her—supreme, superb, magnificent—gathered more and more momentum until it seemed she was everywhere: stardust shooting northward across the sky, pointing the way home.

III
THE PRECIPICE

1910

'Marriage,' Dr Savage said firmly, 'would be good for you. Particularly given your situation. And your age.'

Virginia fixed her gaze on the ground before her, so as not to stare at the way Savage's beard tapered to a fine point, at the way he pulled at it when he made his pronouncements, at the way he arched his eyebrows and lowered his head in an effort to look at his patient over the thin wire rim of his spectacles.

'My situation?'

Virginia's eyebrows were also raised, revealing the extent of her irritation. She knew what he was saying of course: that she was mad and a husband was a cure.

'There is much joy in the institution,' Dr Savage said gravely. 'And,' he looked at her significantly, 'much support that a husband can offer.'

Virginia tried not to burst out laughing. She often did, at the most unexpected and difficult of times. It was considered a symptom of some kind, though of what she didn't know. Perhaps she should tell the doctor that the only proposal of marriage she had considered had been from a homosexual, albeit one as darling as Lytton. She was fairly sure that didn't fit into Savage's many schemes for her.

When Savage spoke to Virginia like this, as he often did, Virginia found herself taking refuge in the most surprising flights of fancy. On this day she imagined she was to be reduced to some kind of liquid metal, copper-coloured, and put into a beaker glass before being distributed into various test tubes so Savage could test which type of marriage, and man, made her the least reactive. But she was grateful for one thing. Her pedigree meant that she wasn't simply to be thrown into an institution, such as the one Savage used to run, and manacled to some bedpost or other until the end of her days.

When she trusted herself, Virginia met Savage's eye then nodded in a fashion she hoped indicated her gratitude, before provoking him. 'I do hope that George's attentions haven't rendered me unfit for marriage.'

Savage reddened at this, taking Virginia's meaning entirely. Indeed he had once given George an extensive lecture, warning him of the danger to Virginia's health if he continued to intrude upon her person. 'Her nerves will not take it, and, I must say that a man such as you should learn to express his—self—outside the home. Have you considered marriage?'

George had mentioned this to Vanessa, who told Virginia, who wondered if Savage spent most of his days going from house to house, advising people to marry. She also recognised, with some reluctance, that Savage had realised what no one else seemed to. A brother, half or not, should not be forcing his affections upon his sister.

She felt the knot in the pit of her stomach tighten. The knot lived within her permanently, it seemed; had begun when Gerald visited her and Vanessa in the nursery, smothering them in kisses, hugging them far too tight, slipping hands up their little pinafores. Of course the nature of what was or was not allowable was no longer straightforward to Virginia, who had only recently, albeit just the once, allowed Vanessa's husband, Clive, to kiss her. Was she trying to drive a wedge between her sister and husband? Was it her sister she wanted to embrace?

Savage's welcome intervention in the matter of George did not change what Virginia was thinking: men like you killed my mother (she died of 'exhaustion'), then my half-sister Stella (you never named her illness) and my brother Thoby (you treated his typhoid as malaria). You are murderers all. She did not even make the moderate observation that she had no intention of looking upon marriage as a profession. She would save that for a letter for the suitor she was soon to meet.

No, Virginia had other questions, more pressing than the one of marriage, but she knew that Dr Savage was not the person to ask: what is a man, what is a woman, and what, if I am compelled to choose between one and the other, am I?

If Virginia ever wrote this scene—perhaps one day she might— she would describe the fine row of redbrick houses in which Savage's surgery was to be found. Outside those houses there would be a cab, looking as much like a horse carriage as a motor, as was the fashion at that time. She would write of a couple, a man and a woman, getting into that cab, holding themselves in relation to each other in a way that suggested both intimacy and wariness. It wouldn't be clear they wanted each other's company, but nor would they be rejecting one another.

. . . are two sexes in the mind corresponding to the two sexes in the body . . .

Virginia Woolf, 1929

She would one day write, would often ask of herself: do they require to be united in order to get complete satisfaction and happiness? Was marriage necessary? That was the question that Virginia would want her scene to ask. Was marriage really necessary?

Instead she said this: 'Thank you, Dr Savage. I do appreciate the advice.'

2018

Alice knew the stories. Chemical restraints, staff shortages, over medication, clients being left to sit in soiled pyjamas. But when Hen took to leaving the stove on, getting lost throughout the streets and parks of Melbourne, and giving herself food poisoning by eating food left out on the bench for some indefinable period, the situation reached crisis point. Alice, Doug and Diana admitted, first to themselves and then to each other, that they couldn't keep an eye on Hen twenty-four hours a day, particularly given they lived in different states.

Diana had children, and ran a bookshop with a cafe in Bermagui. The kind of business that never, not for a minute, would make enough money to live on. Doug looked like a boy version of Alice (tall, skinny, greying-brown hair, hazel eyes), was single and worked as ranger in Far North Queensland. Hen lived in Melbourne, a suburb away from Alice, which meant that it was Alice who got the increasingly regular and confused phone calls and text messages. To spread the emotional load, a group chat called #thetroublewithhen was set up.

What does Hen want?

She's frightened. Changes her mind every day. Doesn't want to be any trouble.

How long has she got do you reckon?

Her body has a few years.
Her brain hasn't long to go.

Doug felt particularly guilty. He was the youngest among them, therefore had been cared for by Hen as a teenager. Hen, this miraculous woman who'd taken on, unasked, the job of loving ungrateful young people. He comforted himself by blaming Hen for her current situation. Suggested that an over dependence on a glittering array of prescription medications had taken their toll.

Is it even dementia? Perhaps she's just drug fucked.

Hardly the point, Diana replied, before confessing that she, like Doug was not in a position to step up. *The kids.*

Doug sent through a shrug emoji to hide the fact he was actually doubled over his phone, somewhere north of Townsville, trying not to weep. Alice, for her part, was realising that not having children had been a strategic error. Lesbians were excellent carers. Everybody said so. Even the married ones were the modern equivalent of a spinster in a Jane Austen novel. Alice made a crack along those lines at which point the group chat fell silent for a few days. Then the siblings rallied, organised power of attorney, a broker, got themselves to Melbourne to look at 'homes', and found a facility called 'Ageing Disgracefully' which sounded fun. Better still it was not far from the botanical gardens. 'For when we take her on walks,' one of them, possibly Alice, said, and they had all nodded in furious agreement. Hen's life would involve oak trees, the Yarra River, black swans and views across Melbourne's skylines.

Hen's life actually involved being the youngest person in a high-care ward. It involved, despite Ageing Disgracefully's promises, a single registered nurse available to an inordinate number of patients. And still this care was so expensive that it had cost Hen a house in Camberwell. Hen, who'd been insisting she could manage (she didn't want to be any trouble) became particularly distressed about the house. 'It's for you,' she protested. 'All of you.'

The three of them assured Hen they didn't need the house or the proceeds from its sale (though in truth Doug did), and that's when Hen started to ramble about their father. His promises. His money.

It was Diana who finally twigged. 'Did Dad pay off your mortgage?'

Hen refused to answer but a few phone calls to the bank clarified that he had.

Why wouldn't Dad have told us?

It's a nice thing he did, right?

It's bullshit. He sacrificed Hen. For us. Paid her off. He was a prick.

Hen attempted a brave face for her first few weeks in Ageing Disgracefully. Cooking classes. Arts and craft sessions. Singalongs. Her desperation escalated. This was not how she wanted things to end. (This was how things were going to end.) The first few times Alice visited, Hen wheedled. Then she begged. Then she yelled. Once she threw a transistor radio at Alice, catching her on the brow. The staff responded by upping Hen's medication and strapping her into a wheelchair. 'For her own safety,' they told Alice. Within months of this torture, Hen had spiralled to a shadow of her former self. Once tall and striking, with a mop of red curls and dark brown eyes, she became shrunken. Grey. More wraith than human.

One evening, as Alice was sitting in her car on Birdwood Avenue, trying to summon up the courage to go into Ageing Disgracefully,

Imaginary Leonard casually opened the passenger door and got in. 'Aren't VWs German?' he asked, before reaching across the handbrake and patting Alice on the hand. 'It's not fun, is it?' he said mournfully, and Alice choked out a strangled sob.

Once Hen was committed—there was no other word for it—Alice unspooled. Her family had broken years ago but she was still trying to fix things, she had to fix things, it was her role to fix things, she had failed to fix things. For a while she stopped trying to fix things and moved interstate, then overseas. At that point Hen developed a number of amorphous conditions, ones that mysteriously shapeshifted. Anxiety turned into arthritis, a sore hip triggered a bung knee, which bloomed over the years into some kind of inflammatory condition. She developed a tremor. 'My body turns on itself,' was how she described it to Alice. When Hen had a breakdown, Alice returned to Australia. It wasn't until Hen was put into care that she was given a label. Parkinson's. Dementia. Or was it Parkinson's Dementia, no full stop needed?

'We can't save them, can we?' Alice said.

Leonard ignored the question. Obviously he had failed to save many of those he had loved. Thoby (typhoid). Virginia (suicide). Lytton (cancer). Julian (bullet). Vanessa (cancer). Cecil (suicide). Bertie (influenza). Bella (old age). 'If you take her for a walk,' he said, always practical, 'I will join you.'

Soon enough Alice was pushing Hen in a wheelchair around the Botanic Gardens. Leonard walked along beside her, his beloved cocker spaniel Pinka trailing at his heels. They headed towards the Ornamental Lake.

'I would like,' he said, 'to see the Moreton Bay figs. Also the swans. Is it true,' he asked, 'that they are black?'

They were. Aggressive, too. Alice decided to let him test that out for himself. Hen indicated that she wanted to see her favourite oak tree on the western side of the gardens.

'You realise, don't you, that your friend Hen was in love with your father?' Imaginary Leonard said, as the four of them strolled, trotted, and rolled down the path. 'She hoped he'd return home to you. And to her. Did he?'

Hen cocked her head, smiled, as if she was listening to the conversation. Reached up to pat Alice's hand where it gripped the wheelchair.

'I have no idea how you are privy to such information,' Alice replied. 'But to answer your question, of course not. My father did not return to her, or us, and then he died of too much booze.'

'Fathers tend to die,' Leonard agreed. 'Or take mistresses. Or both.'

Hen nodded, vehemently.

'When I am in a park as beautiful as this,' Leonard segued, 'I find myself thinking, how did the early directors of these magnificent gardens'—he gestured to a series of names carved into a stone plaque dug out of a cliff face that was some millions of years old—'know just how glorious these trees would become? Take this ancient.' He pointed towards a tall river red gum with a thinning crown and covered with burls, which wore its age with great dignity. 'Which director planted this?'

'None of them,' Alice said. 'It grew here, near the banks of the river when it ran its original course. It predates white settlement. It predates this city.'

'I forget,' Imaginary Leonard said, 'that you are an imperialist just as I was.'

Alice wanted to argue about the ways she was essentially different from him, but then it occurred to her she was not, so she said nothing.

'These gardens remind me of Kew Gardens,' Imaginary Leonard continued. 'And the quality of your oaks! Exceptional.'

By this point Alice had pushed Hen under the massive canopy of her favourite Algerian oak. Its boughs had been allowed to grow naturally, to drape to the ground and support the tree's weight. It enveloped them. Hen, who had been restless, finally relaxed. Alice explained to Leonard that oak trees in the southern hemisphere died younger than they did in the northern hemisphere because they didn't hibernate.

Leonard listened with great interest. 'I noticed this in my own garden. The growth rates of my apple trees from Turkey and Tibet looked very different in an English climate than they would have if they were growing on home ground. But climate and soil does not explain this, I believe,' he gestured at the massive wound in the oak's trunk.

'Machete attack,' Alice said. 'Not so long ago.'

Leonard looked shocked, Hen looked shocked.

Alice had been working on her tendency to overshare, and felt that she had confided enough in Leonard for one day, which is why she didn't explain to him why these gardens, and this tree, was so special to her. For it was here, under this oak tree, that she had married Edith. While the ceremony hadn't been legal at the time, it had felt the best way for Alice and Edith to acknowledge—to each other and to their families—that they planned to stay together from that day forth, in sickness and in health, till death did its work. It had been a bright, hot and late summer's day, the tree's canopy an embrace of green. Diana had been there, Doug hadn't, Edith's parents had flown in from Adelaide and the only other member of the wedding party was Hen. She'd acted as ring bearer, stepping forth with a flourish when required, holding Alice's mother's wedding band in the palm of her hand. The ring was rose gold; Hen was resplendent in a vibrant blue and yellow Marimekko shift. Her red hair sat in wild curls about her face. They'd had a small reception, where more friends joined them, and Hen had made a speech that was so loving and funny that Alice had forgotten she no longer had parents. She had Hen.

The present day was far less perfect, and as Alice stood by Hen's wheelchair, with Leonard hovering near by, she wondered if her recent realisation that Hen had loved her father changed anything. It did not. If anything it only made her miss her father less, and Hen all the more. Instead of discussing any of these matters—as if she needed to, as if Leonard couldn't read her mind—Alice read facts out loud gleaned from the Botanic Gardens website on her phone. 'Four Algerian oaks were planted by the Earl of Hopetoun or members of his family back in 1895. The Earl's son, Charles Hope, planted this wounded one.'

'I was at St Paul's in 1895,' Leonard said. 'Won a scholarship. It was necessary, given the death of my father and our ensuing slide into the lower classes. But a scholarship did not save me from the years of dense boredom that made up my education.'

Hen looked sympathetically in his general direction. Then she indicated that she wanted to get out of her chair. Alice supported Hen, who stood tall for a moment, then crumpled, as elegantly as she could, to the ground. Alice organised her limbs. Made her comfortable. The sun filtered through the leaves. Everyone, even Leonard, seemed to glow a pale green. Hen fell asleep on the bed of leaves and looked, briefly, contented. Alice lay down next to her and began to drift. The last thing she glimpsed before she fell asleep was the ever-vigilant Leonard seated in the wheelchair, so as to more comfortably keep watch.

1911

On Leonard's return from Ceylon he went first to his family home in Putney, saw Lytton shortly afterwards, then, on 3 July 1911 dined with Vanessa and Clive Bell. Towards the end of that evening, Virginia arrived home with Duncan Grant and Walter Lamb. Leonard, who, guided by Lytton's enthusiasm, had already decided he was in love with Virginia, was delighted. He stayed up talking to her—and, reluctantly, to others—until after midnight. Leonard noticed that while Vanessa was the more beautiful sister, Virginia, when animated by conversation was beyond compare. Virginia noticed that Leonard looked as exotic, as fresh from the jungle as Vanessa had promised: tanned, imperious, strong and shy.

Five days later Virginia sent a polite note asking Leonard to join a small group on a weekend in Sussex. Leonard, unfortunately, was soon to be visiting Scandinavia with one of his brothers, but he glimpsed her once more at the Russian Ballet, once again with Walter Lamb by her side. Concerning. However, Lytton soon conveyed to Leonard that Lamb had proposed to Virginia on the very night of the Russian Ballet, and he too, had been rejected.

Enticing. It was not until summer had ended that the two went to Sussex together, with Lytton's sister, Marjorie, to act as chaperone, a role she filled haphazardly.

And so it was that they finally walked alone together across the deceptive slopes of the South Downs: gentle from a distance, demanding when crossed. The escarpment stretched some seventy miles; the vivid green of its heights was dotted with clumps of beech, oaks and yew, atop the dazzling white of undulating chalk that worked its way down to the sea. They admired hedgerow—full of life—old wooden fences, lambs, starlings, wrens and skylarks. They discussed the turf they walked over. Its spring the result of centuries of works by rabbits and hares. They commented on signs of human habitation dating back thousands of years.

Over these early walks Virginia found herself increasingly stimulated by Leonard's presence. She also found that the more she looked at him, the more he reminded her of Thoby. It made sense. The two men had been so close. What had Thoby once said about Leonard after meeting him at Cambridge? Something about him being a violent and savage man. Something about him despising the human race. And then there was this. Leonard had survived typhoid, a thousand miles from civilisation, while Thoby died of the illness in a bed in London. Unless it was a message. Unless it meant something.

Leonard is the wolf and I am his prey, Virginia decided: I must be constantly alert in his presence or he will pounce. The idea, once formed, took on a firmer shape. She was a sparrow. No, a rabbit. No, a goat. She was a knobbly legged billy goat, one that thought it had the meadow to itself, then lifted its sly goaty eyes to find a wolf there, circling. The wolf had a pack, allies—Vanessa, Lytton—all of whom urged the wolf closer. While the wolf appeared friendly, when she tried to gambol away she found herself tethered. She was both anxious and excited.

'Tell me the strangest thing you saw in your time in India,' Virginia asked on a day that he was particularly vivid to her. Her heart raced, her pulse hammered.

'Ceylon.'

'Yes.'

Leonard cleared his throat nervously. 'Would you like to hear about the crocodile and the tortoise?'

Virginia clapped her hands together. 'Excellent!' The wolf was not always gloomy, it seemed. His mouth, she realised, was captivating. She wished she could register what was attractive about him in some visceral way. The visceral way that Vanessa seemed to be responding to a variety of interesting men. Could it be true about Vanessa and Roger Fry? This thought, of course, led Virginia to thoughts of Clive. That kiss. She pushed at the air as if literally wrestling the memory away, was grateful that Leonard did not seem to notice the strangeness of her gesture.

'I was walking with the village headman one day,' Leonard began, 'through very thick jungle near where I lived, for two years, in the dry districts of Ceylon. We often walked out together, this man and I, and on this day we heard a guttural roar. We walked towards the sound for some minutes, before coming, finally to a small pool. Across this pool lay a large dead tree, and across this trunk lay an immense crocodile. It was he who was making the noise.'

'Was the creature frightening?'

'Such a beast, covered in slime and weeds, is primeval in a fashion only rivalled, perhaps, by the elephant. But we weren't afraid of this crocodile, despite its size, because its mouth was wide open—their jaws can hinge, you know, to an angle of ninety degrees or more— and he was staggering on this log, about to lose his footing. Despite his fearsome appearance, it was clear to me that he was suffering considerably.'

Leonard was, Virginia realised, wonderfully different from the other men around her. The advances of queers and ambivalents had been quite exhausting. Such a lack of clarity. Such vagueness of intent.

'He was suffering, you say. So! What did you do?'

'I shot him,' Leonard said, before pausing momentarily. He was not, in his own measured fashion, without a sense of drama.

'And?'

'And on examination of the wretched creature we found an enormous tortoise wedged firmly in his throat. He'd slipped too far in, I suppose, as the crocodile was trying to break his shell.'

'Perhaps he was trying to swallow it whole?'

'It is possible,' Leonard was smiling, 'that the crocodile's eyes were too big for its mouth. As my mother was wont to say of me.'

'Would I like your mother?'

Leonard started, momentarily. 'I think not,' he said, understating the case considerably.

They stood together and looked towards Hove and the sea beyond. 'Could you see the sea from your jungle?'

'You can smell it, you can hear it, but one might as well be a million miles away for all the good that does you. But then there is a break in the scrub and there are boulders spread about and one has to clamber up them. Once your head is above the tree line you see sandy beaches and wide riverbanks all around. From up high you might see an eagle swoop down on a mongoose, or a jackal trotting along at dusk. One day I saw forty peacocks and hens strutting about, the cocks with their tails ablaze like emeralds scattered on muslin. If it was late in the day, I'd see villagers dragging their fishing boats up the shore after a day's work. It is a glorious moment, this moment of release, as one escapes the jungle.'

Leonard felt the quality of Virginia's interest become more intense. It was like an arrow to his heart. Virginia was no conventional woman, all cow eyes and thoughts of marriage. Nothing like his Ceylon 'girlfriends' as Bella liked to call them. No, Virginia was a woman with whom he could share his soul. Their connection was of the mind. When he was with her, he could almost imagine that those dark humid nights—no words, only bodies, only instinct—were just that: his imagination.

'There was a drama to Ceylon, a capitulation from one state to another, that captured me. I hope I don't bore you by going on about it.'

'Quite the opposite.' Virginia understood capitulation. 'But I must defend my own bit of the world, for I think you could walk these Downs for a lifetime and still find some small strange lovely thing to surprise you. Take this,' Virginia gestured towards a slope that looked like a finely worked patchwork quilt and above to a flock of starlings that swooped and swirled. 'It is, perhaps, a more subtle beauty than the flagrant exoticism you have become used to in the tropics.'

'Do not think me unmoved by gentle charm and surprising beauty.' The smile he gave her was so full of feeling she listed, buffeted.

'Tell me more about the Indians,' she said.

'Sinhalese. In the main.'

Virginia was irritated. 'But blacks, anyway.'

'Well, brown,' he said. 'Of varying shades.' He wasn't sure how argumentative to be given that he was trying to woo her, but it seemed to him that distinction was important. 'It was a hard place,' he said. 'But an honest one. Full of beautiful, terrible things.'

'Tell me a terrible thing.'

Suddenly Leonard was finding this whole business of getting to know Virginia quite gruelling. Being in her company was like watching a storm come across the ocean, was like sunlight emerging from clouds after days of tropical rains. For these reasons, and many others, he felt he was sitting an exam, and he had a history of performing poorly in exams.

'One morning, not long after I arrived in Jaffna, the police came early to my door to tell me a boy had disappeared. He'd been seen the day before in a bullock cart, heading in the direction of Kangesanturai some twenty miles away. His parents believed he was to be murdered.'

'What an extraordinary assumption,' Virginia said.

'It seems the young man who had taken the boy was in debt. He kept a dancing girl,' Leonard said.

Virginia's brow furrowed. 'I fail to see the connection between dancing girls and the murdering of small boys.'

'I got on my bike and followed the policeman for some miles to meet with the boy's relations. It seemed that they'd become concerned after someone reported seeing their child with this man, so they'd taken it upon themselves to stop every bullock cart and search it. And that way they caught the young man and had found the boy's jewellery on him . . .'

'Jewellery?' Virginia asked.

'Jewellery,' Leonard affirmed, without elaboration. 'So they took the man and tortured him for information . . .'

'How?'

'By beating him with sticks, by pushing pins under his nails. The tortured man admitted that he had taken the boy to Kangesanturai, carried him out into the sea, knelt on him in the water until he was drowned, taken his gold ornaments, and then thrown the body further out into the sea. Our next task was to look for the body. All day long the villagers and I waded in water, beside and over blinding white sand, in the terrible heat, looking for the corpse. We did not find it. That night I wrote to the captain of the Serendib, the pearl fishing boat that sat offshore, and asked the captain to look out for the unfortunate boy.'

'Did he find him?'

'He did not,' Leonard said. 'Instead he sent me a letter. I remember the postscript word for word: We give a drowned man from seven to nine days to float, but he must have weighed the child down . . .'

'Weighed down how?' Details interested Virginia enormously, Leonard already understood that about her.

'With stones. In the pockets.'

Virginia was thoughtful. Said, 'Large ones, I imagine, would be necessary to keep the body under.'

2018

Another library. This one in Bloomington, Indiana. Three months and a lot of snow. The literary archives at the Lilly Library were different from others Alice had trawled. Expansive as a continent, as deep as an ocean, you could move through generations of western cultural history as you read the letters of soldiers, writers, Quakers, bluestockings, pontificators, fornicators, painters, politicians, failures and random outsiders looking in. Alice could zig-zag from the late 1800s to the late 1960s, could leap from the Victorian era to Edwardian times to the Depression, then, if she so desired, flip-flop between WWI and WWII.

If she wanted to know more about these people's sex lives, she could dash across campus (through a small wood, across a small bridge) to the Kinsey Institute. She could go further afield as well, which she did, sometimes driving over glacial till until she was north of the point where the glaciers crawled to a halt some 10,000 years ago and the plains of the Great Lakes began. Once she drove south-east to stand on the banks of the Ohio River, the body of water slaves had

had to navigate to become 'freed', and tried to imagine the America of that time. It wasn't so hard, with the Ku Klux Klan still around. In the evenings in Bloomington she would drink martinis and eat pizza, imagining herself as some kind of Peggy Olsen, while sitting at bars and arguing with barmen about Donald Trump. She ate Tibetan food at a small restaurant that reminded her of time spent on Freak Street, Katmandu in the early 1980s. As she waited for her momos, she'd sit and exchange messages about her day with Edith, who would, in return, send the latest details of the meltdown—financial, bureaucratic—of the institution she worked at. Messages with Doug and Diana were more fraught as they were overseeing Hen's care. Hen herself would send a stream of messages from time to time—

banking passwords?

Bring yoghurt. NOT FLAVOURED.

cHinese Dr tried to poison me.

Alice? Are you there?

Where ARE you?

—but always seemed to forget she'd sent them by the time Alice replied. Sometimes Alice would find herself wondering about the archives of the future when, rather than the expansive letters she spent her days reading, there would be, at best, these stray assortments of fragmented messages and, at worst, no trace left at all.

Most of her time, however, was spent in the library. Every morning, upon arrival, Alice would heave open the doors of the grand entrance, walk through a foyer to the cloak room, and head towards a second set of plush crimson doors. The room through the plush crimson doors had a panelled ceiling and blond wood tables. Old style card files stood to the left, piles of boxes lay all around, and there was a model of a wasp—or was it a fruit fly?—the size of a small dog. Tumblers of pencils sat on the tables. Reference books on the shelves.

On the first day of Alice's three months she saw a lock of Sylvia Plath's hair, tied up in a bow, sitting in a box with a clear lid as she entered the Reading Room. Maybe it was cut from Sylvia's head the year Alice's father was born. 1939? She didn't know. Could be. But the hair looked more like a teenager's hair. Did it matter? It probably didn't matter.

Alice sat down in front of the materials she'd pre-ordered. There were many boxes.

One memorable morning Alice read about Virginia reading *Women in Love*. Virginia was, apparently,

> *lured on by the portrait of Ottoline . . . She has just smashed Lawrence's head open with a ball of lapis lazuli—but then balls are smashed on every other page—cats—cattle—even the fish & the water lilies are at it all day long. There's no suspense or mystery: water is all semen; I get a little bored, & make out the riddles too easily. Only this puzzles me: what does it mean when a woman does Eurhythmics in front of a herd of Highland Cattle?*
>
> VIRGINIA WOOLF TO MOLLY MACCARTHY, 20 JUNE 1921

Soon Alice was navigating the rapids. Clive Bell was writing love letters to Molly MacCarthy from Paris while Molly's husband, Desmond, was writing them to her from Montdidier, where he was working with the Red Cross during WWI. Molly's young brother, Gerald, a lecturer in Greek, was writing from the Front in France and talking of the pleasures of marching, his love of Shakespeare and the awfulness of the trenches. (Alice switched briefly to her computer and did a search. On 16 September 1916, Gerald would be killed, a small copybook containing biblical translations lying close by his body.) Meanwhile, in 1937, Eileen Blair, wife of Eric Blair (George Orwell), was going to stay at the Hotel Continental on Las Ramblas in Barcelona to be closer to her husband, who was fighting in the Spanish Civil War.

Alice was struck by how easy it was to visit a loved one during a war in Europe in the 1930s. Europeans, the English, were formed by geography in ways she couldn't quite imagine. Perhaps Alice was the wrong woman for this novel. She might as well say it out loud. Critics were certainly going to. In a piece of writing that Alice assumed had been written for the Memoir Club, Desmond MacCarthy gave voice to her concerns.

> *I remember a Bloomsbury period which I called to myself the Dicky-bird period, when a flock of those otherwise harmless creatures descended upon Bloomsbury and pecked conversations to death.*
>
> DESMOND MACCARTHY, UNDATED

After becoming anxious on that particular topic, Alice hung around 1929 for a while.

> *. . . then will there not be the change of life?*
>
> VIRGINIA WOOLF, 16 SEPTEMBER 1929

Virginia asked,

> *And may that not be a difficult and even dangerous time?*
>
> VIRGINIA WOOLF, 16 SEPTEMBER 1929

Yes, Alice screamed across the years to Virginia, menopause is very difficult. Sweats and sleeplessness, depression assured.

In 1939—war about to begin—Virginia compared having her work critiqued by Leonard to being pecked by a bird with a very large beak. Themes were emerging. Alice was pecking her book to death, and then, once done, she would, like Virginia, be pecked to death by critics and readers.

Alice read more of Leonard's letters, during which he reiterated, several times, that *The Lighthouse* was Virginia's best novel, *The Waves* her second best, and *The Years* and *Night and Day* her worst:

> *the facts, got out of control, the book became inordinately loose.*
>
> LEONARD WOOLF, 1967

Suddenly Alice understood: she had to let her facts get out of control. As she had that thought, she found that Virginia was young again, manic, sitting at her desk in 1908 and writing to Emma Vaughan.

> *We laughed till the spiders waltzed in the corners,*
> *and were strangled in their own web.*
>
> VIRGINIA STEPHEN TO EMMA VAUGHAN, 1908

The rapids increased in velocity. Alice was tipped into Box 3, Folder 28 and she was back in the twenties, reading a letter that Ottoline had written to Molly:

> *I saw Virginia yesterday. She comes in as a lovely phantom—a far away,*
> *far gazing lively ghost. But she doesn't seem to wish contacts—or to wish*
> *to probe or thrust herself in one's life, and that is the hidden desire of one's*
> *poor human side. I'm longing for more to be able to get interested in me—*
> *I seem to be so interested in others, but never to be a magnet to their interest.*
>
> OTTOLINE MORRELL TO MOLLY MACCARTHY, 1 NOVEMBER 1927

That was when Ghost Virginia, emboldened by Ottoline's words, sick of all Alice's scraping through the archives trying to wring meaning out of them, sick of all this interest in Leonard and others at the expense of herself, hauled herself out of the soil she'd been scattered in, floated over the North Atlantic in a cloud of ashes, then composed herself into (she liked to think) quite a dramatic skeleton wearing a soiled skirt and blouse in the Victorian style.

Alice tried not to be intimidated by a visitation from such an authoritative, famous writer. A modernist at that.

'Ottoline was impossible,' Ghost Virginia said. 'I've never met a woman with more constant needs. Anyway, aren't you a bit too young to be writing about those of us long dead and out of fashion?'

'I'm only ten years younger than you were when you . . .'

'Let's not dwell on that. It was a cold, distressing and surprisingly painful business that took far longer than I thought it might. I had to jump, actually *jump*, into the water below and it was moving very quickly.'

'What happens next?' Alice asked. When the opportunity presents itself, you have to ask.

'Tedium. Boredom. Restlessness. One doesn't rest in peace at all, I'm afraid to say.' Alice started to take notes. 'Oh stop it,' Ghost Virginia pushed Alice's hand off her keyboard. 'As for Desmond. How did Leonard describe him? An eagle who turned into an affable hawk? Maybe, but he also reduced Molly to a harridan who lashed her husband with her pen in an effort to get him to behave like a real man. So not *that* affable. Let's talk about Lytton, with his charm and talent and his childhood of endless cures'—Ghost Virginia was prattling, Alice was never going to get a word in—'Lytton and I shared that, of course, as we shared so much. All the cures I was subjected to. Milk. Darkened rooms. Leo monitoring my every move. So much rest I may as well have lain in a coma for half my living days. Being dead is hardly less restrictive, I can assure you. Now, to the matter at hand. I don't have much time and I have several requests. Please stop turning me into a victim. Please don't call me a lesbian. Or a feminist. Or whatever other labels you may have saved up for me.'

Alice ran a mental checklist of the thousands of words, many of them labels, she'd written to date.

'And I have a question. OBVIOUSLY,' Ghost Virginia raised her voice. Alice looked nervously around the room. 'Why are you writing about Leonard, when I was clearly the better writer? History supports my assertion here. Leonard really could be quite ponderous.'

Alice had privately wondered the same herself. But railed. 'Good on politics,' she countered.

'A fine political mind,' Ghost Virginia agreed. 'However, I was a woman who fully acquainted herself with the horrors of war. Have you not read *Three Guineas*? I think it's one of my most powerful works. Which means, of course, I understand your writerly problem: if there is too much of me in your book, your own flaws will be highlighted.'

Wisps of hair were floating around Ghost Virginia's skull. Hairy tentacles. Her manifestation was far more dramatic than Leonard's ever were. 'Now I do believe,' Ghost Virginia's eye sockets twinkled as if full of phosphorus, 'that your psychoanalyst once told you that your obsessive affection for your cat Wilson was symbolic of your unresolved feeling for men. You're rather like Leonard regarding animals. But what I want to propose is this: it is not just Wilson that is a vestige of your investment in patriarchy, but this entire project. This so-called novel.'

Alice slumped. She felt increasingly uncomfortable. Not only about her hallucination but also about the fact that Virginia was dismissing not just Leonard's talents but her own.

'The place where Leonard showed the most competence and sympathy, alongside the most patriarchal and authoritative poise, was of little interest to you,' Alice fought back. 'You dismissed his friends as blacks, and described his lusts as disgusting. You accused him of being controlling yet were dependent on him for most things. You were antisemitic. Cruel.'

'Yes, yes,' Ghost Virginia said. 'Men are brilliant, whereas I'm just brilliantly deranged. Heard it all before. I need you to explain,' Ghost Virginia continued, 'why you ignore what you know. That I had to deal not only with patronising if platonic paternalism but with offers of protection from dangerous quarters. You know—all women know—that a man calling himself father, brother, sister, is not the protection the world might like to imagine. Little me, popped up on a table outside the dining room to allow Gerald more access. Older me, doing my Greek lessons and George standing behind me as if to read what I was reading, his hands on my shoulder, pinning me down. The bile rising in my tutor's throat until, more than twenty years later, she vomited as I described what George did to me after Greek lessons. Me! A pubescent girl, in my bed, trying to sleep. George slipping in behind me, smelling my neck, my hair, asking me what I'd done that day, telling me I smelt sweet, his hand moving inside my nightdress. For the world is uninterested in just how cruel family can be to each other.'

Ghost Virginia rattled herself dramatically. Presumably with rage? Alice found it hard to tell. 'Most of the experts who've written introductions to various books about myself and Vanessa say that there is no actual evidence—but isn't our own testimony, the trajectory of our lives, evidence enough? Both of us chose to live our lives with men who did not force themselves upon us. Leonard seemed to think abstinence reasonable and Vanessa's relationship with Duncan was passionate but—other than the night they made Angelica—platonic.'

Suddenly Ghost Virginia changed the subject. 'Once you turn Leo, or me, or any of us, into a story, we are lost. You might as well take up a knife and slit me from gullet to the nethers, then stuff me with cotton wool like wild beasts being prepared for a diorama for all the life you'll get out of us.' She paused. 'I find I am getting quite worked up. It's been a peculiar pleasure to talk. Thank you.' Then, just like that, Ghost Virginia was gone.

The days passed. Alice did her sums and realised that if she kept working on her novel at her current rate she'd be the age Virginia was when she died by the time she finished writing it. On the plus side, getting older meant she was developing insight into what it might be like to feel dismissed as out of touch, as both Leonard and Virginia were in later life, a tiresome generational rite of passage she was determined to work into her writing. Perhaps this explained Virginia's third-person evisceration of Vita's son, Ben, during which Virginia enquired how he was recovering from his 'delightful tour of Italy' after 'his expensive education at Eton and Oxford' in response to his criticism of the Bloomsbury generation as spoilt and out of touch. To be honest, Alice understood why Ben would level such charges.

Alice also found Lytton a useful role model for ageing. 'One has to sleep, eat, digest, take exercise—and after all that, one has to squeeze out one's carefully moulded sentences.' Bowels, as Lytton insisted, were important. And then there was the endless matter of finding desks of the right height, chairs with the right support, and keeping her orthotics dry as she trudged through the melting snow of Bloomington's infinite winter.

Most days Alice woke with a distractingly painful headache. She wasn't sure if they were caused by stress, age, the fact that the coffee she'd been drinking had turned out to be decaf, dehydration from the heating, or the terrible weather. She was always too hot (heating) or too cold (no heating). She stopped along her way—a kilometre there, a kilometre back, back and forth she went, back and forth—and took photos of the ice over buds on trees that were, like her, enduring terrible fluctuations in temperature. Is that what the phrase 'to run hot and cold' meant? Alice, certainly, ran hot and cold.

She walked up the stairs of the Lilly Library, taking care not to slip on the ice. She took off her coat, her hat, her gloves. She stood by the security door waiting for the click which meant she could push, and then she was back in the reading room, its boxes, its card files, its fabulous, bookish, paraphernalia: cardboard to go under the files, shoestring weights, eyepieces, foam supports to rest bound books on.

She organised her cardboard, her weights, her eyepiece, her foam, and took the lid off Box 2, Sackville-West, V., Correspondence 1919, July – 1926. In no time at all she was trawling through Vita's heated murmurings to her husband, Harold.* Harold replied on 'hot rumpled paper'. On Alice ploughed, racing through Vita's affair with Violet Trefusis, sidestepping to read *Portrait of a Marriage* with its filthy travel talk (noses deep in the waves, spray breaking over a ship's deck, the taste of salt water on Vita's lips).

A rose was never just a rose with these people. After a few hours Alice took a break, for she was running very hot indeed. She returned to a letter sent from Vita to Harold on 13 December 1922. It wasn't a crucial letter. Vita's father (Dada) was having romantic problems with his mistress. A former lover dropped around to discuss the end of her marriage. Vita ran out of envelopes.

Alice held her head, the throb above her left temple close to unendurable, but she pushed on because things were now pressing, and soon, in one or two letters' time, Vita was going to meet Virginia.

---

* Sir Harold George Nicolson was married to the writer Vita Sackville-West. He was a diplomat early in his career, and a politician in later years. He was also a writer, prolific letter writer and diarist. Alice liked the drawings he did on his letters to Vita, and also admired his flexibility when it came to marriage, and his devotion to his wife. She did not admire his politics.

Alice breathed in and out. She watched the snow fall outside the window—snow! Still!—listened to the rustle of other reader's pages. She jumped at the muted sounds people's computers made when their emails came through. She found it distracting. Should she say something? She looked at the library interns, silently pleading for them to say something. They would not, she knew, say anything.

Alice made a little move nearer to her subject. She licked her finger—against the rules—then slid her index finger between two sheets of paper. She felt the bow then give of it. She lifted and flipped 13 December to her left. Turned her attentions to 14 December, to her right.

Read carefully.

Nothing.

This was not possible. Seriously, people had no idea what writers endured. How important it was that she see the evidence—of what?—for herself. It was not until 18 December that there was a mention of the historical meeting at a historical dinner party, and it was her husband, Harold who asked, hopefully,

> *I am glad you met Virginia Woolf. Did she look very mad?*

Alice kept turning the pages. Slowly. Carefully—the paper was so fine—until she saw, on 12 January, written not in fountain pen but an HB pencil, Vita to Harold:

> *Darling, I dined alone with Virginia Woolf last night.*
> *O dear, how much I love that woman—*

The relief.

Alice kept reading till closing time. Another two years. Virginia sometimes stood behind Vita as she wrote to Harold, adding to the letters in her distinctive hand, marking her territory.

& if I read over v's shoulder it is by royal license. She is well and very charming.

VIRGINIA WOOLF TO HAROLD NICOLSON, 27 SEPTEMBER 1928

There was a tap-tap on Alice's shoulder. She jumped. Virginia was back.

'Can you imagine it?' Virginia asked. 'Those wonderful breasts, a cigarette dangling from reddened lips? If she opened her mouth too wide, if sparks had flown, well, I really would have exploded. And it is out of respect for the purity of those feelings, which were, I must insist, not simply spiritual, that I ask you to stop trying to tidy Leonard and I overly. Yes, I allowed him to act as my overlord, my commissioner, if you will. But do not think we did not understand the pact our marriage had become. The importance of loyalty.'

'Did Leonard mind, terribly? About Vita?'

'Leonard's primary concern was that I not exert myself. And, of course, to keep me and the garden, alive. What did he say? The bulbs would be coming up long after Hitler was dead and buried. I may have not outlasted Hitler, but the garden most certainly did. I notice you do not ask how Vita felt about Leonard.'

I dreamed last night that you and Leonard had never been really married, and that you decided it was high time to hold the ceremony . . . You did not invite me to the wedding. So I stood in the crowd, and saw you pass on Leonard's arm. For some reason or reasons (not far to seek) this dream made me extremely miserable, and I woke in tears, and have not yet thrown off the effect of it.

VITA SACKVILLE-WEST TO VIRGINIA WOOLF, 16 SEPTEMBER 1926

'Did he know?'

'Know what? Leonard read and reviewed *The Well of Loneliness*. He understood such matters. He was often in Vita's and my company and saw us together. He was at the luncheon at Long Barn when Vita's dear son Ben was explaining that Lady Sackville had told him I'd nearly ruined her daughter's marriage. Which isn't true, but that's hardly the point. Perhaps your question is, did he know about the time I shivered in Vita's arms? Did he know about our kisses and our stroking? Perhaps not.'

Alice sat very quietly. This was an educational visitation. She didn't want to jinx it.

'As for Vita, she was not to be entirely trusted. People think me fragile but I was quite canny when it came to women like her. Which is to say that Leo understood my reservations. Have you read the Forster manuscript? I read it a few years ago when I visited this very library to see what Vita had written about me. In it, Morgan made the observation that it is to the advantage of governments to retain severe sexual laws as it gives them more control over their subjects. Morgan also had very intelligent thoughts on the hopelessness of the novel that seem quite pertinent to your ongoing failure to write an actual novel. He gave up on writing them. In part because he knew he could never be as good as me. Few were.'

Alice piped up. 'Didn't Forster* stop writing because an aspect of his essential self, his—to use your word—homosexuality, meant he could not write novels with the authenticity he felt necessary?'

---

* Clearly Forster should have been footnoted before now. Edward Morgan Forster went to Cambridge with Leonard. His novels include *A Room with a View* (1908), *Howards End* (1910), *A Passage to India* (1924) and significantly, *Maurice*, which dealt with homosexuality. Forster did not allow that novel to be published until after his death in 1970. He was known as 'the Taupe' because his friends thought he looked like a mole. He often wore a tweed cap. When Alice visited the Kinsey Institute soon after she arrived in Bloomington, she saw photos taken of him by George Platt Lynes in 1949. Lynes often photographed men's naked bodies, but the Taupe liked to stay fully dressed at all times, as far as Alice could ascertain.

'That predilection hardly stopped Strachey picking up the pen,' Virginia moved again so she was standing behind Alice, just as she used to stand behind Vita, reading over her shoulder. 'Leonard and I always felt Lytton deserved more credit for this: being himself in a world that despised him. Why don't you write more about this period?' Virginia asked. 'The twenties. When I was sane. When Leonard and I ran the press. When we were furnishing and gardening Monk's House?'

'No threat of war.'

Virginia nodded her skull. 'That's sound, structurally. Of course, I devised such a method for myself in *The Years*. But for my sake. A couple of sentences. Here, I'll write them for you.'

Virginia moved through Alice to the keyboard, and began to type erratically.

'IN 1925 L WeNT OUT INTO TO WOrk IN THE GARDEN AND NEVER CAME BACK. V WENT out INTO VITA BUT DID come BACK. YET STILL, THEiR loVE, thEIR MARRIAGE, ENDURED.'

'Let's go to the greenhouse,' Alice said, standing abruptly. 'The library is about to close.'

The contrast between the frigid air outside and the warm air of the greenhouse was liberating. Alice suddenly felt far more relaxed.

Virginia, still all jangly bones, stood beside a corpse plant, under a fiddle leaf fig. 'I'm not sure why you brought me here,' she said. 'Clearly you have not yet researched my view on greenhouses. Leo and I fought over them. Constantly. He was addicted to them.'

Snow-laden trees could be seen outside, black and white: two-dimensional. The air smelt fleshy and thick. Fetid. They were surrounded by phallic, mottled, purple trunks and stems. The flowers spotted around were equally fleshy and dark, with single petals folded over to form a vessel deep as the cup. Virginia leaned down and reached her hand into the flower. 'None of the delicacy of an English flower,' she observed.

Alice became distracted by the cactus on the other side of the greenhouse, where it seemed that Vita had appeared, breeches around her ankles, and was doing something to make the naked young woman doubled over before her breathe heavily.

'Is that Vita?' Virginia wondered out loud, as she moved closer to look. 'I needed, as you know, the people I loved to be tall.' She peered at the woman being penetrated with, yes, she was sure that was Vita's hand, then realised the woman was Violet. 'Violent Violet. She did bring out the boy in Vita but she could never have written about that boy, like I did.'

Virginia turned to Alice, her posture despondent. 'We were never to share such moments, you know. Though I once held a breast in the palm of my hand. The joy of that affected me enormously. Of course you know. Everyone seems to. These matters were difficult for me. And with Leonard I felt more like a rock than . . .' She gave up trying to talk over the slapping and grunts, a long, loud, Ohhhhhh. Once things had quietened down, she continued. 'Don't think I don't understand the point you are making with all this sordid steamy fecundity. It's a marvellous metaphor. But I think the library is more my natural resting place. For it is there that the power of correspondence, of words, of letters, reside. Did Vita love Violet until the day she died? Not as she loved me, her dearest friend, whose picture was one of the few she allowed in her tower. Not as she loved Harold, her constant correspondent. Not as I loved Leo, my constant companion. The body can betray us, but there are few we can be ourselves with as I was with Vita, as she was with Harold, and Leo was with me.' Vita and Violet were now among the ferns, Vita on her back with

Violet's face buried in her. The sounds they made were more gentle now, but still quite agitating.

'Thank goodness!' Virginia suddenly exclaimed. 'There's Leonard, over by the azalea.' She left the main dome for a room to the side that was cooler. The flowers there were more to her liking. Leonard kept working. Virginia floated around him, reaching out towards him tenderly.

Alice found herself alone. She stepped outside the greenhouse and into the evening to find summer had arrived. She took off her hat, her gloves. She unwound her scarf. She removed her heavy coat and placed it over her arm. How long had she been in there?

Sexed-up squirrels were swishing their tails. Skunks ambled. Deer nibbled on roses. At least a dozen rabbits were lolling about, as if exhausted by the heat. As Alice walked home, the rain started, hitting the hot pavement so that steam floated up, wraith-like, to greet her.

1911

It was to be a modern arrangement. Maynard and Duncan on the top floor, Adrian and Virginia on the second, and Leonard on the first. They would share a cook and a maid. They would eat together. If Leonard was interested, might he inspect some properties with them?

When Virginia wrote to Leonard with this proposal, he hesitated before replying. Would proximity to Virginia allow him to press his suit or would it be a disadvantage? Familiarity did not count in a man's favour, and, as he wrote to Lytton, it was a dangerous move as he would fall in love with her. (He would, he did.) However, the invitation was impossible to resist, and he agreed to join Virginia and Adrian for an inspection of 38 Brunswick Square, and within days they were all living there together. Done. Just like that.

On arrival Leonard went to his room, organised his permissions. An envelope was slipped under his door, the author, Virginia.

Breakfast 9.00am, Lunch 1, Tea 4.30pm, Dinner 8pm

The note left much to be desired.

Gloomy

LEONARD WOOLF, 17 DECEMBER, 1911

By way of enticement, Leonard took to leaving his diary out for Virginia to read, which she did of course, and in among his curt notations Virginia found markings that she could not decipher. Sinuous, foreign.

ව ඳ 92.

He is writing in code, Virginia thought to herself, so I may not know him. It was a titillating notion. Every time she allowed her curiosity to get the better of her, the symbols seemed to have proliferated, interspersed with the initials of whoever it was Leonard had dined with that day. Really, it was quite infuriating. One day she could stand it no longer and drew a series of tight squiggles and swirls which looked nothing like Leonard's but conveyed her meaning well enough. The next morning she awoke to a note under her door: 'Sinhalese. L.'

The matter of the diary—the code, and the notes—was not mentioned over breakfast. It was not mentioned over dinner. It seemed more fun, Virginia decided, to conduct conversations on the page rather than in person, though she did like to sit up with Leonard till well after midnight talking earnestly about books, matters of the heart and the household budget.

'I should really be sleeping now,' she confided, the first night they sat up late together. 'I do put it off sometimes. Some nights I lie awake for hours and it leaves me feeling quite demented.'

Leonard nodded sympathetically, though he, under almost any circumstance, was a man who slept.

'Some nights I take a sleeping draught. It does seem to help.'

Leonard was animated by the thought of being useful. 'Would you like me to mix you some?'

'You'll find it on the dresser by my bed,' Virginia said.

Leonard found talk of bed difficult and dug deep for resolve. But the more he tried not to think of what he could not stop thinking of—fucking a nameless woman from the village on the floor of an abandoned bungalow—the more the details pushed themselves upon him. The hot day. The fact that the room had no furniture, was decorated by jungle, rot and pale green light. He had some idea of what he was capable: the depths to which he was prepared to sink; the give of the flesh he bruised. How would he hide what was degraded about him?

'Tell me exactly where to go,' he stood suddenly, stiff, 'to find your tonics.'

As 1911 drew to a close, a delicate courtship began. Leonard was unable to sustain any subterfuge. He was in love! He did not care who knew it! By January 1912 he had proposed. To describe this proposal as premature would be an understatement. He succeeded in taking the tentative beginnings of their relationship and crushing them, as if with a rock. Lytton's assurances suddenly seemed like the empty phrases Leonard feared they might be. He felt so wretched he did not know himself.

> *If I try to say what I feel, I become stupid & stammering: it's like a wall of words rising up in front of me & there on the other side you're sitting so clear & beautiful & your dear face that I'd give everything in the world to see now.*

LEONARD WOOLF TO VIRGINIA STEPHEN, 24 MAY 1912

Virginia asked for time, for space. Explained that she was trying to finish *The Voyage Out.* Leonard wrote daily letters to Virginia testifying both to the strength of his love and affection but also his self-loathing. She had to understand that he was selfish, jealous, cruel, a liar. Worse. Virginia shared her concerns. He was—she wrote— a penniless Jew. She was—she admitted—unstable. She explained that she felt nothing when he kissed her. That the strength of his desire made her angry. In the space between the lines most people would have understood she was saying, *Stop! Please stop!* Leonard did not read between the lines.

Vanessa, keen to have Virginia off her plate, began to fear that Leonard's persistence would derail their courtship. She spoke to Virginia in encouraging tones of the mystery, the resolve, the intellect of this man from the East who was courting her. She took Leonard aside also. Asked him to show some measure of reserve.

'My sister does not respond to pressure. I understand you need an answer before May, given your return to Ceylon, and you are in truth the only man I can imagine as her husband. But you must go gently,' she said. She did not mention the spells in rest homes, the headaches, the suicide attempts. It would not have made a difference even if she had. Leonard was beyond advising.

'I understand,' Leonard said.

He did not. Failed to understand that he was asking Virginia to change the course of his life. In his letters, his diaries, his conversations with Virginia, Leonard returned again and again to the question of whether he should return to Ceylon for what would be many more years or whether, if he resigned from his job, he would be rewarded by her love.

Each declaration he made, each confession shared, added to her load. Virginia began to bow under the weight of the torrent of his words. Life with Leonard was something she could barely imagine, let alone desire. It was all too much. Leonard was *too much*.

They continued their walks. On these walks Virginia would find herself fighting, fleeing. Leonard, meanwhile, floated along in a state of high anxiety. To call Virginia a woman seemed inadequate, Leonard mused to himself on one such walk. She was a landscape: a hill with snow upon her which no sun had ever melted, no man had ever trod.

'I shall call you Aspasia,' he said theatrically, stopping Virginia, for a moment, in her tracks.

His words were almost lost in a gust of wind.

'Is that really how you see me? How ridiculous.' Virginia threw back her head to let loose her wonderful throaty laugh. This was the problem. She found Leonard, in some profound way, compelling. Giddying.

Leonard's long melancholy face broke into a smile. He was encouraged, and in his smiling transformed. Virginia felt a warmth reach out across the distance between them and rest upon her.

Was momentarily tempted—to do what, she did not know. Leonard reached out, took Virginia's hand with some force, and before she could break away, gathered her up in his arms to better shower her face with kisses.

'Stop!' Virginia said, meeting his force with her own, then walked away from Leonard without another word, leaving him standing there. He watched Virginia retreat from him, then finally seemed to accept defeat. It was over. He set out on the long lonely walk back to their accommodation and, he assumed, the silent judgement of their friends. He was not capable of managing a woman as beautiful, as intelligent, as special as Virginia. And nor, he finally understood, did he deserve her. The voices in his head spilled out of him, tears ran down his cheeks. He was a Jew, nothing but a Jew. He was of a lower class. Worst of all he was intemperate, his passions uncontrollable.

In the face of their dispute Virginia remained in control of her emotions. She walked down to the sea. It was flat and grey. Yet even on the dullest of days there was a sheen that tilted the grey into silver. When the sun came out, the water sparkled and reflected the blue of the sky. In boisterous weather it turned a dark and disturbed green. Foam surged, closer to the shore. One could spend an entire life, Virginia realised, watching the light change throughout the minutes that made up a day, the days that made up the seasons, the seasons that made up a year. The chalk of the cliffs caught colour, bouncing it out to sea: rose petal, steel. The water absorbed and shimmered with those same colours. Then there was the colour of the sky affecting the tones and texture of it all. Racing clouds smudging land, sky and sea. It was overwhelming, some days, the intensity of the light. One could fall into it. One had only to make a choice.

Virginia's body asserted itself. Her debilitating migraines returned and she was removed to a rest home, to better avoid Leonard's devotion. Vanessa banned Leonard from writing to Virginia and further suggested that, on Virginia's return to their shared home in Brunswick Square, he go to the country for some weeks. Not seeing him would aid her recovery.

Leonard, in response to this development, became resolved. He resigned from the Civil Service. He would not return to Ceylon. He would pursue hope in the face of hopelessness. He would do as Vanessa told him.

Rumours as to the reason for the resignation ran amok. Had he inherited a fortune from someone recently drowned on the *Titanic*? (He had not.) But fortune was nonetheless on his side, for it seemed that Virginia's time away from Leonard had achieved what time spent in his company had not been able to. Her feelings for Leonard were growing. If—and only if—they could promise each other a marriage that wasn't second rate, she could imagine having children with, having arguments with, travelling with, writing beside: Leonard.

> *We both of us want a marriage that is a tremendous living thing, always alive, always hot, not dead and easy in parts as most marriages are.*
>
> Virginia Stephen to Leonard Woolf, 1 May 1912

There was a river named Maidenhead. There was a boat. At the end of May, Virginia and Leonard got into it together and he began to row.

'Yes, I will marry you,' Virginia said.

I will marry you. Yes.

2019

Alice arrived at Ageing Disgracefully on Christmas Eve laden with presents, which she put under the Christmas tree. It was a real one, and its piney scent went some way to covering the smell of urine and disinfectant.

When she got to the dining room she found a young aide in tears, trying to force a spoon between Hen's pursed lips. The girl turned to Alice. 'I have others to feed. I can't . . .' Hen had gone on a hunger strike three days earlier. She was throwing meals out windows, at staff, down drains, down the toilet.

'Let me,' Alice said, and sat herself down in front of Hen.

Hen was good at making her feelings felt. She refused to catch Alice's eye, then jerked her arm upwards so it hit the spoon that Alice was manoeuvring towards her mouth. Then, with an enormous effort, she forced two words out.

'Fuck. You.'

Alice ignored the feeling of warm wet soup against her skin. Kept her hand steady. Dipped the spoon into the tomato soup, then lifted it, again.

'Please.'

Hen averted her face, leaving Alice and her instrument of violence hovering in mid-air.

'Hen?'

Hen turned back to look directly at her. 'Fox,' she hissed. 'Hen. Fox.'

'You are not just Hen. Your name is Helena Aetós. Helena for shining light. Aetós means eagle. You could swoop down and take me anytime. You are stronger than me, you always have been.'

Hen swept her arm across the table with sudden force. 'Do. Not. Pat. Ron. Ise. Me.'

Soup went everywhere. It looked like Alice had murdered Hen, or perhaps it was the other way round.

The aide reappeared and began to clean up the mess. Alice sat there, looking at her lap. When she looked up she saw that Hen's red-rimmed but still beautiful brown eyes were full of tears. She put a palm to Hen's cheek, stroked her still fine cheek bones with a thumb.

'Please let me feed you,' Alice said. 'Otherwise it will just take longer. I don't want you to die.'

Hen snorted. 'Die,' she said, but then leaned forward, as a child might. Alice abandoned the soup for something sweeter, lifted some rice pudding to Hen's mouth. Hen gagged then swallowed. Opened her mouth once more.

1912

The honeymoon was not a success. Virginia refused to eat an egg tart at Pasteis de Belém, a tart that the guidebooks insisted was one of the best in the world. Her headaches were relentless. Leonard wrote letters to everyone he could think of, seeking advice on how to better manage Virginia's nerves.

Three days into their stay in Lisbon they caught the train to Sintra, and took a walk through the woods. Leonard felt it might do them both some good.

The cork oaks alongside the path rippled upwards and away from each other while their branches reached across overhead.

'Marvellous,' Virginia said. 'It is as if they are made of pure light. "This Lime Tree Bower, My Prison".'

'The biology of plants is a lot more . . .'

'You are so literal, Mongoose. I talk of the poetry in trees and you try and explain it all away. What I mean is this: it is in seeking and reaching for the light that these plants take shape. They are sculpted by light. Surely you can see that. Or am I not being scientific enough for you?'

Leonard said nothing.

Virginia breathed in then out quite loudly before speaking. 'My point is that I agree with you. There is no God. Light, sun, wind, water, they are our gods. And I confess, they do, at times, make me rather excitable.' She paused. 'We look at things and a feeling is impressed upon us before we register what that thing may even be. Everything we see is made up of patterns of light and shadow, and it is this we must acknowledge. When Vanessa makes such statements, you call her an artist. When I do, you call me mad. Sometimes I'm fairly certain that you find her such a pleasing, such a shapely arrangement of light and shade, that you prefer her to me.'

Leonard watched Virginia carefully as she spoke. She did not tremble, she was not talking too fast. All was well. He could allow the conversation.

'Vanessa is inclined to a form of measured conversing that I enjoy. And perhaps she likes to assert some kind of sisterly authority over you. But as for admiring her form more than yours, that is not true. I could no more enter her bohemia than I could return to Ceylon. Such confusions would be unbearable to me. It is you who are superb. It is you who are perfect. It is you who are my goddess, not the elements you describe.'

This romantic declaration was not entirely accurate. In Kandy, Leonard had overseen a traditional system of marriage in which a woman might marry two brothers and have her time apportioned between them. This had struck him as an interesting way of managing things and returned to the forefront of his mind, on occasion, when he returned to England and found himself standing in a room with both Stephen sisters.

Virginia looked at Leonard, let him take her hand.

'I have read the letters between the two of you.'

'But of course you have, they were not intended to be private, or dishonest. It was you who suggested I seek her advice in the matter of our intimate relations. Though of course it is Lytton who most often wants to give his views on the matter.'

What had happened, on the first night of their honeymoon, was this. Leonard behaved as he assumed a husband ought. He'd taken off her clothes, then his. At the very moment that Lytton, sitting in a public house in Scotland with his travelling companion Henry Lamb*, had wondered out loud whether they would look like two stick insects together—how primordial, how splendid!—Virginia began to shake violently. With the cold, she said. They got under the covers. Leonard persisted, despite the embarrassment of the situation. For a moment he'd thought he was making progress, but then her shaking became even more desperate. Despite this—he'd tried to warn her! She'd

---

* Henry Lamb was born in Adelaide, Australia. He studied medicine, then art, in London. He saw active service in the WWI in the Royal Army Medical Corps and served in Palestine and on the Western Front where he was badly gassed not long before the end of the war. Lytton Strachey was in love with him for a while. Lamb instead accepted the attentions of Lady Ottoline Morrell. He was a war artist in WWII. While an extremely interesting man, and fitting neatly into the unexpected theme of ADELAIDE, Alice could find no particular reason to weave him into any substantial narrative in *This Devastating Fever*.

tried to warn him!—he continued a few minutes longer still until the sounds of her frantic breathing—he was reminded of a hare he'd once seen, caught in a trap—brought him to. Both of them hard as rock where she, the woman, should have been soft. For the rest of their two-month honeymoon, for the rest of his life, he berated himself for behaving like some kind of animal.

Virginia had written of these matters to Vanessa whose response was, frankly, triumphant. She reminded Virginia that she never had sympathised with sexual passion in men. She wrote to Leonard offering lessons on how to pleasure her sister and suggesting he ask Virginia if she was attracted to the female figure. Leonard, an expert on the finer details of male homosexual life, thanks to Lytton, had not, till his honeymoon considered the existence of female homosexuals. Vanessa was more jubilant still when she wrote to Clive, explaining that while they were happy, the Goat's coldness was causing some problems.

Clive then wrote to Virginia, who read, then carefully destroyed the letter. *Vanessa seems inordinately pleased to hear of your marital struggles. How I wish we had been braver, and strayed more. I feel certain, in fact, we would have been rewarded.*

Virginia was angry with Vanessa but could not hate her. To be honest she could barely live without her and had been heartbroken when Vanessa had gone so far to say, 'Surely it is not your intention that I look after you always?'

Virginia stopped, for a moment, to admire the velvet trunks of some particularly mossy trees, buried her hand in the depths of the dark green fronds. 'I do wish, Mongoose, that I felt more, but it is the truth that I do not. I am not able to mirror your passions, and then we are both blundering around. It is useless.'

Leonard winced. He was finding the whole matter inordinately painful.

Virginia continued. 'Vanessa told me she has been having orgasms since she was an infant. I am really not certain I've ever had one at all. It calms me to talk to you clearly on this matter, for we cannot talk clearly when we are under the blankets.'

'It seems to me unlikely that Vanessa was climaxing in her cot, as she'd have us believe,' Leonard said, thinking longer than necessary on the subject.

'Well, Lady Walpole thinks her a slut. And Clive told me that before the baby, they fucked wildly, all the time.'

Flickers of memory strobed as Virginia spoke, so brief she barely registered them. Virginia suddenly found herself having to shake off a spider web, for she had walked straight into one and it caught her in the face. She shivered. 'Either it's cold or I've taken a turn for the worst, I'm afraid. We won't make it to the fortress today.'

In among the letters from home that were waiting for Leonard back at his hotel that evening was one from Roger Fry, asking him if he'd consider acting as secretary for the second post-Impressionist exhibition. To both entice and warn Leonard, he described the first post-Impressionist exhibition which Leonard had missed, presumably, Roger surmised, because he'd been striding through jungles and wrestling leopards to the ground. He'd need this kind of courage, Roger elaborated, to contend with critics. *These men who will describe Cézannes, Picassos and Gauguins as abortions, that will declare that only those with an interest in psychoses will be interested in the work at hand and who will describe the paintings as the output of a lunatic asylum. They will need fending off. Be my Secretary Bird!*

For the rest of their honeymoon, Leonard and Virginia read their books, and corresponded with their friends and family regularly. They found it impossible to keep track of who was sleeping with whom in that late, long summer of the Edwardian Age. Roger with Vanessa, though he had, until recently, been sleeping with the exhibition's patron, Lady Morrell, and it would have been poor form to offend her. Or was it the other way around? Had Roger started with Vanessa and abandoned her for Ottoline? Everyone was at it, it seemed, apart from them.

Once the honeymoon was over they returned home to two single beds placed side by side. Soon after, they moved to rooms of their own. But every morning for the next thirty years Leonard would return to Virginia's room in the morning, carrying a tray with her breakfast. On some of those mornings he would slip into her bed, quiet as a mouse, and they would hold each other, tracing the long lines of each other's faces with the backs of their hands.

Despite protestations of devotion made to correspondents, and to each other, increasing swathes of Leonard's diary were composed of obsessive detail: attesting to, variously, his growing love for his wife, his conversations with Dr Savage, his discussions on sodomy with the various enthusiasts of the pursuit among his friends. He also noted the specific qualities of his wife's excitements; how much she slept, ate, weighed. He tracked her menstrual cycle. (If she missed a period it meant she was underweight, but if it was regular it adversely affected her moods.)

Virginia began to feel like one of those cows, or bullocks, or whatever the beasts were he'd been responsible for in India. Or Ceylon. She forgot which.

She transformed her body into code.

Stopped speaking.

Stopped eating.

2019

'Noisy, aren't they?' Alice was revved, yelling over the chorus. She raced around picking up cicada shells, and finding the occasional live one—jewelled red eyes, vivid green head. She was assisted by a small friend, Pearl, who ran around searching for her own cicadas, before bringing them to Alice as an offering.

'Why are they so loud?' Pearl wanted to know.

'They are looking for girlfriends,' Alice said, before cringing and trying to correct herself, 'I mean . . . actually, don't worry about it. Also, they are trying to scare the birds by being so noisy that it makes it hard for the birds to figure out where they are. If they are loud enough, the birds think they're everywhere, not one place.'

'But they are everywhere!'

'Harder to pick off the fattest and juiciest ones, though, if they all sing together.'

Soon Pearl was building fences out of sticks and had a cicada farm going. That was when Alice noticed two rangers approaching them.

'You need to evacuate. The whole campground does.'

'What about the cicadas?' Pearl asked. Her voice was small and the insect song was big. No one heard her.

'We just got here,' Alice said. 'An hour ago.'

'The cicadas!' Pearl yelled as loudly as she could. 'What about them?'

The ranger looked down at her, shook his head mournfully. 'Sorry, love.'

Soon enough Alice, Edith, their friends, thousands of others, were on the road heading home, evacuated from the mountains and the beach, all of them snaking through the back roads of Victoria.

There was the low hum of the radio: a litany of place names in imminent danger of incineration. The worst fire since 1939, since 1974, 2009. Billions of creatures flew, drove, slithered, hopped, galloped, dug deep into the soil, burnt alive. The dashboard lit up with communications that arrived through Messenger, WhatsApp, SMS. Alice drove. Edith switched between her phone's map and exchanging messages with passengers in other cars in the convoy. No one was sure where to go. No one knew what to do. The air was full of smoke, the wind whipped, the temperatures sat over 40°C.

Alice drove faster and faster but could not, she now understood, ever drive fast enough. Was in danger of losing her grip, had no traction, was concerned her tires, everyone's tires, would melt. Edith read a text from one of the cars in their convoy out loud: Pearl was crying about the cicadas. The radio kept droning. On and on it went. The details were hard to hold on to, but there was this: not so far away, hundreds of people were sandwiched between the conflagration and the sea. They paced the sands. An angel steered a boat across an inlet through walls of smoke. A white horse stood on a beach covered in ash under a sky the colour of blood. Birds fell from the heavens—blue, green, yellow, red—and, like precious stones embedded in black coal, fell at the ash-covered feet of those trapped between fire and water.

On Alice's first long drive, at the beginning of the 1980s, she'd packed her new (old) EH Holden with friends and headed up the Hume then further north again. They'd crossed the Queensland border at dawn after driving all night, and that was when Alice rolled the car. Teenagers spilled out, shook themselves off, got back in, and she kept driving. That memory blurred into the next: 1983, driving back from New South Wales in her boyfriend's Wolseley, the thermometer in the car sitting on fifty degrees. Alice had never been in fifty degrees before. Hoped never to be again. The radio stopped working, suddenly they were driving through flames that flickered in the eucalypts by the side of the road. They drove even faster and soon enough they were safe, and home.

The boyfriend had lasted until Halley's Comet. 1986. He and Alice had stood in the countryside, squinting into binoculars, exclaiming at silvery blobs. They were stoned. The binoculars were poor quality. The comet's tail fell away as it approached earth. Not a good year for it, apparently, which was tough luck as Alice would have to wait until she was almost 100 years old to see the comet on its next go round.

When they were little, Alice, Diana and Doug, used to be taken on camping trips all over Victoria. If they were driving north out of the city, they fell silent as they passed Pentridge—now an apartment complex, a shopping complex, a bar, a cinema—and mouth silently to each other: it's a prison.

In those days the highways were single lane and overtaking lanes were treated with reverence. They'd drive through country towns rather than past them. Every time there was a sign in the road that said 'Dip ahead', Alice, Diana and Doug would bob up and down, like dancing cockatoos. They spied with their little eyes. They played Animal, Vegetable, Mineral. Their Dad played Rod Stewart, Little Feat, Elton John, Steely Dan. They were not allowed to eat junk food *except on long drives* so took advantage: meat pies, hamburgers with the lot, iced buns, milkshakes. Soon after, their parents would yell at them as they threw up by the side of the road.

In spring 2019, there was a spike in the usage of #thetroublewithhen. The messages were nothing to do with Hen, instead gave voice to the thoughts the siblings had been trying to repress, for the bushfires were no surprise. The signs were everywhere.

Where should we buy?

Have you joined Extinction Rebellion?

Should we be more concerned about sea level rise, drought or bushfire?

I can't grow vegetables, can you?

Do you know anything about chooks?

Diana worried about what to say to her grandchildren. She worried about the fact that her youngest grandson was allergic to eggs, chook or otherwise. Alice worried about not having children, being menopausal and therefore being non-essential. Doug reminded her that, evolutionarily speaking, human women live once they are no longer fertile because they can help with the tasks that young families need done. They are useful.

Anyway, how bad could it be?

Bad. And when it happens, it's going to happen quickly.

It was soon after that that all the places they chatted about were eaten by fire and their childhood went up in flames.

1913

'I argued, as you may know, in a recent article, "On Insanity and Marriage", that I would never allow marriage—or children—in a woman with fully organised delusions or hallucinations,' Dr Savage explained to Leonard. 'Virginia comes from good stock, however, so there is less concern about the matter of racial hygiene, though there is, of course, the sad exception of her sister. Half-sister.'

Leonard was confused. 'Sister . . . ?'

'An imbecile. Leslie Stephen's daughter by his first wife. A Thackeray. The child was kept apart from his second family after he remarried and Virginia was born. By the time the girl was an adult she'd been put into an asylum. Nothing else for it.'

'Is she still alive?'

'I believe so. However, on this question of children,' Dr Savage continued, 'my belief is that they would do Mrs Woolf the world of good. Balance out the moral instability that an educated but child-less woman might expect to experience. And more veronal might help with the day-to-day symptoms.'

Leonard's mouth was straight as the horizon. This was not the answer he was looking for. While he trusted Savage on the matter of the veronal—one of his areas of expertise was chemical versus mechanical restraints—he was less convinced the man understood the danger of Virginia having a child.

It had been her joy at a cradle sent as a wedding present, with what Leonard thought was offensive presumption, that first alerted him to the fact that Virginia did not see what was obvious to him. That she was too fragile to manage a child. Leonard was also begin-ning to wonder what crisis of nerves would befall him if they had children, though he did not raise that particular concern with the doctors. He also discussed the matter with Vanessa, who was in full agreement with Leonard, as she was certain that if Virginia did have children, both she and Leonard would be expected to care for them.

Virginia, however, remained determined and had several times now attempted to advance their kissing and cuddling at night into the sexual act that was so distressing to her,

*Old Mandril does want her master so badly and last night his empty bed
was so dismal, and she went and kissed the pillow.*

VIRGINIA WOOLF TO LEONARD WOOLF, 1913

but every time Leonard attempted what he described as the
'complete' act, the trembling began. What he feared, though had not
been explicit about, was the stress the act of penetration would cause
her. He thought, perhaps, it would put Virginia's mind to rest if she
understood that nothing of this sort would ever be expected of her.

He had only to explain.

Next Leonard made an appointment with a Dr Hyslop. Hyslop had
been attending Vanessa during her own troubles and recommended
that Vanessa spend less time with Virginia as the two sisters seemed
to have an adverse effect on each other. Leonard's consequent high
hopes of Hyslop were disappointed when he suggested that they
should wait eighteen months before making a decision but refused
to concede that Virginia should not have children at all.

Leonard turned to Jean Thomas, who ran the rest home where
Virginia often stayed. She was to the point. 'A spot of nerves is no
reason not to have children. Chances are, it'll cure her.'

He moved onto Dr Wright. Wright agreed with Savage.

Finally, Leonard consulted Dr Maurice Craig. 'I am sorry to say,'
Craig said, 'that under no circumstances should Mrs Woolf consider
children.'

Finally armed with rational advice, Leonard felt the time had come
to let Virginia know his decision, though he preferred to describe
it as 'their' decision.

Virginia knew they were circling: the doctors, her sister, her
husband. She understood that all this feeding, these oppressive
attentions, were what was doing her harm.

She was in just such a frame of mind when Leonard found his wife sitting in her chair, reading. Against doctor's orders. Nervous, he steeled himself.

'Stop standing over me,' Virginia said, waving him in the direction of a chair—the looming, she couldn't stand it. Husband and wife sat in silence for a moment before Leonard said, 'The doctors and I are in agreement. We must abandon thoughts of children immediately.'

'This is not your decision to make,' Virginia said. Her relative calm belied the violence she heard in his words. Leonard's tusks had gored her, were tearing her innards out. She began to shake, uncontrollably, from head to toe.

Sometimes the two of them went hours together like this. Two trembling animals on the point of extinction.

It got worse.

Virginia began to keen in a long high-pitched moan, reminding Leonard, for a moment, of women from the village. More animal than human.

'You are murdering me!'

'You are being overly dramatic. You don't like children,' Leonard countered.

'I love my nephews and I would love my own children. It is the children of strangers who get on my nerves. It is YOU,' Virginia's voice was rising to the occasion, 'who does not like children.'

'I like children very much,' Leonard said, stiffly. 'One thing I regret in not being a woman is that I can't bear children. It is, perhaps, the world we would bring them into about which I have my doubts. I don't think you know the terrible things that can happen to a child.'

'Losing a mother at thirteen, isn't that a terrible thing? A half-sister at fifteen, a father at nineteen and a brother who was only twenty-six? Do I not have a half-sister locked away somewhere in a madhouse?'—now she thought to mention it—'Tragedy has haunted my family, yet you talk to me as a woman who knows nothing of the world.'

Virginia knew he thought that life was something she could not see, that she could not understand the meanness and sordidness of it. But what was her illness if not something mean, and sordid? It reduced her.

'I did not mean to suggest . . .'

'You poison things.' Virginia turned away from him, unable to look into his mournful, anxious face a moment longer.

'You must trust me.' Leonard became taciturn. Reason had to find a way forward. 'To make the right decisions on our behalf.'

'I see why we cannot have a child. For I am to be treated like one. I am not one of your blacks, you know. You are not master of me. You are not a gentleman. You are a . . .' Virginia threw him a look of such pure hatred Leonard thought he might vomit, '. . . you are a Jew.'

'Let me get you some milk.' Leonard got up. 'Or something for your nerves.'

'You break my heart then feed me milk, force me to sleep? Why did I marry you, marry at all, if it wasn't for this? For children?'

Virginia imagined life without small humans to distract her. Time stretched out before her, endlessly, irretrievably, like a long straight road through a too-familiar landscape. It stretched on forever, this grinding repetition of sleeping, eating and shitting. What was the point of all those things: the sleep, the food, the bodily functions, if it was not to make a family? She was a failure at everything, it seemed, and she looked down at herself—her dress, her legs, her hands—and saw that she was disgusting. No wonder people laughed at her.

'Didn't we marry for love of each other?' Leonard wondered aloud.

'Love is just a word people say to each other. They open their mouths. Food goes in. Words come out. Love . . .' Virginia swung her arms wildly in the air, like some kind of windmill, and Leonard had to grab her hands to avoid them striking him in the face. He pinned her arms to her side.

Leonard's eyes were wet. Had he not wanted children, hadn't he wanted passion? Was not the loss great for both of them?

But hadn't Virginia written that to him, hadn't she explained— love, children, adventure, intimacy, work. She wanted *everything*.

'Let me consider,' Virginia finally forced the words out, broken glass on her tongue, 'what you say.'

Leonard walked out of the room, found their cook Sophie*, and asked her to contact the doctor. He meant to return to Virginia, but found he could not, and stood in the passageway, chest heaving, with an emotion he couldn't name, for several long minutes.

Virginia became meek. Maybe Leonard wouldn't return? Maybe he no longer loved her? How would she survive if he didn't come back? She began to rub and scratch at herself. She could feel her skin becoming thin, then thinner. Soon she would be nothing but raw flesh, would have nothing to protect her from her husband, the doctors, her so-called friends and family. They would pick her bones clean.

Leonard went for a walk later that evening and met Vanessa in Regents Park, where they sat in silence. A friend, Ka, who was sitting

---

* Sophie Farrell came to work as a cook for Julia and Leslie Stephen when Virginia was four years old. Following Julia's death, Sophie kept a maternal eye on Virginia. She worked for various members of the family over the years until her retirement in 1931. After Sophie's retirement, Virginia sent her a pension of £10 a year.

with Virginia, organised for a message to be relayed to them. Virginia had fallen asleep. She couldn't be woken. A taxi was hailed. A doctor was sent for. Maynard Keynes was sent to acquire a stomach pump. On arrival home Leonard held his wife's jaws open so Keynes could force the tube down her throat.

'This is quite serious,' Dr Head said, when he arrived. 'Terribly serious.'

Leonard found this something of an understatement.

'You don't understand, Len,' Vanessa said. 'This is grounds for committal. Such an attempt . . . well, she could be locked away.' Vanessa was beginning to wonder if she should have given Leonard rather more information before she'd encouraged his marriage to her sister. Instead she made do with explaining that he must remove everything dangerous from the house—scissors, knives, drugs—and that soon such precautions would become routine, but that then, even then, he must never relax.

Vanessa also wanted to make it clear to Leonard, but did not know how, that she did not judge him for a moment. Wouldn't have done so if even the worst was true: that he'd left the drugs out in the hope that Virginia would find them. God knows she'd wanted her gone, if not dead, often enough in the last few years. As she watched Virginia lying there, a doctor hovering over her, Vanessa remembered, for the briefest of moments, how it felt to be lying in her own bed, her body swollen, her breast in her voracious son's tiny mouth. She remembered the way Clive's eyes had passed over her as he'd smiled blandly, and told Vanessa that he and Virginia were going for a walk. They were always going for a walk. So, if Leonard asked her, which he never would, she wouldn't have blamed him for a thing.

'I can ensure this won't happen again,' Leonard announced, to all in the room.

'We need to ask ourselves,' Head said, 'why Mrs Woolf wanted to die. I know Savage would argue this is some kind of repudiation of her duties. As a woman, and as a wife. I am not so sure.'

Wasn't the more pressing question, Leonard found himself thinking, why one chose to persist?

I took out my gun the other night, made my will & prepared to shoot myself.
LEONARD WOOLF TO LYTTON STRACHEY, 21 APRIL 1906

A wave of exhaustion overcame him. Leonard knew people were shocked by his capacity to sleep heavily under any circumstances, but sleep was all he could think of. He excused himself and went to his room. Within minutes he was curled up like small child, his slender hands held in a position of prayer beneath his head, his eyelids twitching rapidly as he fell into his dreams.

It was cool. It was always cooler in Kandy. The hills were green, and it was a particularly beautiful morning. Leonard found himself standing at the prison and looking across the hills surrounding the lake. He'd already brought the condemned man from his cell and read him the warrant of execution. He'd asked the man if there was anything he wanted to say, and the man said only, 'I have been guilty of a crime: I am glad to be punished.' He was dressed in white, with a white hat on his head. Leonard escorted the gently spoken figure, this man in white, to the gallows.

The wooden structure was flimsy and set high so witnesses could see the moment of death. A priest recited prayers requesting that the man's suffering in this lifetime soon be over.

'Drop,' Leonard commanded.

The man fell through the trapdoor as planned, but there was an error of some sort and the descent finished with a sudden jerk, one so extreme that it ripped his head off. Well, not quite off. There was a flap of skin, some tendons and sinew that tethered it to the body as people rushed forward to cut the rope.

The blood, uninterested in the apportion of blame, leapt some four feet high. The priest was sprayed with it, though Leonard managed to leap out of the way. It was so gruesome as to be absurd. Leonard was not sure whether to laugh or vomit. After a few awkward moments—everyone was silent beyond the initial gasp of horror— he'd chosen the latter, and, with a formal nod of his head, raced away to find a convenience.

'Who measured this rope? Who weighed this man?' Leonard called out. There were rules. Precision was essential.

After some extended retching, he returned to his offices, not so far from the temple, and the enormous backlog of correspondence he had to attend to. Leonard had instituted a new rule regarding the timeliness of replying to correspondence. It was a brutal regime and he led by example.

Leonard sat behind his desk. Tea was placed before him. The servant pulled the door shut on the way out and it was only then that it occurred to Leonard that he was terribly tired, and perhaps, if he just slipped under his desk for a moment, he might sleep. Ten minutes, no more. Ten minutes to dream within a dream of riding with Rachel in the cool of the evening after a long, hot and difficult day.

More than an hour later his servant found him there, under the desk, his long lean form curled up as a child's would be, his slender hands held in a position of prayer beneath his head. The servant bent towards him and touched his shoulder, but when Leonard woke and looked at him, he saw that the servant was, in fact, Vanessa.

'Virginia is awake.' Her voice penetrated the fog of his sleep. 'You should go to her.'

2020

In the month after the fires Alice pulled together another draft of her manuscript. She wrote with the urgency of a woman who thought she may not have long to live. She marched. She visited Hen three times a week and took the two hours it took to feed her lunch. She organised a fundraiser for animals affected by the bushfires. She sat down and wrote a list of ACTIONS under the heading WHAT I CAN DO TO MAKE A DIFFERENCE.

A few days after she'd emailed the manuscript to Sarah, Alice's phone rang.

'Hello!' she said, preparing to make light chat before being cut short.

'Okay, I've read it,' Sarah said. 'It's closer, so congratulations. But you're not there yet.'

'It's been a gazillion drafts. Where is there? How do I get to it?'

'Are you saying that nothing is new?'—Was Alice saying that? She didn't know what she was saying—'Are we doomed never to appreciate or learn from the past? This would seem to be a central question in the novel and I'm not sure it's been answered effectively.' Before Alice had time to take this in, Sarah had moved on. 'I have another concern. I know we have argued about the matter of sex before, but the only books I seem to be able to sell at the moment are books about young women having bad sex.'

'But this book *is* about young women having bad sex.'

'Olden-days young people,' said Sarah. 'It's different.'

'Do you think things have changed?' Alice said. 'Or are we all destined to be young people having bad sex? Or worse, just being flat out assaulted.'

'Well I'm an old woman having good sex, and not being assaulted,' Sarah said. 'So I don't know about that.'

'Oh,' Alice said. 'That's great. Though perhaps not the point here. Sexual trauma. War. Political upheaval. Environmental destruction. Radical gender politics. All happened then. All happening now. And maybe I want to say this as well: we need to harden the fuck up. Things have been worse in the past, but they're going to be far worse in the future.' Alice spoke unusually forcefully and was taken aback. She hadn't realised until that moment that she thought this.

'You haven't mentioned plague. The Woolfs lived through the Spanish flu. I want more of that,' Sarah insisted. 'It's timely.'

'Do you really think this new coronavirus is going to be such a big deal?' Alice asked. 'I just don't see it.'

IV
WORLD'S END

1914

Leonard had heard the stories: of women stripped, herded into rooms, sprayed with cold hoses to calm them down when the hysteria rose, force fed. So no, that was not an option, though everyone pressed him to consider it. Many a man had put his wife into such an institution rather than deal with the inconvenience of divorce; the incarceration of an ill wife was no crime at all. But Leonard held firm.

Four nurses, then two, then one.

It was expensive. Alongside the nursing, there was the milk cure. One of the cure's advantages was that it gave a man a precise number to aim for: twelve stone. If Leonard got Virginia's weight up to that magic number she might be cured. And so Leonard presented Virginia with five pints of milk daily alongside enforced seclusion, rest for the intellect (no books), cutlets, liquid malt extract and beef tea.

Virginia, for her part, poured milk out windows and down drains, and spat it at Leonard as he walked in the room holding yet another glass of the stuff.

White. Thick as venom.

During this time Virginia found clothes difficult. The ones she wore hung loose on her frame: a long and faded velvet skirt, a shapeless dark shirt. The outfit was hot. It oppressed her. Her hair was in a bun. She had worried at it, and strands straggled. It was as if she wanted to look as mad as possible, for her derangement to speak with eloquence.

Virginia lost all interest in feeding herself and refused to catch Leonard's eye when he fed her. His hands trembled as he offered her another spoonful. Some days it was an effort to feed himself, let alone his wife. He gave up. Sat by her, a bowl of porridge in his hands, not bothering to lift the spoon to her mouth.

'I am like stones in your pockets,' Virginia could see he was sad, 'dragging you down.'

How often had Leonard regretted telling her the story of the little boy drowned by stones? She returned to it constantly. But he answered her truthfully. 'I can only assume it is you who regrets marrying me. It is I who is a stone. It is you whose pockets are full.'

Leonard's emotion brought Virginia out of herself. Leonard's fingers were long, his body was lanky also. He was like some primordial insect, Virginia thought, waiting to strike (yes, she knew it was the female that ate her mate, but she liked the image all turned about). His melancholy, lined face was, in some ways, a mirror image of hers. All that was loving and soft about him was around his mouth. Yes, her husband had a beautiful mouth, and Virginia could see that it deserved kissing.

'Nessa?' she said her name out loud in the hope that it may provoke an answer. It was Vanessa's kisses she needed most, would need till the day she died.

'You told me she wasn't to visit you,' Leonard said.

'I've changed my mind.'

Leonard said nothing. He was not a man who changed his mind easily and he did not understand the willfulness with which Virginia changed hers. The sheer lightness—yes, that was the word—with which her mind untethered itself. He'd offered himself as her mooring and she'd accepted the offer. Now she tried to shake him off as the bullocks had their plough. Husband and wife both wondered if they understood the nature of the contract they'd entered into. Certainly Virginia never expected this. This intrusiveness. That Leonard would always be there, forcing food upon her.

Virginia lifted her arm with sudden force and the brown muck went over Leonard, over her, and the rest splodged on the floor. They were making her fat, she knew they were, and she was, in fact, right to think that, for by the time that long hard summer was done her body would be plump; fatty folds of milk-white flesh would hang from her. Her brain would be fat also; overfed, lazy with lack of use. There was only this: dull days of beige food and white milk.

'Stop,' she said.

Leonard did not know what he expected of married life, but it was safe to say it wasn't this. He put the spoon down.

'Be sensible, Goat,' he pleaded. 'Otherwise it will just take longer.'

He didn't understand—or wouldn't, or couldn't—that longer made no difference to Virginia. In those hours and days and months, time was all Virginia had. There was nothing else. She moaned softly and looked away from her husband. Why wouldn't he leave her alone? Leonard stood up, bowl in hand, as if to leave, but that too seemed unbearable.

'You won't give up on me?'

'Never.'

Virginia leaned forward as a child might. She sipped. Her mouth was full of the thick stuff. She gagged then swallowed. Her mouth opened again. Her husband put his spoon to it. The operation became mechanical. It continued, this war between the newlyweds, for the next two hours, and, on and off, for the next two years.

2020

Alice was in Adelaide for the writers festival when she understood that she had to take the coronavirus seriously. Just because she was experiencing what experts were calling climate grief did not mean that fucks weren't clustering. It did not mean that shit was not storming.

So. Alice was standing at the juicing section of the breakfast buffet at the Intercontinental, picking over the beetroot, the cucumber, the quartered oranges, the Granny Smith apples. (Crisp. Sour.) She considered the hunks of ginger. The lemon. Sorted them. Leisurely. Using her bare hands. Then she heard a raised voice and lifted her head to see a waitress running towards her. The raised voice was directed at her.

STOP.

THAT.

NOW.

Alice stopped. In the hope of deflecting the anxiety and rage of the hotel staff, she moved towards the hotel's expansive windows. Everyone was looking at her, she was sure of it: a woman who thoughtlessly handled fruits and vegetables as a pandemic was breaking out. Alice looked outside and there it was. The Torrens.

Alice believed her interest in the Torrens could be seen as symbolic of her ongoing inability to focus on the task at hand, specifically the

writing and rewriting of *This Devastating Fever*. The project constantly led
her to interesting tidbits quite unrelated to Leonard or Virginia Woolf,
which meant she still found herself thinking about an article (found in
the Desmond and Molly MacCarthy archives) in which historians such
as Froude fought about Adelaide during the nineteenth century. The
point of contention was the Torrens River, a reviewer of Froude's *Book
of Travel* having claimed that Froude had been wrong to suggest that
Adelaide had a river running through it. The slur stuck, and historian
after historian had quoted the review to prove that Froude distorted
his facts and did not accurately describe what he saw before him.

And here was another thing about Adelaide that was playing on
her mind. It had been here, back in the early 1990s, that she'd had a
meeting with her boss in a sauna of the Hilton Hotel—which hadn't
seemed weird at the time but in retrospect clearly was, and in Alice's
experience growing older was a series of moments that could be
summarised as 'oh dear'—and that had been when her Speedo-clad
boss had asked her who he should employ as a publisher to replace
the irreplaceable one who was leaving.

'Me,' Alice had said. 'I can do it.'

Alice didn't really know what a publisher did when she became
one but she figured it out pretty quickly over the next few months
and years. She occasionally wondered if that was why almost none
of the research she did into Leonard's life was about his significant
work as a publisher, over a career that spanned several decades. She
struggled to be interested in either his career or hers.

When she'd first started *This Devastating Fever*, she hadn't minded
how long it was taking as she thought that the centenary of WWI
would be a good time to launch it, but that centenary had come
and gone. And now the nation was trying to recover from 'once-in-
a-hundred-year' fires and, as she was beginning to realise, heading

into a 'once-in-a-hundred-year' pandemic. She tried to comfort herself with the thought that, even for someone who had not exhibited Olympic-standard levels of avoidance, these were distracting times.

Alice returned to her room and began to doom scroll. Downloaded *The Plague* on her iPad and reread it. She'd first read it for Year 12 English when studying DEATH, at the same time as her mother had been dying. This had led to discussions of EXISTENTIALISM. She had been sixteen. On rereading she was struck all over again by the fact there was a character called Grand, who spent the plague, and *The Plague*, writing and rewriting the opening lines of his own novel, a work that he failed to finish before he caught (but recovered from) the actual plague.

Alice then became fixated on the idea that she, like Grand, would most likely never finish her novel, but instead would catch the plague.

Alice put her iPad down. Had to focus.

In an hour she was chairing a panel in which authors discussed the difference between fiction and non-fiction. One of the authors was famous, and didn't suffer fools. That author was uninterested in discussing the fact that the main character in her recent novel had the same name as her. Was the book a novel or wasn't it? The author would shrug when asked this question. She didn't see patrolling generic boundaries as her job. Alice was inspired by the author's refusal to explain herself.

Alice and the author had a refreshingly scratchy relationship because she'd briefly been the girlfriend of the author's ex-husband. The author and her former husband had exchanged letters on how to 'manage' Alice and the former husband had read the correspondence out to Alice, as they lay in bed. She'd been twenty-five years old.

'She's very young,' the author had written to her ex-husband at the time. 'You need to be more forgiving.'

'It's all very well to tell me to be more forgiving. But sometimes you are impossible,' the ex-husband, who liked to intersperse the letters with short lectures, said to Alice. 'You behave like a child.'

If truth be told, Alice was not much older than a child. Whatever. That had been some decades ago, but Alice had not yet recovered from being discussed and then written about by a couple old enough to be her parents. She had no idea how to protect herself from other people's words and yes, yes, maybe that's one reason why she became a publisher and then a writer but the point is that the panel went well, and Alice and the author had a cup of coffee after the event, in which the author had offered some good advice regarding the saga of the novel that couldn't be finished: stop worrying.

1915

Gerald Duckworth* had started a publishing house, and the proofs of *The Voyage Out* waited for Virginia's recovery in his office. When she was finally well enough to work she negotiated them slowly, working an hour at a time. Leonard continued to hover in the doorway offering glasses of milk. Viscous. Clotted with cream.

Occasionally he would discuss his second novel with his wife, though he had not given Virginia the manuscript for fear she would become

---

* Gerald Duckworth's siblings were Stella and George. His father had died before he was born and his mother married Leslie Stephen when Gerald was eight years old. Julia and Leslie Stephen then had four children, giving the Duckworth children several half siblings: Virginia, Vanessa, Thoby and Adrian. Once they were adults, Virginia and Vanessa accused Gerald and George of sexually abusing them when they'd all lived together. Gerald Duckworth went on to come a publisher and published Virginia's first novel, *The Voyage Out*. Publishing. What a strange and incestuous industry it is.

overexcited regarding his views on women and sexuality. Lytton had read the novel and been relieved by this whiter, more English work.

'So I've read your latest,' Lytton had written—in a letter now unaccountably lost—'on Virgins and their ilk, and I must say, darling Leonard, that it's really quite tremendous. Fewer blacks than your last, as requested, and while I'd say you, by which I mean "fictional" you, is more obsessed with being a Jew than of interest to many, your man is also quite keen on fucking and frankly there simply isn't enough of that in novels these days. Well done.'

There had been other letters of course. The one from Bella had been far less satisfactory and she accused Leonard of writing a book that would inflict extraordinary pain on people he loved.

A third letter, from an eminent critic and so-called friend, was arguably even worse. 'We stand by the truth, us Apostles, and I know you understand this, so I will persist in truth-telling, painful as it may be. You will never be a writer.'

Leonard, in some desperation, felt the time had come to show Virginia his work.

> *I started reading* 'The Wise Virgins', *& read it straight on till bedtime, when I finished it. My opinion is that it's a remarkable book; very bad in parts; first rate in others.*
>
> VIRGINIA WOOLF, 31 JANUARY 1915

Kind words aside, Virginia did not respond well to Leonard's lusty but wooden words about women (like Virginia, unnamed) who were frigid, and those who were more easily swayed (Vanessa? Someone else?). Soon Leonard realised that hiding kitchen knives would not be enough. Most things were weapons if you thought about them hard enough. He took to hiding books, scrutinising surfaces, refusing visitors. Virginia, in turn, refused food and scratched at herself;

nails through skin into flesh until she was bleeding. Towards the end of March she was moved to a nursing home. The day after the move *The Voyage Out* was published. The timing was unfortunate but the contractual terms were exceptional. Fifteen per cent on sales!

> *So much the better—this was death. It was nothing; it was to cease to breathe. It was happiness, it was perfect happiness. They had now what they had always wanted to have, the union which had been impossible while they lived. Unconscious whether he thought the words or spoke them aloud, he said, "No two people have ever been so happy as we have been. No one has ever loved as we have loved."*
>
> VIRGINIA WOOLF, *THE VOYAGE OUT*, 1915

Come April, George Duckworth lent Leonard and Virginia his house in Sussex as it was large enough to house all the nurses.

(Expensive. So expensive.)

Awake.

Asleep.

It made no difference.

Virginia no longer spoke. Leonard's relationship with language fractured. Words floated apart.

Virginia had *B.d.* (bad nights). She became ᚖᚖᚖ. Rupert Brooke died of sepsis on the Isle of Lemnos on his way to fight in Gallipoli. Virginia did not sleep for sixty hours. When Leonard tried to make her sleep she spat at him. Called him a torturer. Herself a prisoner. Said worse things as well. Things that shouldn't be written, though she had written them, in her diary, in letters to her friends. Leonard's diary, in turn, was reduced to cypher, single letters. Meaning disappeared.

> *N.g.d v. conf. No sl w chloroform*
>
> LEONARD WOOLF, 1915

2020

Alice fell asleep while working on a presentation on the sex life of the Bloomsbury Set that she was giving that afternoon. She woke up when the late morning sun hit her face to find that her laptop had fallen sideways onto the bed, she was lying flat on her back, and Ghost Virginia was hovering in the air above her.

'There is an issue I need to discuss with you,' Virginia said. 'Actually, two. The first is a philosophical one. You seem terribly keen to create some kind of trajectory in which Leonard and I were a great romance despite the evidence you have before you.'

'You're about the only Bloomsbury couple not to embark on a fully fledged threesome,' Alice said, sitting up so as not to be at such a disadvantage. 'That's romance of a sort.'

'Putting aside the terrible pressure I was under to give into this view of life, that a woman must have a husband, and the stress it caused me to take on such a relationship, no matter that it turned out well over a period of some decades, I'm rather intrigued to know what you mean by "fully fledged". You seem ignorant about what comprises a threesome. For example, did Lytton ever share the physical act of love with Carrington?'

> *I like being with you more than I can say. You know I love you, and you know I like Leonard. There is a difference between love and like. So you are my love and Leonard is my like. I do like Leonard extremely.*
> Vita Sackville-West to Virginia Woolf, 10 October 1941

'Michael Holroyd says . . .'

Virginia returned the interruption. 'I have no time for Holroyd—I think we can agree that Lytton did "it" with Carrington's husband

Ralph and did not do "it" with Carrington. He instead allowed her to believe she was his great love, leaving her desperate and sad and vulnerable once he was gone. Clive was not physically involved with Vanessa's lovers—indeed Vanessa, for all her carry on about sex in her early years, seems barely to have been touched by Duncan for twenty years. Morgan didn't have sex with that policeman's wife, whatever her name was, in fact I'm not even sure if he had sex with the policeman . . .'

Alice went to interrupt again, but Virginia held up her carpal, metacarpal and various phalanges as if to suggest 'no more', and ploughed on.

'No! This really is quite important, this business of "fully fledged". Perhaps you should have better used your time at the Kinsey Institute and read up what they have to say on the matter of eternal virgins and so forth. Perhaps you could come up with some fabulous diagnosis and, well then, I could certainly REST IN PEACE knowing that you had the matter in hand.'

Ghost Virginia, who had by now lowered herself to ground level, gestured as if she was going to stomp off on her foot bones. 'No doubt you've read this? I wrote it to Leo a year or so after we married, and I think you would agree the note is what, in modern parlance, would be described as "sexy".' Panthea Reid's biography of Virginia appeared to Alice's right, rustled its pages and fell open to:

> the Mandril wishes me to inform you delicately that her flanks & rump are
> now in finest plumage, and invites you to an exhibition.
>
> VIRGINIA WOOLF TO LEONARD WOOLF, 1913

Alice took a deep breath. 'What I am trying to do is resist being overly sentimental about any romantic narrative. Homo or hetero. A narrative that you, in your dedication to your marriage, colluded in.

A narrative that Vita maintained by throwing Violet Trefusis, frankly, under a bus.'

'Under a bus was as good a place for Violet as any. I think Morgan's life is quite the case in point. He failed to write a single novel in more than forty years. His contribution to the world of fiction says much about Leonard's brilliance—he was very encouraging of Morgan's *Passage to India*. I told the Taupe, which was our name for Morgan, exactly that when he popped by in 1970-something, after he died. We chewed the fat, talked about the old days, and compared notes about our respective final resting places. He's over at Canley Gardens. Not so far when you can float around like we do.'

'I thought you didn't like him?'

'I adored him. Though he did call me a disgusting lesbian.'

'He called all lesbians disgusting. Did not say that you, in particular, were a disgusting lesbian.'

'Pedant. Morgan didn't much like women was the real issue. But then who did? Who does? Much the same point that Leonard made regarding attitudes towards Jews. My point is, and I find I'm having trouble sticking to it, is that the heteronormative narrative arc is stultifying. And that we in Bloomsbury worked terribly hard to ignore it.'

Alice didn't want to get into an argument about the fact that the endless cloying correspondence between Vita and Harold was a case of protesting too much. A battening down of the hatches. Nor the fact that the phrase heteronormative did not exist in Virginia's time, though Virginia had made it clear that her education had continued long after her death. For all Alice knew, Virginia had read Maggie Nelson's *The Argonauts*.

'Would you allow me to argue,' Alice asked, 'that you and Leonard had the most passionate friendship?'

Virginia nodded briefly, her jawbone clanging against her rib cage. 'Yes. That is acceptable to me. Though not so much a passionate friendship as an essential one.'

'What's the second thing?' Alice asked.

'This virus business. We've been discussing it up there'—Virginia waved vaguely towards the heavens—'and it is beginning to remind me of the situation we endured when a plague unmatched since the Black Death descended upon us. Our neighbour in Richmond died of it. Lytton abandoned London for the countryside for fear of contracting the virus. I caught the illness in 1919 and was in bed for a month. Everyone loves to imagine that I spent years of my life in bed because I was insane. In fact, half the time I had the flu. It weakened my heart. Far less fun to gossip about. This is an argument I have been having with Freud.* Women who complain of ill health are dismissed as mad, when in fact they have a physical ailment. The flu causes a terrible fog in the brain. Delusions. But it is, nonetheless, an illness, not a personal failing. You've read *Mrs Dalloway*, yes?' Virginia stared at Alice so intently it was as if lasers were shooting out of her eye sockets.

Alice had not read *Mrs Dalloway*. Began to muster excuses, but then her phone buzzed several times. Edith was sending through photographs of a shopping trolly loaded with canned tomatoes,

---

* Alice understood Virginia to mean she'd spoken to Sigmund Freud recently, in the afterlife. The two first met, over tea, three weeks before Freud's death in 1939—the occasion when he'd handed her a narcissus. Freud had escaped from Austria just a few months before and was in England as a refugee. His four sisters were to die in concentration camps. Leonard went on to be Freud's publisher and lobbied the British government when Freud's grandson, Walter, was interned in 1940 as an enemy alien and deported to an internment camp in New South Wales, Australia, that sunburnt country, that land of concentration camps, fire and flooding plains. Australia. What a cruel and mean-minded country it often was.

chickpeas, flour, pasta and rice; of supermarket shelves stripped bare. When Alice looked up from her screen, Virginia was gone.

1915

Lytton arrived at Asheham armed with his ration cards for meat, sugar and butter, as all visitors had been instructed to. It was the only way a person could ensure they would be fed. The man had the habit of sinking deep into whatever chair he found himself in, glasses low on the bridge of his nose. His unnaturally long fingers tapered, his beard draped. He looked for all the world like a Beardsley cartoon.

On this particular day Lytton sat in the living room of George's house in Sussex. He was wearing a bright orange waistcoat, his yellow coat. Leonard wore brown corduroys, a white shirt and cardigan. Virginia lay in bed with either overexcitement, or influenza, Lytton was not sure which, nor why Leonard said it had been a mistake to bring her here. Morgan Forster—hunched, tweedy, dapper in a cap—had already been and gone, leaving Lytton to Leonard and his misery.

The tea was tepid, the scones dry, and war meant there was a shortage of cream. The house was damp and the fire did little, but at least, in winter, the tall grasses died back and let the light in. A fine rain misted the Downs. All was grey, black, the colour of straw, yet there sat this sunset of a man.

'Brookes has left a dozen smashed hearts. I won't miss the person, but I will miss his pretty face. Losing Henry to France is a different matter altogether, though. Men in the prime of their lives should not be heading off to war, nor abandoning those who love them.'

'Henry still lives, Lytton,' Leonard said. This passion for Henry Lamb had always struck Leonard as particularly doomed. Lamb hadn't even an idle interest in sodomy. Leonard changed the subject. 'Molly told Virginia who told me that Desmond hoped to read *War and Peace* and *Tristram Shandy* while at Montdidier with the French Ambulance Corp. However, his job seems to be picking up bodies. I'm not sure a book will help.'

Lytton would not be sidetracked from his grievances. 'I suppose you've heard that Pozzo's hanging around the Treasury making people's lives miserable.'

Leonard knew, but was too polite to say, that he understood Lytton's enmity towards Maynard Keynes had more to do with their shared love of Duncan Grant than his rapidly developing profile as an historian and economist.

'Anyway, I'm stuck on Florence Nightingale. She might be the end of me,' Lytton continued. 'And what of you, Leonard? Is it true you are to move to Richmond? Virginia told me that you don't think she can be trusted with the excitement of Bloomsbury.'

'Do you think she can be trusted?'

'I . . . well, I suppose I don't know. How is she?' Lytton finally enquired, though he knew the answer. Everyone knew, or imagined they did.

'She is incapable of the most basic tasks. Unable to even catalogue her purchases.' Leonard looked worn.

'I can't imagine what you mean.' Lytton was taken aback. 'Is this an administrative issue?'

'She has been doing cooking classes. We have a book in which all purchases are set out. I had given Virginia the job of filling it in. But she just writes "food". These things are important. Food is rationed. I must keep her eating even as half of England is starving.

Did you know it costs 12.5p to buy a loaf, a pint of milk, pound of beef, quarter pound of tea, six eggs and a pound of sugar?'

'I did not. What doesn't our darling Virginia understand?' Lytton was bored by his friend's commitment to bookkeeping. Virginia was also a strain. How long could one woman stay mad for? Years, it seemed.

'Food has types. Meat, diary, fruit, greens.'

'Well, it is all food,' Lytton said, to take Virginia's side, though in truth he knew food to be various and important.

'That is what Virginia said, but she understands other categories. Coal, for instance. And soap.'

'Coal has its own category?' Lytton enquired. 'Could it not fall into a broader category? Such as heating?'

Really, a man could fall into a coma when visiting the Woolfs during this difficult time.

'This does bring me to another matter,' Leonard said. 'I wondered if I may come and stay with you at some point.'

'Well of course,' Lytton said. 'But doesn't Virginia need you?'

'She does not, at the current time, wish to see me at all.' He rubbed at the cut above his eye as he talked. 'Has taken to throwing objects at me. Jugs. Books. Things of that nature.'

'You're welcome any time,' Lytton said. Being married could clearly reduce the best of people to the worst of circumstances. He'd always suspected as much, and this marriage seemed to be the proof. Perhaps bringing these two together had been an error? But weren't relationships made of suffering?

Leonard was embarrassed by how low he suddenly felt. 'It's possible,' he said, 'that I have failed.'

By the time Virginia rose from her bed the war was well advanced. Bertie had died.

Flu. It seemed there was a lot of it around.

The war churned on. Leonard watched as Britain promised Constantinople to Russia, Anatolia to Italy, Syria to France, Palestine to the Jewish people. He threw himself into his work at the Fabian Society. He lobbied for an to end martial law in Ceylon, which had been the British government's response to the rioting that had broken out in Kandy. Few understood why this distressed him so. (Romanis Perera was taken by the British soldiers, tied to a tree, and shot in the presence of his father and twenty-five other villagers; soldiers entered the house of Wafuhenegamage Podi Singho, dragged him from his bed, tied his hands behind his back with his bedsheet, led him to the bank of the Algoda River, and shot him through the heart; English officers and Punjabi soldiers came to the house of Lellopitiyage Sophia and took her husband James Baas, put him in a boat to cross the river, and shot him and two other men within her view on the opposite bank.)

Leonard had walked several hundred miles during these turbulent years, or so it looked to those who saw him walking around the parks of Richmond, through the streets of London, and up and over the Downs. 'What do you think of on your walks?' Bella asked him, for the two now lived quite close to each other and were regular correspondents during her time of grief.

'Tissa. I'm sure I talked to you about it at the time. People walked days, even weeks, to attend the festival there every year. They walked through jungles and across drought-ridden plains while the sun beat down upon them, their feet blistered, and their skin was torn by thorns. As they drew closer to the village they stopped and bathed, and on the occasion that I joined them, there were thousands of people undertaking a precise series of ablutions, before putting on white clothing and entering the village. On the fourteenth night of the festival, under the light of the full moon, a grand procession was held. People prayed for all the things that they hoped for in this life: freedom from suffering, a good marriage, plentiful food, children.'

Once written, these words could not be unthought. Freedom from suffering. A good marriage. Food. Children.

2020

Alice managed to see Hen just the once before lockdown took hold. Hen recognised her, despite the PPE, the moment she walked through the security doors of the ward. A smile passed fleetingly over what had once been her face, then it twisted. Despite the lightness of her frame she lifted herself out of the wheelchair and ran at Alice. The ties that bound her to the chair dug into her wrists. She tried to shrug the wheelchair onto her back, a snail dragging her shell. Her rage was pure. Alice had never seen anything like it. She approached Hen, holding up her hands up in placatory gesture, but Hen managed to sideswipe Alice with the chair before collapsing onto the floor.

'Help,' Alice called out, to the staff moving through the room. 'I need help.' No one looked up, or tended to her, or to Hen. They might as well have been ghosts.

Friends lost their jobs. Comedians continued their shows without a live audience or a laugh track. Cruise ships floated offshore around the world, their customers locked into their cabins, trying to find safe port. People died on the streets of London, New York, Delhi. Burnt forests were logged. Newspapers closed. Hundreds then thousands then millions of people died. She read *The Animals in That Country* in preparation for what she and the author decided to call the first Zoom book launch in the world, then she reread *Station Eleven*, *In a Perfect World* and, finally, *Mrs Dalloway*.

Yesterday, today, tomorrow, she woke at 1 am, she woke at 3 am. Some days she wondered if she would ever sleep again, but when she spoke to others—by SMS, phone, WhatsApp, Messenger, Zoom, or even in person from an appropriate distance down the dark hallway of an old convent where she rented a tiny office—she understood that no one was sleeping, not really, and that the bedrooms of Melbourne, of Australia, of London, of the world, were full of people turning to and fro, people staring at the ceiling, people scared to sleep because they've just read an article that described, in some detail, exactly what the virus did to a person's lungs.

Most days Alice sat on her bed, pillows piled behind her, working on books that were not *This Devastating Fever*. Leonard, however, was still in her thoughts. She remembered his claustrophobia after he left for England after seven years in Ceylon. The way his memories of Ceylon sustained him. The spaciousness of the great lagoons, the sound of the sea pounding on the shore below his bungalow in Hambantota.

The glory of autumn heightened the intensity of this time. Between the hours of five and six, there was a rose-gold sheen to the sky and the quality of the light was a bit like honey. The city glowed. You wanted to reach out, trace a finger in a lazy arc through the sky, then put it to your mouth. But this was not a time to put a finger to your lips, your nose, your eyes. And to be honest Alice couldn't reach out and trace her finger in a lazy arc through the sky because she was sitting in her car, with her windows closed, using her car speakers to conduct a work call. More relaxing than Zoom. Safe.

'Two years ago,' the historian was saying, 'it was almost too hot to walk from the hotel to the festival site. Forty-six degrees or more. This year—well, you were there—the weather was fine but everyone was traumatised by January's bushfires. Now this. I suppose there won't be a festival at all next year.'

These words, these facts, were hard to attend to. Every moment of every day felt hard to be present for, Alice was finding. She looked down her street—one of the oldest in the city—to the edges of the CBD. Pubs sat on most corners, but the corner nearest to her was a former morgue that had become a squat before joining itself to a terrace next door and being converted into a massive townhouse with a high hedge and an elaborate pseudo-Moroccan screen.

Alice thought, for a moment, about morgues. Apparently the Exhibition Building a few hundred metres up the road had been set aside as one in case there ended up being too many bodies. Alice didn't know what counted as too many bodies. She pulled up the notebook app on her phone and typed, with a single finger. *Royal Exhibition Building. Morgue?* Then, concerned this activity would interrupt her call, she stopped and tried to attend, once more, to the conversation. A certain intensity suddenly emanated from the speakers. Alice adjusted the car seat, sat up straighter. Stopped looking at the light, the street, her phone.

'Australia's in trouble, though it's too soon to tell what will happen here,' the historian continued. 'If Italy's economy collapses, then Spain's, then Turkey's, we'll basically lose Europe. Britain's fucked. God knows what's going to happen with China. The United States. Well. There is only one thing that will count as good news this year. One. Single. Thing.'

'That is?'

'Trump dies, and the next day a vaccination is announced.'

'Good times,' Alice joked feebly, talking in the vague direction of her dashboard but lifting her eyes once more to the light. Gloaming, was that the word? Uncanny? Hard, sometimes, some days, some years, to find the right words. The light seemed to be becoming thicker. More like a curtain than honey. Today, of all days, she'd like to pull it to one side. Step through.

Alice's access to the great outdoors was limited, so she took up jogging with neighbours in Carlton Gardens. They would peer at each other through the morning fog, trying to recognise each other by their posture, and perhaps their eyes: masks, beanies and jackets cloaked other identifying features. Alice's jogging habit didn't last long. Her knees were in bad shape. Her favourite Stone Pine was dying and Alice believed that this was a sign jogging was bad for her. Her thinking proceeded as followed: In pre-pandemic times she'd done some classes with a trainer, and the trainer had suggested she stop staring at her feet as she ran and instead lift her head and look into the middle distance. Alice tried, but her gaze slipped, as surely as if weights were dragging it down. Her trainer finally said, 'Look at a tree you like and run towards it.'

She ran.

Alice couldn't quite imagine, though she tried, what it would be like to be living though the pandemic in a city like London, or New York, or Mexico City. She sat in on Zoom calls set up at strange times to accommodate friends, family and colleagues from around the globe. If everyone was on Gallery View it was like a weird version of the Brady Bunch: faces floating in squares with animated hats and animal faces chatting to each other. A friend from London who worked in hospitals appeared to age in fast forward. A friend from New York who hadn't left his apartment for six months had taken to rocking back and forth like a caged animal.

Soon enough Alice was teaching her How to Write a Novel™ class on Zoom as well.

'The pandemic is,' she pronounced, 'plot. Plot is what happens to characters under stress. Do they rise to the occasion or do they not? Do they panic? Do they kill someone?'

(Was she rising to the occasion? Was she panicking? Might she kill someone?)

'Are your neighbours drinking too much and yelling at each other? Are they throwing illegal parties, and if so, are you the kind of person who would dob them in? Are they skulking down the street and glaring at the people to advertise the fact they don't wear masks? Do people break curfew? Have you organised endless picnics outdoors, persisted in having said picnic while it is raining, and held a sandwich in your hand for an hour so you didn't have to wear a mask? Do you walk around with empty takeaway coffee cups in your hand and pretend to sip coffee—again so you don't have to wear a mask?'

(Alice, to her eternal shame, did this. She also enjoyed going to bed at 9 pm. She confessed to neither.)

'Anyway,' Alice continued, 'you get the gist.' Her students had, like her, taken to drinking during class. Wine. Vodka. Gin. They got the gist.

Alice entertained herself and her students by talking about narrative and the fact it was EVERYWHERE.

So: Alice set and joined her students in the following task.

If you tested positive to COVID-19, what would your contact list show?

Predictably, Alice ended up feeling boring. In every list of exposure sites, it seemed, there was a story except in hers. (Greengrocer. Carlton Gardens. Repeat until the end of time.)

People were driving trucks to Shepparton when they shouldn't have. They were going to Bunnings, then brunch, followed by a bar, then several parties. They'd head out again early the next day for breakfast. They ate falafel, headed to Bong On then, bought expensive pyjamas. People visited multiple barbecue stores, made breaks for the border. It was often obvious to the general public that THE ORIGINAL SOURCE OF THE INFECTION CANNOT BE FOUND was code for SOMEONE FUCKED SOMEONE THEY SHOULDN'T HAVE AND NOW THEY CAN'T FESS UP.

After the Stone Pine was removed, Alice replaced the jogging with online Qigong classes, but her tree obsession kept intruding. Qigong taught her that she was Wood element and that Wood element likes to travel.

Inspired, Alice started a travel account on Instagram and invited images from around the world. Hundreds of people sent her photos from exotic places and reminisced about the joys of going to places that were not Australia. Photos arrived from Albania, Botswana, Fiji, Greece, Iceland, Mongolia, Syria, Uzbekistan and Vanuatu. From Arnhem Land, Scotland, Hong Kong, Palestine. The photos taken in the Greek Islands stung the most. In some parallel universe there was a version of herself that had gone to live on Hydra as a young woman and never returned. Had lived a life that was all blue skies, goats, olive trees and rocks. Fish! Retsina! Taramasalata! Her hair had grown long and blonde, she'd worn a golden tan and there'd never been mention—not even a one—of sunscreen or skin cancer. She'd never grown old.

The days began to blur. She and Edith cordoned off different sections of the house so they could work without having to look at each other, having to listen to each other. Her territory was the bedroom, which she barely left.

She watched old episodes of *Dr Who* on iView. Worked with her legs under the doona to keep them warm, but make-up on her face so she could Zoom. Her clothing was similarly schizophrenic. Most days she wore pyjama pants with a cheerful shirt to convey a sense of professional positivity.

On one day in this endless blur of days she joined a meeting with colleagues from Brisbane. Some sat on their verandah in the winter sun, others in board rooms in offices.

'. . . April sales figures, which take in first lockdown . . .'

Behind one of her colleagues she glimpsed a flame tree in full flower.

'. . . different trajectory for commercial fiction and non-fiction.'

This triggered memories of that northern place: snorkelling on the Great Barrier Reef forty years ago. Vibrant. Coral moving with the currents. Colourful fish darting around. A world full of rustles and clicks. After the reef she and her siblings had visited the Daintree Rainforest. Spent time with the cycads and fan palms. Hesitated when in the presence of the strangler figs that stood like scaffolding around the rotted hollows of their host.

'. . . Literary fiction?'

A message arrived through the chat from a fellow board member who'd become a friend: *literary fiction? Lol.*

The geography of Alice's daydream changed. She imagined driving to Bermagui. She'd tried once, twice, three times, but first the Alpine Way was on fire, then the Princes Highway. For two months after that, various sections of road were closed. At the end of March the roads were opened but stage three lockdown restrictions came into play. She planned to go in mid-July, but by then the border had been closed. Would it be years before she could be with her siblings again? Years before she saw the forest of spotted gums that lined the road that swept into Bermagui, before she saw the sleepy town's pelicans, saw the pale-blue armies of soldier crabs pouring out onto the mudflats, before she had the chance to walk the road that had been turned into a nature reserve and left to fall into the sea?

Alice understood that summer fires followed by late summer floods were considered to be part of the cascading effect of climate change. She understood that deforestation led to an increased likelihood of pandemics as surely as WWI had harboured the influenza pandemic a hundred years before. She understood that COVID-19 was now through the aged care system and that Hen would most likely die and she was unlikely to ever see her in person again, but, frankly, understanding didn't seem to make a difference, for she was overwhelmed, couldn't look every which way all at once and anyway it seemed that the genie was out of the bottle, the cat was out of the bag, the tipping point had tipped, and now here she was, here everyone was, living in the territory of the unprecedented, the territory of pivoting, the territory of grief and loss.

Her fugue state came to an end when her elaborate arrangement of pillows collapsed and the entire catastrophe that was her work life was revealed to the board meeting. When asked for her view on a particular issue, Alice found herself making pronouncements, on her back, holding her laptop over her face with outstretched arms.

What the fuck, Alice's friend DM-ed her, *is going on with you?*

People not in lockdown, people not in Melbourne, HAVE NO IDEA. That is what Alice wanted to type into the chat, but did not. Instead she typed: *SORRY.*

The people of Melbourne were becoming impossibly martyrish, entitled and smug. That is what Alice's friend who, as a Boon Wurrung woman, had lost patience with white people's whiny bullshit some years ago, wanted to say. Instead she typed: *Call if you need. I'm here for you.*

After the meeting Alice went back to a book called *The Vegetarian* in which a Korean woman had nightmares about meat and blood. The woman stopped eating animal products, spiralled into a psychosis, then tried, through sheer force of will, to turn into a tree.

As the months went on the claustrophobia built. She called Ageing Disgracefully constantly, to ask how Hen was going, but most days whoever answered promised her Hen was doing well and offered to set up a Zoom call, which was no help at all. Hen had struggled with her computer before she had advanced dementia. These days the best you could hope for was that she didn't throw her iPad across the room. More often than not, the iPad slipped face-down on the bed, Hen said nothing, and Alice would, after calling plaintively into the screen, hang up.

Her dreams were no help at all. She woke exhausted after a night spent walking through her suburb after a nuclear blast. She and Edith rifled through the ash but found no bodies. A bright red fox trotted ahead of them, this way and that. Wilson trotted along beside her, sprightly, as if arthritis and death had not claimed him some months before. Alice burst into tears when work colleagues in Sydney asked her how she was. She and Edith yelled at each other. She was rude to friends who sent her photos of the places she could no longer see. She yelled at strangers. Friends delivered gin to her door. She ate excellent takeaway FOR WAS SHE NOT A CITIZEN OF MELBOURNE? She watched the press conferences. She joined in conversations about whether their premier, Dan, would be wearing a suit jacket or one of his North Face jackets (he'd bought six of them, apparently, at 20 per cent off). She rewrote all the bits of non-fiction writing she'd done that were intended to be commentary on the current moment as the current moment turned to mercury, skidded and pooled all over the place. She stayed at home, did her Qigong classes, learned more about the five elements. They'd gone over Earth, Metal, Water and moved on to Wood, Alice's element. Alice found it hard to discern the gesture she needed to make from peering at her instructor, who was standing in her living room in near darkness. Alice finally summoned up the courage to tell the instructor that she couldn't see a thing.

'Imagine you're hugging a tree,' the instructor said.

Alice opened her arms. Wrapped herself around an ancient oak.

1916

'We're off to Charleston,' Virginia said to Lytton, who was staying for the weekend. 'Will you join us?'

'I think not,' Lytton said. 'I owe Carrington a letter. My missives take some time to craft.'

'Dora Carrington?' Virginia asked.

'The very one,' Lytton said. 'I was negotiating a truce between her and her would-be lover, Gertler. But it seems she is in love with me instead.'

'You encouraged her, no doubt.'

'Being loved is compelling, it's true. One does not have to,' he gestured in a way that may, or may not, have intimated love making, 'feel a passion for a woman to love her. As I hope you understand.'

The couple left Lytton to his dramas, and got on their bikes. Rode through the village of Lewes, of Firle, past the church at Berwick. They never tired of visiting Charleston. The garden, a riot of colour, could distract Leonard for hours. The walls, the furniture, were similarly chaotic: ochre, maroon, olive, blue, sage green, yellow; frescoes, fabrics, ceramics. You could imagine you were standing in front of a Picasso, a Gauguin, the fauves. Asymmetrical faces, hatched and textured lines, naked men, flowers, trees.

When they arrived they found Vanessa so deeply distracted she could barely register their presence. She was obsessed with Duncan, who was obsessed with Bunny, and no matter who was sleeping with whom she was aware that her plans were in danger of falling through. Both men were such unconvincing farmworkers it seemed likely the tribunal would send them to war, or prison.

Bunny explained to Leonard that he planned to tell the tribunal that he'd been born a pacifist. His mother's commitment to pacifism had led her to train under Tolstoy himself!

'By training under, do you mean she once had a conversation with the man?' Virginia asked and Bunny agreed that yes, that was the case.

'I also plan to protest the suggestion that I did not take my agricultural duties seriously. I took them quite seriously.'

'He's going to keep bees, aren't you, Bunny?' Vanessa looked up from where she was sitting by the fire—autumn was setting in and the days getting colder—pretending to knit, though in truth she was watching Duncan, who was sitting opposite her. It was all very awkward, having so many people in the same social circle, let alone the same room, in love with the one man, a man who had that very day been tarred and feathered.

Duncan, used to being the centre of attention, sat listlessly, pulling feathers off his ruined shirt and throwing them into the fire. The smell was enough to make a person retch.

'What will you argue at the tribunal, Duncan?' Leonard asked, keen to know what the options were when his own turn came. Duncan spoke gently into the fire, and while it was hard to catch what he said, his case seemed to hinge in some indefinable way on his personal charm. Bunny moved to stand behind him, running his fingers through Duncan's dark curls to catch bits of tar and twigs. The three of them looked like some kind of holy trinity, glowing in the firelight.

'It didn't hurt nearly as much as I feared,' Duncan offered.

More chat. Cups of tea. A walk out into the autumn evening. Moonrise. It sat on the horizon. Shimmering. Fat as butter.

'It's beautiful,' Virginia said.

'It's dangerous, is what it is,' Leonard said. 'I should have thought. The air raids. They'll be starting soon.'

'The worst thing about the raids,' Virginia said to Vanessa as she got onto her bike, 'is having to talk to the servants. We sleep in the kitchen with them, you know.'

Virginia had described these evenings to Vanessa before. At length. Mattresses lain around the stove in the kitchen for warmth. Sophie, the cook, sobbing gently. Lily curled up, as if trying to hide, in the corner of the room. (Sophie was old; the woman she had worked for since she was a small child had married a fierce and difficult man, and then there was the winter and the war. Lily, for her part, was looking for another job. She knew exactly what her mistress said about her behind her back and had seen the way her master looked at her. Surely a factory would be preferable to the humiliations that each day serving this couple brought?)

Leonard and Virginia cycled through the moonlight. Zeppelins lumbered overhead like some monstrous vision of the future. Downed, one bloomed blood red across the horizon.

'There is no need to be frightened,' Leonard called out, somewhat dramatically.

'I'm not!' Virginia sounded quite merry. The war around her was not nearly as terrifying as the one she'd been waging within herself.

'It is women who drive the zeppelins,' Leonard told Virginia, as they rattled along, 'They are smaller. Lighter.'

'Lucky then, that I've been fattened up for market,' Virginia observed.

2020

There came a night when Alice found herself unable to stop worrying about Hen. Her legs trembled. Her heart raced. She struggled to breathe. Alice was having, she supposed, a drawn-out panic attack. How was she to keep Hen alive? She realised, as she lay on this long, long—oh God would it ever end—longest of nights that she'd spent her entire life worrying about the fact that people might die, and now, it seemed, they were.

She was restless but didn't want to move because Edith needed her rest; her poor wife, who, like everyone, was having a terrible time. Imaginary Leonard arrived. He looked tired. Drawn. Old. He took her hand. Alice shook him off. 'Edith is lying right there!' she said. 'You'll wake her.'

'You feel hot,' Leonard replied. 'Is it a fever?'

Alice realised she'd drenched the sheets, her nightie. She reached for the towel beside her bed. There was a knot of tight, anxious feeling in her throat, down into her chest. Distress radiated throughout her body. These flashes hit once, twice, sometimes six times a night.

'Menopause,' Alice said. 'It's a nightmare.'

'I believe,' Leonard said, 'that some so-called experts on my wife believe that she killed herself because of melancholia caused by the Change.'

'Helpful,' Alice said. 'Thank you.'

'It's not true,' Imaginary Leonard reassured Alice. 'She found it liberating, psychologically, and in other ways. I blame the war. And myself, of course. I dropped my guard.'

'You can't be vigilant for more than thirty years,' Alice said. 'It's impossible.'

'And yet here you lie, trying to work out how you can save your friend Hen from the plague, when millions of people around the world are suffering from this illness, and many of them are dying, most particularly the elderly in these horrendous facilities that seem to be the fashion these days. How do you propose to save her? It strikes me as impossible. Let me read you a section from one of my favourite poems. Rilke,' Leonard said, soothingly. 'Perfect for these "lockdowns" you've been experiencing, though I don't quite understand why you find them so upsetting. Things can get a lot worse, I can assure you.'

Alice felt very small. A child. She briefly imagined that Leonard was her father and that he would look after her.

Alice heard a growling and saw that a cocker spaniel—was it Pinka or Sally? She could barely tell them apart—was by the bed, pulling at Imaginary Leonard's trouser leg.

'I have to go,' Leonard said. 'I am needed elsewhere.'

Alice grabbed his arm for a moment. 'The guilt,' she asked. 'Does it ever stop?'

'Never,' Imaginary Leonard said. 'But you must . . .'

Alice came to with a shock. Was being shaken awake by her wife. 'You're snoring,' she said.

'I can't have been, I've been awake since three,' Alice said.

'Well it's five now. So you must have slept at some point.' Edith leaned over, kissed Alice on the mouth. 'I'm getting up for a run. Need to get my time outside before the crowds hit Carlton Gardens.'

1916

It had been well past midnight when Leonard began to ready himself for bed on the night he heard the sound of muffled laughter—from the kitchen? He thought it was the kitchen—then a crash as something fell to the floor. He didn't believe in ghosts but had heard the rumours. A less rational, more excitable man might have wondered if a distressed former resident, long dead, inhabited his wife. But no, Leonard did not entertain such thoughts. On hearing various reports from Virginia, her nurses, Sophie and Lily, he made careful notes in his diary in case Virginia's interest in tokens (a local word) might be considered a symptom. As for Sophie and Lily's concern, he wondered if their nerves were related to how physically demanding life at Asheham could be. Water to be pumped from a well. Cooking to be done on an oil stove or primus. Servants, nurses, master and mistress alike, had to use an earth closet. The house was cold, so cold it sometimes really felt as if they were living in the dark green depths of the ocean.

I have never known a house that had such a strong character, a personality of its own—romantic, gentle, lovely, melancholy.

LEONARD WOOLF, 1964

Leonard went downstairs in search of the source of the sound. As he got closer, the laughter dropped away to be replaced by something deeper, more guttural. He began to wonder if the noise might have a demonic source when he stepped into the kitchen. The scene before him was more human than he'd been prepared for. It was Lily. She lay in a pool of flour, on her back, on the table. There was more flour scattered on the ground where it had been pushed to make way for her. Her dress was hitched to her hips and her legs were splayed. Her breasts—they were large, Leonard noticed—were spilling out of her bodice. Dishabille. Yes, that was the word.

The soldier tried to move quickly but the pants around his ankles hobbled him. His mouth, recently attached to her swollen, brown nipples, stayed open longer than it should—he was reluctant to let go of the shape of her. Leonard, also slow to react, stared at Lily for far too long—her nipples seemed darker than they ought to be—before remembering that Lily had had a child. This was the reason Virginia had never taken to her. Leonard was less judgemental. Had suggested to Virginia that these things might be a matter of class. Of poverty.

'Lily!' Leonard said her name to bring himself, to bring everyone, to their senses. The soldier stumbled, before pulling up his trousers, grabbing his shoes, and pushing past Leonard. Lily, lush, full, her beautiful cunt plump between legs still akimbo, seemed dazed and failed, for a long moment, to pull her dress down or sit herself up. Courbet's *The Origin of the World* came to mind, give or take a sprinkling of flour. Now there was a fine painter, Leonard thought briefly, before the stark eroticism of the scene disorientated him. Carefully, slowly, he tried to shut himself down before he realised, with a shock that caused him to feel momentarily faint, that he could smell her.

Lily sobbed as the significance of what was happening finally sunk in. Both her shame, and her lover's brutal abandonment. The man was, Lily and Leonard both saw, no gentleman. When Leonard opened his mouth to speak, Lily flinched though Leonard was, in fact, surprisingly gentle.

'Your mistress is ill,' he said, calmly. 'She cannot be alarmed by soldiers running about the place at all times of night. Or believing there are ghosts about.'

'No, sir.' Lily shook her head wildly. 'I am sorry, sir. Please don't dismiss me, sir.'

'I have no intention of dismissing you.' Leonard stepped towards the girl, to comfort her perhaps, but then stopped, turned abruptly, and returned to his room.

Leonard assumed that Lytton, who had an instinct for these matters, would have intuited the traumatic yet sensuous events of the night before, but both he and Virginia were oblivious as far as Leonard could tell.

'Virginia is looking much improved,' Lytton observed over lunch. 'Fat as a zeppelin. One can imagine her rolling merrily over the Downs. But as for me, as for you and me, now conscription has come in, we'll be expected to fight. Which is, obviously, impossible.'

'You could work for agricultural services,' Leonard said. 'Adrian is doing it. Bunny. Duncan.'

'I couldn't possibly work alongside Bunny and Duncan.' Lytton looked outraged.

'Garsington Manor then?' Leonard suggested.

'I'd be bedridden in minutes,' Lytton said. 'The combination of physical strain and the distress caused by Ottoline's prattle would be the end of me. She talks endlessly about her puppies. And, as anyone who knows me well respects, I am much more interested in feline friendship.' He turned to Leonard suddenly. 'What do you prefer, dear Leonard? Cats or dogs.'

'I love both equally,' Leonard said, which was true.

'You really are a very unusual man,' Lytton mused. 'In my experience people are one, or the other.'

Virginia, who'd been standing in the doorway listening, chimed in. She was feeling positively droll. 'Leonard likes monkeys best of all. I'm certain, Lytton, that we could find you work outside and a young and vigorous pacifist to keep you company. Or, as Leonard has suggested, you could join Adrian and pick bugs off currant bushes ten hours a day.'

'I do love this house,' Lytton said, by way of changing the subject.

'It's haunted you know,' Virginia said. 'In summer the grass grows so high that everything turns the colour of corn. And once the candles and oil lamps go on, we are even more submerged.'

'How does the house communicate itself?' Lytton asked.

'It creaks,' Virginia said. 'It sighs. It groans.'

'I'm surprised you are tolerating this conversation,' Lytton said to Leonard who was sitting, peculiarly silent. Leonard, for his part, was thinking of the previous night.

'I was up till all hours,' Leonard said. 'Working on a book regarding the possibility of controlling the availability of armaments as a way of preventing future wars. Ghosts have not been much on my mind. But since you ask, I find these beliefs, carried across the centuries, superstitious. Ridiculous.'

Oh dear, Lytton thought to himself. Pompous Leonard was back. 'I'm dining with Asquith this evening,' he announced, lifting himself from his chair heavily, as if dining with the prime minister was a tedious affair. 'You should join me,' he continued, without offering details as to how they might do that, then struck out to walk across fields to the station, chatting all the while, until his high and quavering voice evaporated into the chill air.

2020

One day, as Alice was conducting phone meetings in her car, Imaginary Leonard plonked himself down in the passenger seat. He was agitated.

'Snowdrops,' he said. 'Forget-me-nots. Runner beans. Tomatoes.'

'Alice?' asked the disembodied voice coming out of the speaker. 'Is that you?'

'Some random has just got into my car,' she said. 'I'll call back when I've a better idea about the timing of the edit.' She hung up. Turned to Leonard. 'You can't just drop in unannounced,' she said, though clearly he could.

'My brothers sent me seeds,' he continued. 'They wrote to me of measles and the flu. Were concerned that illness would get them before the Germans. They sent pressed flowers and told me stories about Foxie. Foxie enjoyed eating rats in the trenches—the military allowed rats to flourish, you know, to eat the corpses. Foxie was like Charles. An excellent dog.'

Then, in his most disturbing performance yet, Imaginary Leonard opened his mouth only for someone else's voice to emerge.

'Paths must be sixty yards wide to a depth of five miles.'

Alice had read the letters. This was Leonard's brother Phillip. Then a second voice that she assumed was his brother Cecil's chimed in.

'It sounds like a lot, but is barely enough.'

'What did your brothers do in the war?' Alice asked, though she knew both the specifics and the generalities. Not many soldiers survived the trenches intact. They lost their minds, their lives.

'They cut gaps in wire fortifications so the army could move through them. They filled in holes caused by shelling so that foot soldiers didn't fall into them. They only had a pick and a shovel. They bridged twenty-six successive lines of trenches in this fashion. By late November 1917, on a six-mile front, checked only at Flesquières, their divisions had penetrated five miles into the defences of the Hindenburg Line. Can you imagine? Can you?' His ghostly face turned red with emotion. He thumped the dashboard with the flat of his trembling hand. Alice flinched.

'Oats and hay had to be pre-positioned for the horses. Think of them, what happened to them. Their fear. Their suffering.' Alice was uncertain, at this point, if *them* referred to the brothers or the horses. 'And what did I do? I sat at home, writing books, nursing a woman who would not love me. I find I cannot get thoughts of Cecil's final morning out of my head. He ate a breakfast of broad beans . . .'

'You know this?' asked Alice.

'I know he planted broad beans successfully. Would not have wanted to waste them before he passed through and operated in open country. The major walked out into the open to revive the men's flagging spirits. A shell blew him to pieces. Phillip and Cecil ran out together to retrieve him, Foxie raced valiantly along by their side. A second shell exploded. More than three hundred thousand died in that battle alone.'

'Did Foxie survive?'

'Phillip liked to believe so,' Imaginary Leonard said. 'But that was his fevered imagination. How could a dog survive what a man could not? Foxie was never seen again.'

'And Phillip?'

'He had a son he named Cecil in honour of his brother. He tried to kill himself many times over. Succeeded as an old man. Despair seems to run in my family. And yours, if I understand the details correctly. I believe you are named after a great-grandmother who killed herself. The one who was on the stage, I believe, in, what do you call it: Kalgoorlie?'

'I have another meeting now,' Alice said.

'I believe your great-grandfather on the other side chose that path also?' Imaginary Leonard said.

'He did?'

'He did,' Leonard pulled the death certificate out of mid-air, as if he were the internet and a poltergeist combined. 'In rooms in a place called Kings Cross—you have such a suburb in Australia, yes?—"Effects of a certain poison, to wit, carbon monoxide, willfully caused by inhaling coal gas".'

'Huh,' said Alice. 'What else do you know?'

'Ah yes,' Leonard said. 'This is what I came to tell you.'

Alice looked out the side window of her car to see that a large crow had landed on her mirror. She looked in through the front window of her house to see that Edith was waving at her, trying to get her attention.

'I'm sorry,' Edith's SMS came through to her dashboard. 'Ageing Disgracefully just called. Hen has tested positive.'

1918–1920s

The Great War unleashed a fatalism and barbarism that Leonard and Virginia admitted deep into their souls. Their own demons, also, had tempered them. Optimism, a sympathetic manner, these qualities struck them as fatuous. They had been forged in the same fire and some alchemy had occurred. Leonard and Virginia were now a couple that only death would tear asunder. The people they'd been on 4 August, 1914 no longer existed on 2 September, 1918.

They celebrated war's end by sitting in Hogarth House* and eating chocolate creams. Their small sacrament. This event was followed by a busy year. They bought Monk's House† in Sussex. It was an excellent year for fruit trees (plums, pears, apples). Leonard stood as an MP for the Labour Party though was, to his relief, not elected. He and Virginia turned forty. They published books under the name Hogarth Press. At the end of 1919, Virginia was hit by the third—or was it fourth?—wave of the Great Influenza pandemic.

People blamed the Spanish for the situation. Something to do with their free press and their dry windy weather. The Americans,

---

* Leonard and Virginia lived in Hogarth House from 1915 to 1924, in part to enable Virginia to recover her health in the calm surrounds of Richmond. Hogarth House was one half of an eighteenth-century mansion. Hogarth Press was named for it, and housed in it. Alice read many books about the Hogarth Press but failed to incorporate this information into her novel in any meaningful fashion.

† Monk's House was named for the fact that monks used the house as a retreat in the fifteenth century. Well, that was the story, a story that Leonard discovered was entirely untrue and led him to meditate on the difficulty of establishing facts when writing autobiography. He believed houses framed phases of a person's life. The house's character determined events that unfolded when lived in them. If this was true, Monk's House was the most significant of all the Woolfs' homes as they lived there, on and off, from 1919 until the day they died.

who had incubated the disease first in towns in the Midwest, then in army camps, then on boats and trains that carried thousands of young men around the country and around the globe, escaped blame. It was hard to get a clear picture of the situation—was it even a situation? Wasn't there flu every year? Rumours of plague rumbled around the world. Trains left stations full of young men who arrived at their destinations some hours later, dead. Corpses turned dark blue to black, blood leaking out of their noses, their eyes, their mouths. It was as if the war didn't end so much as change form. Bullets morphed into viruses that incubated in the bodies of soldiers and spiralled out from the fields of war.

Virginia did not dwell on these horrors. It was horror enough to be bedridden once more. She reacquainted herself with the colours and textures of the wallpaper, and traced the damp stains that bled in the ceiling. On the days she could tolerate daylight, the curtains were opened and she watched clouds float past the window, took in the blue of the sky, or listened to the sound of rain against it.

Virginia feared that those close to her seemed to consider this illness some extension of the essential flaws of her personality. If she'd had more strength she would have explained to Leonard, to Vanessa, that this was not yet another of her episodes, or at least not an episode particular to her, though everyone seemed to experience this influenza privately, had their own constellation of symptoms.

Her brain was a fog. Her joints were swollen. It hurt to lie on her left side, her right, her back, her stomach. Pain was caused by the lightest of sensations. One doctor wondered if she had breakbone, dengue, though that disease was unlikely in Sussex. She lost her sense of smell. She suffered a savage earache and feared she'd be rendered deaf as some, as many, were. She was nauseous for days on end, vomited often enough that dehydration was a serious concern, and Nellie* arrived in her room every hour bearing lemonade she'd made just for Miss Ginny. Lights flashed in the corner of her vision. A cough erupted for weeks, one so violent her ribs were fractured. Her migraine was intolerable, her fever devastating: so high that typhoid, also unlikely in Sussex, was briefly discussed, and Virginia took some comfort in the knowledge her suffering was not unlike Thoby's. She was, briefly, returned to some kind of intimacy with him.

Thoby's form looms behind—that queer ghost. I think of death sometimes as the end of an excursion which I went on when he died. As if I should come in and say well, here you are.

VIRGINIA WOOLF, 14 DECEMBER 1929

Sleep brought visitations. Thoby crushed her skull between his powerful hands like a vice. Leslie stood over her so low his beard scraped along her body, and boomed so loudly that Virginia thought her ear drums would burst. Her mother stood at her feet and gripped her daughter's knees joints, her ankles. Harder she squeezed, harder, her nails digging into Virginia's skin, cutting her

---

* Nellie Boxhall was Virginia's cook from 1916 to 1934. Nellie, like Virginia, had been a motherless child. Nellie, like Virginia, suffered from 'nerves'. The two became locked into a battle that lasted decades, with Nellie regularly resigning, Virginia regularly castigating her both in person and on the page but also giving Nellie cuddles when she needed them (often, apparently) and buying her a pineapple when she was ill. Nellie didn't like Leonard, and accused him of trying to climb in her bed. Few people gave this gossip credence, and Leonard always denied it, saying that Virginia would never have forgiven him if he'd slipped up. After Nellie resigned (or Virginia sacked her) in 1934, she went and worked for Charles Laughton, becoming, by the modest standards of the time, a celebratory chef. Did an excellent roast beef and crème brûlée. Nellie never married, didn't have children but saved enough money to buy her own house. After retirement she shared a house with a fellow servant, a woman called Lottie. Lottie nursed Nellie in her final illness and fell to pieces after her dear friend died. Nellie outlived her former mistress by twenty-four years.

flesh. Then she reached into her daughter's chest and gripped her heart, clenching it tight in her fist.

Virginia came to herself with a jolt and called Leonard's name. Nellie explained he was walking in Kew Gardens. Visiting the fernery. Nellie's words reached Virginia as if from a distance, as if Nellie was standing on the shore calling to her mistress, and she, Virginia, was floating in a boat far out at sea.

Virginia found that she needed and wanted Leonard all the more when reduced like this. Had begun to think of him not as a warder but guardian angel. On his return Leonard joined his wife, bearing cinnamon toast. Virginia felt a moment's disorientation. Was he going to force milk upon her? Wasn't she better? But it seemed Leonard had no intention of forcing food or milk upon her. Those days were done, at least for now. He joined her on the bed. Offered her some distraction.

'I have seen the most extraordinary ferns,' Leonard said. 'With enormous curled ends, fat as caterpillars. Tall as trees. With brown spiky trunks. Some from as far away as Australia.'

Virginia didn't respond. Felt as if she'd floated to the bottom of a deep pond and now lay there with stones weighing down her eyelids, her palms, her feet.

Leonard kept chatting lightly but was feeling nervous. This flu was more serious than any of Virginia's previous bouts, and though the influenza epidemic was generally believed to have become milder with each wave, many were still dying of it, or coming close to death. Leonard put his ear to her chest, her heartbeat seemed erratic. Frantic. He checked her colour. She had not turned blue, thank God, and nor were their alarming flashes of blood red in the corner of eyes or any other orifices. He did not want Virginia to drown in her own foamed and bloody lungs.

'Perhaps I should offer some distraction,' Leonard said. 'I have been working on the year's books. In summary, we now are the owners of two houses. We have published three books. Yours, Tom's and Middleton Murray's. Net profit £26, 3s. 10d.'* He pulled a stub of pencil from one pocket of his tweeds, then a small spiral note-book, torn and stained, from the other. '*Night and Day* received high praise, as did *The Voyage Out*, however neither book has offered us, as yet, any financial return. You have done well from your reviewing work. £153, 17s. I thought you would find that cheering.' He patted her hand hoping she would return the pressure, but she did not.

'I have just been reading Maynard's *The Economic Consequences of Peace*. He has written of his adventures in Versailles some months ago,' Leonard went on. 'He believes that President Wilson had not fully recovered from his own bout of the flu when negotiating. Once brilliant, he seemed unable to fully comprehend the import-ance of the document they were working on. The man saw French spies everywhere. He gave into French and the English demands that the Germans be thoroughly punished. As a consequence the treaty was so punitive, reparations so high, that Maynard fears we will be at war again soon enough. And when I lunched with him the other day, he said there are rumours that Wilson has relapsed, or perhaps had a stroke, either way is now deranged and blind. Edith Wilson is running the country.'

Virginia finally opened her eyes.

'Would you like your toast?' Leonard asked, rearranging the pillows so as better to support her. Virginia took the toast and began to nibble at its corners.

---

* *Kew Gardens*, Virginia Woolf; *Poems*, TS Eliot; *The Critic in Judgement*, J Middleton Murray.

'I find myself quite buoyed,' she said, 'by the news that a woman called Edith is running America.'

After Virginia's recovery, the 1920s passed in a blur of fighting with Nellie, loving Vita Sackville-West, gardening, and the writing and publishing of books: *Economic Imperialism, Empire and Commerce in Africa, Socialism and Co-operation, Queen Victoria, Jacob's Room, Fear and Politics, A Passage to India, The Wasteland, Mrs Dalloway, To the Lighthouse, Orlando, Elizabeth and Essex, Imperialism and Civilisation.* More.

Leonard spent several years on the work that was to be his great contribution to scientific history: *After the Deluge: A Study of Communal Psychology.* It was published in 1931 and received a tepid to cold response. These responses told Leonard that he was no Lytton Strachey. He was no Virginia Woolf. He was no Maynard Keynes. He was not even EM Forster, which was particularly unfair because one could equally suggest that EM Forster was no Leonard Woolf.

The Woolfs saved Hogarth House for publishing and socialising, and Monk's House for the summers, weekends and gardening. Leonard was joined in the gardens by Percy, and they divided them into a series of small sections: trees, shrubs, flowers, vegetables, fruit, roses. Percy was a local man. He'd survived his time as a gunner in the trenches during WWI but was uncertain he'd survive Leonard's pigheaded and inflexible thinking. He hadn't minded being a member of the serving class when he had a clear area of authority. Leonard, in contrast, treated Percy as an equal while insisting on making all the key decisions in the garden. The two men fought for thirty years, with Percy resigning on a regular basis. Despite these tensions they built borders, brick paths, flint walls and fishponds both round and square. A lawn for bowls. A hive for the bees. They made a terrace of millstones, and Pinka took to sleeping there—he loved the way old stones held the warmth of the sun. They built a studio, just for Virginia, with its own garden.

Leonard became increasingly passionate about his orchard. Planted pear cordons against the orchard wall, apple trees, a mulberry, a walnut, cherries plums pears figs. There was spraying, pruning, harvesting. He had had a particular interest in bloodlines since his work in Ceylon, and in light of his discovery of Pinka, the perfect spaniel, he hoped to move into breeding dogs as well. Grafting fruit trees had taught him that the merging of different species of trunk and branch could really be very desirable.

Two elm trees stood in the lower part of the croft field and their upper boughs had looped around each other so from some angles it looked like a single tree. They named the elms for themselves: Leonard and Virginia, and positioned the pond to capture a reflection of the branches.

One evening Leonard came in from the garden to find Virginia in his study, sitting in his chair and reading his diary.

'I can only imagine, Mandril, that you found my latest rather dry.'

She had.

Leonard protested that he'd first developed his interest in the mechanics of soil and composting when he was in Ceylon, but Virginia remained disinterested. However, he understood she was teasing him. Allowed himself to be teased.

Virginia cleared her throat and stood up straight, began to read, as if from a poem:

'Picked slugs off zinnias.

'Returning to Indore method.

'Sir Albert. Early paper 1910.

'The economic significance of natural cross-fertilization in India, Botanical series, volume three, number six.

'Complex sequence of events. Organisms need carbon nitrogen oxygen, go up to 50 to 105 degrees for the first part of process. Then from 105 to 140. Ideal range is 120 to 140.'

Here Virginia paused dramatically so as to catch her breath.

'Earthworm.

'Mycorrhizal association—the living together of fungus and plant root. Absorption of the fungus by the root. Minerals. Manure. Problems caused by deep-rooted trees and plants. Humus the key. Soil health crucial. Carbon—nitrogen ratio—30:1. If carbon heavy, add extra greens or manure.

'Turn

'Turn

'Turn.

'May smoke. DO NOT LET DRY OUT. Cover. Four to six weeks.'

Virginia was building to her crescendo, a phrase that had been firmly underlined by Leonard.

'<u>The health of soil, plant, animal and man is one and indivisible</u>.'

She stopped for a moment. 'What of the elms? Are they deep-rooted?'

'They have roots close to the surface rather than a tap root. They can spread as wide as the crown of the tree, or wider. They're like a mirror, so to speak.'

'Might they not topple in a storm?'

'They might.'

She flicked on a few more pages before settling on another page and beginning her incantation again.

'The history of the propagation and improvement of vegetables by the concurrence of art and nature. Incisions. Shoulder grafting. Grafting in the cleft. Approach grating. Splice. Inoculation.'

'That is a terrible poem.' Leonard looked exhausted. 'My garden's a better one. I'm off to bed.'

'You are such a fine poet I'm inclined to join you.' Virginia moved to kiss Leonard on the cheek, but Mitz, who'd been curled up by the fire with Pinka, dashed up his legs, torso and shoulder, before taking up her position on his shoulder and hissing. Mitz was a small marmoset who'd climbed onto Leonard's lap during a dinner party in 1934. She claimed him with such enthusiasm that her owners offered her to Leonard as a gift. Mitz became extremely proprietorial of her new master, but she need not have worried. Virginia had no intention of getting into her husband's bed. Leonard, flattered by such attention, welcomed both his wife's kiss and Mitz's adoration. A rare and beautiful smile lit up his face.

V
PEARL

2021

Hen died, along with twenty other Ageing Disgracefully residents, that September. The death was as awful as Alice had feared, had been warned, it would be. She never really knew if her messages of love and support had been received, or understood. She did not know if Hen felt abandoned or—and this was possible, knowing Hen—simply relieved. Alice wondered if Hen felt unexpressed resentment that she'd ended up parenting someone else's children. Children who had, in the end, failed her. Though when she asked that question and used that word, failed, in #thetroublewithhen Doug and Diana insisted that was not right. They had not failed Hen. What more could they had done? Alice did not know what more they could have done, so she thanked her siblings, somewhat formally, for their support in this difficult time, and changed the subject. They found her reserve a difficult combination of stand-offish and needy, the chats tapered off, and the siblings all retired to their respective domestic spaces. Caring. Sadness. Death. It turned people into bores.

A few weeks after Hen's death borders opened. Alice took advantage, drove into New South Wales, genuflected at the Murray, and then kept driving to a writing retreat by the Shoalhaven River. She drove past charcoal gashes slashed across hills, the vivid green of epicormic growth moving up tree trunks. This made her hopeful until she noticed the skeletal crowns. These trees—eucalyptus, banksia, wattle—weren't coming back.

On arrival at the retreat she sat down and finished reading the sixth and final volume of *The Complete Letters of Virginia Woolf.*

Again.

The last letters were written on 28 March 1941. The date that Virginia drowned herself in the Ouse River. That reading done, Alice drank some wine, made herself some dinner, and walked down to the river. It was a bright night, a full moon. Wombats barrelled across the path like dodgem cars. They would do her a damage if she wasn't careful.

When Alice got to the beach by the river, the stars of the Southern Cross were before her. Pulpit Rock sat to her right. The blackened branches of the recently burnt stood sentinel around. Once lush, this landscape was now stark. Sculptural. More shocking still was the silence. Only two years ago she'd stood on this very beach listening to a chorus of frogs, cicadas, birds and bats. The splash of the prawns jumping out of the water.

She closed her eyes and felt the cold light of the moon on her body. Tried to take herself back to that orchestra of sound, for she knew it was within her: the movement of the water, the plop-plop-plop of the prawns, the angry rumbling of warring wombats, and the whoosh and gentle thud of the kangaroos. But when she opened her eyes she was returned to this moonscape. This river full of ash.

The next morning was humid. Hot. Felt nothing like autumn. Instead of throwing herself into her tree book, or even her godforsaken novel, Alice was overcome with lethargy. She read Virginia's essay 'The Death of a Moth'. Inspired, she watched a moth, trapped between the flywire and the windowpane, flutter until it dropped with exhaustion. Come the afternoon of her first full day, the rain began to fall. It continued through the night. The river crept closer. The property began to flood in its lower lying folds and valleys. Alice became concerned the wombat burrows would flood, though she had been assured that those robust creatures had evolved some kind of engineering solution to that particular problem.

When there was a break in the weather, Alice went for a walk and became lost in the (unburnt) rainforest down by the Nowra River. The downpour started up again. Her phone was out of range. Alice continued to wander, pinned somewhere between escarpment and river, for the next two hours. When huddling under an overhang she found a small nest, fallen from the ceiling above: a deep cup, it was lined with tiny, fluffy, red and grey feathers, threaded with green mosses and lichens. She put this perfect object in her backpack.

When the rain cleared, and Alice had figured out how to find the road and, by extension, her car, she saw that blood was running down her legs. Two enormous leeches hung off her. One near her ankle, one closer to her knee. Alice knew that you were not meant to pull leeches off in a hurried manner. If their tiny jaws stayed embedded inside you the wound would not heal then became infected. You needed matches and salt. Or something. Alice pulled the leeches off in a hurried manner. Went home. Revised some notes.

Considered Leonard's memories of being a small boy and

a man coming into the room and applying leeches to my back.

LEONARD WOOLF, 1960

of being a grown man, pushing his way through thick, wet grass in the jungle, wearing shorts, and looking down to find bare knees black with leeches.

Once she returned to the cottage, Alice made herself a cup of tea, then finished rereading *The Complete Diaries of Virginia Woolf.* Virginia loved the rain.

To my infinite delight, they bombed our river. Cascades of water roared over the marsh—all the Gulls came and rode the waves at the end of the field. It was, and still is, an inland sea, of such indescribable beauty, almost always changing, day and night, sun and rain, that I can't take my eyes off it.

VIRGINIA WOOLF TO ETHEL SMYTH, 14 NOVEMBER 1940

And yet, despite that infinite delight, that indescribable beauty, she drowned herself, just four months later.

Alice knew about water. When heavy rain finally fell, the water would flow over riverbanks onto the floodplain, carrying debris that had built up over years of drought and dumping it in the river. This kind of flooding was described as 'black water'. She knew that floods were destructive, but that once upon a time they'd meant good things as well. They gave life to river systems and wetlands, they flushed out sediments and salt. Rivers met each other in a rush and their mouths opened to the sea. But as droughts grew longer, black water became more deadly. As temperatures rose, the air held more moisture, which increased the likelihood of intense rainstorms falling upon eroded and parched soil. It didn't seep into the ground so much as skid and skim over the top of it.

Alice listened to the news at the end of the second day with some trepidation. Once-in-a-hundred-year storms, records broken, yada yada yada. Everything was drowning. A woman on the ABC described having to rescue her twenty-four-year-old horse Barney, by cradling his head so he could swim through waters full of dead cattle and bull sharks. He became so exhausted the woman was worried he wouldn't make it.

Alice became worried about fish suffocating, a drowning of sorts, when out of water. She worried about Barney. She saw Virginia rushing out a back gate and across watery meadow. She saw her reach the bank of the river and bend to retrieve large stones.

That evening Alice watched *The Edge of Tomorrow* on iTunes. *Live. Die. Repeat.* She bookmarked *The Butterfly Effect*, *Groundhog Day* and *Palm Springs* for future viewing. A funnel web spider waltzed in across the kitchen floor, high on its back legs. She caught it in a glass and put it out in the rain. Friends told her later that they hinge on their hind legs before lunging, that they were capable of biting through boots, of jumping several feet high. She'd had no idea.

> *L has a purple hyacinth. And the flood has gone. Then the snow came, and I made green holes in the grass every time I came out here to my lodge. We take tea at Charleston: Clive is digging a trench; Nessa feeding fowls; Duncan painting Christ; Quentin driving a tractor—all as it was in 1917.*
> VIRGINIA WOOLF TO MARY HUTCHINSON, 10 FEBRUARY 1941

The next day it became clear that Alice's leech wound was becoming infected. She took a photo of it and sent it to Doug who replied, *that looks bad, you should disinfect that pronto.* Rather than washing the wound, Alice began a new project: drawing a nest a day. Afterwards she finished rereading *A Moment's Liberty: The Shorter Diary of Virginia Woolf.* On 28 March 1941, Virginia drowned herself in the Ouse River.

> *I was saying to Leonard, we have no future.*
>
> VIRGINIA WOOLF TO ETHEL SMYTH, 1 MARCH 1941

Alice took another photo of her infected leg and sent it to Diana, and Edith, to both alarm and amuse them. Both were alarmed. Neither amused.

I'm worried about you, Edith messaged. Alice ignored her, drew another nest, then reread another key text in the Woolf oeuvre which reiterated that on 28 March 1941 Virginia drowned herself in the Ouse River. Alice went walking, up through the bloodwoods to a grove where the casuarina closed in around her. Rainwater coursed over the ground, tracing numerous paths towards the river. A small and intricately patterned snake darted from under a rock, reared at her, fangs ready to strike. Venomous she later read. Also endangered. Everything was endangered these days.

> *So much water has flowed under the bridge that I feel at sea;*
> *and so must conclude.*
>
> VIRGINIA WOOLF TO TS ELIOT, 8 MARCH 1941

Alice dressed her wound and considered a trip along the muddy, possibly flooded, road to the doctor. She drew a nest. She finished reading Quentin Bell's biography of Virginia. On 28 March 1941, Virginia drowned herself in the Ouse River:

> *there's a flood of yellow flowers in the garden—and the view from*
> *my window is like a block of flawed emerald, half green, half*

blue . . . It's amazingly peaceful here, you can almost hear the grass
grow . . . It's difficult, I find, to write. No audience. No private
stimulus, only this outer roar.

VIRGINIA WOOLF TO ELIZABETH ROBINS, 13 MARCH 1941

Vita's budgerigars, she learned, were dying owing to a shortage of bird seed. Louie's* birds were doing much better. She read Leonard's memorandum to the Labour Party in 1941 regarding the aim of Palestine:

Partition is a policy of despair and, under existing circumstances so
desperate as to be almost inevitably disastrous.

LEONARD WOOLF, 1941

She noticed that Virginia, towards the end, began to admire Leonard's persistence, his political work, more than she once had.

I'm glad you liked Leonard's book and gave it to a sceptic. It seemed to me
the only kind of thing worth writing now. Do you find you can read the
novelists? I can't . . .

VIRGINIA WOOLF TO LADY CECIL, 21 MARCH 1941

---

* Louisa Everest, née West, was known as Louie. She was a cook and housekeeper for Leonard (and Virginia) until the day Leonard died, and became an increasingly essential member of the household. She had a diploma in Advanced Cooking, was the branch secretary of the Rodmell Labour Party (which met at Monk's House for many years), and lived in one of the two cottages close to Monk's House that the Woolfe's owned. (Percy lived in the other.) Louie had a black bob, and a strong broad frame. Her demeanour could be contained, stoic, but on occasion she would smile so broadly and warmly that she transformed. Beautiful. Not unlike, in this fashion, her mistress. Perhaps this is one reason why Leonard grew so fond of her. After her husband, Bert Everest, died in the early sixties, Louie married a younger, former German prisoner-of-war called Konrad Mayer. Louie died in 1977.

Now sitting more on water than solid ground, her little cottage a boat, Alice set sail only to find she was temporarily in the doldrums. Remembering that Leonard had sailed a boat while recumbent on a mattress and looking at the sky, Alice lay propped up on a mattress, her leg raised up on a cushion, and began for the fourth time, the final volume of Leonard Woolf's autobiography, *The Journey not the Arrival Matters.* She took exhaustive notes.

> *There we sat in May 1940 . . . Under a hot sun and brilliant sky in the garden. Memory.*
> *The least I could look forward to as a Jew.*
> *Slow-moving catastrophe*
> *If Hitler landed.*
> *There would be no point in waiting; we would shut the garage door and commit suicide.*
> *Drag.*
> *I've a wish for ten years more.*
> *Protracted.*
> *One continues to cook and eat one's eggs and bacon for breakfast.*
> *Reluctant.*
> *Peculiarly painful.*
> *I always remember the extraordinary beauty of the little leopard cub·which I had in Ceylon, so young that his legs wobbled a little under him as he began jerkily to gambol down the verandah and yet showing already under his lovely, shining coat the potential rippling strength of his muscles.*
> LEONARD WOOLF, 1969

It took Leonard almost a hundred pages to get to Virginia's death, in the chapter titled 'Virginia's Death'. Alice seemed to have forgotten she was writing about Leonard, but found she could not escape Virginia, the way she died. (Virginia was alone, Hen had died alone.)

Another problem. It was difficult to extinguish a figure as charismatic as Virginia. Leonard seemed to find that also. There were endless digressions in Leonard's autobiography. There were digressions on the importance of digressions.

> *For the autobiographer to force his life and his memories of it into a strictly chronological straight line is to distort its shape and fake and falsify his memories.*
>
> LEONARD WOOLF, 1969

Digressions were one of the things Alice loved about Leonard. That, and the gardens and the animals and his refusal to put up with bullshit, a quality that united him and Virginia until 28 March 1941 when Virginia drowned herself in the Ouse River.

There were three suicide notes in all, and Leonard believed that all three suicide notes were written on the same day. Others disagreed. This was important because if Virginia wrote some of them in the days leading up to her death, her suicide was more planned than spontaneous.

It occurred to Alice that she could use the power of fiction to write Virginia's end differently. She could save her! (Had Alice saved Hen? No!) No matter that everyone knew the story of the long coat. The walking stick. A single large stone forced into her coat pocket. The ashes, buried under their two elms, elms called Leonard and Virginia, the roots tangled underground, the boughs above laced together.

Alice also had to consider the fact that Leonard loved again. This was challenging but there was no way around it: Leonard replaced his wife with Trekkie Parsons before the war was over.

Two more days passed. The Shoalhaven rose higher. Alice's leg became so swollen she could no longer walk, which was a pity as she'd wanted to go and look at the hundred-year-old rhododendrons at the main house.

> *You could always tell, I think, when she [Virginia] was sad because she walked about very slowly, as if she was thinking. She would bump into things, you know; she might walk up in the garden, not realise she was very near a tree or something like that.*
>
> LOUIE MAYER, 1970

Six weeks before her suicide, Virginia stood firm against suggestions that she had got in a muddle when an editor failed to publish a commissioned piece of work. Some things never change, Alice realised. Freelancing sucked.

> *You now inform me that they do not want: the story, but are 'tremendously keen' about something else. I presume that payment will be made for the story commissioned by you—which will bring in foreign exchange as effectively as if it had been printed.*
>
> VIRGINIA WOOLF, 1941

But, yet again, on 28 March 1941 Virginia drowned herself in the Ouse River.

Alice drew another nest before finishing, for the third time, Victoria Glendinning's biography of Leonard Woolf. She opened a bottle of vodka. On 28 March 1941 Virginia drowned herself in the Ouse River.

> *I know that V. will not come across the garden from the Lodge, and yet I look in that direction for her. I know that she is drowned and yet I listen for her to come in at the door. I know that it is the last page and yet I turn it over.*
>
> LEONARD WOOLF, 1941

1935 and thereabouts

Italy was at the root of Leonard and Virginia's first forebodings about fascism. A recent trip there had been both devastating (Mussolini) and inspiring (the gardens). Indeed Leonard had rebuilt a section of his garden at Monk's House and called it 'The Italian Garden'. It involved questionable statuary.

'Versailles on a quarter-acre, that's what Vita called it,' Virginia told Vanessa, on a day she deigned to visit—an increasingly rare treat.

'Vita is an appalling snob,' Vanessa said. 'Though I do like her. But Harold. Does he resent you?'

'Not me,' Virginia replied. 'Though he seems to avoid Leonard.'

'It's the Jewish business, I suppose,' Vanessa said, and as it happened she was right, though it's not clear she thought that a problem. Certainly the man who was still her husband, Clive, had been known to comment that a Nazi Europe would be heaven on earth compared to Europe at war. The English were an anti-Semitic lot.

Harold's main concern about his wife's friendship with Virginia was that he was expected to be polite to her husband, a man always lurking in some room or other going on about the—admittedly tricky—situation with the Germans. Anti-Semitism, this; Jews, that. Scapegoats. The man wouldn't shut up. Harold had attempted to talk to Leonard reasonably but Leonard remained entrenched in his position: had not his people been on the edges of, worked their way to the centre of, all the greatest civilisations? Wasn't the Alhambra Decree of 1492 still in place? Did Harold understand that, from the thirteenth to the sixteenth centuries, European countries expelled the Jews from their territory on at least fifteen occasions?

Harold had stood for the New Party in the general election of 1931. He did, however, break with the party and with Mosley, when he started the British Union of Fascists. One of the things about being an Englishman was having a sense of proportion. Of perspective. It didn't do to support Hitler—but what decent Englishman didn't have some sympathy for Mosley's position? Some, like Leonard, were decent fellows, but were they worth going to war over? And—Harold had to be honest here—when Leonard kept banging on about the dangers of anti-Semitism, Mussolini, Hitler, the problem of Palestine, the need for rearmament, and the inevitability of war, people just wished he'd shut up.

'I don't think Harold, or anyone really, understands that I am now a Jew,' Virginia said to Vanessa. 'Which is as surprising to me as it is to anyone. Perhaps that is why I really do agree with Leo that the Germans have crossed a line. The issue here, though, is statuary. He does get a bit obsessed with it.'

> *Jews were hunted down, beaten up, and humiliated everywhere publicly in the streets of towns. I saw a photograph of a Jew being dragged by storm troopers out of a shop in one of the main streets in Berlin; the fly buttons of the man's trousers had been torn open to show that he was circumcised . . .*
>
> LEONARD WOOLF, 1967

'I suspect your dermatitis is caused by Hitler,' Virginia said. 'It's quite understandable.'

Leonard stared at the road ahead, saying nothing, so Virginia continued her nervous chat. 'Who do you miss more, Lytton or Roger?'

'What of Carrington?' asked Leonard. 'Is she not on your list?'

'You know I will never recover from the manner of her death. The fact that we were the last to see her. I will never forgive Lytton for letting her love him so. I miss Roger the most but that might be because his death was more recent. And Lytton suffered so much it was a relief in the end.'

Leonard continued to be surly. Silent. Virginia sighed and looked out the windscreen. 'How much longer do you think? We've been some hours now.'

The motor was idling. The top of the Lanchester was down but the cold spring day was telling on them. Getting to the German border had not been easy. But the truth was that the BBC could only be relied on for so much information, and while the Foreign Office had warned English Jews not to travel to Germany, how else was Leonard to understand what was going on? They'd been required to go to the German Embassy in London to get a letter from Prince Bismarck. Bismarck had accommodated the request, pointing out that the Woolfs were Jews of high standing, and would not cause any problems. Leonard was concerned that Virginia may, in fact, cause problems. Virginia was concerned that Leonard might also cause problems.

Leonard had imagined that, as an Englishman, he'd be safe, but now, as he sat on a border of a land where the roads were lined with Nazi flags and banners, he understood he'd been deluded. Being an Englishman was not protection at all, and if his trousers tore he too would be a marked man.

Virginia, frail in some quarters but fantastically resilient in others, had acquiesced to Leonard's request that they motor through Germany to see 'what was really going on' with some enthusiasm. Only now was it beginning to dawn on Leonard that he'd put himself and his wife in quite a spot. But this was no time to dwell.

'I do not blame Hitler for my rashes,' Leonard said, returning to Virginia's early point, which was surprising. Leonard was rarely given to complaints of a personal nature, but in recent times he'd been scratching himself raw. 'But it's like having insects crawling all over me.'

Several times recently, Virginia had remarked that she felt as if ants were crawling all over her. It was to do with the Change of Life, but neither Leonard nor the doctors had taken any notice at all.

She considered pointing this out but the couple became distracted by an argument between a soldier and the driver of the truck in front of them. A cap was flung on the ground. Neither Leonard nor Virginia spoke German very well but it seemed as if the to-do was over the man's refusal to take his hat off as he drove past a banner with the Fuhrer's face on it.

Virginia cocked her ear. Children were singing anthems in the distance. 'Surely children aren't employed on a daily basis to stand around the border waving swastikas,' she commented, though it seemed that they were.

The minutes passed slowly. The Woolfs inched forward. Finally they were at the front of it and a soldier approached them. He was a child really. Leonard, by way of contrast, looked like a figure from the Old Testament.

The soldier stared at the middle-aged couple for what seemed like minutes. Leonard was certain that laws had not yet been passed that forbade the passage of an English Jew through Germany. But who knew? Things changed from day to day. Soon enough marriages between Jews and non-Jews would also be forbidden. Extramarital relations between Jews and non-Jews would be forbidden. Similar laws in Britain would have made Leonard and Virginia's marriage illegal.

The boy broke his silence to point at Leonard's shoulder. 'You travel with a monkey?' he asked, in a somewhat deferential English.

'A marmoset, actually,' Leonard replied, encouraging Mitz to jump onto his arm so he could hold her closer to the soldier. Mitz held out her tiny hand and did a little dip, her head bobbing. She was black and white and, like all of her breed, had enormous eyes. The Nazi was enchanted. He reminded Leonard of Alfred, the boy who worked at the Lewes butchery, who was also partial to Mitz.

'What do you feed her?'

'Mealworms. Fruit. Grasshoppers.'

'She loves macaroons.' Virginia leaned across Leonard to be better heard. 'And tapioca pudding,' she continued, before adding, 'she was a gift from the Rothschilds. Victor Rothschild found her tied up in a junk shop and riddled with rickets. Leonard met her at a dinner party and they fell in love. My husband took her home that night to help manage her health and failed to return her. They have been inseparable ever since.'

Provocative. Confusing. Luckily this boy had heard neither of tapioca pudding nor the Rothschilds. 'By what methods do you train her?'

This really was drawing out too long. Dozens of cars now sat behind them, waiting to be waved through.

'When I trained animals in Ceylon,' Leonard said, with untoward enthusiasm, 'I thought that brute force might be required. Certainly it got me somewhere. But I learned that affection won through force led to hostility and unpredictable behaviour. These days I prefer to rely on patience.' Leonard remembered the business at hand, gestured at the crowds on the road ahead. 'Have we arrived on a special day?'

'Herr President Goehring is expected.' As he spoke the boy looked around and remembered his job. 'Wait one moment.' He ran and took one of the flags from the children, returned to Leonard's car and handed it to Mitz, who took it in her tiny hand, before waving the Woolfs through.

Virginia and Leonard drove on in silence for an hour or two. The traffic moved slowly. Swastikas lined the roads. On the outskirts of each village they passed there was a sign. 'Die Juden sind hier unerwünscht.' In one such village a crowd had gathered, waving flags, presumably for Herr Goehring. Mitz had pissed on her flag and flung it onto the road some time back, but still she caught everyone's attention. Children ran in front of the car to better see her. Leonard and Virginia sat, smiling stiffly, until one girl got it into her head to salute her.

'Sieg Heil,' the girl laughed, raising her hand in salute at Mitz. 'Sieg Heil!' Suddenly there were dozens of children trotting behind the car, giggling. 'Sieg Heil. Sieg Heil!'

Virginia flung her arm up in greeting, nervous. Leonard glared at her until she dropped her arm.

'What are you thinking?'

'I was just trying to be friendly.' Virginia's nerves were stretched.

It was late now and getting cold. There was a break in the crowds lining the road, so Leonard stopped the car briefly and put the roof of the car up. Five minutes after they'd taken off again, a warm trickle ran down his back.

'I think we should let the top down again,' Virginia observed. 'Mitz has caused quite a stink.'

Crowds continued to take advantage of the long spring twilight. Leonard gestured towards them by way of indicating he had no intention of stopping.

'I do believe Mitz saved us today. She bites almost anyone who comes near you, darling. How clever of her to know best not.' She looked across at her husband. Mitz was still perched on his shoulder, grooming his hair delicately so as not to overly distract him. It was her tail that caused the problem. So long as to rub against his rash and to tickle it in a way he found quite infuriating. Or so he liked to say. Virginia was not fooled. Leonard saved his greatest passion these days for Mitz, Pinka and the garden.

Leonard did not take his eyes off the road as he went on, gloomily. 'The League has failed utterly. It's impossible to spend time here and imagine any outcome but war. We can't just sit around saying "The League this" and "The League that" as if the mere invocation of its name acts as protection.'

'Men love war, though they might deny it,' Virginia said.

'I never imagined,' Leonard was trembling quite badly now, not quieted by Virginia putting her hand on the steering wheel over his, nor Mitz rubbing his cheeks gently with her miniature hands, 'that we would be here again. But there will be war. Come the end of the decade, I know it. Did Rupert die for this? Did my brother?'

'Who knows what Rupert died for,' Virginia said. 'For himself, I suspect. Sentiment does not become you.'

And while it seems like a cliché to write that Leonard drove on through the twilight, in the gathering gloom, that is, in fact, what he did. The lush green countryside was illuminated by slate grey clouds which surged overhead through rays of setting sunlight. On Leonard drove, flanked by baby Nazis and their flags. If it were not for the smell of marmoset piss and the gentle snores of his wife beside him, Leonard would have imagined that he was not driving into the future, but the past.

On Leonard and Virginia's return from Germany, Pinka was curled up in her basket by the fire. Dead. Percy had left her there so that Leonard and Virginia could say goodbye. Leonard sat down beside her and took one of her long golden ears between his thumb and forefinger and rubbed it gently. He ran his other hand along her flank. Fire-warmed, he could imagine, for a moment, that she was alive, but there was an essential coldness to her now stiff body that could not be denied. It was a terrible shock, there was no doubt about it.

Virginia hovered around him.

'Leo.' She touched his heaving shoulder blades. 'Mongoose,' she tried again before finally leaving for bed.

Leonard sat with Pinka until the embers of the fire dulled, before taking himself out to the garden and inspecting it, under the light of the moon. It was not so long after this that Leonard's friend, his favourite nephew, Vanessa's Julian, died in the Spanish civil war. (Shrapnel. Infection.) Virginia dropped everything to sit with her sister, who had totally collapsed. Was able, finally, to save rather than be saved. Leonard, meanwhile, had kidney problems. They became so severe he was holed up in hospital, in London.

Vanessa never recovered from Julian's death but, after a time, she crawled out of bed. Leonard checked out of hospital. Everyone dragged themselves closer to the end of the decade. Leonard pursued his ponds and statues. Put electric fires in the bedrooms. Gave lectures on the dangers of anti-Semitism, fascism, Mussolini, Hitler, the problem of Palestine, the need for rearmament and the inevitability of war. He built a rock garden, planted another bed of irises, built a second greenhouse.

On a freezing morning at the end of 1938, Leonard woke to find Mitz wrapped in her ribbons of silk, under the covers, clinging to his bony foot. He lay there a moment, feeling the cold of her hard little body against his warmer one, before scooping her up into the palm of his hand as he had so many times before. Though he knew it was not rational and that she would not, could not, be brought back, he stroked her fur with an index finger. Kissed her all over. When Leonard finally made it to Virginia's room carrying her breakfast on a tray, his long face was longer than it had ever been, the lines in it etched even deeper.

'You have succeeded where the London Zoo has not,' Virginia reminded him. 'You kept Mitz alive longer than anyone else was able.'

She put her breakfast tray to one side and leaned forward to take her husband's hand. The couple sat in silence for a while, then Leonard went out into the garden. Poked at the frozen soil. It would need to thaw before he buried Mitz, so he pruned roses that did not need pruning. Sat under the elm tree and scratched at his disgusting rash.

Leonard's right shoulder would sit an inch higher than his left until the end of his life. Forever poised in anticipation of Mitz leaping onto him. The weight of her realigning his balance.

2021

Alice developed a fever. She was, to use one of Leonard's notations, *n.w.* (not well).

She tossed and turned. Doona on. Doona off. She imagined, or dreamed, that she was being driven down a London street in a hansom cab, which in itself was not so strange, but it was startling when the cab flipped, and the horse continued galloping through the clouds. Alice, still inside the cab, hung suspended. That was when Imaginary Leonard wandered in, a nebulous cocker spaniel trailing beside him, and offered Alice a cup of tea.

'Is this COVID?' Imaginary Leonard asked.

'Leech,' Alice said.

'The look on your face suggests you are also suffering from grief? Might that be true?' Imaginary Leonard looked concerned.

'I miss Hen,' Alice replied, 'but I'm not imagining the leech bite. If their jaws get stuck the infections can be nasty.'

'I liked your friend Hen very much. Her death is extremely sad. However. It is excellent news that America no longer has a fascist leader,' Imaginary Leonard said, in as close to a jolly I-need-to-cheer-Alice-up voice as he could muster.

'It is!' Alice smiled, despite her nausea, her disorientation. She was pleased she'd dreamed up the version of Leonard that disliked fascists, gave apples to children, and liked leopards, rather than the man who once almost beat a horse to death and who tenaciously argued and truth-told until all around him were beaten or bored into submission.

'There is this view that Virginia was not a popular writer,' Imaginary Leonard told Alice, hoping to distract her. 'But by the time I died she'd sold almost 450,000 copies of *To the Lighthouse*, in Britain and the United States.' He beamed. Proud. 'Though of course her first novel, *The Voyage Out*, only sold 479 copies in its first few years, for which Virginia received 26.2s.10d. How many books have you written? Let us do an analysis of effort versus results.'

Alice found it hard to think when she had such a terrible headache. 'Six books,' she said. 'I think. This will be the seventh. Maybe eighth.'

Imaginary Leonard nodded. 'So, let us turn to your dilemma.' He pulled a stub of pencil from one pocket of his tweeds, then a small spiral notebook, torn and stained, from the other. First they considered the royalties made from her earlier books—respectable, but not a living—then they considered her work in progress, *This Devastating Fever.* That situation was much worse. 10,000 days on 100,000 words, or ten words per day. If the equation went something like this: *To the Lighthouse* sales in the forty-two years from publication until Leonard's death in 1969 = approx. $30 a day = a living wage, then Alice had to hope for an astronomical advance, in a time when high advances were harder to come by. Leonard then read out loud wisdom he had imparted towards the end of the final volume of his autobiography, patting her hand all the while.

> *Looking back at the age of eighty-eight over the fifty-seven years of my political work, I see clearly that I achieved practically nothing and I include in that failure my modest involvement in establishing the League of Nations. The world today and the history of the human anthill during the last fifty-seven years would be exactly the same as it is if I had played ping pong instead of sitting on committees and writing books. I must have in a long life ground through between 150,000 and 200,000 hours of perfectly useless work.*
>
> LEONARD WOOLF, 1969

'I leave it to you to consider how much more time to spend writing about a man who was passionate about many things—including the genius he married—was a good publisher, loved animals with every fibre of his being, had a modicum of fame in his later life, but was, ultimately, a failure. Especially in times such as these. It is not so long, perhaps, until you will face more bushfires, or floods, or a beloved pet will die, or the world will be at war once more.'

'War? You're saying there will be another world war?' Alice wasn't sure she'd heard right.

'I am merely attempting to put your choices into some kind of perspective. We never know what will happen next. You lost your parents, and Hen. I lost Virginia and many others beside. Writing is not so important in the greater scheme of things, however the act of writing and of reading can give us reason to live. It is a contradictory pursuit. I hope that, at least, has been useful?' He released Alice's hand, handed her a striped humbug pulled from the same pocket in which the notebook had been living for the last few decades.

Alice smiled thanks at Imaginary Leonard—he certainly *had* put things in perspective—upon which he dissolved, leaving her hanging upside down and alone in her fever-dream hansom cab once more. Alice realised she could not ask much more of them, neither Leonard nor Virginia, both of whom had done their very best to guide her. Leonard had counselled her on meaninglessness and Virginia had warned Alice, clearly and often—was it in person or in writing? Alice could no longer remember—

Nobody cared a straw—and I do not blame them—for the future of fiction, the death of poetry or the development by the average woman of a prose style completely expressive of her mind.

VIRGINIA WOOLF, 1929

When Alice woke the next morning, the sheets, her nightdress, were soaked with sweat. Her fever had broken. Ghost Virginia was jangling beside the bed, looking at her as tenderly as eye sockets in a skull were able to.

'Let's get this over and done with,' Virginia said. 'You need to get back to Leonard. Even I can see that.'

Was this a physical response to Hen's death? The leech? COVID? Was she having a breakdown? The answer to these questions seemed somewhat irrelevant, but she felt porous, light-headed, not quite present, and this seemed like a state of mind that presented her with creative possibilities she should take advantage of. Alice got up, she changed into dry clothes, made a cup of coffee, and moved to her desk. Virginia evaporated as Alice went about her business, only to be replaced, when she sat down at her desk, by a shimmering, translucent, Leonard. 'Just so you know,' he said, 'I always knew my marriage would end like this. Virginia was always going to die, and I, her husband, would fail to save her.'

On 28 March, in 1941, when Virginia was fifty-eight years old, Leonard was in the garden, doing the rhododendrons. Louie was warned about Virginia's state of mind, so asked her to help with the dusting—the better to keep an eye on her mistress. Virginia helped Louie with the dusting. After chores, Louie went to the kitchen to prepare lunch and Virginia put on her galoshes and slipped out the top garden gate, the one that led to the water meadows and the Ouse. It was a bitter day and the long winter had drained all light from the sky, from the land, the plants were husks. No colour. If she'd reached out, Virginia would not have felt anything of substance, the world would have simply given way, a landscape cut out of paper. But she did not reach out. Instead she leaned down, picked up a single large stone.

Alice felt sick to her stomach when she saw Leonard come in for lunch, go up to his sitting room, find two letters on the mantlepiece, one addressed to himself, one to Vanessa. She watched as he opened the one addressed to him, could hear his heart hammering in his chest, see his hands shaking so badly he fumbled. Leonard tried to push down the fear but he already knew what had happened. He knew he should have called the specialist—he'd been going to!—but feared it would provoke her further. Space, isn't that what she had always asked of him?

I can't even write this properly. I can't read. What I want to say is I owe all the happiness of my life to you . . . I don't think any two people could have been happier than we have been.

VIRGINIA WOOLF, 28 MARCH 1941

Now Leonard is running down the stairs calling for Louie. She, in turn, calls for Percy who calls for the police while Leonard runs down to the riverbank just half a mile from the house and sees Virginia's walking stick on the riverbank.

Just there.

No, you're looking in the wrong place, look further along the bank. See how high the bank is? How far she had to jump? Can you hear the water rushing and churning below as it races down to the sea?

After the flood waters and Alice's fever receded, after writing Virginia's death, Alice felt liberated. Instead of returning to Melbourne and flying to Adelaide where she was due the following week, she decided to drive the roads that followed the course of the Murray River. She felt drawn to rivers everywhere, the water that streamed across the planet, ebbing and flowing. They reminded Alice of Virginia, whose mind always seemed to be on the possibilities of rest presented by the bed of rivers, and Leonard, whose mind was always on ways to keep Virginia from resting thereon. And so Alice snaked her way across the continent to the city where the Torrens cut its swathe.

1939

The Munich Crisis: sandbags in the streets of London, men digging trenches, gas masks fitted, the nailing up of shutters, streetlights turned off at night. The children of London were to be sent to the country—many of them to Sussex.

'Are we obliged to take some?' Virginia asked, and Leonard could only agree they were not obliged at all. Then Britain, France, others, handed Germany some bits of Czechoslovakia and the crisis was, for a time, resolved.

Virginia was relieved. Leonard was appalled. Suggested they build a third greenhouse.

'Are you to spend all our income on these monstrosities?' Virginia asked. 'I don't write books so you can build greenhouses.'

Leonard became theatrically patient as he stepped Virginia through his plans for the hundredth time, but Virginia was not having it.

'The greenhouse we have is bad enough. Grandiose. The scheme is impractical. How will we even get the workmen in if there is to be war?'

The argument escalated. The ugliness of these buildings infuriated Virginia. Virginia's obstinance infuriated Leonard. Soon they were both yelling at each other so loudly they had to separate for a few hours, before meeting again, over bowls and cigarillos, that evening.

'Do you think me beautiful?' Virginia asked, by way of apology.

'The most beautiful of women,' Leonard replied.

The argument was of no account. Soon enough war broke out, and Leonard's plans for the greenhouse were abandoned.

'I can't fight a war on two fronts,' Leonard joked to Percy. Percy didn't respond. Leonard did not take such unresponsiveness amiss. He knew that glaucoma was claiming his gardener's sight. That fact would make the most cheerful of men taciturn, and Percy had not been a cheerful man to start with.

'We'll make do with the rock garden,' Leonard said. 'And as I have said before, Virginia and I would like to pay for your operation. If such a thing is to be possible over the next few months.'

'No,' Percy said, then used the last months of his sight to help Leonard with his rock garden, and growing vegetables to support the war effort.

September (outdoors): beans, courgettes, cucumbers, onions, pumpkin, tomatoes.

October (outdoors): broad beans, winter lettuce, onions.

November: peas, onions.

December: broad beans.

January (in the greenhouse—you see, Virginia? Do you understand now?): Aubergine, cabbage, cauliflower, leek, tomato, almost nothing grew outside. Leonard could feel it, they all could, everything closing in, a darkness, the fear that came with it.

Louie's brother went to fight. So did Percy's. Vita's Nigel was commissioned in Leeds somewhere. Back and forth Leonard went, catching the train to London, saying to the politicians he knew, to everyone he knew: *I warned you, I warned you*, but even now they had little tolerance for a complaining Jew.

Petrol was rationed and bowsers shut down so that in the event of a German invasion there'd be none to steal. Food was rationed. Virginia and Leonard biked everywhere. Some days the seven miles to Charleston was more than Virginia could manage, though she tried as often as she could. Vita had petrol rations, so she made some visits, visits most welcome, full of stories of soldiers in towers, parachutists in the fields. Her butler had a breakdown. Louie thought, but did not say: who would blame him? Leonard knew what she was thinking—they had a very sympathetic relationship—and smiled ever so slightly. In fact, the three of them, Virginia, Leonard and Louie, became tighter as the months went on. If they hadn't been of a different class you would even have described them as friends. The three attended endless town hall meetings together, held meetings at Monk's House. There were political meetings. Notice of training sessions was given. Who expected war to be so busy?

How to prepare your house for blackout.

How to wear a gas mask.

How to melt down saucepans.

What to do in the event of an invasion.

They learned how to black out their windows at night, though failed to get this right so that cracks of light could often be seen escaping from the house.

February: (outdoor) carrot, parsnip, radish (greenhouse) so many things! All the things.

March: artichoke, beetroot, cabbage, carrots, chicory, cucumber, leeks, parsnip, broccoli, radishes, rhubarb, sorrel, spring greens, spring onions, watercress.

April: artichoke, beetroot, cabbage, carrots, chicory, potatoes, mushrooms, parsnips, radishes, rhubarb, sorrel, spinach, spring greens, spring onions, watercress.

They learned what to do when the bombers came. (Lie flat. Don't move. Planes fly low and machine-gun people as they run through the streets.)

By May there were artichoke, asparagus, aubergine, chillies, elderflowers, lettuce, marrow, peas, peppers, samphire and strawberries.

Belgium packed it in and left the British stranded at Dunkirk. Leonard found Louie sobbing on the stairs. She managed to get out something about her brother being stuck on a beach. Leonard made her a cup of tea and sent her home. A week later, Louie woke up and opened the door of her cottage and there the poor boy was. No shoes and half-dressed, asleep on her doorstep. He'd been brought across on a Dutch barge, she told Leonard later. A local man had made the fifteen-hour trip over and back several times, sleeping just two hours a day.

Night after night the wail of sirens rose and fell over the sleeping land, wrote Vita.

The Germans made it to Paris. Were expected to cross the Channel and perhaps land at Cuckmere Haven, not ten miles from Monk's House. Leonard became increasingly frantic. The French had given up their Jews. History always gave up its Jews. And that fool Neville Chamberlain with his TREATIES and his keeping 'OPEN THE WAY FOR AN HONOURABLE AND EQUITABLE SETTLEMENT' and his too-late realisation that Germany had no interest in peace. The man was an imbecile. Leonard knew that a Jewish leader—ha! As if that would ever be allowed, unless you counted Disraeli— would not have made that error, was aware of the perils of forgetting what English men thought of its Jews. If England fell he'd be on Sonderfahndungsliste, which meant both he and Virginia would be put into ghettos, or camps, or murdered.

Best to spend days in the vegetable garden before riding into the village, one's basket piled high with produce. Best to pick apples while they were red in the tree. Best to throw apples over fences in the hope that a child might catch one.

Planes flew overhead.

Leonard gardened.

The pear tree was heavy with pears.

Leonard gathered them.

The laughter and cries of evacuated children flowed down the streets of Rodmell, over the stone walls of Monk's House, flowed through the garden to Virginia in her writing room, trickled into the house. Virginia and Leonard became anxious for them for, in truth, they were no safer in Sussex than London.

One night as they sat in the living room, Virginia at her needle-work, Leonard hunched by the radio, Virginia turned to Leonard and said, 'I look back on our childlessness with little regret, though it caused me the greatest pain at the time, as you well remember, Leo.'

He remembered.

Virginia continued, 'However, the thought of London without children feels like the end of the world. It is one thing not to have children. It is quite another to live in a world where they are wrenched, at such a young age, from their family, to go and stay who knows where with God knows who.'

'It may be some consolation to know that not as many parents are allowing their children to be evacuated as the government would have us believe.'

'No consolation at all if they are to be showered with German bombs and blown to pieces.' Virginia was becoming quite agitated, but, for once, Leonard did not try and calm her.

'I agree, Goat, that that is no consolation at all.'

2021

On arrival in Adelaide, Alice was to attend a sparsely attended event (New Normal™!) that was being both live-streamed and recorded for those who'd bought online tickets. The event was a literary lunch, the speaker a writer, who'd won a prize. The wine was good. The prize-winning author was bracing, for she had written a novel was about men murdering women. 'It's a war,' she said. 'In my experience most men hate women.'

One of the men sitting at Alice's table muttered, 'For fuck's sake,' and poured more shiraz. A woman leaned over towards him and murmured soothingly. Alice smiled in a noncommittal way at everyone and tried to gauge the temperature of the room.

'Maybe novel writing won't even exist after the pandemic,' the prize-winning author said, making Alice sit up even straighter.

The following day, sucker for punishment that she was, Alice attended a panel on cancel culture. There was an empty chair to either side of her. The panellists turned to the recent case of a woman who'd committed suicide after years of trauma, triggered by an alleged rape and later the denials of that rape by a high-profile legal figure. Other stories were in the ether as well. A young staffer had been raped in a minister's office. There was desk wanking, online trolling, upskirting.

'Women enter a very vulnerable phase when you combine mental health issues with perimenopause,' one speaker said. 'Sexual assault can increase the risk of bipolar disorder, it can increase the risk of people moving from a depressive illness into a bipolar illness.'

Alice looked up into the leaves of the plane tree by the stage. She remembered being fourteen years old and forced onto her knees by a weedy teenage boy no older than her and certainly no stronger. Suck it, he'd said, or something to that effect, and she remembered thinking that maybe it was okay to do *this* if it made up for not wanting to do *that*. Another memory—violent, intrusive, she started to gag—she was in a room pinned against a wall by a boy who was older, taller, stronger than her. She shouted. She cried. She pulled away and made it to the door but a group of boys were on the other side of it holding it shut. The boy assaulting her suddenly looked defeated. This wasn't fun for either of them. 'Let her go,' he called to his friends. 'She's not up for it.'

Alice was pinned to her seat by the weight of the memories. Clawed at the air as if she could, even now, fight the men off. She felt hot, then cold, by turns. Her chest became tighter and tighter. Perhaps she was having an asthma attack? Had she brought her Ventolin?

'Are you all right, love?' the man a few seats away from her asked.

Love, Alice thought. LOVE?

Being married was no protection. Being almost sixty was no protection. Only the week before, a drunk bloke sat next to her thinking she wanted to talk about sex because she'd once written a sexy novel and then asked her for a fuck. She'd felt quite unhinged with rage. Hadn't slept for a week. That memory was still blooming when another sprung up, then another, and the next, she was in a veritable field of blooms.

Will it never stop? That was the question she kept asking herself. Will it ever stop?

This was the moment—not a good one—that Imaginary Leonard decided to take the empty seat to Alice's right. Same old cords. Mitz his marmoset on his shoulder. Sally the cocker spaniel on his lap. His skin looked bad. Alice felt the heat rise in her chest, up into her throat, she couldn't breathe. She turned red. Was sweating.

Imaginary Leonard, normally solicitous, didn't notice her distress.

'I have been thinking,' he said, 'about the fact Virginia's first publisher was one of the brothers she says put his hands on her when she was a small child. And of course after her breakdown of 1913, after her suicide attempt, her other brother, George offered his country estate to her to recover in. Worse, if I am to understand Virginia's diary correctly, his malefactions were far worse than Gerald's more innocent attentions. I took Virginia to that house and she did not recover.'

Alice sat in silence. Tried to focus on the panel.

'Could a brother rape his sister?' Imaginary Leonard asked.

Alice wondered if she should tell him about a recent conversation with a psychiatrist she had met at a dinner party. The psychiatrist had suggested to Alice that Virginia had Borderline Personality Disorder, most likely as a result of major trauma at a young age, and that she had been treated by the medical community in a way that would have made her symptoms worse. The psychiatrist had reminded Alice that suicide would be the typical outcome in a patient presenting with these symptoms. That is, that Virginia's choice of suicide towards the end of her life supported her insistence that she had been sexually assaulted when young. These decisions were not made lightly. They were not made for no reason.

But the Leonard who listened carefully was not the Leonard who sat beside her. The Leonard sitting beside her was needy. Anxious. Unable to figure it out for himself.

Certainly sisters could be raped. All manner of men, related or not, could hug too hard, too long, pull you onto a knee, climb into your bed, tell you that you were beautiful, as if that were a compliment. Alice found herself thinking of Doug. He had been an excellent brother. Because of him she understood that a brother might also protect his sister, when no one else would or could. When a girl couldn't look out for herself. Brothers could be, and she knew this from experience, much loved.

Ghost Virginia sat in the empty chair to Alice's left, wearing her performative skeletal attire. 'You're correct. It never stops,' she said, wiggling her bony arse so that Alice was wedged down between the two of them. Husband and wife.

'Social distancing wasn't a thing during your own pandemic?' Alice asked, but Virginia ignored her, leaned over her, touched Imaginary Leonard on the cheek and pulled Sally gently by the ear. Leonard continued to sit stiffly, ignoring Virginia, while Mitz hissed. Alice found it strange that they were fighting, given their ashes had been scattered together in the garden at Monk's House for more than fifty years now.

'To be honest with you, sisters can also be problematic,' Virginia said, and Alice, thinking of her on again off again arguments with Diana could only agree. 'But let me tell you something that brothers can do. Brothers can die,' Virginia continued. 'Brothers can be twenty-six and full of life and go travelling through Turkey with their sister and then they can go to Greece and get typhoid and die.'

'They can be blown to pieces in the war,' Leonard elaborated.

By this point Alice's ears were ringing. It was like an alarm had gone off in her head. Alice leaned as far away from Imaginary Leonard as she could.

Leonard turned to Alice. He looked anxious. Old. Long dead. He smelt of piss.

Imaginary Leonard turned to Ghost Virginia. 'I am sorry,' he said, unexpectedly, 'that I did not understand about George.'

Silence means no.

Virginia Woolf to Vita Sackville-West, 4 March 1941

'I am also sorry,' Virginia said. 'I did not fully understand what it might mean to be a Jew.' Neither apology was entirely convincing. Leonard looked angry. Virginia waved her hand to suggest she had no more time for these new-fashioned notions of respect for others and then disappeared. Imaginary Leonard followed suit.

They came. They went.

1940

Peat the Siamese yowled as the planes passed overhead. Leonard learned to identify different planes in his sleep: the regular beat of the English engines, the waves of rhythm emanating from the German Messerschmitts. The wail the throb the waves the searchlights shooting up into the sky, criss-crossing each other, shooting behind and through clouds. His gut churned. If he and Virginia were taken, who would tend the garden? Could Percy be trusted in the matter? The man was almost blind now. Who would care for Sally? Or Peat? Perhaps they could be put in the car with them? The exhaust could take them all out.

Leonard and Virginia still played bowls most evenings, facing south, vigilant. If the planes came over, they threw themselves on the ground and crawled to the cover of elms, flung themselves into garden beds; faces drilled into the dirt; gritted their teeth against the soil.

'We are too old to be carrying on like worms,' Virginia said, on one such night.

They saw a flaming plane spiralling into the water meadows near the Ouse. It was not uncommon for Messerschmitts and Spitfires to fall to the ground, smoke pluming skywards as they did so. As the smoke cleared, they saw a parachute floating slowly down before landing close to the burning wreckage. The two of them loped through the watery fields towards the wreckage, but the man, burnt, almost drowned, began to run in the direction of Germany. Leonard remembered the disease-ridden bullock running frantically—here, there—trying to make it home to die.

Villagers raced towards the man—or was he a boy?—and surrounded him. There was a thud as he was felled with a single stone to the temple. Leonard and Virginia stood in shock for a moment, then walked back towards the house and through the village. They caught glimpses of villagers in gas masks, slipping through the darkness. The atmosphere was surreal, not unlike a Poe story, a Dali, or attending one of Vanessa's debauches a wartime ago.

Virginia remained stoic, cheerful even, but seemed to be detaching in some way. Leonard could feel her slipping away from him, but what could they do? They were all, the lot of them, slipping away from each other.

On one particularly cold evening, bombers crossed Beachy Head, that glorious glowing series of chalk cliffs that cut straight down from land to sea. Flew so low the swastikas on their fuselage could be seen. The noise of them filled the body entirely, filling it with dread. Leonard put Mahler on the gramophone, as loud as it would go, to cover the sound. There was no smothering it, but the strangeness of the music—the whip, the cowbells, the deep bells, the hammer—absorbed the attention.

Virginia hovered close. Picked books up. Let them drop. Then she said something to Leonard about the privy, though he did not hear it, then slipped out the front door, running into the now-familiar darkness. Half an hour later Leonard raised his head to an empty room.

'Virginia?'

Leonard found his wife standing in the street a mile away, in her nightgown, her arms raised to the sky. Leonard did not blame her, for the jungle inched closer and closer, tusked beasts were to be expected at any moment. He took her hand, led her back to the house. 'We don't need to panic,' he reminded her. 'We have the garage, enough petrol, a tube to attach to the exhaust.'

'Adrian has cyanide. So do the Nicolsons. Which do you think would be the better way to go?' Virginia wondered, not for the first time.

A full moon slipped out from behind the clouds and the village lit up in high relief. Everything looked cold. Hard. Her bare feet turned blue.

'Cyanide is surer. Adrian is looking into it,' Leonard tried to sound optimistic.

'Karin probably wants to keep it all for herself. Dreadful woman.' Virginia was putting a brave face on things, chattering away as if they were discussing what to serve for afternoon tea. 'Vita tells me the Queen herself sleeps with it by her bed. In case.'

'What if only one of us were to die?' Leonard asked. 'You'd live without me more easily than I'd live without you.'

'That is not so,' Virginia pressed herself into Leonard's bones. Then it began to rain and the bombs began to drop once more. Not directly overhead but still—too close for comfort.

They broke into a trot.

'We're almost home,' Leonard said.

'I don't want to live without you,' Virginia said, her breath coming short and sharp, 'but more to the point, I don't want to die.'

When they got home the fire had gone out and the house was cold and damp. Virginia no longer had a room of her own. Boxes of manuscripts, books and type filled the living room, the hallways, the kitchen, the bathroom. There was a small printing press. Virginia fell over an old jug and Leonard righted her.

'It smells of cat's piss,' she said, taking care to avoid a tin plate of cat food that was jammed against a box.

It was a death trap really. An open fire. Boxes of paper all round.

Leonard rebuilt the fire. 'Sit,' he said. Virginia sat. Rubbed her bony old knees.

Leonard went to the kitchen and returned holding out an egg that Louie had boiled for them earlier that day.

'My mind tries to comprehend the road Hitler is trying to take us down,' she said, 'but keeps shying away.' As she spoke she gently tapped her egg on the side of the chair. Peat had fallen asleep on her feet despite the steady stream of eggshell chips that were falling into her fur.

Tap.

peel.

Tap.

peel.

Tap.

peel.

2021

The world grew smaller and meaner. The only thing being shared globally seemed to be carbon emissions and conspiracy theories. Friendships fell away. Others grew stronger. People learned the art of picking up where they left off a week or a month or three months after their conversations were interrupted mid-sentence by news of another lockdown.

Vaccination Hesitancy? Alice, otherwise known as @alicelikescats tweeted. *Governance Hesitancy more like.*

Alice soon regretted expending her energy in the world of free-floating anxiety known as social media. Who gave a shit about her hot take in an ever-expanding galaxy of hot takes? Especially when others' hot takes had more historical weight and urgency behind them.

You brought plague with you in 1788. Get vaccinated, and stay away from our community, was one reply. On point. And a second comment. *White people: always have been, always will be, a bunch of fuckwits.*

A year to the day after she'd sat in her car, on Zoom, admiring the autumnal light through her car's windscreen, Alice walked through the Carlton Gardens to receive her first vaccination. She heard, rather than saw, a plane fly overhead. Didn't look up. That world in which she had travelled here, there, everywhere, existed in a galaxy far, far away.

She was upset that Edith wasn't yet eligible for a vaccine. Everyone was being sliced and diced like this: organised into Bubbles and Intimate Partners and those who needed Care, and those who could give Care and those who were Essential and those who could fuck off and die.

As Alice walked through the colonnade of Dutch elms, towards that grandiose duomo, that familiar building, she felt emotional. In recent years the Royal Exhibition Building had hosted SEXPO, pet shows and car shows, though it had once been, according to Alice's iPhone, part of a movement that aimed to chart material and moral progress through displays of industry from all nations. In the late

1980s Alice had seen the AIDS quilt laid out there. Once a hospital, once a morgue, once a residence for the RAAF, now the buildings were a vaccination hub. And as Alice walked towards it, she thought to herself: this is what it is like to live inside history. Everything feels both ordinary and extraordinary at the same time.

> *History may be in a philosophical sense, a fiction, but it does not feel like*
> *that when we miss a train or somebody starts a war.*
>
> DAVID LODGE, 1977

So few people were being vaccinated before Delta arrived that Alice didn't need to book her shot, didn't even need to line up once she arrived. Instead she was pointed in the direction of a booth, then sat and talked to the nurse—his name tag read 'Omar'—for a while. Neither of them was in any hurry. He looked like a former boxer, which he possibly was. Omar and Alice discussed the building's 140th birthday plans and the fact they'd had to be pushed back. Alice liked this idea—that a building could have birthday plans. Apparently the promenade on the roof led you around the dome. The intention had been to open it again after 110 years of closure, but the date of the celebration kept being moved forward. The plan was, Alice assumed, to wait until the things were BACK TO NORMAL, but she, Omar, many others, knew there was no BACK TO. Normal was over and New Normal™ was not going well. Omar suggested the pandemic was Buddhism at work—we are being forced to live in the moment—Alice thought the last few months had been more demoralising than Zen allowed for. Omar showed Alice photos of the last trip he had taken overseas. India! They reminisced about that country a while, chatted about the time Alice caught dengue fever. Meanwhile, of course, any number of Sri Lankan refugees were trapped in a similar but far more threatening bureaucratic limbo: on bridging visas that did not allow them to work, or leave for fear of being denied re-entry. Alice and Omar got into it for quite a while before Omar remembered he was representing his government and probably needed to zip it.

'Time to get on with it,' he said.

Alice took off her shirt, took quite a complicated selfie of the needle hovering near her shoulder, got the jab, and then posted it to Instagram. It was all over before she felt a thing.

After that Omar and Alice farewelled each other, and then she went and sat among the carefully spaced out rows of chairs. She had to wait for fifteen minutes to make sure there were no ill effects. She could have slayed a cup of tea or lollypop but, it seemed, those days were gone. To while away the time, she leaned back in her chair and looked at the details of the recently repainted ceiling. It really was something. Pale greens and olives, pinks and gold. Victorian Boom Style. Byzantine. Bling. The longer she stared at it, the more the paintwork seemed to fade. The frescoes blurred and became more grimy and indistinct. The heating must have gone off because the hall, already cavernous, felt damp and cold. Alice leaned back further in her plastic chair and stretched out her legs, but it was as if she was setting back her car seat and it just kept on going. Now she was lying in a narrow iron cot with a single cotton sheet pulled over her. An electric light bulb swung overhead.

Alice hadn't heard about this side effect. Wouldn't Omar have warned her if the vaccine caused hallucinations?

Alice turned her head to one side and saw two men carrying a stretcher walking past. She peered into the darkness: many stretcher bearers, carrying what looked like human bodies, were navigating the spaces between the rows of beds.

Some white starched headgear loomed over her. It was a nurse, carrying a pot plant under each arm. She placed one of them on the table beside Alice's bed.

'To cheer you up, dear,' she said. 'For you are one of our fortunate survivors.'

'What year is it?' Alice asked.

'1919,' the nurse replied.

'Bollocks! It's 1930,' yelled out a man who looked as if he was starving, was wearing pants and a shirt so worn through it may as well have been rags. He was sitting at one of more than a dozen tables set out to feed the hundreds of people sitting around him. Having established he was living through the Great Depression, he looked at the stew on the plate in front of him then began to shovel it into his mouth.

'He's wrong,' said a softly spoken woman, dressed in an RAAF uniform, sitting on a nearby bed. She was looking down at her boots, lacing them. She looked up. 'It's 1942, luv. We're at war.'

Alice struggled to sit up and better understand what was going on, but some strange force, a weight on her chest, seemed to leave her flattened and made it hard to breathe. Perhaps it was the smoke. 'Is that a fire?' She pointed towards 1953 and an enormous aquarium. 'You need to do something about the fish!'

The nurse interrupted Alice's trip, or dream, or whatever it was. 'Look,' she said. 'You have a visitor. After you've chatted to him we'll fumigate you with steam and eucalyptus, then you can be off. He tells me he has a car waiting outside.'

Alice knew, given the difficulty of parking in Carlton, her visitor was unlikely to have brought his Lanchester. Imaginary Leonard looked tenderly down upon her. Gave an apologetic smile, then sat gingerly on the bed next to her. Social distancing was not in his vocabulary, but he was wearing a gas mask, circa WWII, to protect them both.

'I brought this.' Leonard pointed out the obvious, then held up a second mask. 'And I have brought along Virginia's. She'd be honoured if you'd take it. She's become very fond of you.' He put the mask to one side of Alice, then took her hand. Patted it.

'I don't think I've ever spoken to you of Marjorie Ritchie. Trekkie Parsons, you might know her as. I met her, of course, when she designed a cover for her sister Alice's novel, back in 1930. *Occupied Territory*. A lovely book. I had the opportunity to fall in love with her because I took to visiting Alice Ritchie in hospital as she lay dying in 1941. Cancer. It was not long after Virginia, a matter of months. I'd always been frightfully fond of Alice. She was alone, and needed help getting her affairs in order. I would sit by her hospital bed and hold her hand, much as I am holding yours. Trekkie, who was far younger than I, not to mention decidedly beautiful, was very grateful to me for visiting her sister in her final days.'

This version of Imaginary Leonard had something of Darth Vader about him. His voice rattled through the gas mask.

'Was this like Vanessa and Virginia all over again? Were you in love with two sisters?'

'I suppose I was,' Leonard said. 'But Alice was far too ill and of course Virginia had just . . . I'd rather not talk on the matter anymore. It was just your name, and this hospital, and your hand, that got me to thinking.'

Alice felt squeamish. Was Imaginary Leonard making a pass at her?

'This building makes me feel quite at home. Your pandemic really does remind me of our war effort.' Leonard looked around the hall.

'Except we're too lame to do it properly.'

'I've noticed,' he said. 'Your government does not seem to understand how serious a virus can be. Almost four hundred people died of it in just this one building! Here, in an inconsequential nation on the wrong side of the globe! In Europe the situation was so terrible that Herbert wrote a book about it.'

'Herbert?'

'You know him as HG Wells, I believe. The book was *War of the Worlds.*'

Leonard turned his gas mask towards Alice. 'Virginia's mother died of the flu—of heart failure caused by the flu. In 1916 and 1918 Virginia caught the same flu that killed Bertie. She then contracted the pandemic-form influenza at the end of 1919. Many times over in the years that followed. The flu kept coming back for years to come.'

'Why is it that you never wrote about this? Given that people you knew died. Given that Virginia was so ill. Did you not consider that it might explain her weak heart? Her fragile health?'

'Her weak heart certainly,' said Imaginary Leonard. 'But the neuralgia? Well, the thought never occurred to me, though perhaps it should have, given Maynard's stories about President Wilson. It's true that delusions were a symptom of the disease. Something to do with the severity of the fever and the swelling of the brain. But I think it's fair to say that Virginia was delusional before she became ill. And we were unaware, at the time, of quite how serious the situation was. It was just an extension of the war. All of us were at war in those years, given one thing or another. Whatever the case, it was hardly the worst thing to have happened to us.'

'A hundred million dead? More? And not the worst thing to have happened?'

'People are always dying,' Leonard said. 'Of terrible things. Every day. The flu is just one more way to die.'

1941

The bombers unloaded themselves onto the docks of East London, upon Bloomsbury. Leonard and Virginia went into London to try and save what was left of their house, but it was weeks before they were allowed to pick through the ruins. They were looking for books and paintings, diaries and jugs.

'We had too many things, anyway,' Leonard said.

'My books!' Virginia was stricken.

A stranger offered them a cup of tea from a thermos as they walked, in shock, through Mecklenburgh Square*. Leonard looked around and saw people drinking tea while perched on piles of rubble. He did not like people very much but more recently he had been struck by their kindness.

They walked past Tavistock Square.† All that was left was a pile of dust and bricks, and an old wicker chair that they had once owned sitting on top of it.

'Why did we leave that chair, dearest? I liked it.'

Leonard shrugged. He couldn't remember. He noticed that the colourful walls of what had once been their sitting room were now exposed to the air. Duncan and Vanessa's work. All those Bloomsbury houses with their repurposed spaces, hand-painted walls and stark pieces of furniture. At the time they had talked about such decorations as one small part of a larger vision, a new world. Places where they

---

* Leonard and Virginia lived in 39 Mecklenburgh Square from 1939 until it was bombed in 1940, though spent much of that time outside London, at Monk's House.
† The Woolfs lived at 52 Tavistock Square between 1924 and 1939, and ran Hogarth Press from there.

made themselves. Places where they had imagined lives not shackled to the past.

They returned to Sussex. Winter came.

It rained.

It snowed.

The snow melted.

The Ouse became swollen. Burst its banks. Water raced through the paddocks for miles around as evening fell. The setting sun came out from behind a cloud and turned the pane of water gold. Seagulls wheeled in great loops across the sky.

2021

The skies began to fill with signs and wonders. Or perhaps it was simply being away from light pollution. The stars were clearer in the ranges, and on their first night living there, Alice and Edith had stood outside their new (old) cottage and watched Venus rise. Starlight shot with red, green. Scintillating.

There were lots of reasons for the move. COVID. Alice wanted a garden of her own. Offices were on the way out and Zoom was still a thing. This allowed Alice and Edith to pursue their long-held fantasy to move to the country. At the very least it struck them as a good way to see out the pandemic, though in truth it seemed that the pandemic was more likely to see them out.

They moved in April, just as the weather was turning. In time to plant: cabbage, lettuce, rocket, spinach, carrots, celery, cauliflower, leek, turnips. The ground was harder than ideal. Bulldozing after major fires forty years earlier had churned clay and volcanic topsoil together, resulting in earth that alternated between too hard, or a bog. She bought bags of horse shit from a stall by the side of the road and spent her days digging and composting a section of paddock at the back of the cottage. She listened to music as she worked, The Avalanches' latest. It was floaty, ethereal, and, as far as she could discern, about ghosts. She felt seen.

Her next project was the planting of an orchard. The drier, hotter temperatures predicted over the decades to come made Alice's orchard a risk, not to mention the fact they were heading into winter, but she couldn't resist the idea. Bought saplings of apricot trees, nectarines, apples, mulberry—even a walnut. The trees were staked for support and protection against the wind, but would stakes be enough? Wind gusted wildly on Mt Macedon, Geboor, an extinct volcano an hour out of the city. A place famous for its nineteenth-century English gardens, though its history was far deeper than that, and the marks of stone axes could still be seen in boulders at the mountain's base if you knew where to look. Mt Macedon wasn't far from Hanging Rock, that rocky cathedral made of lava and snow gums, of time slip. Rocks and rifts had rippled and rucked through the entire region millions of years ago and now lay open to the heavens covered with lichen and moss.

Concerns about wind and associated risk analysis turned Alice's mind to other things. She had a quick conversation with Imaginary Leonard on the subject and he, most usefully, suggested a greenhouse. Edith, usually calm to the point of sainthood, was furious. Told Alice that it wasn't just going to cost a bomb to build and a bomb to run, it was going to be ugly. Alice mounted a passionate defence involving solar panels. She came up with a compromise that required hoops, PVC and rope: caterpillar tunnels. She painted a word picture for

Edith, promised shade in summer, freedom from frost and protection from pests and the wind. Edith did not believe caterpillar tunnels would manage high winds. The conversation looped back to Alice justifying her original suggestion of an actual greenhouse, one with foundations and structural integrity. This was followed by a drawn-out discussion regarding fencing, wind barriers and wind tunnels. Edith raised the rights of native animals, such as kangaroos, to graze on vegetables. Alice raised the spectre of wild deer, talked about working on the cutting edge of agriculture in difficult times, the possibility that they might succeed in expanding the climate envelope for the successful growing of vegetables. Edith resorted to sarcasm. We're farmers now? And scientists? How marvellous. I had no idea, etc. Alice was upset by Edith's tone. Mentioned her hope that her nearly finished novel would provide an injection of cash. Edith rolled her eyes. Literally. Alice had never seen such a dramatic eye roll before.

The argument was so heated that Alice became concerned some actual damage had been done. The lockdowns were taking their toll on couples all around them. There was no reason to assume they too wouldn't be collateral. Alice was reassured when Edith woke her at three the next morning. 'I want to show you something,' she said. Alice didn't ask questions. Complied. Put on her beanie and Ugg boots and stepped into the frosty night.

'Look.' Edith pointed north, high. 'A meteor shower.' Alice looked up to see stars shooting across her field of vision, glorious.

'What's that noise?' Alice wondered, for she could hear a repetitive bonking noise.

'Frogs?' Edith wondered.

Yes. Definitely frogs.

It was 25 May, the night of the blood moon, the night before another lockdown. 'Full moons meant air raids. That's one thing that working on my interminable novel has taught me,' Alice said to Sarah, who was standing beside her, in person.

It was the first time they'd been in each other's physical company for two years, and Sarah looked far older than Alice remembered. She'd grown her bob long, allowed it to go white, and pulled it back off her face into a bun, which highlighted how strained she looked. Lines had sunk deeper into her face. 'I think I would be enjoying this moment more,' Sarah said, 'if I wasn't here to enjoy a few hours of freedom before the lockdown tomorrow.'

'It's not definite, is it?' Alice asked, but Sarah just shrugged. Of course it was.

'I probably should tell you,' Sarah said, 'I'm thinking of closing the agency. There wasn't money in the work before this shit show and now . . .'

'I thought books were doing well?'

'Not the books I represent,' said Sarah. 'Or maybe I'm just depressed. Me, my writers, we're yesterday's news. The main reason though is I'm almost seventy. I want to travel.'

'A cruise, perhaps?' Alice suggested.

'Fuck off,' said Sarah. Then the two women burst out laughing. As if the publishing industry was a war they'd survived together rather than what it was: a pile of words about stuff that went in and out of fashion, that were largely ignored, but every so often changed people's lives.

Edith came out of the cottage carrying three Negronis and passed them around with due ceremony. 'Blood moon. Bloody beverage,' she said.

'Blood moons were often considered a bad omen,' Alice said. The radio that morning had told her that the Inca believed the moon turned red at these times because it was being attacked by a jaguar. Alice liked that idea.

'Do we need omens?' Edith asked. 'We're there already, right? Inside the bad.'

They were. Edith was, as usual, right.

'There's another thing,' Sarah said. 'The moon used to look bigger. It was closer to the earth. A million years ago it would have been twice as big and twice as bright. Much more menacing.'

'And in the future?' Alice asked.

Sarah described an extinguished moon. One so old that it no longer orbited a dead planet, but was still being dragged around an ancient sun, a red giant, a sun that was exhausted, was dying.

You'd have thought all this talk of end times, on a night close to freezing, before a lockdown, would have killed the mood, but no! The three women were transfixed as they watched the earth's shadow slide slowly across the moon. Alice, head craned, looked at the tiny dark red globe and imagined other people, in other centuries, leaning back as she was, seeing what she was seeing. The shadow highlighted the curve of the globe, threw the craters into relief. The darker the night became, the brighter the Milky Way; the more silver the smear of stars, the redder the moon. Alice looked at the ground for a moment, to take the pressure off her neck, but became worried she'd miss the flare of totality and lifted her head again. The moon was, by now, made up of bloody darkness wearing a halo of cold white light.

'Was there a flare?' Alice asked. 'Did I miss it?'

'I'm not sure there is going to be one this time around,' Edith said. 'Does it matter?'

It did not.

The blood moon didn't exactly cause the mouse plague, but, in Alice's mind at least, it seemed that one led to the other, and as millions and millions of mice swarmed through southern Queensland, into New South Wales and northern Victoria, Alice became concerned that the swarm would make it further south. Edith had lived through a mouse plague when she was a child. 'It's the smell that hits you first,' she told Alice. 'Dead mice. They're everywhere.' And if they were to believe what they saw on the news, which they did, that was true. There were tails sticking out of hubcaps. People being bitten in their beds, grain consumed, prisons being evacuated because the number of decomposing corpses made it unsafe to sleep or work in the buildings. Baited mice crawled into water tanks, streams and rivers to die, poisoning water supplies.

Alice tried to wrap her head around the various issues the mouse plague raised: genetic biocontrol research, pesticide use. The excess of mice was also disgusting, there was no doubt about it. It had been a recurring problem since house mice hopped off the first fleet. The only good thing about the mouse plague was the consequent owl boom. Owls. She could never get enough of them.

Early one morning, after Edith had headed to the shed, aka to work, Alice began to read *Silent Spring* and learned about the way chemicals lay in the soil, and passed through living organisms one to another, killing vegetation, sickening cattle, poisoning birds, and working *unknown harm on those who drink from once pure wells.*

Imaginary Leonard saw that Alice was reading this significant book, one that had made quite an impact on him when he had first read it. He decided to join her. This was the oldest Leonard to visit Alice yet. His hair was whiter, his frame stooped, his voice softer.

He had a newspaper with him and, with no ceremony at all, began to read from it. 'In January of last year, a worker from the Rentokil factory presented veterinarian Douglas Good with two Labrador puppies, which had died from ingestion of a suspected, but unknown, poison. One of a high yielding and well-managed herd of twenty-six Friesians, a cow has unaccountably collapsed. Three other cows died soon after, to be followed by the deaths of several more cattle over the following months. Good called in the Veterinary Investigation Officer from Wye, Kent, who, in turn, requested the services of the Biochemistry Department of the Central Veterinary Laboratory.'

'Your point?' Alice asked.

'This problem of pesticides has been with us since the war's end. Rentokil began in an apple-pulping factory. Their product was an apple spray. Yet I do not need poison to grow good apples. Dozens of dogs and cats have been poisoned in Wales. Have you ever lost a dog to poisoning? Shooting them is the only kindness one can offer. Some of the dogs died because they were fed dead cows to see what the effect was. The poison, once ingested, goes everywhere. From the river to the soil to the grass and the cows. The paper even has a cartoon,' Leonard pushed the paper across the table to Alice. Pointed to a cartoon of two men standing over a dead dog. It wasn't funny.

Alice turned on the radio. 'Let's listen,' she said. Leonard took up his position. A series of experts on breakfast radio explained why the New South Wales government should be allowed 5000 litres of bromadiolone to poison the mice. The two of them leaned in closer to listen to conversations that had been raging since the 1960s, since the 1950s and the 1940s.

Alice had turned, during the course of the pandemic, into the kind of woman who stood, in a flannel nightshirt and Ugg boots, yelling at the radio. All rage and no arse (it happens), hands on hips, shouting into thin air. Her hair, once brown, had turned grey. Leonard, similarly incensed, slapped his thighs in exasperation.

'It is as if eighty years of debate has never happened,' Alice shouted. 'Billions of animals died only a year ago. Native animals have been left in extremis. The owl boom is going to turn into owl carnage.'

'I have been talking about the dangers of pesticides ever since the days of the Rodmell Horticultural Society,' Leonard shouted back. 'It was the war that started it. We needed to produce more food. But these chemicals are not the answer. I am treated as a crank but I am not. And these dead dogs, these dead cattle, are the proof.' He spoke as if the deaths of the bullocks in Ceylon in 1910, the cattle of England in 1961, were still present to him. As if he were not also dead. He turned to Alice, looked tired. Drawn. He asked: 'Have you considered a beehive?'

Alice had written about cyclones and trees and flooding and plague and dying koalas. But interestingly, as she pointed out to Edith, after a storm had been raging for several hours, and after an olive tree fell onto the bedroom window, she had never before been in a cyclone, albeit a small one. So from that perspective, a tree falling on the cottage followed by days without power was a useful experience. The early decades of the twenty-first century were proving to be quite something. Not to mention giving Alice the pleasure of being able to use the word 'tempest' without any exaggeration whatsoever.

'What a time to be alive!' the women joked, nervously, before moving to see out the rest of the long dark night away from the windows. FluffyShark joined them under the doona and the three of them huddled together, hoping the world wasn't going to end.

Which it didn't. In fact, it turned out that despite the fallen tree and two days without power—no heating, stove, hot water or wifi—Alice and Edith had got out of things lightly. They considered, briefly, driving to the city to get warm and buy a cup of coffee, before remembering it was all a moot point. They were locked down, locked out, roads were blocked, travel limited, proof of addresses needed, couldn't visit anyone, no one could visit them and, perhaps worst of all, neither woman had any way of charging their iPhone-MacAir-iPods.

'Do you think this is how it is now?' Alice asked Edith, and yes, Edith agreed. This is how it was now. They put on their raincoats and made sure that the newly planted fruit trees had survived (some had), then tried to pick as many black olives from the prostrate tree as they could before the cockatoos got to them.

After the tempest receded, sometime after lunch, they went for a walk along the road up the mountain, which was zig-zagged with the trunks of mountain ash and manna gum that had fallen root-first, or, worse, snapped somewhere in the middle of the trunk. Most people wouldn't have power for days. Others, according to the news, would be waiting for months. Houses were smashed. Cars were smashed. Tens, hundreds, thousands of trees were down, all across the state. Lighting a fire was the only way to stay warm, which struck Alice as ironic given that eighteen months ago the smell of burning wood had smelt of nothing so much as: death.

Polar blast. A once-in-forty-year storm. A statement that, when repeated on breakfast radio, led to Alice yelling out loud, 'Once-in-forty-year storm *bullshit*,' after which she felt slightly better, before getting back into bed to keep warm, and getting on with her book. It was coming together now. She was sure of it.

1941

My Darling, I have just had the most awful shock . . . He says . . . she was
terrified of going mad again. He says 'It was, I suppose, the strain of the
war and of finishing her book and she could not rest or eat.' Why, oh why,
did he leave her alone?

VITA SACKVILLE-WEST TO HAROLD NICOLSON, 31 MARCH 1941

Vanessa told Vita that Leonard wanted to see her. Vita did not want
to see Leonard, but she went to Monk's House, whereupon Leonard
made her a cup of tea and led her to the sitting room. Virginia's
needlework lay on the chair, her coloured wools hung upon their
rack. There was her thimble, sitting on the table. Her scribbling
block. And when Vita looked out through the window, she had a
view of the river that had taken her love, her friend.

'I don't like you being here, alone,' Vita said.

'I have no choice,' Leonard replied, and Vita saw that this was true.

He joined Vita by the window, where she looked out across the
water meadows. They stood there in deep affection—well, hers for
him. Leonard, at this point, was frozen. When he thawed, relations
would become less cordial.

'Do you know how the meadows work?' he said to Vita, for they
had been on his mind. 'Some of them are a thousand years old.'

'Surely not these ones?' Vita knew all about water meadows but
she let him explain them to her once more. Leonard was fond of
lecturing people on subjects on which he had expertise, and even
those he did not.

'I became interested in irrigation when I was in Ceylon, but the
way these meadows work is quite different. These are known as
bedwork systems and they are most likely from the early eighteenth

century. They're suited to wide alluvial valleys and flood plains, and the chalk-land rivers of southern England. The channels act to ensure the grass becomes covered with a flowing film of water, which then delivers nutrients, warms the soil, and encourages growth. This is known as floating downwards. If the meadow floats upwards—that is, the water sits stagnant—the grass might drown. The men who had this skill, the ones that understood water, who made the water float down, not up, were known as drowners. And that's what I am, don't you think?' he said, turning to Vita, his face drawn into a despair so sharp she flinched. 'I should have watched more carefully. You understood what Vanessa and I have always known. Vigilance was required at all times. With the war, the bombs, the possible invasion. I lost sight of her, perhaps.'

'Virginia could swim.'

'She could,' Leonard said.

'Vanessa mentioned a hat? That it was well made. That it would have stayed on her head. Gone down with her.'

'It is true,' Leonard said, 'that we have not found the hat.'

Leonard's voice became harder to hear, for planes were streaming overhead, as they always were. It was relentless, this war, and had years to go. The thuds, the bangs, the pops, the crashes, the bodies, the whir of engines, the silence.

'We can only hope,' Vita said, 'the body is carried out to sea. That it is never found.'

'The river is tidal,' Leonard said. 'It's possible I suppose.'

But, of course, two weeks later Virginia Woolf's body was found, and Leonard saw what remained of his wife a final time.

VI
DAYS OF MIRACLES AND WONDER

2021

Alice walked through a grove of oaks. A hawthorn hedge lined the edge of the property; some crabapples had been planted along a creek. Young lemon-scented gums and angophora were dotted around, a contrast to the sterner Stone Pine and cypress that had been planted a hundred or more years ago: survivors of the fire that had incinerated the landscape in 1983.

The storm had swept down an eclipse of bogong moths. They lived short and demanding lives and once clustered in their millions, but their numbers had dwindled precipitously. This year, they were back, albeit in modest numbers. Alice was keen to see them.

The moon was a bright crescent you could hang a hat on, its cold light picking out the muted smudge of greys and browns of a bogong moth. Its long fat body sat lightly on the earth. Alice picked it up carefully, making sure not to knock the dusty scales from its delicate wings, and put the moth high on the trunk of a tree. Wondered how it would find its way home. Once clouds of the moths had set off at dusk, night after night, flew high into the mountains, how did they guide themselves? Did they use the stars? Would they live long enough to right their course or did the high winds and storms condemn them to death before they reached their destination?

The moth fluttered its wings ever so slightly as if in thanks. Alice heard the rush of them as it lifted up and off the tree to make its way deeper into the forest, out of her reach. There was such a rustle it seemed as if it was not one moth, but dozens of them, lifting up around her.

At just that moment a stag towering out of sight, between the oaks and a stand of cypress, made a break for it and ran across the open grassland, a thread of moonlight catching its horns. Alice's heart raced. She knew that deer had become pests, but she'd never seen them before; not like this, anyway. The foxes—large, with lush long tails and golden eyes—were at home too. Alice couldn't see them on this evening but knew they moved along the fence line up to her left where she often saw them at dawn: russet red against the silvery frost. The scene was so bucolic, so English, that Alice could have been walking through Kew Gardens, which is, perhaps, why Imaginary Leonard joined her, looking the age he was when he'd lived in Richmond.

'I do believe I have seen a fern from this place,' Imaginary Leonard said, 'growing in the greenhouse at Kew. Collected some years before I was born. You are lucky to live here. This is very much the land-scape Bertie tried to cultivate in the botanic gardens of Kandy. The silhouette of these hills adds to the effect.'

'We call them mountains.'

'Mountains then,' Imaginary Leonard said mildly, dissing the Australian landscape as only the English could. 'And am I right in thinking that your forebears settled here in 1910?'

'Apparently,' Alice said. 'The property is no longer in the family.'

'I have come to discuss the future of the novel with you,' Imaginary Leonard said, 'as well as the future of your novel. You are aware, yes, that the kind of novel you have been trying to write is a product of our imperial culture? Virginia had the skills to try and present a new vision in her work, and I have been shocked to learn that literary fashion has returned to the Victorian model—after all we did to break free of it.'

'I'm not sure I'm a novelist,' Alice said. 'Perhaps you could have been? *The Village in the Jungle* really is remarkable.'

Imaginary Leonard shrugged. 'A fine book, maybe, but barely a novel.'

Alice was keen to know more, but Leonard held up his hand as if to shush her. Had stopped in his tracks; his face full of wonder. 'Is that a . . . kangaroo? Virginia loved kangaroos. Used to talk of creeping into their pouches. I have seen them at the London Zoo but I had no idea they would be so . . .' He seemed more ethereal than he had on previous visitations. His long bony fingers were translucent, as if he were lit from within, spun out of moonlight. Alice could almost see through him.

Leonard turned to Alice and looked directly at her. His eyes were not kindly, as they had been in previous imaginings; they glowed with a cold white light. He had no pupils.

'To business: one of the reasons I joined you tonight is because Virginia often used to go moth hunting. We are both of us touched that you have taken such an interest in moths.'

'We?' Alice asked.

'For some decades after my death we did not speak. There were complicated supernatural reasons for this, but also, if I am to be honest, we were unresolved about some private matters.'

'Didn't Virginia's ashes live under the elm named for her at Monk's House? And your ashes next to her, if not scattered close by? Did that not make communication easier?' Alice asked.

'Reconstitution is easier if you have not been incinerated, but as I say, there was more to it than that.'

Leonard stepped out from under the canopy so he could see the stars more clearly. 'I have missed that constellation,' he said, pointing at the Southern Cross. 'Ceylon sits very close to the equator. We had that constellation there. I would, by the way, like to see your orchard, but I fear it will distract me from my mission. I have, I must say, found our conversations delightful, but the time has come for them to end. I won't be back,' Leonard said, 'and there is something I've been meaning to mention to you. Have you read Virginia's first novel, *The Voyage Out?*'

'A long time ago,' Alice said.

'In that novel, Terence Hewet dreams of writing a novel of his own, a novel "about Silence . . . the things people don't say". Virginia and I discussed this advice, and she has sent me as our emissary. Maybe you should say less? Or just—and please forgive me for saying this—stop? As much as I've enjoyed the attention, this novel, it doesn't matter. We don't matter. Nothing really does.'

Alice hoped he might follow up that advice with a fatherly pat on the arm. But no. They stood together a few minutes, basking in the looming shadows of the mob that lived on the land. Big Boy, as Alice called him, was, as ever, standing tall. Alert to danger. One of the smaller kangaroos moved closer to them. Alice had noticed her. A tiny thing. Barely out of the pouch.

The joey skittered away as two of the adolescents began to box; cuffing each other around the ears; rearing up, kicking out. They opened their throats and flung their heads back. Made guttural grunting sounds.

'All that life. That fight. Glorious,' Imaginary Leonard said.

'Look.' Alice gestured at the mother standing at the edge of the group. They could just discern the outline of the joey peeking out of her pouch.

'Oh my,' Imaginary Leonard said. 'Oh m—'

Alice didn't interrogate the sudden silence that fell. She leaned down to pick up her pandemic kitten, now a fat cat, who seemed to materialise just as Leonard evaporated. Alice flung FluffyShark over her shoulder for the walk home. His large white paws perched firmly as he stared intensely at the kangaroos, the trees.

As they approached the house Alice saw the light she'd left on to guide her way was shining so brightly that it had confused the moths. There were hundreds of them, crashing into the bulb, throwing themselves against the windows in search of the light. She hadn't needed to leave the house to see them all, and it seemed by leaving it she had lured them towards death.

'I'm sorry!' Alice shouted into the night. 'I'm sorry!' Then she gripped the now squirming FluffyShark and dashed into the house. Turned off the lights in the hope that not too much damage had been done.

> *One could only watch the extraordinary efforts made by those tiny legs against an oncoming doom which could, had it chosen, have submerged an entire city, not merely a city, but masses of human beings; nothing, I knew, had any chance against death. Nevertheless after a pause of exhaustion the legs fluttered again. It was superb this last protest, and so frantic that he succeeded at last in righting himself. One's sympathies, of course, were all on the side of life.*
>
> VIRGINIA WOOLF, 1942

1942–1950s

When alive, Virginia had been uncertain as to what was worse. Pints of milk thickened with beef stock and malt, stomach pumps, or American journalists lurking in the gardens at Monk's House and then writing an article full of intimate assumptions that seemed to characterise her as a mad woman. After due consideration she scrawled a final wish in the margins of one of her suicide notes—'Will you destroy all my papers'—and after due consideration Leonard ignored that wish.

Leonard had believed that Virginia's death would not be survivable. But he found that it was. Most things were. There were societies to join: Royal Horticultural, Ancient Monument, the National Cactus and Succulents, the National Trust, the British Pteridological Association, Zoological Society of London—quit over an argument concerning the definitions of distances and the ways a crow might fly—Sussex Beekeepers' Association, Sussex County Cricket Club. He joined the India Club and the Athenaeum, was a Fellow of the Royal Society of Arts and the Royal Society of Literature, the Council of the Fawcett Library Trust and the Society of Authors. Closer to home he was president of the Monday Literary Club of Lewes, Clerk of the Parish Council of Rodmell and both founder and President of the Rodmell Horticultural Society. There was Virginia's estate to manage, and collections of her work to publish: essays, diaries, letters. (Best though, to edit, so as to save some from the sharpness of her pen.)

There was endless correspondence to attend to: the press, critics, friends, family, and an increasing number of Virginia's fans who began to flock to him. Virginia was being made, and remade, over and over. Modernist, lesbian, feminist, snob, anti-Semite, pacifist, a woman with views so outmoded she might as well be declared extinct. A woman so visionary in her understanding she was a revolutionary. Leonard was, as he always had been, diligent about replying to letters.

Bella sent condolences, from a castle in West Africa. Words failed her. Her heart ached. She was distressed at the news. She'd attempted sleep in her room next to dungeons, but been kept awake by the sound of waves pounding relentlessly at the base of the castle walls. He and Virginia had had, she suggested, one of the most perfect companionships that ever existed. If not for the war she would come to his side once more.

His brothers were less forgiving, accused him of selling his wife's tragedy for gold. And then there was everyone else.

No, Virginia did not kill herself because she was a coward.

Yes, I sleep well. I eat well. Fish, macaroni, fresh eggs, vegetables I have grown, honey from the bees I have raised.

No, Bloomsbury was not a group of like-minded people who were hopelessly out of touch with the modern world.

Yes, it is true that Virginia and I did not get on well with her brother, your father Adrian, and it pains me that was so.

No, I do not believe in an afterlife, you sanctimonious arrogant, complacent, uncharitable, religious fool.

Yes, it is wrong to shoot dogs just because they are fat and old— unless, that is, you also intend to shoot fat old humans.

No, Virginia was not an unpopular writer. Would you like to see her sales figures?

In truth, Virginia was a happy person, extremely amusing and frequently gay.

I would rather that you, Miss Evangeline, desist from sending me letters every day. I would rather you desist from flying from

Los Angeles to London, getting in a cab, putting plants on my door-step and then returning home to the United States. It is . . . unsettling.

No, you may not read Virginia's diaries.

No, you do not have my permission to write Virginia's biography.

No, she did not care overly for Freud.

William, is it true that I predicted the outbreak of WWII, almost to the day? I must say it doesn't surprise me.

TS Eliot was anti-Semitic, but wasn't everyone?

No, Vita, you may not publish the letters between my wife and yourself. No, I don't know when I will publish my wife's letters, her observations were sharp and will cause others pain.

No.

No.

Yes, I agree that letters and diaries do not reflect some absolute truth. We are all many people within one and we present different faces to different people. We are, in that, not unlike the Hindu Gods.

Yes, Virginia did read Tolstoy.

Yes, Lytton Strachey's homosexuality was irrelevant to our friendship.

Yes, some things are private.

I agree, Baroness, that it is not proper to discuss the use of chloro-form snorting at orgies, among aristocrats.

Yes, you may call your play *Who's Afraid of Virginia Woolf?*

Yes, I will leave all Virginia's affairs to you and your sister, for there are not many people I trust.

Yes—confided, in private—Virginia was a lesbian.

And, to a much younger married woman with pale blue eyes and light brown hair, a woman who tucked that hair up into her motor-cycle helmet before riding to a secret department in the war office every day, he wrote:

I wish you were with me to see the pond covered with the bloodred & the cream waterlilies & bright blue sky, reflected in it.

LEONARD WOOLF TO TREKKIE PARSONS, 1943

The two never discussed their relationship publicly. Nor did they share a bed: Leonard had prostate problems and Tiger—for that is what Leonard called her—remained loyal to her husband. However, it was not just gardening that Leonard wanted to share, but his life. He suggested they bring their Siamese cats together to mate; he told her he loved her despite the fact she was married, that he wanted to kiss her toes.

From 1951 Monk's House was open from time to time as part of the National Garden Scheme. Leonard planted charming crocuses and daffodils to misdirect those wandering the gardens. He planted a mulberry and a walnut which, had Virginia been alive, she would have objected to on the grounds they'd block the view of the water meadows from her writing room. Percy had gone blind and resigned. No Virginia and no Percy meant Leonard had two fewer people to argue with about the garden, but nonetheless he waited some ten years before he revived his plans to build another greenhouse or conservatory. Whatever he called it, Virginia would have hated it. When done, the glass lean-to sat under his balcony in hedgehog tower, tucked along the sides of the house, ruining its rustic lines. Leonard didn't care. His early work in that structure was tentative. He planted orchids, which, while larger, more colourful, and possibly more crass than those that preferred cool weather, were relatively respectable. It was not long, however, before he picked up the pace. There was the matter of cacti, which, over the years, became increasingly obscene with their great fleshy slabs, needles like spines and flamboyant blooms. There were great leafless trees that looked like a tangle of spider's legs—smooth, bright green, strangely jointed. When a limb snapped, a milky, viscous fluid flowed out. Vines twined up the trunks of larger plants until they were pushing, along with the tree canopy, a great green mass at the roof, threatening to smash through the glass and bring the winter rushing in to lay waste to the tropical profusion. But, though the glass bulged and buckled, it held. Down below a thorny tangle sprung up through the floor that threatened to attack all who entered.

Virginia never really left him during these years. She ran a cool eye over his letters and reviews. Offered comments on the books he was reading. Chided him from time to time. Many an evening he would be, say, picking apples, and he'd swear that he could see her, coming out of her studio, walking through her garden to join him, cheroot in hand, before stalking off into the mist when she saw Trekkie, or caught a glimpse of the conservatory. As for the maple, it filled her with rage. Leonard would talk to no one about this phenomenon. He had no evidence for it, was not sentimental, and certainly did not believe in ghosts. It was simply some human weakness that was bothering him. If he ignored her, it would go away.

> *Whatever hour you woke there was a door shutting. From room to room they went, hand in hand, lifting here, opening there, making sure—a ghostly couple. 'Here we left it,' she said. And he added, 'Oh, but here too!' 'It's upstairs,' she murmured. 'And in the garden,' he whispered 'Quietly,' they said, 'or we shall wake them.'*
>
> VIRGINIA WOOLF, 1921

Leonard's arrangement with Trekkie meant that he had the weekdays, and her husband, a publisher in London, the weekends.

It served them both well, but Trekkie was as frustrated with the conservatory as Virginia would have been. Leonard began to fill the small glass rectangle of a room with flora indigenous to Kandy: Bulu, Nawa, Hora, Telambu, Walu Kina. Trekkie remonstrated that these plants would destroy the structure—some of them could grow to thirty metres—but Leonard claimed it was fine, and it seemed it was, though, as Trekkie couldn't see through the undergrowth, she had no idea if the larger rainforest trees had even survived.

Some days they would garden together. Other days Trekkie would go to her painting studio—where Virginia once wrote—and then at sundown would stand by the conservatory door, a G&T in hand, calling to Leonard. She had introduced drinking into their daily schedule, and Leonard took to this with some enthusiasm. Drinking with Virginia had required him to be vigilant. Drinking with Trekkie did not.

Despite the smallness of the space, she often couldn't see him, often couldn't even hear him. She could, though, hear distant clicks, slithers and rustlings, and once, she swore, the shrieks of monkeys. It seemed Leonard had developed the ability to move through that thorny, leafy place silent and unscathed.

Leonard was, in short, an ill-tempered, old and pedantic man, and not everyone understood why a woman as beautiful, kind and warm as Trekkie spent so much time with him, especially as she already had a husband, albeit one who had a mistress. Others didn't understand why Leonard had taken up with a woman less complicated, less brilliant than Virginia, but they misunderstood him entirely, for Leonard was nothing but grateful for the uncomplicated love and care that she provided him for more than twenty years. Their friendship. Those years were such a gift. Trekkie was such a gift.

1960

An old man was curled up on a planter's lounge. A large hat lay over his head, covering his face. He wore a rumpled white shirt that was half tucked, half hanging out of loose cotton pants. A cup of tea and plate of short eats sat, untouched, on a small table beside him.

The man's secretary hovered a short distance away. She remonstrated with their driver. 'He's exhausted,' she said. 'We must leave now.'

'But Mr Fernando was very clear. The itinerary, also, is very clear.' The driver held up a timetable. 'It says, "We are all very excited to meet Mr Leonard Woolf".'

Two young civil servants sat on the terrace close by, drinking tea. They weren't excited, but they were on the itinerary.

The civil servants, named Mr Senaratne and Mr Jayaweera, looked around. A rambunctious family, including several tiny and badly behaved children, were yelling at each over fish puffs. The sleeping planter, a dried-out husk of a man, who looked somewhat like the carapace of large praying mantis, had left. It's possible they made a joke at his expense. The country was littered with old white people who had not left in 1948, as they should have, had been lulled, perhaps, by the myth. Ceylon: a model colony, gained independence peacefully, a member of the British Commonwealth.

Time was passing. The men called the keeper of the rest house over. Did he know if Mr Woolf had arrived? Had he, perhaps, left a message cancelling his visit?

'You did not see the little old gentleman sleeping on the hansi putuwa when you walked in? He has just left. This very minute.' The keeper pointed towards the dust on the road. Dust that rose in the wake of a car that was now out of sight.

Ah.

Mr Senaratne and Mr Jayaweera asked for the bill, got in their car, and sped the twenty miles up to Bandarawela in pursuit of the illustrious Leonard. Let the record books show they caught up with him and dined with him that evening. Let the blogposts suggest they were underwhelmed.

Leonard and Trekkie had arrived at Ratmalana Airport a week earlier, whereupon they had been met by the Permanent Secretary in the Ministry of Industries, Home & Cultural Affairs, Mr Sheldon Fernando. Mr Fernando swept them up, showered them with care, and whipped them into a whirlwind of ceremonies. They met the governor-general, the prime minister, countless dignitaries. Everyone went out of their way to praise not just Leonard but all administrators of his ilk—those from the beginning of the century. It was during the next generation, Leonard was informed, that things had gone wrong.

Leonard had not expected such kindness, and allowed himself to forget, over the weeks of his trip, that colonial administrators were unpopular, unfair, severe and ignorant. Riots, of increasing frequency and intensity, had erupted in the years since Leonard had left, and the British government made internal tensions worse. The most recent of these had been only two years ago: the 1958 riots which had done the British government untold reputational damage. There was the widespread murder of Tamil men, and rape of women. A priest was burnt alive. The Tamils retaliated. The British government did not intervene to stop the attacks and punished those who did: security forces were given permission to shoot rioters if necessary. Almost every senior Tamil politician was arrested. More than 10,000 Tamil refugees poured into camps down south. In June the government moved refugees from those camps back north, to Jaffna. Created a ghetto.

2021

Alice was working on her new lap desk, in her pyjamas, under the doona. It was extremely cold. FluffyShark was snuggled up beside her, his chin snug against her computer. The shed was too cold to work in so Edith now worked in the cottage and occasionally arrived in the bedroom bearing cups of tea. They wore headphones so as not to be distracted by the sound of each other working. The two women had been working in the same space, on and off, for more than a year now. It was lucky that they loved each other. A miracle, in fact.

'Didn't Virginia Woolf write in bed on cold mornings?' Edith asked.

'It was the secret to her genius,' Alice replied, as if joking, though she secretly hoped her writing might, through dint of circumstance, turn into a quality comparable to Virginia's. 'I'm stuck,' Alice said. 'On the scene I've put off writing for ten years.'

'Is it traumatic?'

'Not even.'

The wives returned to their respective computers. Alice returned to wondering why Leonard Woolf in Ceylon in 1960 was so impossible. Was it because the Colombo Alice had visited in the early 2000s was a land of war, of cars, of air-conditioning? Was Colombo then as Michael Ondaatje had described? The louvres all being opened and a breeze sweeping through the city as evening fell? Did Leonard and Trekkie sit on the chequerboard terrace of the Galle Face Hotel, under a palm tree at the end of hot days? She saw in her mind's eye the railway track that Leonard and Trekkie would have seen if they'd sat in the same spot she had. It traced the coastline, north to south, straight as an arrow, and had become the site of the largest single rail disaster when the tsunami hit in 2004. This detail, of course, was not relevant when writing a scene set in Colombo in 1960, but a detail that kept intruding nonetheless.

Alice went through the copious notes she'd written years ago to see if they'd help. It seemed that younger Alice had established that on Leonard's return to Ceylon in 1960:

1. He spoke very softly when he was interviewed.
2. He would glance at his 'private secretary, Mrs Parsons' when he answered questions as if she might be able to help him find the answer.
3. Was in Ceylon for three weeks and visited all his old haunts, including Jaffna, Kandy and Hambantota.
4. He met the prime minister and other dignitaries and was toured around the country.
5. He became close to a senior civil servant, Mr Shelton Fernando. Fernando joined the Ceylon Administrative Service in 1950 and went on to hold many senior positions including Assistant Land Commissioner, Deputy Director of Plan Implementation, Commissioner of National Housing and finally serving the Public Service Commission of the Western Province. (Mr Fernando's children remember parties with music and dancing. They remember living in outstations around Ceylon. They remember that their

father respected people regardless of race, religion, caste or social standing. They remembered that their home was run like his office: they had a daily timetable that was always followed.)

6. Bella Woolf/Southorn died at the end of 1960. After her death, Leonard fulfilled her wish that that he speak at the Association of Ceylon Women.

7. 'Standing under the great trees and among the ruins of the ancient city of Polonnaruwa, which . . . Nazis.'

dot

dot

dot, Nazis?

Clearly, Alice was in trouble. She had not intended, back when she began her project to write about the older Leonard. Entire boxes of documents had remained unopened when she was at the University of Sussex. Now that Australia had reverted to type—a prison, people locked up, people locked out—she wouldn't be getting back to Sussex any time soon. She googled the archives at the University of Sussex, where she had spent time more than a decade ago and found a list of documents she'd not asked to see during her time there:

1. A hundred letters from Shelton Fernando and Leonard's replies, sent between 1960 and the time of Leonard's death. These letters discussed Leonard's career in Ceylon, his work in the decades since on behalf of Ceylon, his writings on Ceylon, and included a discussion between them of the attacks made on him in the Ceylon papers in the 1960s. They also, from time to time, discussed personal matters.

2. Correspondence with others met on the trip, about the trip.

3. Twenty-five letters regarding arrangements for the trip in 1960, including itinerary, timetables, bills, receipts etc.
4. Correspondence with the *Ceylon Historical Journal* about their publication of Leonard's Ceylon diaries.

Having had access to such documents would have allowed Alice to write this important sequence of the novel far more vividly. As it was she was compelled to trawl her memory, blog posts and old newspaper articles, and if it hadn't been for the pandemic, Alice would have leapt on a plane and returned to Sussex. But those days were over. So many of her years of travel already seemed remote. Places that were a long way away and been visited a long time ago. Maybe she'd dreamed these places? Maybe she'd made them up?

Alice turned to her emails in the hope of distraction. There was one from a friend, a writer, who was writing an oratorio about a gay academic who'd been thrown into the Torrens by a group of men later identified as police officers. The academic drowned. The police officers were tried for, but acquitted of, murder. It was going to premier next year, apparently. Some days Alice found it hard to believe there was going to be a next year, let alone feel herself able to imagine what kind of year it was going to be. She moved on to a morning exchange on the sibling WhatsApp group in which she used the phrase 'the Before Times'. Diana and Doug both informed her they'd been using the phrase for *weeks*. Everyone had. Clearly, she was out of touch.

Alice turned to a different window of her computer, refined her search terms, and found an interview Leonard did with Michael Roberts in 1965. Roberts was a self-described thuppahi (of mixed ethnicity), an academic who trained in social sciences at Peradeniya

University and ended up in the Department of Anthropology at the University of Adelaide. (Adelaide. Again. Did Michael Roberts live by the Torrens?)

Alice found reference to a correspondence between the two men held at the University of Sussex, but did not know where the interview had been conducted, and as Imaginary Leonard no longer dropped by, he could not enlighten her. Alice liked to imagine that the interview took place in a hill station by a fire, though that had occurred some years after Leonard's visit. Michael Roberts was still alive. She could email him and asked where he had interviewed Leonard Woolf. She needed to know if she was going to tease the scene out into fiction. She did not, however, email Michael Roberts.

Other observations included in Roberts' papers were that Woolf was smart. He was reasonable. He did not suffer fools. He came across as arrogant but that was, perhaps, because he was plain-speaking. Woolf was an impressive, possibly exceptional, man. A fair man.

Alice was saved from this latest rabbit hole by a phone call. These days phones meant: therapist or Sarah. At times the two were indistinguishable.

'So where are you at?' Sarah asked.

'I read a really interesting article from the *Sri Lanka Times* yesterday,' Alice launched in. 'An interview with the granddaughter of the village headman from Leonard's time there. He used to hold court under a massive, gnarled tamarind tree, which formed a large canopy by the roadside. His files were bought to him by bullock cart. He loved the villagers, the article says, and like to watch the herds of deer drinking at the tanks.'

'You're still researching?'

'I am. Here's another thing—did you know that Arthur C Clarke played Leonard in the film of *The Village in the Jungle?*'

'I did not,' Sarah said. 'If *This Devastating Fever* attempts to tackle sex tourism it really will implode. Anyway, googling is not research.'

'I'm not allowed into the city,' Alice said. 'I can't access my books.'

Thought, not said: I can't access my life.

'You don't need the scene,' Sarah said. 'Send me what you have by the end of the month, then I'm submitting it to publishers, then I'm retiring on all the money you're going to make me.'

'Got it,' said Alice. 'Definitely.'

1960

'Once,' Leonard said, 'a man's knowledge of the world was determined by the number of miles he could walk in a day, or, perhaps, as far as his bullock cart could carry him. The average man's universe was ten miles' radius from his village, at best.'

'Did you not use cars in 1910?' Trekkie asked. She had only been two years old when Leonard had arrived in Ceylon in 1904. Nine when he left it. She was fifty-eight now. Leonard was eighty. The number of years since he'd left Ceylon was almost fifty. The number of years that Ceylon had been self-governing, was twelve. It would be another twelve years before it was known as Sri Lanka.

'No. And I'm pleased. I knew the villages because I walked and rode among them. I sat under trees and talked to them. These days administrators cover thirty, forty miles a day.'

Leonard and Trekkie were standing on the footpath on Galle Road. Leonard had stepped in front of a car, almost been hit by it, but was now safely on the footpath. He pulled out a hanky, wiped the sweat off his brow. Found he felt quite shaken.

Trekkie, his dearest Tiger, really was a marvel. He would not have been able to manage this latest trip without her.

'Perhaps a G&T would help?'

They were walking towards their final social engagement of the trip. A light but early meal with Shelton Fernando at the Galle Face Hotel. Normally, Mr Fernando ate at ten at night but he was far too polite to point that out. Yes, Mr Fernando believed in a Christian God, yes he loved parties and dancing, and neither God, nor parties, or dancing, were of interest to Leonard. In other ways, though, the men were similar. Gentlemen, hard workers, great believers in justice. They had both studied literature at university. They had both established entire villages. They were both passionate about administration.

> *the most precious flower and fruit, the essential mark and prerogative of the independent, sovereign state.*
>
> LEONARD WOOLF, 1916

They sat together on the terrace. How did Mr Fernando hear Leonard over the sound of the ocean, the wind? How close did he have to lean towards Leonard's lined face if he were to have any hope of hearing a word he said?

'In 1911,' Leonard told Mr Fernando, 'I stood on the deck of a ship looking back at this coastline and watched the Indian Ocean crash against coral reefs.'

It was so vivid to him, this memory. Standing there with his sister by his side, gripping the rail until Colombo disappeared into a shimmer of sea mist and heat. He became lost in the memory, and Trekkie touched him lightly on the arm, bringing him back to the present and a question from Mr Fernando, who had heard of Leonard's perspicacity and wanted to know if Leonard believed the world was safe now, or if there might be a third world war.

Leonard was tired. 'I believe it is impossible to underestimate the human race. Their capacity for sheer idiocy and their refusal to learn from history leads me to believe that extinction is always a distinct possibility.

'And civil war? Here?'

On that matter, Leonard confessed, he needed Mr Fernando's expertise. And so, after establishing that Leonard was now to call Mr Fernando 'Shelton', the two men discussed the causes of the 1958 riots in some detail. Leonard understood that a Mr Aluwihara, the Government Agent of Polonnaruwa, had been one of the few government officers who had acted with complete impartiality. Halted rioters. Saved lives.

'What happened to Mr Aluwihara?' Leonard asked.

'He was dismissed,' Shelton said.

'And the army?'

'The army is withdrawing from civilian areas. Except, perhaps, for Jaffna, where they may stay a while longer.'

'I believe you were responsible for the opening of a school for 186 Tamil children, seventy-five of them girls,' Shelton said. 'That showed a commitment to female education that England often failed to achieve for its own girls.'

'At the time,' Leonard said, 'there were objections to the funding. The costs of building were covered by the sale of opium. And in truth it is my sister Bella who exhorted me to commit to matters of female education, though I am very pleased that she did so.'

Shelton enquired after Mrs Southorn's health. He knew her by reputation, of course. Her second husband, Tom Southorn, had gone on to be Secretary of Hong Kong. Governor of Gambia.

I treasure the memories of my time with you and at Peradeniya and am always grateful to you for giving me my first taste of the East.

BELLA SOUTHORN TO LEONARD WOOLF, 1960

'My sister and I differ on matters of self-rule and some family matters. But mutual affection overcomes this,' Leonard said. He felt Bella's presence everywhere on this trip, had stored up stories so he could write to her in detail. What he did not say was: Tom has died. I did not like him in Jaffna in 1904 and didn't warm to him in the years thereafter. Bella is eighty-three, bereft, blind. Soon she will be dead as well.

A waiter approached.

Was Mr Woolf available to talk to a Mr Wijesinghe?

He was.

Mr Wijesinghe approached the table. He reminded Leonard of an event that had taken place when he'd been a local administrator and Leonard a general administrator. It was during the time of the rinderpest epidemic. A diseased buffalo was wandering free and Leonard asked the owner of the buffalo, a village headman, to shoot it. The headman refused. Leonard then handed a rifle to Mr Wijesinghe, grabbed the buffalo using considerable force, and led it into range of the shot. 'Shoot,' Leonard had said.

'I shot that buffalo,' Mr Wijesinghe said. 'You made me shoot a man's livelihood, his transport, his friend, before his eyes. Why did you do this?'

Leonard sat quietly.

'Was it just, sir? Was it just?' Mr Wijesinghe was now a very old man. He was also an angry and insistent one.

'It was,' Leonard said softly. But he was trembling. 'But it was also cruel.'

After Mr Wijesinghe left, his long face was longer than it ever had been. Trekkie glanced at him in concern, but didn't want to be oppressive so turned away to let the men talk for a moment. Ordered herself another glass of wine.

'This,' Leonard told Shelton, 'is why I left. We were paternalistic. We were severe. We treated your people like children.'

2021

As Alice wrote the scene in which Leonard has tea with Shelton Fernando she found it hard not to write what she knew happened next. The army would stay in Jaffna for another twenty-five years. This would lead to civil war. Alice's country, Australia, would spend millions of dollars to keep a single Tamil family on Christmas Island, on the grounds they were not refugees. The violence they fled had begun last century, on Leonard's watch. Alice did not yet know that soon things in Sri Lanka would become even worse and the nation would be on the brink of ruin. Alice did not know how to keep her writing where it belonged. She found she was writing faster and faster but could not, she now understood, ever write fast enough, was in danger of losing her grip, had no traction, was concerned her words, everyone's words, would empty of meaning.

A shot rang out. Alice was jolted by the shock of it. She put her computer to one side, got out of bed, pulled on a baggy jumper to cover her pyjamas and stepped outside of the cottage to see what was going on. She looked towards the road, in the direction of the sound. There she saw the large body of the alpha male kangaroo she'd so admired. Once this powerful beast had stood tall as a man, though built far more heavily in the biceps and chest. But when Alice moved closer to his body, she could see a woman standing about ten metres away, her shotgun now pointing towards the ground.

'Kindest thing,' she called out to Alice.

'Car?' Alice asked.

'Fence,' the woman said.

Alice tried to hold the gaze of the big roo's eyes as the light in them faded, as his blood flooded onto the road, but could not. She saw the bones sticking through his feet where he'd become tangled in a fence and infection had set in. His haunches had shrunk. The woman asked Alice if she could help, and together they rolled the body onto a canvas sheet and lifted it, with some difficulty, into the van.

As the woman drove off, Alice held a hand aloft, then walked down towards the dam. So much life. Ducks (or were they geese? This was a matter of some contention). Ibis. Heron. Cockies. Rosella. Magpie. Butcher birds. Crows. And, just over there, flamingos were lifting off the far banks of the tank.

At first only a dozen rose up into the air.

2005.

Suddenly there were hundreds of them.

1960.

Then there were thousands, the air was thick with the flurry of wings, downy feathers, floating before her, light as dandelions. Pink, black, white. Larger, stronger, longer feathers floated down, also transcribing a wider, more controlled trajectory. Flight feathers. Cutting through time.

1910.

1969

Over his final decades, Leonard's friends and family took to dying. Lifting themselves out of the earthly realm much as the flamingos had: in modest numbers at first, then in large flocks. Maynard Keynes (heart attack, overwork), Adrian Stephen (in his sleep, he did not suffer), his wife Karin (suicide). Phillip Woolf (suicide), Harold Woolf (suicide), Flora Woolf (suspected suicide). Vanessa Bell (cancer), then Clive Bell (cancer), who Leonard had thought a fool but nonetheless had been a man who, like him, had loved Virginia, had loved Vanessa. Charles, Pinka, Sally, Mitz and Peat had been followed by dozens more: cats, dogs, monkeys, fish and assorted reptiles.

During his lifetime, empires had risen—Australia, swathes of Africa, Canada, Ceylon, Egypt, India, swathes of Malaysia, New Zealand, Singapore—and some had fallen. His own nation had carved up the map and offered bits of various countries to other countries as if the world was their personal board game.

Prime ministers came and went: Gladstone x 3, Gascoyne-Cecil x 3, Primrose, Balfour, Campbell-Bannerman, Asquith, Lloyd George, Law, Baldwin x 3, MacDonald x 2, Chamberlain, Churchill x 2, Eden, Douglas-Home, Wilson, Heath.

He received honorary doctorates from universities. He got his papers in order. He became a bestselling author. This matter of the autobiographies was a strange one. Both unexpected and satisfactory. Leonard's bearing witness to the end of a way of life was paying off. He described a class (his) and way of life (the villages') that was practically extinct. The first world war had almost succeeded in destroying them. The second world war had finished the job.

And then came a summer day, in 1969, when Monk's House garden was open to the public. People came through in large numbers, poking through the garden beds. They admired the clematis, the roses, the red-hot pokers. Leonard worked in the apple orchard and refused to catch people's eye. Words floated towards him.

Virgin.

Suicide.

Mad.

Bloomsbury.

Literature.

Secretary?

Threesome.

Misogynist.

Cruel.

Leonard remained focused on netting his apples. He was particularly enamoured with the Black Diamonds, small nuggets the colour of aubergine. Extremely rare, Leonard had them sent all the way from Tibet. Or China. He was no longer sure what the correct title of that small, high country was. Whatever it was called, Sussex was far too warm for apples of this type, and yet, under his care, they thrived.

The next day, Vout, his latest gardener, found him lying under an apple tree. Vout called Louie, no spring chicken herself, who was in bed, recovering from cancer. Despite her illness she leapt up and ran to Monk's House, arriving in time to stop the ambulance from taking Leonard away.

You get to an age when if you plant a tree in your garden, you will not be
alive to stand beneath its branches.

LEONARD WOOLF, 1969

'He wouldn't want it,' she said, standing by her prostrate employer. Leonard lay on the ground, groaning in agreement, though, as it turned out, this was only the first of what would be a series of small strokes that would peck away at his brain.

Trekkie was concerned the stroke had been caused by the stress of the open garden, but the more likely cause of his dying was inevitability. Leonard was almost ninety years old. With the exception of EM Forster and Bertrand Russell, Leonard had managed to outlive his generation.

On the days when Trekkie could not be there, a young woman called Virginia—yes, everyone commented—often stayed, and worked quietly on her own projects while she kept an unobtrusive eye on him. Leonard slipped into the conservatory more and more.

Ghost Virginia would sometimes attempt to join him, though she was careful to look as she had when still alive. She hoped they could converse, as they once had, with depth and affection, but it didn't work out. Leonard had explicitly told her on many an occasion that he did not believe in life after death. He told others as well, just so there was no mistaking his position. Insisted there was no evidence that the mind can exist separately from the body, or that the personality can survive death.

'Every time he goes in,' Young Virginia told Trekkie after one of his longer forays into the conservatory, 'I worry he'll die in there and I'll have to scramble through the thorns to find his body. By the time I get to him he'll be a pile of scattered bones, gnawed at by wild pigs, and trampled by elephants.'

'Nothing would make him happier,' Trekkie observed.

Leonard kept up his reviews, his reading and correspondence. He won six first prizes for his vegetables at the local show only a few weeks after the first stroke. Six!

Despite these successes, Leonard felt his mind creak and his body crack, as his fault lines ground together, lifted up, gave way. While most of them opened into a darkness, or perhaps just a nothingness, he could also feel a brightness, a lightness, working its way in. He could truthfully say—indeed often did, to whoever would listen—that his future and imminent extinction caused him no fear or pain. 1969 was further away from 1880, the year of his birth than he'd ever imagined he'd get.

On the last morning of his life, Leonard stayed in bed and attended to his correspondence. This had once been a tedious affair, as various insults were hurled his way, but now everyone was polite. Leonard assumed this was because he was so old that people were afraid of him. Too late to wish it otherwise now. Regret would get him nowhere.

This morning's pile of letters approached a dozen or more. He picked up the first.

'Dear Mr Woolf, I am studying Feminist Philosophy at the University of California but am taking study leave at the University of Sussex. I'd be terrifically grateful if you could make the time to see me to discuss the work of the late Virginia Woolf. Perhaps you'd like a chance to give your side of the story? Cheers, Virginia.' (Virginias were everywhere he looked. Most of whom, as far as Leonard could gather, were named for his wife.)

His side of the story?

Leonard glanced at a second letter and saw that it was from Vanessa's daughter, his beloved niece Angelica. Angelica suffered from a surfeit of fathers, none quite up to the job. She thought of Leonard as close to one as she was ever going to get. He picked up a third envelope. This, from Mr Nallaperuma's grandson, with whom he'd been corresponding since his visit in 1960. A fourth was from Morgan, whose handwriting was now so tremulous it resembled an insect trail through fine dust.

Leonard had woken up with a headache that was steadily getting worse. Now, words danced up and down on the page and, alarmingly, seemed to disappear altogether. He called to Louie before remembering that she had gone home after leaving him with a fresh cup of tea only ten minutes ago. It was still tolerably warm.

He turned to his proofs. He'd indexed the first three volumes but wasn't up to that task anymore. Still, he wanted to reread his final book. In it he recommitted to his philosophy of not crying over spilt milk. And there had been so much milk in his life.

'Louie?'

Milk spilt and thrown.

'Trekkie?'

Forced upon.

'Virginia?'

Silence.

His mind was wandering. Virginia, his Virginia, Ghost Virginia, took the opportunity to insert herself into the cracks, cracks that were turning into chasms. Something substantial was giving way.

'Which theory do you like the most, Leo? Was I mad because molested, because I was a repressed lesbian? Was I a modernist genius or a failure? Who is the better writer, that wretched James Joyce or me? Would the women libbers have saved me or simply bored me to death? Was I not breastfed for long enough by my dear mama? Is that why you would force so much milk upon me?'

'I regret the milk cures, Goat. And the removal of books. I wish I had never told you about the small boy who had stones put in his pockets so as to weigh him down. And I fear,' his voice started to tremble, a single teardrop, the shape of Ceylon, ran down his cheek, 'that I may have been rather harsher than was ideal.'

Leonard was a man who had often been wrong during his life. Virginia knew this to be true, but she also knew that there were times when he had been far wiser than most. Because of this, Virginia told Leonard what he wanted to hear. 'What I remember is that you saved me. And that together we found happiness.'

'You don't mind Trekkie?' he asked.

Virginia hesitated. 'I mind her quite a bit.'

Leonard pulled himself together, tried to stand up to her a final time. 'There is all manner of talk about you and Vita. There are articles. Books. Plays.'

'More spiritual than physical. She was a terrible snob.'

'So were we all, if I am to believe what I read. We've really fallen out of fashion,' Leonard paused. 'I think I would like to die before all these academics and critics and their damned theories force the life out of me.'

Leonard had a cup of tea in his hand. He couldn't remember where it had come from. He was standing in the conservatory. Everything was becoming very vague. Virginia realised she did not have much longer to ask him the questions she needed. There were more important things to consider than the hundreds of thousands of words—maybe millions of words—written about her and her husband. How many, if any, of those words were true? No two have been as happy as we, is what she once wrote him. No two have been as much written about, is what she'd pen now, if she had the chance. If she hadn't been mad to start with, she would have gone mad with irritation had she lived.

'Do the swallows still swarm and swoop at dusk, gathering, then fragmenting in mesmerising rhythm? Has the summer been warm? Do the rhododendrons still bloom? Has there been enough rain this season? How is Angelica? Why do we allow war to take our young men? Why do we allow our women to be raped and then expect them to act as if it doesn't matter a fig? Why did Trekkie paint over the colour of my room when that blue-green really was quite perfect? What did you plant in the elm's stead after it blew over? A magnolia? The roots, when I reach out for them, seem to me to be that of a magnolia.'

It was remarkable, really, how vivid she was to him.

'Look,' Virginia was speaking more loudly now, calling to Leonard from close to the edge of the cliff, one of the deep green flanks of the Seven Sisters, which billowed all the way to Eastbourne. Emerald green set atop dazzling pure white—chalk cliffs plunging down to pebbled beaches. When he reached her he saw the violet stars— tiny daisies perhaps—growing, so it seemed, out of the chalk itself. Vermillion. White. It seemed that everything was like this when he was with her. Saturated. Clear. Her beauty took his breath away. It did from first meeting to last.

They were walking, he realised, towards Birling Gap on the way to Beachy Head. Leonard felt distracted as he pondered the intricacies of Virginia's luminescence, as he searched for the right words to describe that quality, at the same time as keeping up with her long, gangly gait.

He felt a sweat coming upon him as it often did in the heat of Ceylon. But here he was, in Sussex, so there was no accounting for it. Virginia had some kind of authenticity of being that excited him. She was, as he had imagined she would be, supreme. There was nothing phenomenal about her.

Virginia walked fast and talked faster. Today she wanted to convey the similarities and differences between writing and painting. Something about the need to capture shape and light and colour with words in the way an artist does with her brush. And yes, there was more to it than that: it seemed that now was the time to change the very shape of things. There was a gap in history's relentless grind into which they might insert themselves. Might make a difference.

'Imagine,' she said, 'that our childhood was a time spent in a dark stone mansion, one that lets no light in.'

It wasn't hard for either of them to imagine this; it was close enough to the truth.

'And now think of a house that is, well, like some kind of beach shack or bather's box. Small and painted bright yellow! Yes, that's it! The colour of sunflowers. Just a small square wood shack with its front door open and the sun streaming in and we are all running out the front door in our ridiculous swimmers ready to embrace the new century. To leap right into it.'

Leonard often thought of houses himself. Monk's House, centuries old, had absorbed him into its wooden bones. There were his London rooms in the year after Virginia died—bombed, grey, dank, no ceiling, windows boarded up, the ruins of Bloomsbury all around. Further back, a lifetime ago, were huts that gave way unless constantly maintained. Vines pulling on the walls until the whole structure crumbled.

Virginia sat down above Birling Gap and surveyed it proprietorially. She was overwhelmed by the fluid dip of grass and earth down into pebbles and the channel. Leonard could see that she was transported and dared to hope that she, like him, was taking pleasure in the company as well as the scenery.

'Do you agree?' she asked, turning towards him open-faced, 'that there is possibility?'

And he could see that, yes. The Victorians were done and the sons and daughters of that era of international domination and overstuffed lounge chairs were coming into their time. The future looked bright. He reached out, as he had on many an occasion, for Virginia's hand. For once she did not remove it.

Leonard leaned towards her and she did not recoil. Virginia looked at him and smiled, and so he kissed her, gently. Pressed his beautiful mouth against her soft lips. Their first kiss was, and would always be, the most extraordinary, most illuminated, the most tender moment of his life. He saw the future, he embraced it, and together they began their voyage.

Thorn bush was biting into his tweeds, unravelling the cloth. Leaves were slapping him in the face. In the distance he heard the clack of a leopard's jaw—really, there was no other sound it could be. As for the boar, he smelt it before he saw it. His tea sloshed from the mug before slipping from his grip altogether. He felt his face, already drooping, slacken even further.

This really wasn't as bad as I feared it might be, he thought, not as bad as poor, long-suffering Lytton had warned him it would be. His body followed the mug, down onto the forest floor. He felt little pain or even sadness. He would miss Trekkie, there was that. His main concern was that he had fallen, slumped and twisted in a way that suggested distress and would alarm Louie—with him for some thirty-seven years now—when she found him. Not quite the elegance of the reclining Buddha, but it would have to do.

'Was your drowning painful?' he finally summoned the courage to ask, but Virginia didn't seem to hear him, was now striding along way ahead of him on the clifftop. Mitz appeared to have joined her, was bobbing away on Virginia's shoulder, tail swinging from side to side. 'You must remember, dearest,' she called out, 'you kept us both alive for longer than anyone expected.' And with that she disappeared into the distance and Leonard was on his own again.

Leonard fell back, cliffs melted, he drifted out to sea. He found himself reclining on a mattress on a raft while the sun beat down upon him. A whiff of rotting oysters jolted him momentarily before being replaced by a combination of coconut milk and curry leaves, a smell so mouth-watering he considered hanging on a while longer, but then that smell faded also. He was becalmed, abandoned, entirely alone, floating on the smallest of boats on the largest of oceans. He dozed under the immense canopy of the Milky Way. He watched as his brothers leapt out of the trenches on the western front and ran over open ground, watched the explosion of a shell as it landed upon them. He held Lytton's hand as he lay dying, pulled Pinka's ear, kissed Mitz's tiny face. He walked through the ruins of his bombed house, he saw the remains of his wife's body a final time. There was Trekkie, in her studio, standing back from her latest painting, assessing it with her head cocked to one side. He was on a headland in a distant land, craning his neck to watch as a comet skated by, brilliant and bright. He reached out and grasped it by the tail.

2021

Alice never was clear if the students in her How to Write a Novel™ course learned anything from her, but they did seem to get some pleasure in her company and that was not the worst thing in the world. She read Tips by Famous Writers™ and shared them. Take John Updike. In one of his novels he'd killed a baby, and at the time he drowned a fictional baby in the bath, his third child had only been three months old. This experience had been 'unsettling' but had, nonetheless, been manageable as the fictional baby was 'only a few sentences and adjectives on some pieces of paper'. It was not, therefore, a real baby.

Alice and her students discussed this awhile. If a character was cobbled together with sentences and adjectives, bits of paper, did they exist in the 'real' world? For Alice, and many of the students, it felt as if they did. However, to dodge the class collapsing into a discussion of what constituted the 'real' world, Alice decided to pass on a particular writing tip, one that had been playing on her mind: that death was considered a good way to keep people reading, but not necessarily a good way to finish a novel. Apparently George Saunders' debut collection contained almost forty deaths, though these included the repetitive murder–suicide of four ghosts caught in a paranormal glitch.

Alice sat down and considered the matter of deaths—direct and indirect—in her own novel.

- Thoby Stephen.
- Virginia's parents. Her own parents.
- Robert (Bertie) Lock.
- Rupert Brooke.
- Cecil Woolf + 300,000 at the battle of Ypres alone.
- Battle of the Somme (which included Ypres). One million. Give. Or take.
- WWI. 40 million.
- Spanish flu. 100 million?
- Virginia Woolf.
- WWII: 75 million.
- COVID-19. Hen and millions more. Ongoing.

Alice decided to move from human deaths to those of other species. She googled articles on the revision of the death numbers of Australian native animals during the bushfires upwards from one billion to three billion.

She turned her head to avoid the images of burnt, dying, dead echidnas, koalas, kangaroos.

It was too much.

'What should I do?' Alice said out loud, to her cat, to her pot belly stove, to the whisky—Writers' Tears—sitting by her side.

Silence.

'Perhaps Alice could die in *This Devastating Fever*? Of COVID? It has a poetic ring to it.'

Silence.

'Leonard?'

The silence elaborated itself around her: it doesn't matter. She heard a chittering, an undercurrent of sound.

'Virginia?'

FluffyShark's attentive face alerted Alice to the fact that the under-current of sound came from the tiny bats that lived in the wall. It seemed that even Leonard and Virginia, her long-time companions, her mother and father, her therapeutic visions, these parts of herself, these icons of history, these irrelevant individuals, really were done with this drawn-out exercise. This so-called novel.

Thinking time over. Business Uggs on. Alice's students' faces popped up, in studies, living rooms, bedrooms and kitchen tables around Melbourne and regional Victoria. Alice smiled to see all these smart people, these excellent writers, sitting before her. It was a joy to talk to them. She fought, as always, her instinct to say: DON'T LISTEN TO ANYTHING THAT I HAVE TO SAY. JUST WRITE

THE FUCKING THING. But WRITE THE FUCKING THING was not a business model. It wasn't a goal or a KPI.

FluffyShark jumped onto her desk and did a catwalk in front of the camera. Alice waved. 'Get your tea,' she said, 'your wine. I'll set up the whiteboard on my iPad.' She no longer asked them to mute their mics. The noises of humans going about their business was reassuring.

A dog barked loudly in the house of the third student to Alice's right. FluffyShark jumped off the desk.

'Okay, I've been looking forward to this one. Our surprise finale. Are we ready?'

She shared her screen.

THE ART OF FINISHING YOUR NOVEL, Alice wrote, then underlined.

She knew that none of them were close to the ending. Not her students, not her, not her novel, and not the planet. What she didn't know was what they were at the beginning of. (Tipping point had been reached. They stood on a precipice. Geological time collapsed into human time.)

Below Alice's declarative statement, was a drawing of a tree. Yet another of her plot visualisations, one she'd prepared earlier. Some students were smiling. Others looked bemused. One was wrangling a toddler. Someone's screen had frozen. Another wandered off screen to look for their wine glass. Alice could hear someone crying off screen. Yet another asked everyone if they had heard what was happening in Sydney and read out a tweet she'd read that morning by a writer who lived there.

Time has never meant less. The Gregorian calendar is a guidebook to the lost city of Atlantis. All around is the end of possibility. We go

through the motions, never going anywhere. Glaciers melt, we are frozen.
Time is stuck.

RICK MORTON, 2021

Alice found herself fighting the strange sensation that she'd been teaching this one class not just for minutes but for years, for decades. New strains, dying forests, dying oceans, catastrophic floods, heat bubbles, disappearing glaciers, collapsing ice sheets, talk of war, actual war. Would it ever stop? It would never stop. Not in her lifetime. Not in the lifetime of the children she hadn't had, but knew and loved nonetheless.

Alice was fritzing. Admitted as much to her class. She set a writing exercise and a timer for half an hour, then she turned off her video. Muted her mic. Stepped out of the cottage into the darkness, a heavy coat thrown over her classic Zoom ensemble: sparkly jumper, tracksuit pants. The oaks had thrown golds, ambers and crimsons at Alice throughout autumn, but the colour was done now. The winds were coming up and Alice remembered there had been a warning on the news. The largest wind gusts for a hundred years, maybe a thousand, who the fuck knew? The last power blackouts were just a taster. Secure your premises. Ensure your homes are safe from treefall.

Secure.

Safe.

Not possible.

Didn't matter.

Alice looked south. Clouds gathered on the horizon. Lightning flickering through them with the intensity of the tropics. Melbourne glowed, hunkered down under the sky, but then there was a flash—the moment before blackout—as the lights went out. Not just the lights of Melbourne, but the lights of the cottage, the lights up and down her street.

Edith called out from inside: 'You okay out there?'

She was.

As Alice's eyes adjusted to the darkness the stars seemed to grow brighter. The dome of the southern hemisphere held her. Her mob of kangaroos bounded past. A fox and her pup dashed by. She could make out several stags, in the distance, galloping into the forest. FluffyShark must have slipped out of the house and was trotting past the oaks and down the hill towards her. The earth began to shift under her feet. She heard thunder and rumbling. Was this an earthquake? A storm? A nuclear war? Alice braced herself. Widened her stance and held her arms out wide, to allow the cold, beautiful violence of the rising winds to play upon her skin. Then she heard it. A powerful owl, so close it was as if he didn't know or care that she was there.

'Woo hoo,' he called. 'Woo hoo.'

Acknowledgements

As this project drew to conclusion during the global COVID-19 pandemic I developed a deeper understanding of the importance of the Australian writing community to my work, and my life. Thanks to all of you who I've had conversations with about my work, and this novel in particular, over the years. You know who you are.

This project was completed over so many years that I need to thank those who supported the project in its various stages. Mandy Brett, Jenny Darling, Gillian Ford, Michael Heyward, Chandani Lokuge, Norman Mackenzie, Pauline Nestor, Walter Perera, the staff in the archives at the University of Sussex, in particular former staff member, Elizabeth Ingliss. Also the staff of Lilly Library at Indiana University and (also from IU) Catherine Dyer. Thanks also to staff at the British Library.

Particular thanks to those who were with me from the start of this project to the finish: Ian Britain, Michelle de Kretser, Helen Murdoch, Virginia Murdoch.

Those who read the manuscript, or sections thereof, and offered feedback at crucial stages include Donica Bettanin, Emily Bitto,

Ian Britain, James Bradley, Chris Brophy, David Carlin, Kate Cole-Adams, Saul Cunningham, Rebecca Giggs, Jane Gleeson-White, Becky Harkins-Cross, Philippa Hawker, Lorna Hendry, Toni Jordan, Michael Livingstone, Lenny Robinson, Meredith Rose.

Residencies enjoyed during the writing of this manuscript include McCraith House (thank you, RMIT) and Bundanon (thank you, Bundanon Trust). This novel began, somewhat accidentally, at Pemberley Estate in Sri Lanka (through the support of an Asialink scholarship in 2004 and host Brendon Gooneratne).

Financial and other support was provided by the following organisations over the course of writing this novel: I was the recipient of the United States Studies Centre–Indiana University Creative Arts Fellowship in 2018 and spent three months in the wonderful Bloomsbury archives at the university's Lilly Library. I worked in the Leonard Woolf Archives, which are a part of the Special Collections at the University of Sussex Library. That trip was supported, in part, by a Monash Research Graduate School Travel Grant and, in part, by Helen Murdoch. I was also the recipient of an APA scholarship in 2006–2007 to study Creative Writing at Monash University and received a grant to write this novel from the Australia Council in 2008.

Finally, I would like to thank my agent, Jane Novak, and the amazing people at Ultimo Press. Most particularly to my editor Brigid Mullane, whose belief in this novel after so many years is one of the reasons it turned into a real book. Finally.

Copyright

Copyright is managed by, and permission given, to quote from the works of Leonard Woolf by the Society of Authors on behalf of the Leonard Woolf estate. As well, The Society of Authors manage the Virginia Woolf estate and granted me the right to use her work (with the exclusion of diary extracts). Permission to quote from the diaries of Virginia Woolf was given by Granta Publications. The Society of Authors are guardians of the estate of Lytton Strachey and gave me permission to quote him. Permission to quote Vita Sackville-West was given by the managers of her literary estate, Heritage Curtis Brown. Quotations from the Desmond and Molly MacCarthy Collections and Vita Sackville-West's manuscripts appear courtesy of the Lilly Library, Indiana University, Bloomington, Indiana.

Thanks too to Rick Morton and Geoff Dyer for allowing me to use their words. (And also to Brigid Delaney for suggesting to me that I read Dyer's *Out of Sheer Rage* when I was trying to finish this novel.)

All reasonable attempts have been made to seek other permissions that may be required.

A note on sources

While many books were important to the writing of this novel, I was particularly reliant on the scholarship and writing of Anne Olivier Bell, Victoria Glendinning, Yasmine Gooneratne, Hermione Lee, Michael Ondaatje and Frederic Spotts.

I am aware that some readers will be frustrated by the lack of detail regarding the original sources of quoted material. This was out of deference to the fact that *This Devastating Fever* is a novel, albeit one which draws on the real writings of Leonard and Virginia Woolf. However you can find a full bibliography on my website, www.sophiecunningham.com. If you have particular questions or concerns about source material, you can email me on feverfeedback@sophiecunningham.com.

The following details may also help you pursue a closer reading of quoted material.

The quotes from Leonard Woolf dated 1913 are all from his novel *The Village in the Jungle*. The quote dated 1916 was first published in *International Government: Two Reports by L.S. Woolf with an Introduction by*

Bernard Shaw. All quotes dated 1960 are from his first autobiography, *Sowing.* All quotes dated 1964 come from his third autobiography, *Beginning Again.* The quote dated 1967 came from his fourth auto-biography, *Downhill All the Way.* Quotes dated 1969 come from his final autobiography, *The Journey Not the Arrival Matters.* Leonard's (and one of Lytton Strachey's) quoted letters can be found in Frederic Spotts (ed.), *Letters of Leonard Woolf.* Lytton Strachey's second letter, regarding the death of Thoby Stephen was quoted in *Lytton Strachey: The New Biography* by Michael Holroyd.

The 1915 Virginia Woolf quote on p. 166 regarding *The Wise Virgins* is from her diary and was also quoted by Victoria Glendinning in *Leonard Woolf: A Life.* Reproduced here by permission of Granta Books. Virginia Woolf quotes from 1921 are from her story 'A Haunted House'. Virginia Woolf quotes from 1929 on p. 99 and p. 230 are from the essay 'A Room of One's Own'. All other quotes from 1929 are diary entries, have been dated, and can be found in the 1990 edition of Anne Olivier Bell's *A Moment's Liberty: The Shorter Diary Virginia Woolf.* They have been reproduced by permission of Granta Books. The quote from 1942 can be found in the essay 'The Death of a Moth', which was published after her death. The letters of Virginia Woolf can be found in Nigel Nicolson and Joanne Trautmann, (eds), *The Letters of Virginia Woolf, Volumes One to Six.*

Vita Sackville-West's letters to Harold Nicolson can be found in the archives at the Lilly Library, Indiana University. Her letters to Virginia Woolf can be found in Louise DeSalvo and Mitchell Leaska (eds), *The Letters of Vita Sackville-West to Virginia Woolf,* 1985. Molly and Desmond MacCarthys' letters can be found in the archives at the Lilly Library, Indiana University. Letters from the Vita Sackville-West and the Desmond and Molly MacCarthy Collections have been used courtesy Lilly Library, Indiana University

Alice's transcripts of Leonard's and Virginia's material is based on notes I took when working in archives, but have also been adjusted to highlight the difficulty of deciphering hand-written archives.

Sophie Cunningham is the author of eight books including her recent collection of essays, *City of Trees* and has written both fiction and non-fiction for adults and children. She has a passion for trees, walking and broader environmental issues, and every day she posts an image of a tree on her Instagram @sophtreeofday. A stalwart of the Australian literary scene, Sophie also works as a writing teacher and was a co-founder of The Stella Prize, former editor of *Meanjin*, and former chair of the Literature Board of the Australia Council.

She lives in Melbourne.